MW01616908

DRAGON MAGE

RIDERS OF FIRE DRAGON MASTERS
BOOK TWO

EILEEN MUELLER

CONNECT WITH USA TODAY BESTSELLING
AUTHOR, EILEEN MUELLER

EileenMuellerAuthor.com

Website, newsletter and free books,
including *Bronze Dragon* and *Silver Dragon*,
Riders of Fire prequel novelettes

Facebook:
www.facebook.com/groups/RidersOfFire

Follow Eileen on BookBub:
www.bookbub.com/authors/eileen-mueller

RIDERS OF FIRE DRAGON MASTERS
IS THE PREQUEL SERIES TO THE AWARD-WINNING,
BESTSELLING RIDERS OF FIRE SERIES.

DRAGON MAGE

RIDERS OF FIRE DRAGON MASTERS

BOOK TWO

USA TODAY BESTSELLING AUTHOR
EILEEN MUELLER

Dragon Mage, Riders of Fire Dragon Masters book 2 © 2021 Eileen Mueller
Typesetting © Phantom Feather Press, 2021, American English
Cover Art by Christian Bentulan © Eileen Mueller, 2021
Dragons' Realm Map by Ava Fairhall © Eileen Mueller, 2018
Phantom Feather Press Logo by Geoff Popham, © Phantom Feather Press, 2014
Paperback ISBN: 9780995137417

Phantom Feather Press
29 Laura Ave, Brooklyn, Wellington 6021, New Zealand
phantomfeatherpress@gmail.com
www.phantomfeatherpress.wordpress.com

PHANTOM FeatHer PreSS

Magic, every time you turn the page.

Dedication

Keep on striving. Never give up hope.
When the stars fade and your dreams shatter
After the dark, there is always a new dawn
and the sun will shine again.

DRAGONS' REALM

Red Guards

GREAT SPANGLEWOOD FORE

Tooka
Falls

Fores
Edge

Devil's Gate

Monte
Vista

Waldhaven

DEATH VALLEY

THE TERRAMITES

THE FLATLANDS

N

W   E

S

NAOBIAN SEA

*Fieldhaven is known as Last Stop years later in *Riders of Fire*.

DRAGONS' HOLD

Blue Guards

NORTHERN GRAND ALPS

Montanara

River's
Edge

iddi's

seshoe
d

nglewood

River Forks

Last Stop

WESTERN GRAND ALPS

Western
Settlement

Lush Valley

LUSH VALLEY

Southern
Settlement

NAOBIA

Crystal
Lake

Green Guards

Naobia

Silent Assassins

THE WASTELANDS

Prologue – A Year Ago

Giddi caressed Ma's hand, his sit bones aching from perching on the hard chair next to her bed all night. He'd stayed up, keeping vigil. There was no one to relieve him, so, apart from short privy breaks and grabbing food for both of them, he'd been at his mother's bedside for days.

At least now she was sleeping peacefully. Her breathing was so quiet he could hardly hear it, like the whisper of a faint breeze through a strongwood on an almost calm day.

Crisp footfalls sounded in the hallway. The bedroom door opened. Master Mage Balovar entered and closed the door quietly. "How is she?" he asked, nodding at Ma, his dark eyes concerned.

Ma's eyelids fluttered. "Hello, Balovar," she said, her voice as weak as a hatchling's wings.

Balovar leaned over the bed and kissed her forehead. "How are you doing today?"

She smiled, her eyes drifting shut and her hand slipping out of Giddi's onto the quilt.

Balovar pulled up another chair, gingerly placing it next to Giddi's. "A messenger bird from your father arrived for Starrus today," he said quietly. "This time, he enclosed something for you."

"He did?" Giddi burst out, then hushed as Ma stirred.

Pa had finally contacted him. It'd been moons since he or Ma had heard from his father. A year ago, when Starrus had returned from a secret quest without Giddi's father, he'd told them Gideon—Starrus' trainer and Giddi's father—had been delayed on secret business.

Maybe Pa was finally coming home.

Balovar passed a piece of creased parchment to him. Giddi was so excited, he nearly dropped it. He ran his thumb across the imprint of a flame in the honey-yellow wax seal. Yes, it was Pa's seal, all right. Eagerly, he broke the seal.

Dear Giddi,

I've hurt my hand, but I trust you can still read my script. My apologies for passing this message on via Starrus, but he's the only one I can trust to deliver it safely. If anyone else knows my whereabouts, I'm at risk of being endangered.

Son, you're of age now.

Giddi puffed up his chest. He was eleven summers' old, now, and proud of it

Because I can't be with you, I'd like Starrus to train you in my absence. I've taught him everything I know, and he's an honorable man. Heed him, and learn well. I hope to be back with you and your ma soon.

Until your flames light up the night sky,
Your beloved,
Pa.

'Back with you and your ma soon?' Giddi could scarcely believe it. Ma had always told Giddi that Pa would come back, but he'd been gone twelve moons, now.

EILEEN MUELLER

Hang on. If Pa was coming home soon, why would Starrus need to train him? Giddi sighed. Pa's words were a platitude to make him feel better, not a promise.

Balovar leaned in, "Do you mind?" He plucked the letter from Giddi's hand and read it aloud to Ma, his voice a gentle murmur.

Then he passed Giddi back the letter and stood. He tousled Giddi's hair—as if he were a littling.

When would adults see he was grown? Giddi didn't need to be petted like a newborn dragonet. He rolled his eyes at Balovar's back as the master mage turned back to Ma.

"I hope you get better soon." Balovar nodded at Ma, then strode to the door. On the threshold, he paused. "You know you're like a son to me, Giddi. Come and see me if you need anything." He turned the doorknob. "You can start training tomorrow with Starrus. I'll meet you both in the clearing at noon."

As Balovar shut the door, Ma stirred and tried to sit up. She coughed, spasms rattling her chest, then slumped even deeper in to the pillows. Her eyes bright with tears, she whispered, "I miss Gideon."

All these moons, Ma had never said that once. She'd comforted Giddi, told him Pa would be home again soon. Never once had she shown sadness.

Giddi squeezed her hand. "Like you said, Ma, he'll be home soon." Although, from the sound of things, that was highly unlikely. "Don't worry. Just rest, so you can get better."

"I want to see him again." Tears spilled from her eyes. She grasped the covers. "Find him, Giddi. Find your father." Her chest rattled with a mighty spasm, her head lolled to one side and her breathing stilled.

"Ma." Giddi picked up her limp hand and felt her wrist for a pulse.

Nothing.

His heart thundering, he touched her neck. Still nothing.

And her chest was still. No breath ghosted from her lips.

"Ma, no!" he whispered.

Eyes stinging, he placed her hand back on the quilt and kissed her cheek. "Good bye, Ma." He was enveloped by the scent of her lavender soap.

Her last words burned through him. *Find him, Giddi. Find your father.*

He had to be brave. He had to find Pa.

BOUND FOR NAOBIA

G iddi sighed and dipped his mop in the battered pail. He wrung it out and shoved it back and forth across the bloodstained deck. Gods, this was a gruesome job. It had been bad enough seeing the needless slaughter in battle. They'd barely cleared the corpses of dead pirates and sailors away before Starrus had started ordering him about, putting on airs in front of the ship's captain as if Giddi were a slave—not a mage in training. It was as if Starrus was oblivious to the carnage, the dead people, the heavy weight of grief weighing on Giddi's chest.

Luckily the captain was goodhearted, not like the Scarlet Hand. The pirate's hands had been tanned, not red but it didn't take much imagination to guess how he'd earned his name. Rumors said the new scourge of the Naobian Sea ate the hearts of his enemies. After seeing the bloodshed and carnage from their short battle today, Giddi believed it. The man was ruthless. He shuddered, suppressing the memory of a young green rider whose body had been sheared in two on dragonback, he and his injured dragon falling into the sea for the sharks to devour.

Giddi shrugged and kept on mopping. There was nothing for it. Hopefully his luck would change when they reached Naobia.

Sailors called to each other as they reattached the rigging to the newly-mended main mast. It'd been lashed together with ropes after a green dragon's tail had caught in the rigging during their battle earlier that day against the Scarlet Hand—a bloodthirsty new pirate captain. Without the mast and sails, the ship had lolled on the sea like a good-for-nothing layabout, rising and falling on the swell, a miasma of burned flesh and charred timber hanging over it.

A few green dragons darted around the boat, their riders catching ropes from the sailors below and leaning out at daring angles to attach them to the spars or throw them to sailors up the masts.

Goren, leader of the Naobian green guards, wheeled on his emerald dragon, calling out to the other dragon riders. He'd been at it for the past hour, and his voice was nearly hoarse.

Giddi mind-melded with Goren's dragon, Rengar. *"Why doesn't he mind-meld with their dragons instead of yelling? That'd save his voice."*

"The riders and dragons can't hear him when he mind-melds. Only I can," Rengar replied. *"We can hear you, of course, because you're the dragon mage. Other than that, we only hear our own riders. Besides, sometimes Goren prefers to bellow to give himself an air of authority. He's rather young to be leader of the green guards, you know."*

Even though Goren was young, he was at least ten summers older than Giddi, and the dark-haired dragon rider barely needed more of an air of authority. There was a toughness about him, as if he'd grown up on the streets, that made Giddi more than a little wary.

Finally, the sails were furled and ready, and the crew awaiting the captain's instructions. The captain prowled along the damp deck, running an eye over the shrouds.

Giddi plunked his mop back in the old wooden pail and leaned against the railing. He mopped his brow. It was much warmer on the Naobian Sea than back home in Great Spanglewood Forest. Thank the Egg he'd stowed his mage cloak in a hammock below deck.

"Trim the sails," the captain bellowed, "but don't put too much strain on that mast. It has to get us to Naobia."

Sailors sprang into action, heaving on the ropes. The mast creaked ominously as they unfurled the mainsail. The soot-stained fabric snapped and caught in the breeze; the edges charred from the fiery breath of Scarlet Hand's sea dragon.

Giddi shook his head. Who'd have thought a pirate could tame a sea dragon.

The captain stalked along the deck, inspecting his crew's handiwork. Giddi snatched up his mop and swabbed another dark stain on the planking. As the captain passed him, water crested over the side of his pail and splashed the captain's boots and breeches. Odd. Giddi hadn't noticed the ship tilting on the swell.

The captain spun, his jaw snapping shut, and glared at Giddi.

"Sorry sir, I must've kicked the bucket." He grinned and added, "Not metaphorically, but literally." Although his foot hadn't been anywhere near it.

The captain's face broke into a wry smile. "Come on, boy don't be sloppy. You're not drowning those stains, you're cleaning them." He shook the water from his boots and strode off.

There was a muffled snigger behind Giddi's back. He spun. Sure enough, he hadn't nudged the pail at all. Starrus was grinning, his hands twitching. His flaming trainer had used his magic to slop water over the captain on purpose.

Scowling, Giddi dunked his mop and kept swabbing.

Later that afternoon as Giddi was tying off a rope on the boom, the end of the rope whipped out and lashed his wrist. A nasty red welt rose on his inner arm. By the flaming First Egg, it stung. As he rubbed his stinging flesh, his eyes meet Starrus' gaze.

There was a malicious glint in his trainer's eye. "I hope you're all right," Starrus said. "There's not much you can do when ropes catch in a gust of wind."

What gust of wind?

Starrus always played dirty when no one was looking. And no one was here to reprimand him. They were far from the Mage Council or any other mages—except Master Mage Findal, the Naobian mage who'd been kidnapped and was on the Scarlet Hand's ship heading for the Wastelands. Starrus was right—there was nothing Giddi could do.

Giddi snatched the end of the rope again, determined to ignore Starrus. It slid through his fingers, burning his palm and leaving a trail of torn skin. Giddi's belly burned with rage. He thrust out his injured hand. "Look what you did." His anger surged, rushing down his limbs. Energy coiled in his palm and wind gusted from his fingers across the deck.

Starrus, caught by the sudden gale, flew backward, slamming his back on the rail, then landed on the deck on his backside. He clambered to his feet, face thunderous.

Giddi hastily tied off the rope, picked up a pail, and strode toward the newly-appointed first mate. The last one had been buried at sea only a few hours ago. The first mate was talking to a sailor who was bent over a barrel, nailing a lid back on.

"How long until we get to shore, sir?" Giddi asked.

The first mate squinted. Shading his eyes with his hand, he looked up at the creaking rigging. "The best part of five days, depending on whether the mast holds. If not, it could take a week or longer."

Giddi groaned. A week with Starrus? These past few hours already felt like forever.

§

On Giddi's third day on the merchant ship, the wind died. The ship's sails drooped, hanging flaccid. The timbers of the ship gave the odd creak, but the shrouds hung slack. Occasionally, a small puff of breeze made a sail flutter, and the crew hopefully stirred, just to have their hope die as the breeze did.

EILEEN MUELLER

The sky was a clear and cloudless carpet of endless cerulean-blue. Giddi yearned to soar on dragonback over the sea. No such luck. He was still here, trapped under Starrus' watchful gaze. There was no glade nearby to wander off into, no clearing where he could escape unnoticed for a few moments of peace. Nowhere to go where Starrus couldn't find him—only this shrotty ship.

The ample-bellied cook ambled out of the galley toward the captain, cursing under his breath. His ruddy complexion was marred by a ferocious scowl, the paleness of his sun-bleached eyebrows almost comical. "By the shrotty lice-infected tail of a cranky dog. Captain, the hold is overrun with rats. They've eaten the hardtack, all but a wee barrel, and dirtied our supply of flour."

"What of the dried beef and salted pork?" the captain asked.

"We used the last of the beef yesterday and a rat gnawed through the last barrel of pork. The water ran out of the hole, then they got in to soil it, so now it stinks of rat dung."

The depth of the captain's scowl matched the cook's, but his was anything but comical. "How did this happen? I thought someone was on hold duty."

"Ook was killed in the battle, sir, and no one thought—"

"Of course, no one thought." The captain sighed. "I'm the only one who thinks around here. How bad is it?"

"We've enough for a bite of supper tonight and some broth in the morning, sir." The cook yanked off his hat and wrung it between his hands. "We're still at least three days from shore." He gazed at the limp sail. "If not more."

"All hands to the oars," the captain bellowed.

Sailors rushed down into the hold.

"My oarsmen will be hungrier than a nesting dragon with all that hard work."

Giddi nodded. Pulling oars would be much more strenuous than running up the rigging and trimming a few sails.

The captain spun on his heel, all business. "You two!" He waved a hand at Starrus and Giddi. "Get down to the hold too."

His straw-blond hair glinting in the sun, Starrus drew himself up, puffing out his chest as if he were a master mage. "I hardly think that the best use of a mage's talents is pulling on the oars to get us to shore." He quirked an eyebrow gazing down his nose at the captain.

"I know that," the captain snapped. "Which is why you're on rat-killing duty. If we can't find anything else, at least we can eat rat."

Ugh. Giddi's stomach churned.

Starrus reeled back, grimacing. "Surely you can't expect us to—"

"You'll do what I ask, and you'll eat what you're given. Now, get to it, and stop those rats from ruining whatever else we have left." The captain disappeared down the hatch to the main hold.

Green guards swooped down to the ship, taking turns to alight and let their riders down to help with the oars. Goren gave them a grim nod as he and his team of riders descended into the hold to have their turn at the oars. Their dragons wheeled back into the sky above the becalmed ship.

Cook shrugged. "The food's kept down there." He gestured at the aft hatch. "I'll get back to the galley and scrape together something for when the men finish their shift. Bring me up what you can salvage."

Starrus flourished a hand at the rickety ladder leading down the narrow hole into the hold.

Giddi grabbed the rungs and headed down into the gloom. When he was halfway down, Starrus' boot landed on his back. Giddi tumbled down the rungs, smacking his shoulder and hip, and landed on the planks with a thud that knocked the wind out of him.

EILEEN MUELLER

Why, of all the stinkiest tricks! Anger burning through his belly again, he scrambled to his feet. He couldn't dare let a single spark slide from his fingertips. He'd be tried for insubordination. He was only a lowly trainee mage; Starrus was his better.

Giddi settled for a snort and let a tiny ball of green mage flame flare from his fingers. He gently set it free. The mage light bobbed around the stinking, stifling hold, casting an eerie glow over an assortment of barrels, bolts of cloth, chests, and jars. Ominous squeaking and the skitter of scurrying feet made Giddi's back ripple with goose flesh. It wasn't that he didn't like rats...

Gods, it was warm down here. The air was fetid with the stench of rat droppings. The taste clung to the roof of his mouth. Jammed itself down his throat, making his stomach roil.

Starrus' boots thunked as he clambered off the ladder and leaped to the deck. "That was a bit clumsy of you. Still, accidents can't be helped. I'm sure you'll be fine."

Giddi refrained from rubbing his throbbing shoulder, not wanting to give Starrus the pleasure of knowing he'd hurt him. "I'm fine."

Red eyes ventured out from the shadows behind a chest, gleaming in the glow of Giddi's mage light. A tail disappeared down the center of a bolt of gold-and-blue striped fabric.

Giddi held his hand high, more light flaring from his fingers.

There was a shrill squeak. Suddenly, a horde of rats scampered out of their hiding spaces from behind barrels and chests, the patter of their feet drowning out Giddi's thundering heart. The hold seethed as they raced over a sack of flour that had been gnawed open, the contents littered with dark droppings. Sharp teeth gleamed in the dark. Vermin swarmed over bolts of cloth and skittered across trunks, a massive, furry tide.

Light flared from Starrus' fingers. "Kill the shrotty vermin," he rasped and flung a bolt of green flame. His trainer's mage flame hit a rat, blasting a hole in its side. The rat dropped to the planking, its body smoking. Others squeaked and fled, scampering behind trunks and barrels, worming their way through tattered bales of cloth. One dived into the half-open sack, and others followed, until the sack twitched and bulged like a dying corpse.

Starrus thrust his hands out and set the sack ablaze. It crackled, the scent of charred meat filling the hold. He closed his fingers into his fist and the flames died, leaving a pile of smoking flesh, fur and ash.

Giddi's eyes watered and bile rose in his throat. He coughed, trying to swallow his gorge. He flung out a finger and shot a bolt of fire at a rat slinking along a beam on the hull. Engulfed in flame, it landed on a bale of golden cloth which flared to life, burning with a vengeance. Giddi twisted his fingers, pulling the energy back inside himself. The flames died.

A rat skittered along the ceiling and launched itself at Starrus. The rodent sank its teeth into his trainer's shoulder. Starrus bellowed. Giddi threw a tiny fireball at the rat and its body fell at Starrus' feet, twitching and reeking of mage flame. Three more took its place, leaping at his trainer, but this time, Starrus was ready. Hands out, Giddi's trainer let out a swathe of blistering fire that killed all three rats. He mopped his brow then extinguished the burning carcasses. "Filthy vermin," Starrus snarled. He kicked one of the rat carcasses across the hold. It thudded against a trunk, spraying ash and charred fur.

Giddi spun as a rat scampered across his boot. Flame seared from his fingers. The rodent's fur lit up like a ghostly green halo. The rat's shrill squeal rang through the hold, nearly slicing his ears in two, then it was silent.

Five rats rushed at Giddi, their high-pitched shrieks ringing in his ears. His pulse pounded. Energy boiled in his core and coursed through his arm. He thrust his hand out and a bolt of flame shot out of each fingertip, the luminescent green light making Giddi squint as it hit the rats and neatly sliced off each off their heads. The headless carcasses ran in circles, their necks cauterized by the mage flame and stinking of cooked flesh. Then they dropped dead. Giddi spun to fend off another attack, flinging out his hand and severing another five rat's heads.

"How in the egg's name did you do that?" Starrus gaped. "Have you been holding back?"

Of course, he'd been holding back. Starrus was so jealous, even the slightest display of power had his trainer cracking down on him. And of course, they had to control the fire or they'd set the ship alight.

Giddi swallowed, his throat as tight as a hangman's noose. "I don't know. No, sir." He stared at his hands, hoping he looked perplexed. "It just happened."

"So, you didn't even try?" Starrus sneered.

Giddi shrugged and spun as another wave of rats leaped from a bale of cloth at him. He blasted the rats backward into the side of the hull with a gust of wind that also knocked Starrus sideways. His trainer hit a pile of barrels with a sickening crunch.

"Are you all right, sir?"

"Of course I am," Starrus snapped, nursing his hip. He stalked over to the ladder and clambered up the rungs to perch halfway up. He narrowed his eyes at Giddi. "I'll supervise your training from here. By the time I count to thirty, I want twenty rats dead."

Starrus began to count in slow, measured tones. Flame danced from Starrus' fingertips illuminating the hold as the rats charged Giddi. His trainer made no move to kill them, counting in an icy monotone that made Giddi's neck prickle.

A rat leaped at Giddi's leg, teeth bared. Giddi smote its head off then slit the gut of another with a burst of flame.

By the time Starrus had reached twenty-five, Giddi had only killed ten rats.

He mopped his face. "Sir, could we swap places? I'm exhausted."

"Ten more to kill in five seconds. Twenty-six…" Starrus kept counting, flame dancing at his fingertips, a nasty smile on his face.

Giddi spun, shooting flame, but the rats kept coming.

When Starrus reached thirty, he started from zero all over again.

Giddi soon lost count of how many times Starrus had reached thirty and how many rats he'd killed. He slumped against a barrel, panting, sweat dripping down his neck. "Could I please have a rest? Or a swig of water?" He motioned at the waterskin hanging from his trainers' belt.

Starrus smiled and sent a plume of mage flame toward Giddi's boot. Giddi jumped aside and the barrel exploded into flame, the stench of burning rum roiling through the hold. Giddi swayed, the fumes making him dizzy.

"Sorry, I was aiming for a rat." Starrus said. Smiling grimly, he extinguished the flame.

Last time Giddi had checked, he hadn't resembled a rat in the slightest. For the sake of the First Egg, the sooner he was off this ship, the better. He pursed his lips and staggered behind a wall of chests shoulder high, to the darkest corner of the hold.

His mage light reflected on hundreds of gleaming pinpoints of light. Holy dragon smoke! He let his mage light flare higher. The rats had shredded huge bales of cloth. Hundreds of rats of all sizes were scurrying away from the green luminescence. He'd found their nest.

The sight of the nest and the injustice of Starrus' treatment rankled, making Giddi seethe. He channeled his anger, letting power course through his arms, and set the nest and every rat alight. The mage fire blazed like a funeral pyre, the cloth and squealing rats engulfed in licking tongues of flame that devoured them. For a moment, Giddi wished it was Starrus who was aflame.

His cheeks burned with shame. He'd never had such vile thoughts before. He monitored the fire, making sure the ship's timbers didn't catch, and quenched it, reeling the *sathir* back inside himself until the last flame sputtered and died.

He stood for a long moment, casting mage light over the charred remains. Sweat soaking through his shirt, he was so exhausted he could only summon a faint yellow glow—yellow, the color of a beginner. In a flash, he was back in Fieldhaven at the archery tournament where he'd met Anakisha and been so excited to compete that he'd accidentally let a wall of green flame rip at the target. He shook his head. If only he'd kept control—if only he'd hidden his abilities—his trainer wouldn't be so venomous. With a stab, he realized he'd just made the same mistake again.

Giddi shrugged and shone his pale-yellow light into the corners. Not a single rat was twitching. All dead.

He stood, his breath rasping, gathering his strength. His insides were hollow, his power depleted. Giddi wanted to curl up on a soft pallet and sleep. But Starrus was waiting, so he stood and breathed, counting until he'd inhaled a hundred times.

Now that the rats were still, through the bulkhead he heard the splash of the oars and soft chant of the sailors as they heaved. He massaged his shoulder which was still throbbing where Starrus had kicked him as they'd descended into the hold. That seemed like a lifetime ago.

Slowly the soles of Giddi's feet began to tingle as he drew in new energy from his surroundings. With every breath that rasped through his aching lungs, Giddi let the life force of the sea and the air around him trickle back into his aching body. His fingers tingled. Slowly his lungs stopped aching. Burnout—he'd never been this close before, but then again, he'd never released that much *sathir* with such wild abandon. He'd contained his talents, worried others would be scared of a boy with so much raw power.

Worried his trainer would hold back and not reveal his precious secret—the secret that drove Giddi to obey him.

Slowly the well of *sathir* in his belly replenished until he had a humming coil in his middle. The stench of charred rat flesh coated his mouth. He spat and stole out from behind the wall of sea chests.

Starrus was still sitting halfway up the ladder, languidly examining his nails. "Oh, there you are, boy. Are we done?" His trainer stretched out a hand and took one last look at his manicured fingernails—nails that had likely never seen a pail or mop, nor done a day's honest labor.

Giddi picked his way through the smoke-hazed hold, his boots slipping more than once on burnt rat corpses—the squishes underfoot making him shudder.

He nodded at Starrus, too tired to speak. Hopefully, his trainer would be happy with him now.

Starrus pointed at a chest. "You missed one." A nose poked out from behind the chest, twitching. Starrus aimed a thin stream of mage flame at the final rat and killed it. "Next time, make sure you get them all." He turned and clambered up the ladder.

Giddi gaped at the ungrateful wretch's back, his fingers twitching with temptation. Gods, what was he thinking? He'd never wanted to blast anyone before, let alone hit someone in the back like a coward. Starrus brought out the worst in him. Giddi grabbed the rungs and climbed the ladder. It was ironic: trainers were supposed to tease the best out of you.

Starrus scrambled out of the hold and Giddi followed, squinting in the bright sun.

"How's the situation down there?" the captain asked.

Giddi remained silent, letting his trainer do the talking.

Starrus grimaced. "Not good, sir. The rats are fine—we killed them all—but many of your goods have perished and there aren't any decent foodstuffs left."

We killed them all! Giddi refrained from snorting. Starrus had only dealt with a handful.

"I was afraid the food was spoiled." The captain shook his head and yelled to the first mate, "Bring them some lines, so they can do something useful."

Starrus smiled ingratiatingly. "Captain, if you have a spare sack, I can volunteer my trainee to clean up the rats and toss them into the sea."

He what?!

The captain ran an appraising gaze over Giddi. "Good idea, but don't throw the carcasses overboard. And when he's done, you may choose a finely-carved chest as a token of my appreciation."

"Thank you, sir." Starrus' smile was as oily as roast eel. And twice as stinky as a raw one.

Overhead, Rengar furled her wings, her emerald scales flashing as she dived down to the ocean. She plunged her neck in the water, then backwinged and ascended in a spray of water, a silver fish flapping in her dripping jaws.

The first mate came up to the captain, a sack in his hands. "Here you go, Captain."

"What's good enough for a dragon is good enough for us." The captain reached inside and handed Starrus a short stick that had twine wrapped around it with barbed hooks on the end. The captain leveled a gaze at Giddi. "We'll need the rats as bait. It's time you both caught us some fish."

A FINE CATCH

W hen Giddi emerged from the hold with a sack of burnt rats, the captain handed him a fishing line. "With no wind, it'll take us longer to get to shore than we thought." He gave a grim chuckle. "We'll have no choice but to start eating each other unless we catch some fish."

Giddi had fond memories of fishing with his father when he was a littling, before Pa had disappeared on his quest. He smiled, remembering.

It was a hot summer's day. Giddi and Pa sat on the edge of the riverbank watching the fish flit about the swimming hole.

"How old are you now, son?" Pa asked, a cheeky twinkle in his eye. "Seven summers? Eight? Old enough to catch us a tasty supper?"

"C'mon, Pa." Giddi poked his father's ribs, making Pa twitch. "Stop teasing. You know I'm already nine summers." He puffed out his chest and thumped it. "I've been practicing. Watch this." Giddi held up his fingers and shot a thin stream of mage fire at a rock on the far side of the bank. A spray of sparks ricocheted off the rock and fell onto the surface of the water, making the fish scatter as if they'd been stung.

"Nice flame, there, but you'll never catch a meal like that, boy." Pa laughed. "I'll show you a trick." Pa took off his boots and stockings and rolled up his breeches, then dangled his legs off the edge of the riverbank, wriggling his toes in the water. "If you hang your toes in here long enough, an eel will come out from under the bank to have a nibble and then you'll be able to catch one."

Giddi arched his eyebrows. "Are you serious?"

"I'm serious." Pa's mouth twitched.

Giddi rolled up his breeches and dunked his toes in the water. Even though the day was warm, the water was chilly. "By the dragon gods, it's nippy Pa."

"Excuse my pun, son, but nippy is the last thing you want when you're luring eels," Pa teased.

Giddi wriggled his toes, and sure enough, after a while a large eel stuck its head out from under the bank, nosing around his foot.

"Quick, pull your feet—"

"Ow!" Giddi yanked his feet onto the bank and examined the bite on the edge of his big toe. "It's bleeding, Pa."

"Now," Pa urged, "use your mage flame." He yanked his feet above the water. The eel reared up out of the river, jagged jaws wide, trying to snap at Pa's feet. "Quick, son."

Giddi sent a flaming bolt of mage fire at the eel's head. The blast hit its head behind the eyes, instantly killing it. As its body slumped into the water, Pa reached an arm into the river and grabbed it. Although the eel was dead, its body twitched and contorted in his father's hand, lashing his arm with its tail.

Giddi shied back.

"It's all right, lad. They always do that when they first die. I reckon the eel's telling us life is worth fighting for." Pa winked. "Life is always worth a fight, whether it's your own life or someone else's. Remember, that with great power comes the responsibility to protect others."

Giddi looked at the eel forlornly. "I didn't protect him, did I?"

Pa's belly laugh boomed across the river, startling a fawn, which fled through the trees, its white tail flashing. "No, this eel is providing our family with sustenance so we can protect others." He ruffled Giddi's hair. "Now fetch me that stick you whittled so we can cook this delectable fellow and surprise Ma when we get home with supper."

"Come on, boy, stop dreaming." Starrus' voice cut through Giddi's thoughts.

Giddi passed a burnt rat to Starrus, the smell of the carnage making his belly churn. The only consolation was that Starrus looked just as queasy as he drove one of his hooks through the rat's upper lip and flung his line overboard.

A flurry of silver shapes shot toward Starrus' rat, making the teal ocean ripple.

Starrus' line went taut. "A fish, straight away," Starrus crowed, his face triumphant as he wound the line on his stick, heaving on the twine to pull the fish in.

Giddi cast his line out.

Starrus grunted and yanked, his face turning red and the veins in his forehead standing out.

"Not too fast," the captain cautioned, "or you'll break the line." He strode off, leaving them to it.

"Shrotty fish!" Starrus gave a mighty yank. His line broke and he flew onto his backside. A large fish sped off, its silver scales glistening as it made away with Starrus' bait and hook. Starrus got to his feet rubbing his backside.

Giddi smothered a snort and Starrus spun, his glower hot enough to strip skin. "What are you laughing at? Go fetch me another hook."

Giddi reeled in his own line, pocketed it, careful not to snag the hooks on his clothing, and strode over to the first mate who was inspecting a sail while openly guffawing at Starrus.

The mate passed him some hooks. "Trap for young players, these fish," he called out, before lowering his voice. "When you get a bite, let the line run out so the fish thinks its got freedom, then slowly pull it in."

Giddi refrained from saying that he already knew that, in case Starrus overheard. The crankier Starrus got, the worse it would be for him later. Besides, Starrus had knowledge he needed. Desperately. "Thanks for the hooks."

EILEEN MUELLER

Giddi wandered back to Starrus, threaded some new hooks onto Starrus' line and passed him back the fishing stick.

Starrus grunted and threw the line overboard. Further along the deck, a few sailors cast lines overboard too.

Before Giddi had a chance to cast his own line into the sea, Starrus' line went taut again. His trainer grinned. "See, boy, I have the magic touch."

Scowls rippled across the faces of the sailors hanging over the railing with their own lines.

Starrus let the fish take the line, playing it out. When the line slackened, he slowly turned the stick to wind it back in.

A moment later, his line broke again. "Shrotty, scum-sucking bottom dweller," Starrus cursed.

The sailors laughed.

Flinging a hand out at the ocean, Starrus raked his fingers toward the ship. A swell built on the sea, racing toward them. A freak wave rose over the side of the railing, splashing Giddi's breeches and depositing the miscreant fish—the twine still hanging from its mouth—onto the deck with a solid plop at Starrus' feet.

"See," Starrus sneered at the gaping sailors, dripping, but triumphant.

The enormous fish flopped, the pink of its gills flashing as they opened and shut in a vain attempt to draw air. Starrus struck the fish on the head with the heel of his boot, killing it, and then grasped it by the tail and waved it above his head. "Here, Captain, that'll feed some of your crew tonight."

He wasn't wrong. The fish was a fat one, as long as his arm, still twitching. Its scales gleamed on Starrus' wrist. "The rest of you no-good loafers haven't caught anything," Starrus gloated, his eyes raking over Giddi and the other sailors.

"Much appreciated, Starrus," the captain said dryly. "The rest of you may as well put down your lines and we'll let the mages do the fishing."

A way off from the ship, a dark shape undulated under the ocean, driving a school of fish toward their boat. The rushing school of white bodies gleamed with promise beneath the pristine aquamarine sea.

Giddi didn't want to stand here stuck at the rail all day, or have to swab the deck with the other men fuming. Maybe he should try Starrus' trick. He channeled *sathir* down his arm and whipped out his hand, then raked his fingers, pulling his arm toward him. An enormous wave, as wide the boat's length, swept up the side of the ship and splashed over the rail, drenching the sailors. Men scrambled out of the way as fish thudded to the deck along the length of the rail. Giddi gaped—there were at least twenty or thirty fish flopping on the planking.

He strode along the rail, throwing the smaller ones back, feeling Starrus' glare burning twin holes through his shoulder blades. Despite being wet, the sailors cheered enthusiastically and whacked the fish on the heads with their fishing sticks. Men clapped him on the back as they collected the fish in large wooden tubs.

"Cook'll smoke these. "

"They'll make mighty fine eating."

"Good work, lad."

The captain's bellow rang out, "Well done, lad, you saved the day. We now have enough food until we reach Naobia."

While the crew were busy with their backs turned and the captain was overseeing them working, Starrus stalked along the deck, fuming and gazing out to sea. He spun. A blast of wind issued from Starrus' hands, thrusting Giddi backward across the slippery, fish-laden deck. His back slammed into the rail. Giddi gasped as pain rippled down his spine. Starrus tugged his hands. Giddi slid toward him. Then Starrus flicked his arms, spinning Giddi around. Wind blasted Giddi's back. He hurtled into the rail, smacking his ribs, his breath knocked out of him.

And then Giddi saw what'd been rippling beneath the surface and causing the fish to flee. An enormous multi-tentacled creature blacker than ink was swimming alongside the ship.

Starrus let out a crazed shriek, waving his arms. *Sathir* whooshed from the sea past Giddi toward Starrus.

A huge wave higher than the tallest strongwood rose from the sea, carrying the beast with it. Water gushed over Giddi, dousing him in brine. Salt stung his eyes and filled his mouth. He spluttered and coughed, taking in more water, then waved his arms, trying to drive the water back.

"Sea monster," a man's strangled cry reached Giddi over the water thundering onto the deck.

There was a flash of black groping tentacles over the rail and a shudder as the beast hit the outside of the hull. The monster's thick tentacles flipped over the edge and wrapped themselves around Giddi's arm and chest. The beast hauled him against the rail, smacking his ribs again. The ship tilted. Giddi's heart pounded like a battle drum as the creature's vice-like grip tightened, the pressure driving the air from his lungs.

Spots danced before his eyes. Gods, he couldn't breathe.

The creature squeezed him tighter against the ship's rail. With a stab of pain, one of Giddi's ribs popped. He shrieked.

Sailors' cries rang out. A sword slashed past Giddi's head and bounced off a tentacle. The sea monster pressed him tighter against the planks, leveraging itself higher up the ship's hull until its misshapen head towered over Giddi. An arrow zipped into the beast's fleshy forehead with a wet thunk. The sea beast ignored the arrow, and opened its gaping maw, a foul briny stench washing over Giddi.

Giddi's knees grew weak and he slumped. The monster lifted him from the deck, his feet swinging in midair as it drew him toward its cavernous mouth. An enormous hooked beak glinted within the folds of its maw, growing ever closer.

Giddi turned away from the foul stench. Sailors were yelling, running, slashing at tentacles that writhed across the deck seeking more victims. Starrus was smirking, making no move to help—of course not, he'd dragged the monster from the sea.

Hot breath wafted over Giddi's cheek. Gods, he had no chance. He strained to bring his hand up. No use—the beast's grip was too tight. He tried to summon his magic, but fear froze the heat in his belly, turning it into a ball of ice.

This was it—he was going to die.

Arrows hit the beast's head with fleshy thwacks, peppering it like a pin cushion. Pain shuddering through its body, the monster tightened its tentacles and jiggled Giddi like a rag doll. For a moment, it loosened its grip.

Now! Giddi heard Pa's voice as if he were a littling all over again, learning to control his magic in Spanglewood Forest. *You can do it. Go on, son.*

Giddi lifted his thumb. A jagged bolt of flame seared from his thumb, flying into the monster's neck. Giddi channeled everything he had into that flame, making it just as fierce as the wall of fire he'd loosed at the targets in Fieldhaven; brighter than the flame he'd fired at the rat's nest; as hot as the sun.

His mage fire blasted the monster's head to smithereens.

Dark chunks of flesh showered the deck, inky blood spraying over the sailors. Its tentacles twitched madly, loosening their grip. Giddi fell to the planks among a writhing nest of tentacles thrashing in the frenzied throes of death. Tentacles wrapped themselves around sailors, masts and the boom, and then released, slumping lifeless to the deck.

Giddi kicked at a nearby tentacle and closed his eyes, glad he could breathe again.

"What in the First Egg's name was that?" captain bellowed.

"I don't know," Starrus replied mildly. "A freak wave probably washed that beast aboard. Luckily my trainee killed it."

With the wounds on his neck still raw where the sea monster had gripped him, Giddi spun, enraged, and thrust his hands up in front of his chest. He blasted Starrus backward with a gust of wind that knocked his trainer into the mainmast. The sails fluttered then billowed with air, making the repaired mast creak.

"Oi, you!" the captain cried, rushing at him. "What are you doing?"

Oh, by the dragon gods' claws, he'd probably be whipped for insubordination or trying to harm his trainer. Giddi stammered "I— I—"

The first mate approached, rolling up his sleeves. "The captain asked what you think you're doing."

Giddi gnawed his lip, staring at his feet.

The first mate clapped him on the back. "Whatever it was, do it again."

The captain laughed. "Stop looking so scared. You made those sails billow, lad. That's just the type of wind we need to get us to the mainland." The captain jammed one fist on his hip and flung his other arm up, pointing at the sail. "Now come on, mate. Get blowing."

Giddi gaped, but the captain thrust his arm out again. "This boy's going to power us to the mainland," the captain said, proudly beaming at Giddi.

The first mate clapped him on the shoulder again. "You're all right, aren't you, lad?" He nodded at Giddi's neck and tattered shirt. "Lucky you killed that monster." He gestured at the chunks of flesh on the deck.

"I'm fine." Far from it. All Giddi wanted to do was slink off down to his hammock and lick his wounds, but now he was stuck. However, with everyone's attention on him, he'd be safer than where Starrus could get his hands on him. As he thrust out his hands, Starrus smirked.

Giddi harnessed *sathir*, tugging the energy from the air and letting it thrum through him. A puff of wind gusted from his fingers and tickled the sails, making them flutter.

"That's not how you do it, lad," Starrus blustered. He pushed Giddi aside and swept his straw-blond hair off his forehead. With a grandiose flourish, he waved his arms at the sails. Wind rushed from Starrus' hands, tousling the crew's hair as it swept over them and hit the fabric. The sail snapped to life and the ship surged forward.

Starrus grinned. "See, boy?" he cried above the gale roaring from his hands. The mast creaked and the ship shuddered.

They were underway, going so fast waves surged alongside the ship leaving trails of creamy-white that tossed the remains of the sea monster's head on the ocean's surface.

"Hey, not so fast!" The captain shot Starrus a narrow-eyed glance.

"Why not?" Starrus sneered. "Are you afraid of the speed?" Sweat broke out on Starrus' forehead as the wind grew fiercer, whipping off a sailor's hat and sending it flying out to sea. The mast creaked ominously. The sail strained at its tethers.

By the First Egg, no!

Rengar roared, flapping her wings and diving toward the ship.

With a shriek of timber, the repaired mast splintered and hung off at a wild angle. Dragged by the sail, it crashed to the deck.

Crew scattered. A man was trapped under the sail, limbs floundering like a white-sheeted beast.

The first mate tackled Starrus and knocked him to the deck, then straddled him. Starrus blustered and fumed, his face turning crimson, but the first mate had a blade to his throat before he could lift a hand or cast a spark.

"The captain told you to stop," the first mate said through clenched teeth. "And that means stop."

"Throw him in the brig," the captain bellowed. "No matter how great his power, a mage who won't listen is no use to me."

A couple of crew members grabbed Starrus.

Goren and his green guards stormed out of the hatch above deck. Goren's eyes flew wide as he took in the collapsed mast. "What happened?"

"That mage happened," the captain snapped, tossing his head toward the sailors dragging Starrus away.

"Your shirt's ripped." Goren narrowed his eyes and seized Giddi's arm. "What are those marks on your neck?"

Giddi touched his stinging skin and winced. "A sea monster reared over the side of the ship and grabbed me in its tentacles." If he claimed Starrus had summoned it, no one would believe him.

"Tilt your head up." Goren examined Giddi's skin. "They look like sucker marks. I've seen them on a fisherman who slashed his way free from such a beast's slimy grasp. You're lucky to be alive." He gazed at the beast's remains. "It looks like it was a big one."

Rengar passed over the boat, the breeze from her wingbeats stirring her rider's black hair. A vivid memory shot into Giddi's mind: Starrus from above, magically thrusting Giddi against the rail and creating the giant wave that flung the sea monster at him.

Goren's dark eyes flashed as he glanced up at his dragon. He clenched his jaw and strode toward the broken mast and crumpled sail. "Come on, Let's get this ship-shape. The sooner we get back to Naobia, the better."

Giddi couldn't agree more. He couldn't wait to get back to Great Spanglewood Forest.

§

It took the rest of the day to mend the broken mast and set the sail right, even with the help of the valiant green dragons. The mighty creatures were tiring as night fell.

"Are you all right, Rengar?" Giddi asked.

"Perfectly fine," she said. *"Except that this ship is making so little progress. It's exhausting to fly in circles all day around a craft that's barely moving. I wish there was some way we could help."* She dropped the last rope for Goren to tie off and ascended, her wingbeats ruffling the newly set sail.

Goren scratched his head and addressed the captain. "Our dragons will need to rest soon. They've been airborne for hours. There's a small isle nearby where they can land."

Giddi cocked his head. "If I create some wind to propel us there, perhaps they could help tow us to the mainland after they've rested. We can't be far off."

Goren raised an eyebrow. "I'll have to ask Rengar."

Rengar interrupted. *"No, you don't. The dragon mage and I have already discussed it. I'd be happy to help and so would the others. But we'd like to start now. The sooner we can get to the isle to rest, the better. We dare not leave you here. The Scarlet Hand and his sea dragon are still at large."*

Rumbles of assent issued from the other dragons' maws.

Goren, Giddi and the first mate harnessed the dragons to the ship by fastening ropes around their haunches and tying them to iron rings mounted on the top of the hull.

Giddi flung his arms up, aiming them at the sail and braced himself. Powered by *sathir*, the energy from his surroundings, a steady wind gusted from his hands at the sails. The fabric snapped as the breeze caught it, the sails taut and bathed in the golden rays of sunset as the ship headed toward the nearby island.

NAOBIA

The rest of the trip passed without event. Starrus spent most of his time locked in the brig, scowling out over the water, speaking only when he had to. Giddi made sure he kept out of his trainer's way.

After half a day of using his wind power and the might of the dragons to help the ship make progress, a breeze rose, then grew into a steady wind that blew them toward Naobia.

A couple of days later, a cry came from the crow's nest. "Land ahoy! Naobia's in sight."

The sails billowed in the wind and the mast creaked— but now, no one cared. Land was in sight and the ship would soon be docked for repair.

Giddi ached to be back on dry land. Although he wouldn't be free of Starrus, it would be better than being confined on this ship under his trainer's thumb. He winced, testing his sore rib.

Emerald and jade dragons wheeled over the town, then roared and flew out to meet Goren and the green guards. Giddi let his mind remain open and heard them greet each other.

"Thank the Egg you've returned," cried one.

"What took you so long? We've been back for days," teased another.

"My daughter, you've returned with your cargo safely," crooned an enormous jade dragon to Rengar.

Cargo? It was odd that the dragons thought of the ship and its crew as cargo.

"The dragon mage is on board," a young dragon mind-melded, bounding about in the air, and flicking his tail. *"I'm Kevin. Nice to meet you, Giddi."*

"Nice to meet you too." Although it'd been a long and wearying journey, Giddi couldn't help grinning.

The port was a thrumming hive of activity. Horses clopped along the road to the pier. Sailors unloaded crates of spices, brightly-patterned fabric, carved chests and barrels onto merchants' carts. Voices rose in a hubbub of haggling, sailors calling commands or embracing loved ones waiting at the docks. Gulls wheeled overhead, swooping down to snaffle scraps of fish as a group of fishermen unloaded their catch from a small boat with faded blue sails.

Starrus, who'd been out of the brig for an hour, stood at the rail, squinting, the wind ruffling his straw-blond hair like wheat swaying in a storm.

Their crew tied the ship to the pier and lowered the gangplank. In a flurry of wingbeats, Rengar swooped down and landed on the pier. Kevin landed beside her, stomping his feet and raking the dock with his talons. The other green dragons departed, flying out over the city. Goren dismounted, patted Rengar's neck, and strode up the gangplank as if he were the King's Rider.

The captain pounded his fist on his heart, his weathered face creased in a smile. "Thank you. Your dragons provided valuable service: first in battle, then by assisting us to get safely back to port."

Goren nodded. "The pleasure is ours. I hope your ship will soon be repaired and that you'll be able to traverse the Naobian Sea safely again."

The captain's face tightened. "What of the Scarlet Hand?"

Goren frowned, his mouth grim. "We'll put an end to his antics, I swear it."

The captain thumped his fist on his chest again. "I'm at your service, should you require aid."

Goren raised an eyebrow. "Much appreciated. If you will, could I request a word with the mages?"

The captain inclined his head. "Be my guest."

"Thank you." Goren approached Starrus.

Giddi rushed over, eager to hear what the leader of the green guards wanted. *"Rengar, what is it?"*

"Wait and see. You're a powerful young mage, the only dragon mage in Dragons' Realm. With so much power at your hands, you don't want to rush into things foolishly. Patience would be a virtue that's worth cultivating."

Giddi rolled his eyes and took his place at his trainer's side, his neck prickling as he realized it was the first time he'd been near Starrus since the mast had snapped.

Goren eyed Starrus without smiling. "If you'd like to fly back with us, I can arrange lodgings with the green guards for both of you."

Giddi grinned eagerly. The ship rose and fell gently on the swell as Rengar mind-melded. *"We'd love to have you stay with us. As for him…"* The emerald dragon appraised Starrus. Her snort was carried by the breeze from the pier. *"I guess he is a skilled mage."*

"I'm learning from him." Giddi tried not to let his dislike of Starrus color his thoughts. There was no point in making his feelings public. He had to remain in training with Starrus.

"I'd love nothing more." Starrus' clipped tones broke through Giddi's mind-melded conversation with the mighty emerald dragon. "However, I arranged alternative lodgings for us in town before we left." He nodded brusquely at Goren and strode off, calling behind him, "Come on, boy, fetch our things."

Goren clapped Giddi on the shoulder. "Good luck with him, lad." He stalked back to his dragon, cursing Starrus under his breath.

"I'm sorry you can't stay with us," said Rengar as she unfurled her wings and shot high above the ship, heading inland, her emerald scales catching the sun like sparkling jewels.

Giddi sighed. He had no choice. He had to stay with Starrus to find out the whereabouts of his father. A powerful mage, his father had been gone on secret business for the mage council since Giddi was a littling of ten summers and hadn't been heard of since. The entire mage community had refused to speak of his father's disappearance, saying only that he was on an important quest.

When Giddi's Ma died, Master Mage Balovar, the head of Great Spanglewood Forest Mage Council, had taken Giddi under his wing and assigned Starrus as his trainer.

"Bring our luggage ashore, boy." Starrus stalked down the gangplank, his midnight-blue cape billowing in the salty breeze, leaving Giddi with his own possessions in an old sack balanced on top of the fancy chest that Starrus had received from the captain as a reward for killing the rats. As if Starrus had killed them. Giddi bit his lip and refrained from snapping something rude at Starrus. He nudged the chest with his boot. It wasn't too full—they'd come here on dragonback with only a few possessions—but it was large and unwieldy. Trust Starrus to choose something ostentatious instead of practical.

As Giddi bent to pick up the chest and sack, the first mate clapped him on the back, making him wince as his sore rib twinged. "Good luck, lad. You're going to need it with that trainer. A bit of a dandy, isn't he?"

"I'll be fine." Giddi hefted the chest, the handles cutting into his hands as he peered around the sack to make sure he kept his footing. "Thank the First Egg it isn't stormy or I'd lose my footing on the narrow gangplank."

"That mage is more slippery than any gangplank will ever be." The first mate shook his head. "Watch out, lad. I don't trust him."

"Neither do I, but thanks for the warning."

Starrus was gesturing impatiently from the dock. Giddi marched down the gangplank, back straight as an arrow, not wanting to give Starrus the pleasure of seeing him struggle. As he reached Starrus, his trainer unfastened his cloak and draped it over the sack and chest, neatly obscuring Giddi's view.

"Lose that and you'll pay with your life," he snarled softly. His voice rose. "Come along, boy, we don't have all day." Starrus strode along the crowded pier, shouldering his way through a group of sailors unloading bales of cloth and skirting a rag tag bunch of workers lifting barrels onto a cart, his straw-blond hair bobbing above the crowd.

Giddi hurried to keep up. "Excuse me." He edged past a man with a hand cart stacked high with bolts of golden cloth decorated with hatching dragonets, bursts of lush flowers, and seascapes, then made his way past a sailor haggling with a merchant over a case of necklaces and earrings.

"But they're the finest, crafted by artisans in Metropoli," the sailor exclaimed, lifting a glittering necklace with a dragon pendant encrusted with red glass beads from the chest. "Look, these are rubies—I swear it."

The merchant hooked his thumbs over his belt under his giant belly, his yellow satin shirt spotless, unlike the sailor's grubby garb. "They're nothing but glass. I'll give you a silver eagle for the lot."

"That's daylight robbery," the sailor cried. "This chest is full of precious jewels and worth at least ten golden dragon heads."

Giddi peered around the edge of Starrus' blue cloak. Where was his trainer now? He could barely see past this stupid cloak or through the throng of people. There was a flash of pale blond hair further along the road by the pier. Dragon's claws, Starrus was hoofing it. Giddi adjusted his grip on the chests' handles and pushed his way through the crowd to the other side of the road where it was less crowded. If only his load wasn't so cumbersome. Perhaps he could re-jig it. He stopped at the edge of a winding street edged by multi-storied stone buildings, and put down their belongings. Starrus' cloak slid off the sack and chest onto the dirty cobbles. Hurriedly glancing around to make sure his trainer hadn't seen, Giddi scooped it up and draped it over his arm. Of course Starrus hadn't seen—he was a barely-visible flash of pale blond among the dark haired Naobians cramming the road. A horse nickered, clopping past with a cart piled high with barrels.

Phew, the air was humid, fetid with horse dung and garbage, occasionally redeemed by the fresh salty tang blowing off the ocean and the wafting scent of peaches from a nearby fruit stall.

"Lovely juicy peaches!" The rotund middle-aged woman at the stall grinned at him. "Want one?"

"No thanks."

"Need a hand, sir?" a voice piped up behind him.

Although Giddi was tall for his twelve summers, who'd be calling him sir? He spun.

A grimy-faced littling with dark eyes and a mop of tangled black curls edged out from the shadows of the building and grinned at him. "New to Naobia, sir?" The lad's clothes were tatty and his fingernails were as black as his hair.

Not that Giddi cared. The boy was probably after a copper. Giddi had a couple in his pockets. It wouldn't hurt to help someone who was down on his luck. "Here, hold this for me, will you?" Giddi passed the lad a copper and thrust the cloak into his grubby hands. "I'm in a bit of hurry and need to repack my goods." He flung the chest open and stuffed his sack inside. It fit nicely—with enough room for Starrus' cloak. Giddi turned. "Please pass me—"

The lad was scampering off down the side street, dashing between the stone buildings, his little boots echoing off the cobbles and Starrus' cloak firmly in his grip.

Oh gods! Starrus would kill him. Giddi snapped the chest shut and flung it at the peach seller's feet. "That boy's stolen my master's cloak. Could you look after this?"

"Of course. Get after those street rats. Those blighters stole a sack of my peaches this morning."

Blighters? There was only one, but Giddi didn't bother correcting her. He thundered down the road after the rascal.

The boy ducked down an alley, scampering through the shadows, and took another twisting lane uphill behind a bakery and a butchery. Giddi raced through a cloud of buzzing flies, the pungent scent of rotting meat scraps from the butcher's discard pit sticking in his throat as he gasped for breath. This little lad was fast.

The littling bounded down a narrow lane between two buildings and clambered over a wooden fence.

As if that would stop him. With ease, Giddi vaulted the fence.

He landed on hard-packed dirt, in a small courtyard edged by the back and sides of three stone buildings. And faced a band of five masked youths in dark cloaks with swords gleaming at their hips. The boy smirked at Giddi and tossed Starrus' cloak to the biggest one, a barrel-chested lout with shoulders as broad as a draft horse's.

"Thank you, Lennie," the big lout said, catching the cloak and throwing it to another man who chucked it onto a heap of spoils piled against a wall. There were sacks, beautiful cloaks trimmed with ermine, two small chests and an assortment of blades. One of the sacks was open, revealing the stall holder's peaches. A dark stain blotted its side and the sweet aroma of peach juice hung in the air.

They'd been busy today. No doubt, Giddi wouldn't be their last victim. "I see you have a few fine goods that you've traded today," Giddi ventured. "Perhaps you don't need my tatty old cloak."

"Tatty?" the big lout sneered. "That cloak will fetch a silver eagle in the marketplace tomorrow. Or did you have a better offer?" His hand rested on his sword hilt in a not-so-subtle gesture.

"I already paid the littling a copper." Giddi held one hand out, palm up, and slowly reached into his pocket with his other hand

and drew out his last three coppers. "This is all the coin I have. Let that be payment for my cloak."

The lout curled his upper lip and gave Giddi a look that made him feel as if he'd just crawled out of dragon dung. The other thugs on either side of the lout laughed, and the lad, Lennie, sniggered. They spread out in a semicircle, flanking Giddi.

"I checked, like you said, Marco." Lennie gazed up at the lout. "He's unarmed."

Unarmed indeed. Giddi refrained from twitching his fingers and, instead, tugged on the *sathir* in the sweltering air, drawing the energy inside him.

The ringleader, Marco, grinned and advanced, drawing his sword from his scabbard with a scrape that made Giddi's blood run cold.

"How about you go about your business or we chop you into tiny pieces and put you in the butcher's offal pit?" Marco's dark eyes glinted. He waved the sword as if it were a natural extension of his own arm.

Dragon's claws! This guy knew what he was doing.

Lennie, bolstered by having five big cronies with him, gave Giddi a cheeky grin. "He was so dumb, he gave me his cloak. Can't have wanted it."

"You brat. I—"

"Don't you insult my little brother," one of the thugs roared, reaching for a dagger at his hip.

"If you really cared about your brother, you'd help him choose a better career." Giddi snorted. "Teaching him to steal and run with a gang on the streets isn't brotherly."

The man's blade flashed past Giddi's head and thudded into the fence behind him. Another thug whipped out a blade and threw that. Giddi ducked and rolled. Someone kicked his ribs and suddenly, there was a sword tip at his throat. Giddi swallowed, his gaze traveling up dark breeches and tattered shirt, taking in Marco's bulging muscles.

"How did you get those scars on your neck?" Marco asked.

Giddi shrugged one shoulder against the hard ground beneath him, careful not to move his throat. "I'm fresh off a merchant ship. I, ah, tangled with a sea monster."

"And lived to tell the tale?" Marco jerked his head at Lennie's brother. "Check him."

Marco's sword pricked a little harder. A warm trickle ran down Giddi's neck, emitting a coppery scent.

Lennie's older brother knelt down and checked the sucker scars on Giddi's neck. "It's a sea monster all right. His wounds are just like the ones your pa had when his body washed up."

"You should've stayed on the boat," Marco snapped, paling. "Not gone swimming in the sea."

"I did stay on the ship." Giddi raised an eyebrow. "The monster clawed its way up the hull of the ship and strangled me with its tentacles, trying to devour me."

Marco's face turned ashen.

Lennie piped up. "How'd you fight your way out?" He leaned in, eyes shining.

This time, Giddi waggled both his eyebrows. "With my bare hands."

Marco's gaze fell to Giddi's hands as if they held magic.

They did. But Giddi wasn't about to let them know that.

Marco was still pale and his jaw was clenched. "I suggest you get to your feet quietly, get back over the fence, and mind your own business," he ground out, drawing his sword away from Giddi's throat.

"Sure," Giddi croaked.

Marco held his blade at the ready as Giddi scrambled to his feet.

Gods, he had to do something. The dragon gods knew why, but Starrus prized his fancy-colored cloak above all else. Giddi cleared his throat. "Thank you. Ah, I can't leave without that cloak. It belongs to my master and he'll skin me alive if I return without it."

"Then fight him off with your bare hands," Lennie's brother sneered.

"Shut up, turn around, and put your hands on the wall," Marco snapped.

Giddi sighed and complied. "Are you sure you want to do this?" he muttered as another thug ran his hands down his breeches and shirt. He winced as rough hands patted his sore rib. The brute took Giddi's last three coppers and a piece of fishing twine from his pockets.

"Hurry up," Marco snapped. "We've been here long enough. The green guards will be flying patrol soon."

"We could take his cloak, too," Lennie said. "It's not as nice as the other one, but it'll still fetch coin at the market."

That was the final straw. Giddi spun, shoving out his elbow and smacking the frisker in the jaw. The man reeled back, clutching his chin. The gang of street rats yelled. More swords scraped from scabbards.

Giddi flung up his arms. Sathir churned down them and a wall of roiling flame shot from his fingers and encircled the five older street rats.

Lennie shrieked and cowered against the wall, trembling. "Don't hurt me," he cried.

"I won't, if you get me my cloak and the peaches," Giddi replied.

Lennie raced over to the wall and snatched up the cloak and sack of fruit.

"Pass them up to me." Giddi swung himself onto the fence, groaning as his ribs ached. He leaned down to grab Starrus' cloak and the woman's peaches off Lennie.

Now all he had to do was find Starrus.

§

Yanir sat down and leaned back against the trunk of an oak. He stretched his arms, the sun lighting his sandy-blond hair like a halo. By the dragon gods, he was beautiful. Why had Anakisha never seen it before? She knew the answer: she'd only had eyes for Justan, the son of Fieldhaven's ex-arbitrator.

But not anymore.

Yanir—and Zaarusha, the dragon queen—had changed all of that.

Grass rippled as the sea breeze wafted from the ocean. It was strange, scenting salt in the air after growing up on the edge of the village square in Fieldhaven. Anakisha had never even seen the Naobian Sea until she'd fought the Scarlet Hand on dragonback just over a week ago. Mind you, she hadn't been on dragonback much before that either. Or seen much besides the inside of the *Dancing Dragon*—the tavern she'd grown up in.

Poppies danced in the warm breeze. The garden outside the cottage Yanir was staying in while he recovered from his battle injuries was pretty, in a wild unkempt way, with swathes of poppies growing alongside winding paths under huge oak trees. These poppies were different from the scarlet ones at home; some were the bright yellow of buttercups; others were orange, cobalt or amethyst.

Anakisha grinned. Naobia was a whole new world.

Yanir's gray eyes danced, too, as he smiled at Anakisha and rotated his shoulder. "There. Happy?"

Anakisha was ecstatic. A week ago, he'd had a burnt hole the size of a fist on his chest and an arrow in his shoulder. Now, he was fighting fit, thanks to the local healer and the wonder of piaua juice.

"You'll do," she said. Grinning back at him, she sat down and leaned against the tree. She took his hand, lacing her fingers with his.

He reached across his body and stroked the back of her hand, his fingers creating delicious shivers that ran up her arm and made her want to melt.

He shook his head. "I'd heard that piaua juice burned, but I didn't imagine it would be that bad. How did you bear it when I healed you back at Fieldhaven?"

"Everyone knows women can bear pain better than men," she teased, poking him in the ribs.

He twitched and laughed, shaking his head, his sandy hair falling over his shoulders. A slow smile spread across his face, and he leaned down. "Then, let's see how well you withstand pleasure," he murmured, his words ghosting across her cheek. His lips brushed hers.

Anakisha shivered and arched up to meet his kiss.

The latch on the gate clicked. Someone coughed.

Anakisha jerked back, pushing Yanir away, as guilty as a littling caught stealing pastries at the market.

Giddi strode through the gate into the pretty garden, his long legs racing along the path. His dark hair was tied up in an unkempt tail and he was in his mage cloak, his shirt stained with damp patches. There were odd red circular marks on his neck.

"Good morning, Anakisha. Nice to see you, Yanir." Despite his gangly limbs and frame, Giddi bowed, sweeping an arm in an elegant flourish. "Good morning, my honored King's Rider and honored Queen's Rider."

Anakisha burst out laughing. "Welcome back. Since when have you been so formal?"

He shrugged, his intense eyes regarding her—a peculiar shade of evergreen that was so dark they could pass for black if you didn't look twice.

Anakisha leaped to her feet and enveloped Giddi in an enormous hug. She pulled back and looked at him. "I swear you're getting taller," she said. "Every time I see you, it seems like you've grown."

Giddi grinned. "I'm nearly thirteen summers old. I'm in my growth spurt. Maybe I'll tower above you tomorrow."

"It'd more likely be from a mage potion than a growth spurt if it happened that fast." She didn't want to embarrass him by asking about the strange welts on his neck. Perhaps he'd got them in battle.

Yanir got to his feet and hugged Giddi too. "Nice to see you, Giddi. Did you bring the merchant ship home safely?" He narrowed his eyes peering at the cocky young mage. "What happened to your neck?"

Anakisha cringed.

"The ship's here, safe and sound." Giddi gingerly touched one of the fierce oval marks on his throat. "We ran into a tentacled sea monster who gave me a rather slimy hug."

Yanir clapped Giddi on the back. "Thank the dragon gods you made it back to shore. Let's grab a bite while you tell us all about it." He slung an arm around Giddi's shoulders and led him along a path through the trees to a bench that overlooked the shore.

The housekeeper had laid the table earlier with a cloth, a basket of fresh pastries from the market, and a pitcher of orange juice. Anakisha and Yanir sat at the table. Giddi winced, a hand flying to his ribs as he sat down.

"Are you injured?" Anakisha asked.

He ignored her, wolfed down a pastry and reached for another. "Thanks. We ran out of food on board because we were delayed by the broken mast. We ended up fishing for our dinner, which is how I encountered the sea monster."

"So, you fished a monster from the sea?" she asked.

His eyes slid away. "Something like that. Anyway, I managed to fight it off with mage flame."

"He's hiding something," Yanir mind-melded.

"*I agree. Give him time,*" she replied.

Yanir changed the subject. "You were brilliant in battle, Giddi. Thanks for helping to save me."

Giddi hung his head. "Well, actually, Zaarusha chided me."

"Zaarusha certainly did chide you," Anakisha agreed. "What were you thinking, leaping onto Syan without asking?" She lightened her words with a friendly cuff on his shoulder.

Giddi sighed. "Yes, well, there was that, too."

Yanir shook his head. "Don't be so hard on yourself. You tried to save my life with a heroic leap onto dragonback."

"He nearly yanked you from the saddle by accident!" Anakisha said. "But you wouldn't have known. You were unconscious."

Giddi let out a sigh that wracked his frame, his shoulders slumping as the air rushed out of him. "I was just trying to help. I always make a mess of things…"

Anakisha was taken aback. What had happened to the cocky young mage who'd blasted a wall of flame at the targets in Fieldhaven? "Hang on. What's going on? Has Starrus been giving you a hard time again?" Pursing her lips, she eyed Giddi. "At least you're safe with us now. By the dragon gods, I'm glad the Scarlet Hand's dead."

Yanir cleared his throat. "About that," he said. "I've been thinking long and hard about the three men in frock coats we saw aboard the *Fiery Dragon*. I know at least one of those men dressed in a fancy frock coat that we killed was only a dummy stuffed with rags and tied to the rail."

Anakisha shook her head. "No, I'm sure we killed the Scarlet Hand. We achieved what we set out to do."

Giddi's eyes flitted between them. "Anakisha I—" He paused with his mouth half open, then snapped his jaw shut.

"Come on, Giddi, you know you can tell us anything," Anakisha said softly.

Giddi's eyes darted around as if there were spies lurking behind the oak trees. Anakisha was suddenly aware of the distant hiss of the waves on the shore and the gulls squawking.

The young mage leaned forward and whispered "I agree with you, Yanir. As the *Fiery Dragon* sailed off, I saw a young man—dressed in shirtsleeves and bloody breeches—ordering the crew about."

A chill rippled down Anakisha's neck. "And?" Her hands clenched her thin summer dress.

"You know the Scarlet Hand has a sea dragon?" Giddi's bushy eyebrows rose. "And you know I can hear dragons?"

"Yes, of course." Anakisha's heart pounded. She clenched the fabric tighter.

"Well, that sea dragon mind-melded with me, telling me our battle wasn't over yet." His bushy eyebrows drew down in an ominous frown and he chewed his lip. "Anakisha, I wish it were over. I keep remembering that dragon rider." He gulped, his cheeks paling.

An image shot into Anakisha's mind of the young rider's body shorn in two, he and his dragon plunging into the sea to be devoured by sharks in a seething flurry of foaming pink ocean. She shuddered. "Did you realize you just mind-melded with me? Thank you for sharing that."

Yanir arched an eyebrow and mind-melded with Anakisha. *"So, you and the dragon mage can mind-meld?"*

"It's news to me, too. That's the first time it's happened."

"You saw that?" Giddi mumbled. "I'm sorry. I'm feeling overwhelmed. My thoughts must've leaked."

"Leaked? Gods, he must be powerful." Yanir shook his head, then spoke aloud. "I didn't dare tell anyone I suspected the Scarlet Hand was still alive. I didn't know if I was delirious and seeing

things after being injured, but thank you for confirming what I knew in my heart."

The poppy heads nodded in the warm breeze.

Giddi cleared his throat. "So, I guess you're both heading back to Dragons' Hold?" He shifted on the bench and winced, his hand cradling his ribs.

"Are you injured?" Anakisha stood and moved around the table, taking a seat on the bench beside Giddi.

Giddi shuddered, and a vision ripped through Anakisha and Yanir's minds.

A mighty beast rose from the ocean, its tentacles sprawling over the side of a ship and wrapping around Giddi, squeezing his body. His chest ached. His lungs were tight and his throat was constricted.

Anakisha grasped her own throat as if her air was about to be choked off. Beyond the tentacles thrashing in front of her face she glimpsed Starrus smirking.

The vision faded and Giddi sat panting, sweat rolling down his forehead. "Sorry, I think I leaked again. Every time I think of that monster, I break out in a cold sweat."

"Which monster?" asked Yanir. "The kraken or Starrus?"

"A kraken? Is that what it's called?" Giddi replied.

Anakisha bent down. "Those red marks on your neck..."

"Suckers. And on my arms and torso," Giddi said. "It was a flaming close call."

"You examine him and I'll get the piaua from my bedside cabinet." Yanir strode back to the cottage.

"Piaua juice?" Giddi asked, pulling up his shirt. "How did you get your hands on that?"

Anakisha sucked a sharp breath through her teeth. Massive purple and yellow blotches marred the skin down Giddi's left side. He stood and turned, showing her more bruising on his spine and red sucker marks across the pale skin on his shoulder.

Yanir returned and passed Anakisha the vial of piaua juice. "Well, Giddi, if you came off better, I'd hate to see what the kraken looks like."

Giddi chuckled, then winced and clutched his ribs. "Let's just say that monster is missing a few tentacles. And most of its body. The sharks feasted well that day."

Anakisha's throat was too choked to speak. He was so young. Only a few summers older than Stella, her sister back in Fieldhaven. Giddi's injuries were far worse than the damage the Howlers had done to Stella, yet the memory of her sister crying at the tavern's kitchen table, her cheek marred with a bruise, made Anakisha's belly surge with anger all over again.

What was wrong with her? Another memory battered at the door in her mind. She refused to let it in, but it broke through anyway: Justan, standing at the back door of the Dancing Dragon with her bloody, dead brother Jacob in his arms.

Anakisha swallowed hard and blinked, then swallowed again. Justan—the man who'd murdered her brother and fooled her into thinking he loved her. And Starrus smirking as Giddi was in the kraken's grip. She'd seen his trainer bully Giddi more than once. The nagging feeling that Starrus had orchestrated the monster's attack wouldn't leave her.

"Lie in the grass," she said gruffly, spreading a cloak on the ground for Giddi. A gull swooped down to the table, diving at the pastries. Yanir waved his arms to shoo it off.

Giddi hissed as Anakisha dropped drops of the pale-green juice into his skin and rubbed it in. "Flaming eggs and claws, it burns." Green sparks flitted from his fingers, and leaped into the grass, making it smolder.

Yanir stamped the sparks out. "Watch it or the whole cottage will go up."

The bruises on Giddi's skin slowly receded, then disappeared. He stretched and flexed his side. His face lit up. "It worked. I feel better than I have in days." He sat up and twisted his torso. "Hey, piaua is amazing. Thank you."

She grinned back. "You're welcome, Giddi. Anytime."

Giddi's face clouded. He cleared his throat. "Do you mind if Starrus and I travel back to Dragons' Hold with you both, instead of me traveling with him alone?" His eyes flitted between them.

Yanir's pewter eyes met Anakisha's. *"I'd been hoping to get to know you better on the return journey,"* he mind-melded. *"But I'd do anything to help Giddi get away from Starrus."*

"So would I." Anakisha smiled at Giddi. "You're welcome to travel back to Dragons' Hold with us. We're leaving tomorrow."

Yanir ran a hand through his hair. "We'll address your trainer's behavior with the mage council at Dragons' Hold."

Giddi scrambled to his feet, his body rigid. "No! You can't do that. Whatever you do, you can't let on to Starrus that you know."

Anakisha planted her hands on her hips. "And why not?"

Giddi's gaze slid away. "You just can't. That's all."

"What's Giddi hiding?" Yanir mind-melded.

Overhead, a dragon roared. Leaves rustled in the wind from Rengar's wingbeats as she swooped down. Her feet thudded down on the trail to the cottage's gate, scattering pebbles. Goren swung out of the saddle and strode through the gate.

"Anakisha, Yanir. And you." He pointed at the young dragon mage. "Meet us by the docks as soon as you can. There have been reports of pirates attacking a ship near an isle off the coast."

A shiver of fear rippled down Anakisha's spine. Yanir's warm hand closed around hers as they surged to their feet.

"Yes, Goren, we'll be there," the King's Rider answered.

"There's no time to waste. Let's go," Giddi cried, his eyes shining brightly.

Thank the Egg, she'd just healed him.

To the Rescue

S oon, Anakisha, Giddi and Yanir were gathered near the docks with a troop of green guards and the few blue guards who'd remained behind to help patrol the coast. Beyond them fishermen were unloading their catch, sliding fish into barrels and loading them onto a cart bound for the market.

Giddi sniffed, breathing in brine and trying to quiet the agitation flitting through his belly. He wasn't even a qualified mage, yet he was fighting his second battle against pirates in as many weeks.

Goren stabbed the horizon with his finger. "See that smoke from behind Talon Isle? We suspect pirates have set fire to a boat. Hopefully they haven't taken everyone captive for the slave trade in Metropoli, but if they have, we'll hunt down our people and rescue them. Our young dragon mage, Giddi, can ride Kevin." This time his finger stabbed toward a young green dragon. The green shifted on his hindquarters, his talons skittering across the cobbled dockway.

Butterflies erupted in Giddi's stomach, beating his insides with their wings. By the First Egg and the mother of all dragons! He was riding a dragon on his own into battle! He casually strolled toward the glorious emerald dragon. The green was young, like himself, not fully grown but still large enough to ride.

"He's in training," Goren barked. "Like you." He shot a stern glance at Giddi. "No hi-jinks. Be brave, but be careful. We don't want either of you injured."

"I'll take care of them." An older blue guard nodded at Goren from the saddle. His dragon's cobalt hide was marked with scars from many battles and his gray hair rose around his head in a halo the same shade as his bushy beard.

"I'm Giddi, a trainee mage from Great Spanglewood Forest." Giddi strode over and reached up to shake the rider's hand.

"I'm aware," the rider said dryly, leaning down from his saddle to meet Giddi's handshake with a firm grip. "You're the young dragon mage, aren't you?" Giddi nodded, and the rider continued, "I'm Frugar of Lush Valley. I was the arbitrator there until I imprinted with Garthox." He patted his dragon's scaly cobalt neck and chuckled. "That was a change in my life. My son, Joris, is the new arbitrator now. He's raising a family, but his child is much younger than you—a newborn babe in fact." He shot Giddi a shrewd glance. "Stick by us and we'll make sure no harm comes to you both."

Kevin snorted and preened his emerald scales. Giddi twitched as a mellow, honeyed voice flowed through his mind. *"As if I'd let any harm come to my rider."*

Giddi couldn't help grinning.

"Very well, Frugar." Goren faced Giddi. "Pay heed to Frugar. He knows what he's doing."

Giddi nodded. "Of course."

"So, they think we need babysitters. We'll show them, won't we?" The dragon lowered his head and sniffed Giddi's hair. He pulled his head back and narrowed his eyes. *"What are those shaggy things above your eyelids? Are you in the habit of carrying spare caterpillars around for a snack?"*

Giddi burst out laughing. *"No,"* he mind-melded. *"Those are my eyebrows. I've always been teased that they grew faster than the rest of me."*

The dragon eyed him from head to toe. *"I dispute that,"* he said. *"I think you've grown perfectly well. You're just the right size to ride me. My name is Kevin."*

"I know, you greeted me when we first docked. Nice to see you again." Giddi laughed again and scratched the skin at the base of

Kevin's horns. Kevin tilted his head, a low rumble echoing through his throat. His eyes slitted in pleasure, he angled his head so Giddi could reach better. As Giddi's fingers caressed the ridged scales, a comforting warmth stole across his chest, making him smile.

"Come on," Goren called, already in the saddle. "You'll bond fast enough in battle."

Giddi clambered up his dragon's side and fastened himself into the saddle, relieved that his sit bones didn't ache the way they had after his first three days on dragonback when they'd raced out to fight the Scarlet Hand.

Rengar tensed her haunches and sprang into the air. Zaarusha, Syan and the green and blue guards followed her like a satin ribbon unfurling across the harbor.

Giddi gulped. They were off to battle again. With no bow at his disposal, Giddi was reliant on the power coursing through him. Kevin tensed his haunches and sprang, wings flapping. Giddi's teeth snapped shut and his belly dropped so fast it landed in his boots.

They shot over the fishing boat, Kevin's talons nearly scraping the tip of the mast. A fisherman gave a shrill whistle. Another yelled. A cheer rose from the dockworkers, and a few waved.

Garthox's voice was instantly in Giddi's and Kevin's minds. *"Not so close to those ships,"* he growled. *"We're rescuing those in trouble, not doing dragon acrobatics."*

"Of course," Giddi replied as Kevin wheeled in a mad frenzy, dancing out over the sparkling ocean.

§

Kevin winged through the sky, zipping between the other dragons, dancing with excitement. Giddi held on, his hair ruffling in the wind and his heart soaring as they sped over the sapphire ocean. A school of flying fish broke out of the sea, arcing out of the water in a spray of crystal droplets. An immense dark shadow rippled beneath the surface, chasing the silver fish.

The hidden creature lurking in the vast ocean's depths reminded Giddi of the sea monster. He shuddered, feeling the grasping tentacles on his throat and chest all over again. His windpipe tightened and his hand reflexively flew to his ribs. Thank the dragon gods Anakisha had healed him so he was fit for battle.

"Don't fear," Kevin said. *"If any creature attacks, I'll deal with it. You're safe in my talons."*

Giddi hadn't even realized he'd shared his thoughts.

"We'll have to work on you shielding your thoughts when you have strong emotion," Kevin said. *"Being able to mind-meld at will is an unusual talent, but if you can't control it, it could become a fatal weakness."*

Thank the Egg, Starrus wasn't with them now. The last thing Giddi wanted was for Starrus to know his weaknesses. His trainer was like those hidden creatures lurking in the vast ocean's depths, ready to strike anytime.

Giddi lifted the flap on a saddlebag and pulled out some cheese and an apple. "Do you want some?"

Kevin snorted and dived.

Giddi grabbed the saddle, losing his grip on the apple. It plummeted into the sea. Kevin followed, wings furled and tail flying out above them as they dropped. When the next school of flying fish broke out of the ocean, Kevin plucked some fish in his talons and threw them into the air. Catching them in his maw, he snapped them down. He dived again and snatched up another fish. *"This one's for you. I assume you don't like fish raw—although I can't understand why."*

Giddi chuckled. "Certainly not—unless the raw fish is marinated in soppleberry jam and apple vinegar and basted with honey—but even then, I prefer my fish cooked."

Kevin snorted and flung the fish into the air. He speared it on his talon and shot a moderate orange flame at the fish, roasting it.

Giddi caught the fish, throwing it from hand to hand to cool it as Kevin ascended back up to fly with the other dragons.

Ahead, a black pall spread across the sky, and the scent of burning timber drifted on the air. They were rapidly approaching Talon Isle.

Giddi munched down the succulent fish, juice running down his chin. *"By the First Egg, that was delicious, better than anything I've had in weeks. I could get used to this life."*

"So could I." The dragon rumbled beneath him. *"I know we haven't imprinted, but I'd be honored if you were my rider."*

"Thank you." Giddi shrugged. What else could he say? Although he felt a warm affection for this dragon, they hadn't had the glorious rush of emotion that true riders spoke of when discussing the bonding process. While he could detect Kevin's thoughts and some of his emotions, from what he'd heard, imprinting was a lot stronger. He snorted. As if speeding across the ocean on dragonback and mind-melding with a magnificent creature wasn't enough. This was glorious.

Soon, wisps of smoke curled around Kevin, Rengar, and the other dragons.

"Dragons' claws!" Goren called as they shot above the smoke-bound isle.

Yanir flung an arm toward a burning ship on the far side of the isle, calling. "Dragons, speed to that ship."

Rengar, Zaarusha and Syan shot down toward the craft. Flames licked up the masts. Figures dashed across the burning deck. Through the smoke, Giddi glimpsed a three-masted ship sailing off toward the horizon. His heart thrummed at the thought of encountering the Scarlet Hand again.

Smoke engulfed the other dragons as they dived to rescue the crew on the burning ship.

Giddi mind-melded with Kevin, *"That pirate ship's getting away."*

"It is indeed. Those vagabonds should pay for setting this ship alight." Giddi wiped the sweat from his face as Kevin shot out of the smoke and across the ocean, tearing after the three-masted ship.

§

Dirty smoke stained the sky like an ugly inkblot. The boat's sails were on fire, fierce flames devouring the fabric. The mast and hull had caught fire too. Anakisha leaned low as Zaarusha angled her wings and sped down toward the burning craft. Four figures scrambled about on deck, trying to douse the flames with pails of seawater. Even as they lowered their pails on ropes and dunked them into the sea to pass the buckets back to their crew mates, she knew it was too late.

The fire crackled. Thick plumes of smoke rose from the hold. Any moment now, the craft would be nothing but a smoking ruin on the water.

"We have to save these people," she cried, mind-melding with Zaarusha, Yanir and Syan.

"We can't save the boat," Yanir agreed. *"Let's get them out."*

Syan's dark wings flapped. He and the King's Rider vanished into the roiling smoke.

Anakisha's heart pounded, her eyes smarting as Zaarusha followed Syan into the blistering heat.

§

In a flurry of hot orange sparks, the burning mast crashed onto the deck. A strangled scream cut through the smoke. The mast had landed on a sailor, pinning his leg to the deck. Yanir barely snatched a breath before Syan dived.

His sleek scales flashing, Syan angled through the fumes. Yanir's eyes watered. Heat roiled over them as Syan grasped the sailor in his talons and dragged him out from under the mast. The

EILEEN MUELLER

man screamed and his head rolled back. Syan wrenched him up in his talons, and swooped. Flames leaped along the man's breeches, burning him alive.

"*Hold on.*" Syan said.

Yanir's stomach lurched as they dived over the edge of the ship toward the sea.

Syan plunged the man's lower body into the water, then they were airborne, flying back to Talon Isle.

§

Anakisha's hair whipped her face, tendrils of smoke wending up her nostrils, making her cough and splutter. She wrapped a scarf over her nose, mouth and chin.

"*Hold on!*" Zaarusha rumbled and dived, her rainbow-hued scales dimmed by dark smoke.

Anakisha leaned forward and slid her hands through the hand holds on Zaarusha's saddle. They zipped through the smoke and heat, then swooped over the deck. A Naobian woman was beating back flames with a blanket.

"*We must help that woman!*" Anakisha mind-melded.

As Zaarusha wheeled to turn around, the blanket burst into flame and the woman's clothing and hair caught alight.

"No," Anakisha's scream was drowned out by the woman's piercing shriek.

Zaarusha dived to the ocean, filled her maw with water and spewed it over the woman's head. The flames fizzled and died. The woman gaped up at them, her garb drenched and her forehead blistered.

Zaarusha plucked her in her talons and flew through the black, choking smoke toward the golden sands of Talon Isle.

§

Frugar leaned low over his dragon, Garthox, as she angled her wings to miss the worst of the smoke and shot around the burning mizzenmast. Since he'd left Lush Valley, he'd admired the sleek fishing craft and trade ships along the Naobian coast. What a waste of a fine boat. He pulled a cloth up over his nose as they swooped along the deck.

The captain was valiantly battling flames at the aft end of the hull, but he had no chance. The entire craft was about to go down with its goods and the lives of its crew, if they didn't save them.

Frugar tossed a rope down to the captain and bellowed. "Up here!"

The captain didn't hear him. The roar of the fire and the crackling flames were deafening.

A throaty bellow issued from Garthox's throat.

The captain glanced up. Relief etched on his soot-stained face, he grasped hold of the rope. Frugar strained, hanging onto it as the man clambered up the rope and eased himself up behind Frugar into the saddle. He collapsed against Frugar's back, panting. The man's heart thudded against Frugar's spine. "Th-thank y-you."

Garthox flapped his wings, cutting through the smoke high above the burning craft. "It's all right. You're safe now," Frugar patted the man's arm as the captain shuddered against his spine.

"Shrotty pirates," the captain cursed. "We should burn the Scarlet Hand himself."

"As much as I'd like to run down those scoundrels for ruining your fine livelihood, we need to get you all safely back to shore. Saving people's lives is more important than chasing down those filthy pirates." Frugar shook his head, frustrated.

Out of the corner of his eye, he caught a flash of green winging out over the horizon. *What in the Egg's name are that stupid young dragon and dragon mage up to?*

"We'd better find out," Garthox replied.

"Hold on tight," Frugar bellowed as Garthox flew after Kevin and Giddi, speeding across the ocean toward the pirate ship.

EILEEN MUELLER

§

Zaarusha deposited the woman on the golden sands edging a beautiful lagoon. The beach was fringed with palms, but even this idyllic isle was overshadowed by the thick pall of smoke.

Yanir and Syan landed and helped a man sit on the sand nearby, with Yanir tending him.

Anakisha fetched a waterskin and slid off her saddle. "Here. Let's use this on your forehead."

"Thank you." The woman bowed her head and let Anakisha tip water over her singed hair and the angry skin on her forehead. The lady hissed as rivulets of water tracked clean trails over her char-streaked face.

"I hope that gives you some relief." Anakisha fastened the empty waterskin, doubting much else would help. Half of the lady's hair was singed to a crisp, the remnants standing out in a blackened halo on one side of her head.

The Naobian's dark eyes flew wide. "It's you. From Fieldhaven."

"You know me?" Anakisha asked.

Yanir wandered over with the other crew member.

Anakisha squinted at the woman. She did look familiar. That was it! "You sold me my first coconut and pineapple."

The woman gave her a shrewd glance. "Yes, but you were with another man, not the King's Rider."

Anakisha's throat tightened at the mention of that traitor Justan.

Yanir slipped his arm around her shoulders. "Not anymore," he said simply. "Now she's the Queen's Rider and flies at my side. Hopefully for many more years." He bent and kissed her hair.

Anakisha's heart swelled.

"Thank First Egg, you're here." The woman rushed forward and flung her arms around Anakisha. "Thank you, honored Queen's Rider."

"I believe I recognize you from the *Dancing Dragon*," Yanir said to the woman. "You and your husband told me about the Naobian pirates."

"I'm pleased to see you. We've been set upon by more pirates. Now our ship's burned to the waterline. They boarded us and took our best goods then made off, torching our craft as they left." She gestured at the smoking wreckage on the water, her face creased with worry. "Have you seen my husband?" Panic edged her voice.

Anakisha mind-melded with Zaarusha. *"Could you check with the dragons whether the ship's captain has been saved?"*

"Certainly." Moments later, Zaarusha mind-melded again. *"Garthox says he's carrying him behind Frugar. He's injured, but he's alive."*

Anakisha shared the news. The woman's answering smile was the best thing she'd seen all day.

§

Goren's throat was tight with the acrid fumes of the burning boat. Near the fiercest flames, was a young man tossing water into the raging inferno. His paltry pailfuls created clouds of steam that hissed and billowed over his face only to disappear as the roiling heat drove all the moisture from the air.

Goren squinted against the smoke smarting his eyes as Rengar lunged to the deck and snatched the lad's shoulders in her talons.

His feet swaying, they took off, Rengar's wings beating furiously.

The mast cracked, a shower of sparks flying over Rengar's wings. Via the imprinting bond, Goren felt pain searing through his dragon. He snatched up his waterskin and flung the contents over the embers, extinguishing them before they could burn the flimsy membranes between her wing struts and plunge them into the sea.

"Rengar, are you all right?" Gods, if he lost his dragon...

"I'm fine. Thank you for the shower, though." Rengar always downplayed her injures, but she couldn't fool him. That'd been a

close call. She ascended high over the open ocean, the sea a carpet of moving living emerald and indigo beneath them. *"He's getting heavy. Ready to play catch?"* she asked.

Goren looped a rope under the saddle straps, ready for the lad. *"I'm ready, but he might not be."* He chuckled, then called out to the lad, "Get ready, we're going to catch you."

Rengar dropped the lad. She furled her wings and dived, her snout facing the sea and her tail streaming out behind her. Goren's eyes watered in the downward rush. Rengar caught up to the lad and broke his fall by slapping his backside with her tail.

He flew up into the air, screeching.

"Now," Goren yelled. "Get ready. We're going to catch you."

Surprise shot across the lad's grimy face. He floundered, legs flailing in midair. Rengar slapped him again to break his fall again and dived neatly under the boy.

With a shriek the lad's body slapped onto her neck where he clung, shuddering.

Goren flung his arms around the boy and hung on tight. "Stop screaming," he instructed, "you're safe now. Relax and hang onto her spinal ridge."

The boy wrapped his arms around the dragon's spinal ridge. Goren secured his rope around the lad's waist, tying him onto his dragon's neck. "No point in you falling off before we reach Naobia," he said.

"Our ship," the lad groaned. "What will become of it?"

The fire below was raging through the vessel, the timbers charred and already disintegrating. Those vicious flames would leave nothing but a broken hull to be scattered upon the sea.

"I expect it will burn itself out soon enough," Goren said matter-of-factly. "There's not much we can do, except get you and the crew safely back to shore."

The lad gritted his teeth. "And those pirates who set fire to our boat? What of them?"

It took skill enough to aim an arrow accurately from dragon-back. It would be nearly impossible burdened with injured passengers. "Don't worry. It won't be today, but we'll track them down," Goren growled.

Rengar interrupted. *"What are those two up to now?"*

Goren spun. The dragon mage and Kevin were a streak of green shooting across the ocean toward the pirate ship, Frugar and Garthox on their tail. He squinted. *"Does Frugar have a passenger on dragonback?"*

Rengar melded. *"Yes, the captain, who's badly injured."*

An injured captain, a silly young dragon, and a dragon mage who was nothing more than a sapling were going up against a cutthroat band of pirates?

"May the dragon gods help them," Goren muttered.

FRUGAR

Frugar hunched low over Garthox. *"That shrotty dragon mage and that silly dragon."*

A growl built in Garthox's throat. *"Headstrong and foolish, if you ask me."*

The captain spasmed in pain against Frugar's back, but clung on tight, his arms clenched around Frugar's waist.

Who did that dragon mage think he was, going after a pirate ship on his own? It was a brilliant way to get himself killed. A shiver ran through Frugar, as if someone had walked over his grave. He flexed his shoulders. "Please lean back a bit, would you?" he said to the captain. "I need to access to my quiver."

As the wounded captain leaned back, Frugar swung his quiver free, angled it over the outside of his shoulder, and nocked an arrow to his bow. Ahead of him, the dragon mage and that foolish young dragon sped across the ocean, descending toward the pirate ship.

§

Giddi's heart thrummed, fire burning through his veins and sparks flitting from his fingertips as they sailed through the air toward the pirate ship.

"Hey, stop!" Frugar bellowed behind them.

What was Frugar thinking? They were almost within firing range.

Kevin bucked in midair. *"We can we ignore him, can't we? We're so close."*

"I agree. Those pirates harmed innocents. They deserve what's coming."

Now, Giddi could clearly see it wasn't the Scarlet Hand's ship, the *Fiery Dragon*, but another pirate they were chasing. Instead of blood red sails, the ship's were white. A dark flag of a dragon skull flew from the topmast. The figurehead wasn't a dragon, but a carved mermaid with flowing locks of hair that partially obscured her shapely torso and draped down to her scaled tail.

"Are we close enough?" Kevin asked, excitement thrumming through his mighty scaled body as they swooped down.

"I think so!" Giddi unleashed a plume of green flame from his fingers. It shot through the air and sizzled into the sea. Flame it, they weren't close enough.

"We need to go nearer so I can burn them," Kevin mind-melded, shooting forward with a surge of speed that nearly blew Giddi's bushy eyebrows off.

"Do you think we should swoop lower?" Giddi asked.

A pirate yelled.

Dragon's fangs, his flame had alerted them, so they'd lost the element of surprise.

Pirates poured out of the hold, hollering and seething across the ship. A few swarmed the rigging like monkeys, and clambered into the crow's nest. They nocked their bows and released a volley of arrows. More shot at Giddi and Kevin from on deck.

Arrows zipped through the air. Kevin swooped to avoid being hit.

"Lower," said Giddi. *"I'm still out of range."*

Kevin swerved and Giddi ducked as another arrow whistled past his head. By the Egg, that was a lucky miss.

More arrows headed for them. Giddi blasted a swathe of flame. The arrow shafts crumpled to ashes that fluttered on the breeze. Kevin rushed forward, his wings scattering the ashes as the arrowheads dropped into the ocean.

"We're finally in range!" Giddi blasted mage fire at the ship. The sail caught, green flames licking along the edge. Pirates heaved pails of water at the sail and the fire died.

Giddi leaned back to avoid an arrow whizzing for his chest— another narrow escape. There was a cry behind him. A dragon roared. Kevin wheeled and shot up. Giddi spun in the saddle. Frugar was on Garthox, his bow hanging from one hand, his other hand clutched at his breast, the arrow protruding from between his fingers.

Beneath his splayed fingers, a scarlet stain spread across Frugar's riders' garb.

The old dragon rider gazed at him, stricken. His eyes rolled back in his head. He slumped forward over his dragon's neck, revealing an injured man he'd rescued from the burning boat.

The captain of the burned ship reached forward and shook Frugar, but it was too late—the old rider was dead.

Horrified, Giddi's throat constricted as Garthox let out an anguished roar.

Anger kindled inside Giddi's belly. He kicked Kevin's sides. *"Let's get down there and kill those shrotty pirates."*

"We'll teach them a lesson," Kevin growled. Kevin's anger coursed through Giddi's body, making him tremble with rage. Fire whirled from his fingertips, exploding into an enormous sheet which sped toward the pirate ship.

But the wind changed, the pirates tacked, and his fire blew off course, sweeping past the edge of the ship's rail.

Garthox roared. Her voice sliced through Giddi's anger like a glacier. *"Stop your foolishness. Our lives are more important than your revenge. Turn back at once and head for Goren. You may not care about your own life or this captain's, but at least you could consider Kevin's. He's a young dragon and has hundreds of years to live. Don't waste them with your petty vengeance."*

Before Giddi could answer, Kevin spun and followed Garthox back toward the burning ship and Talon Isle. With every wingbeat, Frugar's blood slid down his cobalt dragon's side, crimson dripping into the sea.

GOREN'S WRATH

Kevin and Giddi landed in a field outside Naobia, joining Goren and his troops of green and blue guards. Garthox landed beside them and let out a mournful howl. The captain's eyes flew wide as he fumbled with Frugar's harness. Goren rushed over to assist him.

Giddi slid from the saddle, legs trembling, and strode over to help Goren lift Frugar's body from his dragon's back. Goren got his arms around Frugar's chest. His belly churning with nausea, Giddi took the weight of Frugar's legs, and they lifted him down. The older rider's congealed blood smeared over Goren's riders' garb as other blue guards grasped his body. They carried him across the meadow.

Giddi's head spun. It was his fault Frugar was dead. His rashness and stupidity had ended a seasoned rider's life.

"Lay him here," Goren said.

They lay Frugar on a blanket. Goren folded the blanket and covered Frugar's torso with it, leaving his face open to the air. "We'll leave his view unimpeded. It's only right that he should face the sky that he loved to soar through with Garthox." Goren thumped his fist over his heart and bowed his head. "May Frugar's spirit soar with departed dragons."

Frugar's lifeless blue eyes stared up at the sky.

"May his spirit soar with departed dragons," the blue and green guards echoed.

Giddi tried to mumble along with them, but he was struggling so hard not to vomit, he could barely manage. Dead. Dead. Dead. All because of him.

"Come with me." Goren led them a short way from Frugar's corpse. The riders silently followed, forming a ring around Goren when he stopped.

Goren turned to Giddi. "Rengar has relayed what Garthox saw. You fool," he hissed. Veins stood out on Goren's temples as he pounded a fist into the palm of his other hand. "You've lost an experienced rider—and for what? Your pride?"

Giddi grimaced.

The silence drew out between them for long moments before the leader of the green guards broke it. "More like your stupidity. You were under my command, and yet you rode off after that pirate ship as if it were no threat at all, endangering yourself and your dragon." He waved an arm at the captain, still perched on Garthox's back. "We were supposed to be saving people, not seeking revenge." Goren's jaw clenched, the muscles twitching as he ground his teeth and regarded Giddi with slitted eyes.

Giddi stood tall, his hands clasped behind his back, and held his head up, meeting Goren's gaze. He deserved every drop of Goren's wrath. "I acknowledge that Frugar lost his life due to my foolish actions." A tear leaked from the corner of Giddi's eye and tracked down his jaw.

Goren didn't say a word, merely stared at him as if his burning gaze could ignite Giddi's body and engulf him on the spot.

Yanir shifted on his feet. "Anakisha said you were warned against such foolishness by the dragon queen herself when you tried to rescue me in battle." Yanir's gray eyes were as flat as slate. "Zaarusha told you then to think before you act, to consult with your dragon—or any dragon for that matter." His cheeks puffed up, then he released an exasperated breath.

There was no point in mentioning that Giddi had asked Kevin.

"*I encouraged you.*" Kevin's head drooped, his scales dull. The poor young dragon felt just as guilty as he did.

Goren's eyes finally broke from Giddi's and met the King's Rider's gaze. "Frugar is the former arbitrator of Lush Valley settlement."

The King's Rider nodded. "Giddi, the price of your foolishness has been a man's life—an honest man, one who is far from his home. You will accompany me and Anakisha to visit Frugar's family and inform them that their father has fallen in battle, so they can pay their last respects."

"And their grandfather," Goren snapped. "His son's first littling was born two days before he left Lush Valley to come to our aid. Now he will never see that littling grow up. Never have the happiness of seeing his wife or any of his progeny again."

"Rengar has arranged for supplies to be brought here so you can leave at once," said Goren, motioning at two incoming green guards, flapping out from the city toward them. "You'll be riding Kevin. He deserves to face their grief as much as you do." He rubbed a hand over his forehead and turned to the gathered riders, his shoulders slumped. "Prepare Frugar's body for the long flight."

Two of the green guards secured Frugar's body in the blanket, covering his face, then tied him to the back of Kevin's saddle.

"If you learn from this, perhaps Frugar's death will prevent you from endangering others. Perhaps from killing many. Make his sacrifice count." Goren strode back to Rengar, mounted, and flew off toward the city.

Green guard riders assisted Yanir and Anakisha to transfer the supplies from the incoming green guards' saddlebags to Zaarusha's, Syan's and Kevin's. Green guards took the ship's crew back to Naobia to see a healer.

The blue guards helped the captain to dismount from Garthox and led him to a waiting green dragon. They gathered around as Garthox pointed her snout skyward and let out another howl that made goosebumps ripple along Giddi's arms and his neck hairs stand on end.

A heavy weight pooled in Giddi's belly. He stood numb, no one looking at him, as the dragon howled again.

Garthox slid into his head. *"Due to your foolish antics, my rider has died. You may as well have shot him with mage flame yourself."* She snarled, the muscles in her sinuous throat rippling, and bared her fangs at Giddi.

Giddi stood his ground, not moving a finger's breadth. He braced himself and met her gaze. If this was it, he'd die acknowledging the consequences of his actions. *"It's my fault."*

Her head lunged down toward him. She opened her maw and hot breath gusted past her yellowed fangs, blasting over Giddi's face. *"He died, trying to protect you from your recklessness."* Her fangs clashed shut, a hand's breadth from his cheek. *"No one will trust you again until you prove yourself,"* she snarled.

Ice slithered down his back. His thirteenth name day was tomorrow, and already, his hands were stained with blood as scarlet as the red poppies that had been bobbing in Anakisha and Yanir's garden that morning.

He tried to clear his throat, but couldn't speak. Instead, he nodded, meeting the dragon's golden gaze.

Her tail whipped out and struck Giddi's thigh, making it sting. She held her head high, turned her back on him, and stalked across the meadow.

LUSH VALLEY

After two days of arduous flight with Frugar's body strapped across Kevin's haunches behind Giddi's saddle, they circled over Lush Valley settlement with heavy hearts.

Zaarusha, Syan and Kevin landed in the village square, their talons skittering on the cobbles. Frugar's dragon, Garthox, landed too—standing alone, her head held high, her saddle empty.

Villagers wandering through the square stopped to stare. People rushed out of stores and a crowd built. Murmurs rippled through the villagers. From somewhere beyond the square ringed with wooden and brick two-storied buildings, drums started beating. Their booms echoed through the settlement and people flooded the square until they could barely move.

Guttural cries rent the air. "Frugar!"

"No, not Frugar!"

"Quick, fetch Joris."

Anakisha and Yanir dismounted. Giddi clambered off Kevin's back and went to stand near them. The crowd parted to let a man in his late twenties through. Joris strode toward them, his gaze grazing Garthox's empty saddle and his mouth set in a grimace. "Where is my father?" he demanded.

His eyes darted to Frugar's body slung across Kevin's haunches, and his mouth sagged. Shock rippled across his features. He addressed Yanir. "The first visit King Syan and his new rider pay me is to bring back my dead father?"

Yanir cleared his throat and met the man's gaze, thumping his hand on his heart. "I'm Yanir, Syan's new rider. Your humble servant, sir."

"Tell me what happened." Joris strode to his father's dejected dragon and patted her snout, then spun and stalked to Kevin. He snapped his fingers, and three farmers rushed to help him untie his father's body and lift it down. He stood, cradling Frugar against his chest. His fierce blue eyes met Yanir's. "How did he die?"

The crowd was silent.

Yanir cleared his throat again. "He died valiantly in battle, defending innocent people against pirates." The King's Rider's eyes met Giddi's but he said nothing of Giddi's part in Frugar's death.

Giddi hung his head in shame. Gods, if only he could take back his actions, turn back time, or magically make everything better. His chest grew tight. There was no magic that could bring back the dead.

A woman bustled into the square holding a sleeping babe swaddled in blankets. She walked to Joris' side and touched his arm.

"My father's dead." Joris gazed at Frugar's blanketed body, grief cracking his voice.

Joris' wife gasped. "No, he'll never see little Klaus walk."

Harsh lines etched the sides of Joris' mouth. "No, he won't see anything ever again. And it's all the fault of those flaming dragons," he said bitterly. "I told him they'd be the death of him."

An older woman with graying hair pushed through the crowd, then. Clutching at her chest, she stood motionless, whispering, "No, no, no," over and over again, tears tracking down her face.

Giddi's insides turned to ice. He blinked, squeezing his eyes tight, searing this moment into his brain. He could never forget this. Never act rashly again.

"No, no, no." Her grief-stricken plea echoed through his bones.

Kevin's rumble drifted through Giddi's head. *It's not our fault. We only wanted to fight the pirates and right the wrongs they'd caused. They nearly killed the ship's crew.*

EILEEN MUELLER

"I know, but they didn't succeed," said Giddi, "which makes my actions worse than theirs. I actually killed someone."

A low rumble ran through Kevin as he shared a memory of a pirate aiming his bow from the crow's nest. The arrow zipped past Giddi, and Frugar cried out. A flood of warmth enveloped Giddi, thawing the ice in his chest. "You didn't shoot the arrow that killed him."

But Giddi steeled himself against the comfort Kevin was offering. "No, but I may as well have."

§

Frugar's widow collapsed against her son. Sobs wracking her body, she embraced him and her dead husband. Two men hastened out of a nearby store, carrying trestles and planks of wood. The crowd edged back so they could set up a makeshift platform in the middle of the square. Joris laid his father's body on the planking. Frugar's wife pulled back the blanket from her husband's face and kissed his pale waxy cheek, her tears falling over his hair.

Yanir watched the grief-stricken scene, helpless. Would this be his fate one day, to be carried back to Dragons' Hold for Anakisha to mourn him? He shook off the thought. She hadn't even been to Dragons' Hold yet. Maybe they wouldn't even get there.

Anakisha's thoughts floated through his head. "Yanir, don't be so glum. I haven't been to Dragons' Hold yet." She slipped her warm hand around his and squeezed it. "We still have a lot of life left. Look, Frugar had children and a grandchild. Hopefully, we'll have that one day too."

Yanir couldn't help a sharp intake of breath as Anakisha shared a memory with him. "You know I've seen our children in a vision," she said.

Yanir walked toward Anakisha in a meadow in the basin at Dragons' Hold. He was holding a babe, and a littling girl of a few summers was clinging to his riders' breeches.

The sun warmed Anakisha's face, her heart leaping at the sight of them.

"Mama, look!" the girl squealed, gazing up at Anakisha. "She got a tooth."

The girl clinging to Yanir's breeches had her eyes and his sandy hair. The babe in his arms grinned, a pale tip peeking through her top gum. Yanir crooned, "That's why you were crying." He kissed the babe's forehead and asked Anakisha, "How is Esmeralda now? All better after her fall?" He nodded at her hip.

Anakisha shifted, hefting another little girl on her hip, the spitting image of Yanir.

Anakisha's eyes shone with tears. "Don't worry, Yanir, things may look grim now, but we'll get there."

Giddi was standing stoically, as if he were about to take a beating. He'd been aloof since Frugar's death, barely eating and refusing to talk. The poor lad was too young to be carrying an accidental death on his conscience. They'd all been shocked. Perhaps they'd been too hard on him. At that age, Yanir could guarantee he would've raced after the pirates. Perhaps Goren would've too.

Frugar's widow was now openly weeping, her head on Frugar's chest and her arms wrapped around his body. Garthox twitched on her feet, obviously eager to give her rider his proper send-off.

"I'm the village arbitrator," Joris declared, pounding chest. "And this is my father." His voice boomed across the square. "My father was a fine and just arbitrator before me—before he became entranced by that dragon." He pointed a trembling finger at the keening cobalt dragon. "He spent much of my adulthood away from home, away from my mother, and away from those he loved. He protected people we do not know and fought for good across the realm." He bowed his head, his hand still on his chest. "I'm proud of him."

His mother's head snapped up, revealing her tear-stained face. She pushed herself off her husband's body and stood. "I'm not," she shrieked, her voice trembling with rage. "I'm not proud. Frugar's been killed. I never want to see another dragon in my life. These beasts have taken my beloved husband. Taken your father. Taken our beloved ex-arbitrator. How dare they darken our valley with their presence?" She turned, pointing a trembling finger at Yanir. "You, King's Rider, are no longer welcome here. Your dragons are not welcome within these alps." Her arm swept around them to encompass the horseshoe of Grand Alps around the peaceful verdant valley.

Joris' face darkened, anger rippling across his features. "Mother?"

Yanir stiffened, Anakisha squeezing his hand. Thank the Egg, Joris didn't agree. He'd soon talk some sense into his poor grieving mother.

Frugar's wife whirled, eyes flashing and her gray hair flying from her bun. "Yes, son?"

Joris nodded. "I agree with you." His quiet affirmation carried across the silent square like a gong.

"What!" Anakisha's shock seared Yanir's mind like a hot brand. *"Surely they can't mean that. Pirates killed Frugar, not dragons."*

Joris drew himself up to his full height and clambered onto the platform his father was lying on, standing near his father's boots.

Giddi stepped forward.

Yanir's eyebrows shot up and Anakisha squeezed his hand tightly.

Tall for his twelve summers, the lad pounded his fist on his heart and bowed. "Honored arbitrator and honored wife of Frugar, it's my fault your husband died. He and I were pursuing pirates when we were attacked. A fatal arrow hit him." To his credit, the lad's voice rang clearly across the square, even though his hands were shaking.

Joris' blue eyes turned icy. "How is this your fault, then?"

Giddi tripped over his words. "I-I was t-too rash. My young d-dragon and I raced into b-battle and Frugar followed me to try and st-stop me, so I'm responsible for his d-death." He nodded at Frugar's widow then met Joris' gaze. "I apologize deeply for your pain. I'd do anything to make up for it."

Joris stiffened. "If it weren't for you, my father would be alive. Who are you?"

"Trainee mage Giddi, sir, of Great Spanglewood Forest."

"I curse you. No mage may set foot in Lush Valley as long as I'm arbitrator, and the long shadows of dragons and riders must never darken Lush Valley again."

Murmurs spread like wildfire through the crowd, building in the square.

Joris puffed out his chest and hollered, "As long as I live dragons will never be welcome in Lush Valley. Any dragon or rider who ventures over the Grand Alps will be shot on sight."

Yanir dropped Anakisha's hand and leaped onto the makeshift platform next to Joris. "Wait!" he bellowed. The crowd turned to him, but the murmurs didn't still. He yelled above them. "It was an accident. We've traveled two days to bring Frugar home for a decent funeral. Please wait. Let us set our differences aside until after his funeral."

"Wait for what? More deaths?" a man yelled.

Another waved a pitchfork.

"I say a talon for a talon, and a fang for a fang!" Joris' face was flushed. His icy-blue eyes, gleaming. "Kill the lot of them!"

A battle drum beat a frantic tattoo. Villagers cried, their faces contorting with fury. Mothers screamed, herding their littlings out of the square. People grabbed makeshift weapons, rushing at Yanir, Anakisha and Giddi.

"Stop, please." Yanir tried to yell over them. "Listen to reason."

Anakisha grabbed his hand and yanked him off the dais as an arrow whistled overhead. *"Quick! Run. To our dragons."*

He, Giddi and Anakisha shoved their way through the confused crowd, rough hands grabbing at their garb. They burst free, sprinted to their dragons, and clambered into their saddles.

"Archers, fire!" Joris bellowed, shaking his fist.

Syan, Zaarusha, and Kevin sprang above the crowd. A volley of arrows shot at them.

Garthox roared and leaped above the square, releasing a swathe of flame that burned the arrows. She swooped and plucked up Frugar's body, and winged off toward the Eastern Grand Alps.

Yanir's heart pounded against his ribs as Syan's dark wings beat skyward, leaving the Lush Valley Settlement seething. They winged high above the valley, heading along the chain of the Western Grand Alps. *"Anakisha, are you and Zaarusha all right?"*

"A little shaken, but fine. I'm more worried about Giddi."

"Although their reactions were surprising," the queen of the dragons said, *"I've endured worse."*

Yanir glanced across at the young dragon mage who was slumped in his saddle, his chin on his chest. "Giddi!" The lad didn't turn his head or give a sign of having heard him. Yanir called again. *"Syan, please ask Kevin if Giddi's all right."*

"I already have," the onyx king replied. *"He's not answering either."*

Yanir sighed. *"Well, that was a waste of time bringing Frugar home. He didn't even get his funeral."*

"Oh, he'll get one all right. Garthox will give him a dragon's send-off and scatter his ashes across the alps so his soul can fly with departed dragons," Syan replied, winging high in the sky until

Lush Valley Settlement was only a speck beneath them. *"I'm more worried about the living—our dragon mage and Kevin. If they don't stop blaming themselves, this could scar them for life."*

Kevin's emerald scales and Zaarusha's colored ones caught the sun as they headed south, back to Naobia. Syan spread his onyx wings, as if he could shelter the others beneath them.

Naobian Mage Council

After two days in the saddle, eating on dragonback, and barely stopping to sleep, Kevin, Syan and Zaarusha reached Naobia in the evening. Goren flew out to meet them on Rengar and guided them back to the city square.

Kevin landed on the cobbles of the Naobian square as the sun was sinking behind the buildings. Yanir, Anakisha and Goren's dragons landed with a thud beside him and their riders dismounted.

Goren approached them and shook Yanir's hand. "Thank you for seeing Frugar home."

"You're welcome." Yanir gave a terse nod, but thankfully didn't say anything about the animosity in Lush Valley.

Giddi's heart sank. There'd be time enough for that. He slid off Kevin. *"Thank you for letting me ride you."*

Kevin nudged Giddi's hand. *"Good luck. I'm sorry about Frugar, but anytime you need a dragon, let me know."*

Giddi nodded and watched the green dragon and Rengar wistfully as they rose over the buildings and winged off toward the hills. Zaarusha and Syan settled on their haunches in the corner of the square.

Anakisha patted Zaarusha's flank. "We'll meet you in the orchard when we're done," she said aloud.

The royal dragons sprang into the air and circled over the town before disappearing behind the buildings to the peach orchard outside the city wall.

Giddi raised one of his eyebrows. "Where do you live?" he asked Goren, gesturing at Rengar who dipped her wings—the sunlight turning them into a blaze of shimmering emerald.

Goren scratched his mop of curly dark hair. "In a cottage outside the Naobian city wall."

"And Rengar and the other green guards?"

Goren shrugged. "Sometimes she sleeps in my garden, but often she and the other dragons stay overnight in a cavern in the hills north of here. They're still close enough to mind-meld if there's a problem."

"Aren't those the hills where jewel beetles are found?" Giddi asked. "Do you think she'd bring me back one?"

Goren laughed and clapped Giddi on the shoulder. "You're so tall for your age and have so much power, sometimes I forget you're only twelve summers old."

"I'm thirteen summers, now." Giddi bristled. He was no boy anymore—he already had a man's blood on his hands.

"Are you, now?" Goren chuckled. "The caverns are filled with jewel beetles, so I can ask if you like." His mouth took a grim turn. "But first, let's get you to the mage council."

"The mage council?"

Goren nodded. "Apparently there was a complaint laid the morning you and Starrus arrived. Some local troublemakers reported that they were encircled in a wall of flame in a back alley. They said a young mage who attacked them was gangly with dark hair and bushy eyebrows." Goren raised one of his own eyebrows. "I don't know many other mages who fit that description. The mage council and your trainer, Starrus, want to hear your account of how Frugar lost his life and all about this flaming incident."

The weight of a boulder lodged in Giddi's gut.

Anakisha shot Giddi a sympathetic glance. "Yanir and I will come and lend our support."

Giddi gave a terse nod and followed Goren through the winding alleys, tugging his cloak around him, although the evening was sultry and warm. Anakisha and Yanir and Goren tried to talk to him, but his throat was so tight, he could only grunt in reply.

In a piazza with a pretty fountain of two stone dragonets at play, there was a large yellow stone building wedged between two gray slate houses. Goren halted in front of it and mounted three steps. A sculpted brass archway of flaming dragons framed a grand wooden door. There were six wooden panels on the door at eye level, each ornately carved with men and women manipulating the elements: a woman thrusting wind at a sail; a young boy forming a wall of ice; two mages shooting fire from their hands at a wolf; a girl cleaving a snake's head with a flying branch; and a man with his arms outflung, using his powers to create a furrow in the earth and spit a volley of dirt at an attacking swordsman.

Although those five panels were impressive, it was the center panel of an old mage holding up a sphere with beams of light radiating from it that drew Giddi's eye. His face and the small globe he was holding were infused with light that shone like the sun.

"What's that?" Giddi asked Goren, pointing at the sphere. How was it possible to infuse an object with *sathir* and make it powerful?

Goren shrugged. "Not sure. Never really thought about it. A mage talisman, I guess." He lifted a heavy brass knocker shaped like a dragon's head and rapped on the door five times.

Giddi swallowed and tried to smooth his rumpled clothing.

Anakisha laughed. "You might as well not bother. You can't smooth the wear of two battles and a trip to Lush Valley and back out of your garb that quickly."

Yanir chuckled. "You'd be better off washing the mage soot from your face."

Giddi's eyebrows shot up. He'd had no idea his face was dirty. "Good advice." He dashed down the steps to the fountain, splashed water over his face, and slicked back his hair.

"Hurry up," Goren hissed as Giddi raced back to the doorway, drying his face on his sleeve.

Footsteps thudded behind the door. Anakisha pushed Giddi up the last step into place beside Goren, while she and Yanir remained on the step below, like warriors flanking their rear in case of attack.

The door opened on well-oiled hinges revealing a tall man with a mass of dark curly hair, dark eyes and olive skin, wearing a mage cloak. A thin braid on the side of his head was adorned with mage crystals of turquoise, jade, amber, ruby and amethyst—showing he was a master mage, fully qualified in elemental magic of all disciplines. He peered down a nose shaped like a hawk's beak at Giddi, reminding him of a raptor about to pounce. "Ah, Goren, I see you've brought the culprit."

"Good evening, Master Mage Takoda." Goren said smoothly. "Giddi's hardly a culprit until he's been tried."

"W-what do you mean, *tried*." Giddi blurted. "Is this a trial? M-mine?" His voice squeaked embarrassingly.

Goren shot him a glance that would've frozen a lake over.

Giddi snapped his jaw shut.

Yanir cleared his throat. "Excuse me."

Takoda's eyes flew to him. He bowed deeply. "My honored King's Rider, it's a pleasure to host you." He flashed a smarmy smile.

Yanir inclined his head. "A pleasure to meet you, too, Master Mage Takoda. May I introduce the new Queen's Rider of Dragons' Realm, Anakisha of Fieldhaven."

"Nice to meet you," Anakisha smiled.

Takoda took Anakisha's hand and kissed it. His dark eyes glittered as he ushered the King's Rider and Queen's Rider inside.

What a leech. Giddi followed Goren over the stoop as Takoda led Yanir and Anakisha along a broad hallway lit with vanilla-scented candles in golden sconces. Doors lined the hall, each embellished with one of the carved symbols that had been on the front door. Crystal dragon sculptures littered the broad space, their scales shimmering with all the colors of the rainbow.

"Opaline crystal from Naobia's own Crystal Lake," Goren murmured.

They marched past oil paintings of mages in battle hung in gilt frames. In one, flame roiled from a mage's fingers at an army of warriors. Another mage stood on a beach, hands out, creating a waterspout that towered over a fleeing pirate ship.

Giddi's shabby boots echoed on the tiled floor. And he'd thought he could smite those pirates on his own. He had no idea how to wield a quarter of the power of those mages in the paintings. He wanted to shrink in on himself and disappear. If only he could transmogrify into a mouse and sneak under one of those fancy carved doors.

At last, they came to the end of the hallway and a wrought-iron door engraved with dragon scales dusted with flecks of gold. Flames wreathed the door frame. If the door was supposed to be intimidating, it was working.

Takoda pushed the heavy door open and ushered Yanir and Anakisha inside with a sweeping bow. He nodded to Goren as the leader of the green guards strode confidently into the chamber, then he disdainfully waved Giddi inside.

The door clanked shut behind them, making Giddi's nerves fire with the urge to bolt. He held himself steady as Takoda ushered Yanir and Anakisha to some elegant chairs at the side of the room.

Giddi squinted in the blazing light from a chandelier holding at least a hundred candles. Takoda sat next to four other master mages, who were seated behind a table in ornately-carved chairs with backs that towered behind them. One of the center seats was empty. A symbol from the front door was carved on the back of the chairs above each of the mage's heads—and the same symbols, inlaid in gleaming gold, copper and silver, were on the table in front of each mage. Carvings of flames licked up the edges of the huge table's legs and along the edge of the tabletop.

And he'd thought the door was intimidating. Giddi gulped, sure every mage in the room could hear him.

The empty chair and the place on the table in front of it were carved with the wind symbol. With a jolt, Giddi remembered the mage on the Scarlet Hand's ship using *sathir* to fill the bloody-red sails with wind and power the *Fiery Dragon* away from them, across the Naobian Sea toward the Wastelands. That must be Master Mage Findal's spot.

Findal had been kidnapped by the Scarlet Hand, who was forcing him to work for him. Starrus and Giddi had been tasked with retrieving the Naobian Master Mage. And they'd failed.

Goren stood with his legs apart, shoulders back, and his hands clasped behind his back. Giddi wiped his palms on his breeches, thrust his shoulders back and clasped his hands behind him in an imitation of Goren's confident posture—but he felt anything but confident. Sweat instantly broke out on his palms.

"Good evening, master mages." Goren bowed and Giddi followed suit. "You requested the presence of our dragon mage?"

"Dragon mage?" a short mage sitting by the water symbol snapped, his wizened face ornamented with an absurdly-shaped beard that reminded Giddi of a mushroom. The mage's brown eyes flitted about the room then landed on Goren again, who flourished a hand at Giddi. The man's thin eyebrows nearly disappeared into his thatch of dark hair.

"Yes, Master Mage Quam, the young lad is a dragon mage," Goren said.

The mages all turned their gazes to Giddi, scrutinizing him as if he were a jewel beetle shell at the marketplace.

Sod being a mouse—he'd rather he was an ant so he could scurry off undetected. The silence stretched. Giddi's pulse hammered at his throat, counting off each moment.

The wrought iron door behind him clanged open and shut again. Crisp steps sounded on the tiled floor, and Starrus' straw-blond hair came into view. His trainer towered beside him. "Good evening, honored master mages of Naobia. It's my pleasure to be summoned to your highly esteemed council." Starrus gave an elegant bow and stood between Giddi and Goren.

A willowy woman with regal bearing and dark hair stood at the center of the table. She nodded at Starrus. "Now that Starrus has arrived, we may begin our proceedings. It has come to our attention that there was an unfortunate incident in the slums of Naobia upon your arrival back from battling the Scarlet Hand."

"My warmest greetings, honored Master Mage Lucinda." Starrus bowed again. "If I may be so forward as to inquire, what sort of incident are we discussing?"

"A conflagration. We thank you for vanquishing the Scarlet Hand from our shores." Glaring at Giddi, Lucinda drew herself up to her full height. "However, unruly mage fire must not go unchecked."

On one side of him, Goren twitched.

Starrus' dark gaze glittered as it rested upon Giddi's face. "Is that so?"

An icy trickle slithered down Giddi's back. Oh gods, he was in so much trouble. Giddi refused to meet his trainer's gaze, staring straight ahead at the mage council.

"In the poorer quarter of town near the docks, a mage matching this lad's description circled a group of youths in a ring of fire." Lucinda shook her head. "He terrified them out of their wits."

"So that's where you got to," Starrus muttered, glaring at Giddi. He addressed Lucinda. "My trainee was delayed by the docks, but he never explained what he'd been doing when we met up at our lodgings."

And if he explained now, Starrus would punish him for losing his precious blue mage cloak.

"The youths also say he stole their belongings," croaked a crone with bushy gray hair seated in the chair carved with the earth mage symbol. The rings on her fingers flashed with mage crystals.

"Thank you for telling us, Flisa." Starrus' glare sharpened, a blade about to strike. "You stole their belongings? I had no knowledge of any of this." Starrus twitched his midnight-blue mage cloak around him and raised an eyebrow. "Boy, come clean and confess your misdeeds to the mage council. Are these accounts true?"

Giddi nodded. "In part." Exactly which part, he didn't want to say—or Starrus would learn about his stolen cloak and be forever on his back, tormenting him with more than a sea monster. The dragon gods knew why, but Starrus was exceptionally fond of his cloak.

"He should be given the severest punishment possible to prevent him from abusing his power in the future," Starrus said, denouncing him.

Abusing his power? That was what Starrus did, not him. Giddi rubbed the newly-healed skin on his neck.

Next to Flisa the crone, a wiry, ruddy-faced Naobian sitting by the carved mage talisman shifted. "Shall we hear what the young mage has to say? After all, if he's really a dragon mage, he has a part to play in the future of Dragons' Realm."

"That's ridiculous, Jaedak." Starrus snorted.

There was a rap on the door. A green guard Giddi didn't recognize strode into the chamber. "I have an urgent message for you, Master Mage Lucinda."

"Can't you see we're busy? We're holding a trial."

"The information I have is pertaining to this trial," the rider said, flushing as he met Goren's stern eye. He delivered a roll of parchment to Master Mage Lucinda. "This mage missive arrived from Great Spanglewood Forest. I also have a verbal message."

"Very well."

The guard straightened, avoiding Goren's glare. "The young green dragon who took this mage to Lush Valley is distressed. Kevin's been disturbing all the green dragons in the caves with his nightmares."

"We're not here to hear about a dragonling's nightmares," Takoda snapped.

"I know," the green guard said, "but he's mind-melding with all the other dragons and sharing memories of him being attacked with arrows in Lush Valley. And he's howling about a rider that died. When they woke him, he confessed that he and this young mage had accidentally killed someone in battle, and that the man's death has started a feud between dragons and Lush Valley."

Starrus whirled and grabbed Giddi by the collar, shaking him. "You did what?"

Yanir leaped out of his chair. He and Goren yanked Starrus away from Giddi.

Giddi reeled. Stumbling, he placed his hand on the council table to brace himself.

Anakisha rushed to his side. "Giddi, are you all right?"

He pushed her away and stood. "I'm f-fine," he snapped, straightening his spine and awaiting the council's judgment. It was true, all of it. He'd flamed the youths, caused Frugar's death and started a feud. His stomach jumped like a dragonet. Gods, he wanted to puke his guts out. Oh no, the floor was spinning. He was going to be sick all over the tiles.

Anakisha grabbed him and pulled him into a chair. "Place your head between your knees and the feeling should pass." She laid a soothing hand on his damp forehead.

He bent, his pulse pounding at his temples and the tiles still turning.

"Breathe deeply," Anakisha whispered.

Goren was speaking, his voice sounding as if he was at the end of a distant tunnel. "Those pirates burned a boat and nearly killed a captain, his wife, and two crew. Young Giddi did act rashly, showing a lack of judgment when he charged after them. Frugar, a blue guard and former arbitrator of Lush Valley, followed Giddi to protect him and young Kevin. However, Frugar was killed by the enemy, not Giddi. It was an accident."

Giddi couldn't believe his ears. Goren—who'd been so wrathful at Frugar's death—was defending him.

"Are you sure the lad didn't get him killed on purpose?" Starrus' slick voice twined through Giddi's ears. "Maybe he was scheming to start a feud with Lush Valley. The boy has always been trouble."

That slimy toad. Giddi kept his mouth shut. If he argued with Starrus, he'd never find out where his father was.

He saw his mother's dying face, her eyes bright with tears as she slipped into the next life, whispering, "Find him, Giddi. Find your father."

Her last words burned through him all over again. He had to be brave. To face this for her. Despite Anakisha's protests, Giddi struggled to his feet and faced the council.

The green guard spun to Goren. "You were angry when Frugar died, but now your tune has changed. Why?"

Goren cleared his throat. "Despite Giddi's mistakes, Kevin, the young dragon Giddi flew with, told Rengar that Giddi handled himself admirably in Lush Valley, taking full responsibility for Frugar's death." His eyebrow arched. "A feat that wouldn't have been easy when faced by archers with nocked bows."

Yanir spoke up. "I can confirm that."

Anakisha joined in. "He's been very brave and faced up to everything. He's young and made a mistake."

"A mistake that has turned a whole settlement against us," Takoda snapped.

Anakisha stood, her cheeks blazing. "Did none of you make mistakes when you were twelve or thirteen summers old? Did you never break something, accidentally hurt someone or do something rash and foolish?" She thrust out her hand. "Look at him. He's seen the grief resulting from his foolhardy actions. He's not himself. Guilt is eating away at him and has been since Frugar died. Giddi feels worse than anyone, and he will carry this burden his whole life. He doesn't need your condemnation. He needs training."

Giddi couldn't believe his ears. Training?

The ruddy-faced mage glared at Starrus. "Mages require discipline. You are responsible for his training." He slammed his hand on the table, sparks skittering from his fingers across the tabletop and bouncing across the tiled floor.

Giddi flinched as a spark bounced against his tatty boot.

"How old are you, boy?" Lucinda asked.

Giddi stared at the floor. "My thirteenth name day was yesterday," he mumbled.

"Tall for your age, then." Lucinda nodded. "Young mages can be foolhardy. I thank the Queen's Rider for reminding us of the dragon mage's age."

"Dragon mage?" Starrus sneered. "What falsehoods has this boy been spinning? Surely you don't believe such lies." Beneath his bluster, his trainer was pale.

"Good point. How do we know he's a dragon mage?" the crone demanded.

Yanir spoke quietly but his words carried through the chamber. "Syan has mind-melded with him."

"As has Zaarusha," Anakisha added.

"They're royal dragons," Starrus replied. "Their abilities may have accounted for that, not his."

It was now or never. "Please give me a moment," Giddi said.

He stretched out his mind, opening his senses and reaching out for Kevin and any other dragon within range. *"Can you hear me?"* he asked.

"Of course I can," Kevin replied.

The other dragons piped up, rumbles, squeaks, and roars ricocheting through his mind. Gods, his head was going to burst.

"Enough! I hear all of you." Giddi panted, relieved when his head was quiet again. *"The mage council doesn't believe I'm the dragon mage."*

Snarls and angry bellows ripped through the air outside. Talons skittered on the rooftop. A dragon smacked the roof with its tail, sending a boom through the council chamber. Roars built as dragons on the outskirts of Naobia flew back to the city. The walls shook.

Footsteps thudded down the hallway, people yelling.

"Stop this at once." Lucinda commanded, eyes flashing.

"Thank you," Giddi mind-melded with the dragons, his knees shaking. By the First Egg, the dragon gods and the flaming butt of a dragon with belly gripe, he'd never expected that.

Starrus opened and shut his mouth like a stranded fish. Shock was etched on the faces of the master mages, but Anakisha gave Giddi a sly smile.

She believed in him.

"That was a trick, a pre-arranged signal," Starrus cried. "He's only a minor trainee with no skill at all. Why, I have ten times the power he does."

Anakisha quirked an eyebrow. "Both Yanir and I witnessed the wall of flame Giddi let loose at the Fieldhaven archery tournament when he got overexcited. As did Zaarusha and Syan."

Yanir stood, saying mildly, "I urge you not to doubt the testimony of the King's Rider or Queen's Rider again. Now, I believe our business here is finished..." He took Anakisha's hand and started toward the door.

"Not so fast." Lucinda said. "We are yet to decide the consequences for Giddi's actions, and resolve the question of his training. We also have yet to read the missive this green guard has brought. I suggest we do that while we deliberate."

Yanir and Anakisha sat again. "Very well," the King's Rider said, "but I won't have aspersions cast upon the only dragon mage the realm has seen in years."

"Understood, and I agree." Lucinda unrolled the scroll of parchment and held it up. "The Great Spanglewood Forest mages have a message for Starrus."

Starrus puffed out his chest, smiling. "Yes, honored Master Mage Lucinda?"

Her mouth twitched. She compressed her lips, regarding him over the parchment for a long moment. "It pertains to Master Mage Findal, the leader of this council, and you."

No wonder the Great Spanglewood master mages had wanted Findal back—he was the Head of the Naobian Mage Council. Lucinda must be leading in his stead.

Lucinda cleared her throat and read:

Starrus,

We trust we find you in good health. We remind you that we sent you to Naobia to rescue Master Mage Findal from the Scarlet Hand and instructed you not to return until you found him.

It appears that the highly-esteemed Mage Findal is still in the clutches of this vile pirate. Hence, we instruct you further to traverse the Naobian Sea and hunt him down.

We do not expect you or your trainee to return until you have restored Master Mage Findal to Naobia.

Master Mage Balovar, head of the Great Spanglewood Forest Mage Council.

She rolled the parchment up, her fierce gaze sweeping the room. "It appears that the mages of Great Spanglewood Forest have made a difficult decision for us. Starrus and Giddi, our young dragon mage, will both leave Naobia tomorrow and sail to the Robandi Desert. Even if you have to go all the way to Metropoli, you are to find Master Mage Findal and bring him home to Naobia—a fitting punishment for your misdemeanors."

Oh, gods. Giddi's heart plummeted.

The room was silent. Not even Yanir spoke.

Lucinda stared at Starrus. "When you return, we expect a full report of what training you have given Giddi enroute." She switched her gaze to Giddi, her black eyes boring into his. "And a demonstration of what you have learned."

ROBANDI STRAIT

"**L**and ahoy," a sailor called from the crow's nest.

"You can stop shooting those useless fireballs into the sea, boy," Starrus barked. "Get ready for landing."

Giddi was relieved to stick his hands in his pockets. Starrus had made him shoot flame into the water every day of their journey on *Wave Runner*, a merchant ship bound for the Wastelands. He claimed he was teaching Giddi control, but he hadn't given him any pointers yet—well, not useful ones.

The captain sauntered over. "Are you sure you want to seek out the Robandi assassins? It's not an action I'd recommend. A band of ruthless killers don't seem like the right people to ask for information about the whereabouts of pirates."

What! That was their destination? The Robandi assassins were a cutthroat group of men and women who robbed and slaughtered hapless travelers in the Wastelands. "I thought we were traveling to Metropoli," Giddi ventured.

Starrus ignored him, answering the captain. "My dearest captain, they're the right people to ask. No one else lives around here, and pirates and assassins are all of the same creed, so I'm sure the assassins will know of the pirates' movements." Starrus rubbed his hands, grinning.

The captain scratched his grizzled beard and squinted at the orange terrain showing on the distant horizon. "Before we can get to land, we have to get through the Robandi Strait. Two strong opposing currents meet here, making it the trickiest stretch of ocean between here and the Wastelands." He pointed at the water ahead.

There was a band of smooth ocean, but beyond it, the ocean's surface was broken by a churning mass of water.

"See that turbulence? It's caused by a current that pulls to the South and another that flows from the east. Where the two meet, are the most treacherous waters known to man or dragon. There are more shipwrecks under the Robandi Strait than throughout the rest of the entire Naobian Sea."

Giddi piped up, "Is there any pirate treasure on those boats?"

"Don't be stupid," Starrus sneered.

The captain chuckled. "If there is, not many have dared to hunt for it. The oceans here are infested with sharks, especially closer to the cliffs." He pointed to a distant orange strip jutting from the sea. "The Robandi silent assassins throw the bodies of their victims off the top of those cliffs, keeping the sharks well fed, so those nasty wee fishies like to patrol the waters here."

Giddi gulped. There was no way he'd go swimming off that coast.

"You two would do best to stand at the front. You're less likely to vomit or be thrown overboard. Hold on tight. We're about to hit the troubled waters." The captain stalked off to talk to the first mate.

The sea ahead rippled and bucked like a river racing between narrow rocks. At the center where the two currents met, a giant whirlpool spun—ten times wider than the boat's length.

Giddi clung to the rail, staring at the violent sea. If something bad happened now, even his magic would be no help.

Where the currents clashed, the water was raging, slapping into wavelets that siphoned into the wild whirlpool—something Giddi would have thought impossible—except he was witnessing it.

The captain bellowed orders. "Below decks, now! Man the oars!"

The crew rushed into the hold and readied themselves at the oars. Below decks, a chant started up. "Heave ho, heave ho." The oars slid out of their hatches and dipped into the water, stroking swiftly.

"What are we doing?" Starrus demanded of the captain as the ship's prow angled toward the whirlpool at the center of the turbulence. "You're not taking us through that thing, are you?"

"Of course, I am," the captain replied. "It's the only way ahead, or the currents will wash us onto the treacherous rocks hidden beneath the surface. Many unfortunate captains haven't known the secret of the Robandi Straits. This whirlpool is nicknamed the Eye of the Robandi Storm. The only place calm enough to sail across the strait is through its center."

Calm—if that was calm, Giddi was the mosquito on a dragonet's backside.

"Heave, double time," a sailor bellowed below. "Come on, heave."

The oars sped up.

As the ship hit the rough water, it bucked and tossed like a dragon wanting to shake a rider loose. The prow rose and then dropped. The currents tugged its timbers, making them shudder and groan. Giddi's stomach dropped and then bolted up into his throat and then dropped again. He lost his footing and fell, his backside smacking into the planks.

Starrus laughed, then fell over too, smacking his forehead on the rail.

Giddi smothered a snigger and lurched back to the rail, holding on with a white-knuckled grip. He peered over the edge, the choppy waves making his head spin. *Wave Runner's* nose plowed into the current, and the sailors heaved, angling the ship toward the massive whirlpool.

"Starboard oars only," the captain yelled. The oars on the port side rose from the water, pointing to the sky and dripping with brine. "Hard to port!" The prow dipped and rose as the ship swung around into the swirling vortex of water.

"Starboard, heave!" the captain bellowed. The first mate below shrieked his command at the oarsmen who rowed in a frenzy, angling *Wave Runner* straight into the center of the whirlpool.

The aft end of the ship spun, turning the prow around to face where they'd just come from. By the dragon gods, the captain had lost control. Giddi clung to the rail, his limbs shaking as the ship spun.

"Starboard oars, lift," the captain cried above the rush water. "Port oars down. Hard to port."

The first mate was bellowing at the top of his voice.

"All oars row," the captain bellowed.

Men were grunting and yelling, but the oars kept digging into the sea. They shot through the eye of the Robandi Storm and spun again.

"Faster, faster," the first mate yelled at the oarsman. "Heave, heave, heave."

The captain stared at the horizon, pale-faced, not uttering another word as a wall of water on the southern side of the whirlpool rose to meet them.

The vessel rose on the swell then dipped, spinning again. Giddi lost all sense of direction. The rush of the water drowned out his thundering heart. Salty spray hit his face and chest, drenching him to the skin. He desperately clung with frozen hands to the rail, praying to the dragon gods that he wouldn't be tossed like an egg shard into the swirling mass of sea.

Below decks, the first mate's rhythmic cries blurred into a maddened frenzy.

Oars hit the sea, digging deep.

The ship sped across the water and shot over the lip of the whirlpool and into the choppy waters beyond.

Giddi's head stopped spinning and his stomach stopped lurching as *Wave Runner* rode the churning water of the straits.

A cheer rose from the first mate, and a ragged reply came from the exhausted oarsmen as they rowed toward calmer waters.

§

Wave Runner slowed, stilled, and bobbed on the water. At last, they were through the Eye of the Robandi Storm. "That was incredible," Giddi turned to Starrus, but Starrus hadn't heard him. He was clenching the rail and puking over the side, his face a violent shade of green.

Giddi smothered a grin and strolled a few paces upwind, gazing at the distant coastline of the Wastelands. Orange cliffs rose from the sea, still far-off, but now visible, as if an artist had daubed jagged tangerine blobs above the sea.

Under the guidance of the first mate, the exhausted oarsmen trooped above deck for fresh air, a bite of cabin bread and a dipper of water.

The captain offered Giddi a piece of cabin bread and leaned on the rail beside him. "I see your trainer's had a rough voyage." He chuckled. "He's a bit hard on you. Have you thought of training under another mage?"

Had he ever. Giddi shrugged. "I still have much to learn from him." Especially the whereabouts of his father. He changed the subject. The last thing he wanted was Starrus to hear. "How long until we arrive at the coast?"

"About an hour of smooth sailing. We made it through the whirlpool just in time. The next half hour is critical because the tide is about to change, and when it does, if we're not far enough away from that stir-crazy water, we'll be sucked right back into the Eye of the Robandi Storm."

"Help." A faint voice shot through Giddi's head—a dragon. He spun and searched the skies, but there wasn't a wingtip in sight.

"Help, please." The cry came again.

Giddi whirled, casting his head from side to side.

The captain followed his gaze, startled. "What is it?"

"A dragon called for help," Giddi said. "I'm trying to figure out where it is."

"I don't hear any roaring." The captain snorted. "That trip through the Eye of the Robandi Storm has addled your wits."

Giddi's hands clenched. "No, I heard one."

The captain cleared his throat. "Well… I'm sure if you can hear a dragon, you're capable of asking it where it is." He nodded and left to talk to his crew.

Wave Runner's sails billowed and snapped in the wind as the vessel headed into calmer waters, on course straight for the Wastelands.

Starrus retched again and wiped his mouth, still bowed over the railing.

Giddi stretched out his mind. *"I can hear you but I don't know where you are."*

"I see a shadow on the water," the dragon replied. *"You're approaching me."*

"What?" Giddi gaped at the water but couldn't see anything.

"I'm trapped in a net in a shipwreck. Please, help me."

"You're underwater?"

"Yes, I'm a sea dragon. Quick, your ship is almost overhead. Do something."

Giddi spun. "Captain, quick! Cast the anchor overboard. A sea dragon is trapped below in a shipwreck."

"A sea dragon?" The captain's eyes flew wide. "How do you know that?"

"I'm a dragon mage," Giddi whispered so Starrus couldn't hear. "I mind-meld with dragons."

The captain scratched his beard. "I've seen sea dragons in the distance before, but never met one. How can we help?"

"You're almost above me. Jump in and set me free."

Fear clutched at Giddi's throat. He tried to speak, but only gargled.

"If you don't help me, I'll die here, stranded, far from the other sea dragons. Quick!"

"Prepare to cast the anchor, Captain." Giddi mind-melded with the sea dragon, *"Tell us when we're directly overhead."*

"You're going to jump, aren't you?" The captain nodded. "Ready the anchor," he cried to his crew. "The boy's jumping overboard to save a sea dragon."

Starrus whirled, still green about the gills. "What mischief are you up to now, boy? I can't even be sick for a moment without you concocting some shrotty tale." He sneered. "Even if there was a sea dragon, there's no way you can help. You can't breathe long enough underwater to do anything useful."

He could breathe for eighty counts underwater, last time he'd tried in the river near Horseshoe Bend. Giddi looked his trainer in the eye. There was nothing but contempt on Starrus' face. He was worthless in his trainer's eyes. "I know," he said, "but I have to try."

Giddi strode after the captain and three crewmates to the end of the ship where the anchor rope was coiled on deck. Starrus trailed them.

"You don't have long," The captain said. "We have to set sail soon or we'll be caught by the tide. If we're dragged backward into the eye, we'll end up in the briny deep as skeletons guarding decaying cargo—instead of being bound for Metropoli. When you see the anchor ascending, grab hold or we'll lose you." He clapped Giddi on the back and gave him a grim nod. "Good luck."

"It's simple, boy," Starrus said. "If you're not done by the time the captain is ready to sail, we'll go without you." He muttered to the captain, "That fanciful idiot always thinks he's hearing dragons."

The sailors bent to heave the anchor overboard.

"Don't cast it over yet. Just unwind a few lengths," Giddi said. His plan was crazy, but it just might work. Then again, it might also kill him.

The scrape of the anchor rope being tugged free sent a chill down Giddi's spine. He shucked off his shirt, boots and breeches, leaving him clad in only his undergarments.

"I'm warning you. If you die, I won't be accountable." Starrus' eyes glinted.

Taking deep breaths, Giddi edged around Starrus, and climbed on the rail near the anchor. He perched there, waiting. The sea was full of murky shapes and shadows. He closed his eyes and took a deep breath. Then opened them and took another.

"You're nearly above me," the sea dragon called.

"Now!" Giddi yelled.

The sailors hefted the anchor and threw it overboard. As the roped uncoiled, Giddi lunged over the rail and grabbed it, hurling himself off the ship. The rope burned his hands. He hung on, twisting his legs around it so he didn't lose his grip, and sucked in a huge lungful of air. His body hit the water and he plunged into the sea's icy embrace.

The salt stung his eyes. Everything was surrounded in a murky blue haze. The anchor sunk like a stone, the sea turning greener and darker as they descended—until *Wave Runner* was a distant shadow on the surface surrounded by a glimmer of light.

Giddi clung to the rope as the anchor rapidly sank toward the ocean floor. *"I'm coming. Where are you?"* He counted. If he only had eighty counts, he'd have to swim back to the surface at thirty or he'd run out of air.

"*I'm beneath you, trapped in the net of the shipwreck.*" A tiny spurt of flame lit up the gloom below him, illuminating a dragon among a tangle of seaweed suspended between the masts of a mighty galleon that was resting on the ocean floor.

The anchor thudded to the sandy bed and dragged Giddi closer to the galleon before snagging on rocks. He was already at twenty counts. Ten or twenty to go before he had to swim for the surface.

"*Don't panic. With me, you'll be able to breathe underwater.*"

He kicked off and swam toward the galleon and the enormous emerald-scaled sea dragon bound by seaweed-draped ropes. "*I need air to breathe. I'm not a sea dragon.*" He hadn't plunged all this way only to run out of air before he could help, but, hopefully, it would only take a moment to free her.

"*Trust me. You'll be able to breathe.*"

"*That's impossible.*" His lungs were straining. A tiny flow of bubbles escaped his lips. Gods, his ears hurt down here. Luckily, he could mind-meld with this creature so he didn't have to use them. Giddi trod water by her head.

"*You're a dragon mage, yet you believe it's impossible? I'm Queen Aquaria of the sea dragons.*" Queen Aquaria was tangled in the rigging. Festooned with seaweed and limpets, the ropes were barely visible in the gloom. The queen regarded him with golden eyes and snorted. "*You must trust me or you'll die, and I'll be stranded here and die too.*"

Forty-five counts.

Giddi's chest tightened as if someone was pulling a band around it. He gazed through the emerald gloom of the ocean depths to the distant glimmer of light on the surface. His lungs burned.

He had thirty-five counts left. Maybe less.

Air bubbled from his nostrils. Gods, no, he had to hold his air in. He was losing control, his instincts screaming at him to open his mouth and take a shrotty breath of salty water. The anchor had propelled him down here so fast, but it was further than he'd thought. If he tried to reach the surface now, he'd die trying. He couldn't do it. He couldn't save her or himself.

Starrus was right. He was a fool for even trying.

HOMEWARD BOUND

"**W**e should visit Lush Valley on the way home," Yanir mind-melded, his tawny hair shifting in the breeze from Syan's wingbeats.

Anakisha felt like rolling her eyes. Yanir had been insisting for the last day that they stop off and see Joris. *"It's not like he's going to bake us a cake and ask us in for soppleberry tea,"* she replied.

"Or even a haunch of goat," Zaarusha chipped in.

Anakisha burst out laughing, and Syan and Zaarusha joined in.

"It's been nearly a week. He's had time to cool off. I think we should at least try," Yanir insisted. *"I mean, what could we lose?"*

"Our lives," Anakisha said. *"I value mine and Zaarusha's—and yours, of course, except when you're being this stupid. Joris threatened to shoot us on sight—and any other dragon that came within sight of Lush Valley."*

"He was in a grief-fueled rage."

"Yes, one that had archers shooting at us within moments. I don't think that will have changed in the last six days."

Yanir was silent for a while as they flew alongside the Western Grand Alps—the border to the greater Lush Valley area that contained Lush Valley Settlement, Western Settlement and Southern Settlement. The chain of alps stretched from south to north, the pristine white peaks gleaming in the sun, the foot of the alpine chain carpeted in lush forest.

To the west, plains spread out in a variegated patchwork of fields dotted with a few isolated villages that looked like handfuls of pebbles from up here, rather than dwellings. Fieldhaven was the first major town—visible as a blob of brown surrounded by fields in the distance.

Zaarusha soared higher, skimming along the spine of the alps. Syan followed, dancing along the peaks.

"Why do you prefer flying along the mountain chain instead of beside it?" Anakisha asked.

"Warm air rises up the mountain from both sides" Zaarusha rumbled in her mind. *"Where the two currents meet, these wonderful thermals occur."*

"Sure, thermals are warmer, but what's the fuss?"

"Warm air rises, so we get a natural lift and don't have to work so hard," the dragon queen replied. *"Watch this."* Zaarusha stopped flapping and angled her wings, tilting them so the right one was higher. The breeze caught her and she slowly spiraled upward, her wings barely moving.

The dragon's exhilaration rushed through Anakisha, making her blood surge through her veins. She grinned. *"Now I get it. This is fun."* They spiraled higher, Syan receding below them.

Then King Syan, too, angled his wings and caught the thermal, spiraling up beneath them. Yanir gave a whoop.

Anakisha laughed. This was the life—way better than serving ales to drunken patrons in the *Dancing Dragon*. A fierce pang of homesickness hit her. She missed her sister Stella, but they were on their way home, so she'd see her and Pa soon enough.

"We can't stay long, though," said Zaarusha. *"There are pressing duties at Dragons' Hold."*

"Like what?"

"Training you, for a start," Zaarusha said. *"And that's going to take long enough. Then maybe you'll be good enough to do some real work."*

Anakisha slapped Zaarusha's shoulder. *"You cheeky queen."*

Zaarusha snorted and spiraled higher. *"You'll love Dragons Hold. It's beautiful."*

Anakisha's head spun.

"Are you all right?" Zaarusha asked.

Dizziness swept over Anakisha. She started to slide from the saddle.

"Anakisha," Yanir yelled. "Hold on."

His yell jolted her eyes open. Gods, she'd been about to pass out.

"Sorry, the air might be a bit thin for you up here," said Zaarusha. *"Hopefully you'll be fine when we descend. Hold on tight."* The queen's wings furled and her head dipped.

Anakisha's stomach rushed into her throat as Zaarusha dived.

Yanir was right at Zaarusha's wingtip, riding Syan, soothing Anakisha via mind-meld. *"Hang on Anakisha. Hold on. I'm right here beside you. You'll be all right soon."*

Anakisha clung on, her head swirling and the landscape blurring. Zaarusha slowed her descent. Opening her wings, she floated out over the alps. Anakisha's head cleared and air rushed back into her lungs. *"I'm fine now."* But the incident left her rattled. What if she fell off Zaarusha in midair? She'd be impaled on a branch or dashed upon the mountainside into tiny pieces. She shuddered.

"We can train at Dragons' Hold," suggested Zaarusha. *"You can practice jumping off my back and I'll catch you."*

"What!" Yanir's bellow ripped through all of their minds. *"You'll do no such thing, Zaarusha. I'm not letting Anakisha be speared upon a pine or drowned in a mountain lake."*

"You may not have a choice," Anakisha mind-melded. *"I'll decide what I attempt. I trust Zaarusha's judgment."*

"So do I," said Yanir, *"but—"*

"Are you going to trust my judgment?" she asked.

"Are you going to trust mine?" he retorted. *"I believe we should try going to Lush Valley to visit Joris. We need to make peace with him."*

Anakisha gazed across the Western Grand Alps and sighed. Western Settlement was below. Further east was Lush Valley.

Syan mind-melded. *"It might be worth a try. We've never had a feud in Dragons' Realm before. As King of the Dragons, I'd like to mend the rift."*

"Exactly how I feel," Yanir said.

Anakisha nodded. *"Fair trade."*

"What trade?" Yanir asked.

"We'll try our luck in Lush Valley, if Zaarusha and I get to make decisions about my training."

"But you've no experience," Yanir said.

"Exactly," Anakisha replied. *"So, I'm not prejudiced against new ideas and I don't hold any biases. Besides, I have a wise dragon queen to guide me."*

Zaarusha laughed. *"There's no way you're going to win this one, Yanir."*

"Nor should he," Syan interrupted.

"All right," growled Yanir. *"But make sure she stays safe."*

"Always," said Zaarusha.

"Safer than trying to bargain with Joris," Anakisha slipped in slyly.

There was a cry below them. An arrow zipped past Zaarusha and struck Syan's shoulder. He roared. Pain ricocheted through Anakisha's head until Syan broke mind-meld. *"Syan!"*

Another arrow flew up and pierced Yanir's jerkin sleeve, hitting him in the upper arm. He cried out, grasping the arrow shaft.

"Yanir!" Gods, not again. He'd barely recovered from his last wounds.

"It's my bow arm." He grunted.

Anakisha snatched her bow from her saddlebag and nocked it with an arrow from her quiver. Gods, they'd been caught off guard, busy bantering and dancing along the alps without being vigilant. There were five archers in the snow on Western Pass, near an enormous unlit pyre. A small brazier was burning in a metal pail nearby.

One of them bellowed, his voice carrying up through the air. "Get the colored dragon! She's their queen."

Anakisha aimed at the leader, but as she released the tension on her bow, Zaarusha twisted to avoid an arrow aimed at her tail, and Anakisha's shot went wide.

The archers shot high. A volley of arrows rained at them. The dragons ducked and zipped, making it impossible for Anakisha to fire at the men.

With a bellow of pain, Syan grabbed the arrow in his shoulder with his teeth and snapped it off. He tossed the broken shaft into the air, set the fletching alight, and batted it with his tail. It careened into an archer and his jerkin burst into flame. The man dropped and rolled in the snow, extinguishing the fire.

The men dipped their arrows into the brazier. "Aim. Fire!" the leader yelled. Flaming arrows shot toward Zaarusha.

Anakisha ducked as a fiery arrow zipped past, leaving the stench of her singed hair in her nostrils. Zaarusha swooped, breathing a swathe of fire, but she was out of range.

"Lush Valley was a bad idea. Let's get out of here," Yanir mind-melded. Waves of pain swamped Anakisha's mind.

"They're both hurt," said Zaarusha. *"He's right. We must go."*

With Yanir clutching his arm, slumped over Syan's back, the huge onyx dragon roared and wheeled away, heading down the mountainside toward the forest and the plains, away from Lush Valley.

"Yanir, are you all right?"

He turned in the saddle. His face was paler than her mother's finest lace 'kerchief. *"Thankfully, it's only my arm,"* he grunted. *"It hurts like wildfire, though."*

"We have to find a healer," Anakisha said. *"Zaarusha, lead us to the nearest settlement."*

They descended, Syan losing height rapidly.

Gods, first the pirates had damaged Syan's wing, and now his shoulder was injured.

"They hit my bow arm," Yanir said, "otherwise I would've shot them right back."

Snowy boulders rushed past them as they headed down the mountainside, the trees looming ever closer, their tips like upstanding spears waiting to impale them.

"Syan," Anakisha mind-melded, "can you make it to that cluster of houses in those trees?"

The forest was looming ever closer. The onyx dragon swung his head and angled his wings to swoop toward five or six houses on the edge of a clearing in the forest at the base of the alps.

Syan's wingtip nearly brushed the trees as he landed. A moment later, Zaarusha thudded down beside him. Anakisha leaped out of the saddle and ran. Yanir slid awkwardly from Syan's saddle, stumbling as he hit the ground. Anakisha grabbed him, and helped him sit.

She knelt to examine his wound.

"I'm all right," Yanir said, leaning back against Syan's rear leg. "Take care of Syan first. His wound's deeper."

The onyx dragon's breathing was labored. Anakisha rushed over to his shoulder. Gods, he'd broken the arrow shaft off level with his flesh. The only way to extract it would be to dig it out and sew the wound together. She gulped. She was no healer.

"Sorry, Anakisha, but with my arm injured, I'm not much help," Yanir mind-melded.

"Neither am I," huffed Syan. Blood oozed from around the wound.

If she pulled the arrow out, would it bleed more? What if she damaged his tissues by extracting it? Gods, she didn't know what to do.

A door smacked open and two littlings ran from one of the houses into the clearing. "A dragon," a thin boy yelled, racing out to meet them.

His littling sister clapped her hands with glee. "Two dragons," she cried, her dark braids bobbing as she ran.

The boy reached Syan and Anakisha first. "This dragon's hurt," he said. "We should fetch Ma."

Anakisha spun and addressed the littlings. "Is your Ma a healer? Where is she?"

The girl beamed. "Out in the forest collecting remedies."

The boy nodded. "She's the best healer in our settlement," he said proudly, flourishing a hand at the six houses on the edge of the forest.

In such a tiny place, that didn't mean much, but it was better than nothing. "Come with me, and we'll collect your ma," Anakisha cried, grabbing their hands and racing to Zaarusha. She flung the children up in the saddle. "Strap yourselves in." She clambered over Zaarusha's shoulders and wedged herself between two of the queen's spinal ridges.

Zaarusha tensed her haunches and sprang above the trees, her wings flapping.

"Where does your ma normally go?"

"Along by the river," the girl said.

They swooped up over the trees. *"Yanir, how are you doing?"*

"I'm managing," he mind-melded, pain and anxiety cascading through his thoughts. *"I'm worried about Syan though. His breathing's slowing."*

"We'll be quick, I promise." A promise she had no idea whether she could keep.

Zaarusha tilted her wings. *"There, through the trees,"* the dragon queen mind-melded. *"I spy a red cloak down by the water's edge."* Zaarusha swooped and landed in the river, her weight making the stones rumble like a landslide and torrents of water gush around her legs.

On the riverbank, a woman shrieked, dropping her basket, her hand flying to her mouth. "What are you doing with my littlings?"

The littlings waved. "Ma," cried the dark-braided girl. "Please help the lady. Her dragon's injured."

The mother picked up her basket and appraised Zaarusha. "She looks healthy enough to me."

"No," the boy called. "Not this dragon. The other one."

"There's another one?"

"Syan, the King of the Dragons, lies injured in the clearing near your home," Anakisha called. "Please come quickly."

Zaarusha extended her tail, making a bridge to the riverbank. The woman clambered onto the thickest part of Zaarusha's tail, and Zaarusha lifted her onto her back behind the littlings. Still hanging onto her basket, the littlings' mother slid between the queen's spinal ridges.

With a clatter of rocks and a splash, Zaarusha was airborne, winging back to the clearing. The foliage blurred as she sped over the treetops.

"I'm Anakisha, the new Queen's Rider. King Syan and his rider Yanir were struck by arrows near Lush Valley. We need your help."

"I'm Arabella," the woman said. "Who was firing upon the protectors of the realm?"

Anakisha grimaced. "The people of Lush Valley are angry because Frugar, their former arbitrator, died on dragonback while fighting the Scarlet Hand, a nefarious pirate who's terrorizing the Naobian Sea."

The woman shuddered. "News of the Scarlet Hand reached us last week. They say his dragon picks the bones of littlings clean."

"I'm not sure about that." Anakisha sighed. "But pirates did kill Frugar, and now the citizens of Lush Valley are angry with all dragon riders."

"What twaddle."

Exactly—but somehow, Anakisha didn't think Joris would agree. "Hold on," Anakisha called as Zaarusha dipped a wing and spiraled down to land near Syan.

Arabella slid off Zaarusha's back and strode briskly to Syan. As she examined the wound on his shoulder, Anakisha helped the littlings down.

"Eliona, grab my healing kit from the kitchen table. Borlan, you break this clean herb into a pail of water and bring it to me." She thrust a handful of herbs at the boy. The littlings scampered back to the house. "Quick, give me your blade. I don't want the littlings to see this." Arabella held out her hand.

Anakisha thrust her blade into it.

"The arrow shaft's broken off level with his skin. It's not going to be pleasant or easy to extract it. Could you lean on his foreleg to hold it still and push your hands on the skin around the shaft, while I try to prise it out?"

Yanir staggered to his feet and lurched over. *"Anakisha, let me help."* Without a word to the healer, he leaned against Syan's foreleg, his body warmth seeping into Anakisha, comforting her and his dragon.

"Thank you," Syan thrummed.

The healer's movements were deft. Moments later, Syan let out a roar that shook the nearby branches, making the leaves rustle. With a fleshy sucking squelch, the healer drew the bloody arrow from the wound and dropped it onto the grass.

Suddenly, the girl and her brother were back with their supplies, gawking with wide eyes.

"Water first, please," Arabella called.

The boy stepped up to help his mother wash the wound.

"Needle."

The littling girl threaded a needle with twine and passed it to her ma. "It's pig gut," she whispered conspiratorially to Anakisha.

"Don't tell his rider. His best friends are pigs," she whispered back. Anakisha had the distinct feeling it wasn't the first time the littlings had helped out.

Yanir was hovering over the healer, getting in the way, the arrow still sticking out of his upper arm. Gods, that must hurt.

"Yanir, come and sit over here." Anakisha led Yanir over to a tree trunk and eased him down.

"I'm fine," he said, making a poor attempt at protesting. He leaned back and closed his eyes. "Oh, it's good to sit. I thought I was going to keel over."

Once Arabella had finished stitching Syan and had treated his wound with piaua juice, she came over to Yanir. "You're both lucky I have a fresh supply of piaua juice."

Yanir gritted his teeth, grasping Anakisha's hand with his good hand while the healer extracted the arrow, stitched the wound and sealed it with piaua juice.

"Dragon's claws, this stuff burns," he muttered as the wound in his arm knitted together before Anakisha's eyes. *"I don't think I'll ever think of piaua juice without seeing you in the* Dancing Dragon *fighting the healer and saying you were fine."* He shook his head. *"I was trying hard not to laugh. You had that huge bleeding dragon egg on the back of your head and were obviously dizzy and weak, yet you summoned up enough pluck to fight with the poor healer."*

She slugged him. *"I hope you never need piaua again. Between us, this is becoming quite a habit."*

"I'd prefer to indulge in other habits," he agreed, his eyes straying to her lips.

Anakisha blushed. At least she was distracting him from his pain.

Arabella beamed at them. "Well, that's a job well done," she said, putting her needle, herbs and piaua juice into her basket as the littlings gathered up her other supplies. "You've had a bit of a shock, so, although you're healed, I think you should both stay the night in our home before traveling on. That will also give King Syan some time to recover his strength."

Eliona and Borlan broke out in squeals of delight, dancing on the grass.

"We can't really say no to that, can we?" Yanir asked, arching an eyebrow.

Anakisha smiled at Arabella. "If you're happy to have us, nothing would please us more."

RESCUE

"*Climb on my back, little one.*"

Little one? Stars danced before Giddi's eyes. His legs slowed, his arms sluggish in the water. He clung to the breath in his burning lungs.

"*Now!*" Queen Aquaria snapped. "*I can only help you breathe if you sit on my back.*"

Giddi clenched his jaw, his throat screaming with the effort of keeping it closed. Spots whirled before his eyes.

The queen thrashed in the rigging, limpets scattering and floating off through the water. "*I said climb on my back. Hurry, before you black out.*"

Giddi swam past her head and ducked between the seaweed-covered ropes, his legs floating out behind him. As he touched the dragon's hide, a pale silver bubble of *sathir* enveloped him.

"*Breathe,*" the sea dragon queen commanded.

Giddi's mouth flew open and his lungs filled with air. "Oh gods, thank you. Thank you." Within the silver bubble, tears of gratitude ran down his cheeks. "I thought I'd die."

"*No, I need to thank you. I thought I'd die down here too,*" said Queen Aquaria. "*Now, how can you get me out of this trap? I can't burn these things without burning myself.*"

The ropes were strung tight around her throat, belly and tail. Ripped sails hung like limp laundry from jagged masts, the fabric undulating on the current. Giddi yanked one of the ropes trapping Queen Aquaria, but it held fast.

"*How did you get stuck?*"

"I was searching for new feeding grounds for my sea dragons when I spotted a school of fish flitting through the seaweed. I dived between this ship's branches after them and this trap got me."

Branches? Oh, masts!

"You're a dragon mage. The realm hasn't had one of those in a long time. How will you free me?"

He'd jumped overboard without even thinking—and not even brought a blade with him. How could he rescue anyone? What a fool. Giddi glanced back up at the surface, the pale light endlessly far away—too far for him to swim in eighty counts. There was no way could reach the surface without her help.

"Yes," Aquaria said, "you do need my help to reach the surface. Now that we've settled that, let's get to work." She thrashed her tail and limbs, trying to yank the slimy ropes from the masts, but the more Queen Aquaria wriggled, the tighter the rigging became.

Giddi clung to her spinal ridge as particles of seaweed swirled in a flurry around them. "Stop, you're making me seasick."

Aquaria stopped thrashing and hung in the rigging, her head drooping. "I can't free myself. You'll have to use your powers, young dragon mage, whatever they are."

"I have the power of flame, but it doesn't work underwater," he replied.

"I don't see why not," the dragon said. "I just let out a short burst of flame."

Giddi channeled *sathir* from the ocean, drawing it inside him, and letting it build in his hands. A small yellow fireball darted between his hands. Only yellow? A weak flame would never survive the water outside this bubble of *sathir*, but he hadn't produced enough power to release a green one. "I'm not strong enough," Giddi panted.

"You have to believe in yourself," the dragon said. "Try again."

He tugged more *sathir* out of the ocean until energy thrummed from his core through his arms. Green light shot from his fingertips forming a roiling ball of flame. He spun and forced it out of the silver bubble. The fireball shot toward the rope that secured Aquaria's tail, but it fizzled and died.

"Try harder. I know you can do this. You have to. There is no other way."

"How long will the air in this bubble last?" Giddi asked Queen Aquaria.

"Probably not long enough," the queen admitted.

Giddi's next fireball hit the edge of the rope and disintegrated into a shower of sparks, barely singeing the rope before it died.

These ropes were waterlogged. It was going to take more than his usual effort to burn through them. A cool current swept past them. Giddi glanced at the anchor. The captain had said the tide was turning—if he wasn't quick, *Wave Runner* would leave without him.

His next fireball built quickly. He thrust it out of the bubble, and it hurtled toward the main rope ensnaring the dragon's tail. The flame collided with the rope and caught, flames licking along it. The rope was cast asunder from the mast, the long end drifting in the sea.

Queen Aquaria lurched, her hindquarters drooping toward the aft end of the ship.

"No, my throat." An awful gargling noise came from Queen Aquaria's throat. Bubbles sped from her mouth. Gods, no. She was choking! The queen would die. He couldn't get to the surface alone. They'd both die, trapped here in this awful rigging.

§

"My dearest Captain, although he's a fine lad, we can't risk your cargo or the lives of your entire crew for one wayward boy." Starrus smiled, turning on his charm to convince the captain. "Sir, I'm afraid we must reel in the anchor. Look, the tide is turning." Starrus flicked a fleck of dust off his sleeve and pointed at the swirling current.

The idiot captain and first mate peered into the sea near the anchor rope. What were they waiting for? This was as fine an opportunity as Starrus would ever get to be rid of Giddi, the so-called dragon mage. Imagine a mere boy claiming talents like that. A boy who could shoot a wall of fire out of his hands as wide as a meadow and then channel it into a flaming spear that he'd accidentally shot at the onlookers in Fieldhaven. The entire mage council had been rattled to see Giddi's power erupt. Starrus would make sure it never happened again.

"The boy's your trainee. You're obliged to care for him." The captain glared. "You're too tough on that boy, by far."

"Powerful mages are always forged in fiery furnaces, Captain. It's good for the boy to have a tough trainer." Starrus said. "Furthermore, Captain, I am not obliged to consign your entire crew to death due to my trainee's fanciful notions."

The captain's brows drew down. He scowled at the outgoing tide, then gave a brisk nod. "The boy couldn't have survived this long. I shouldn't have let him try." He grimaced. "You're right. As much as I hate it, we can't risk everyone's lives." He turned to the first mate. "Set the sails and haul in the anchor."

"Yes, Captain," the first mate replied. He issued instructions to the crew.

Starrus smothered a smile, painting his face with concern as three sailors rushed over to haul in the anchor.

§

Giddi harnessed *sathir*, tugging it inside him until his core was molten. He let the energy build and thrust it along his arms until his palms were hot. And still he let it build further, tugging more *sathir* from the water, drawing the energy inside him until his body shook and his head thundered.

There was a metallic flash near the rocks. Before Giddi's eyes, the anchor started to ascend toward the surface.

"*Sorry…*" The queen's gargling stopped and her head slumped.

Giddi thrust his hands above him through the bubble—and let go.

Lightning and fireballs shot from his hands hitting the rigging above, shearing through the ropes. A spear of fire flew into the mainmast and it cracked and sagged like a broken limb.

Giddi and the sea dragon queen fell through the water and hit the deck. The planking splintered beneath the queen's mighty limbs. She shook herself. Fragments of rope and chunks of seaweed floated away, drawn by the cool current of the outgoing tide.

"*I knew you could do it.*" Queen Aquaria turned her long sinuous neck to him, her golden eyes gleaming. "*Hold on.*"

Giddi gasped, limbs shaking as he clung to her spinal ridge.

With a mighty thrust of her hind legs, Aquaria launched them from the deck, splintering the wood underfoot, and swam, her limbs and wings propelling them toward the surface. Fish scattered. Sharks loomed in the distance.

Giddi barely noticed. The bubble of *sathir* surrounding him was shrinking. He was dizzy. The air in his lungs was thin and unsubstantial. He grew faint. Bright spots appeared before his eyes. He was running out of air, yet they were nowhere near the surface.

"*Hold on, Dragon Mage. Please, hold on,*" Queen Aquaria called as his vision went dark.

§

Wave Runner's sails billowed as they sped away from the Robandi Strait toward the Wastelands. Starrus' stomach had stopped roiling, although he still tasted bile at the back of his throat. Thank the Egg, he'd gotten rid of that stinking young dragon mage.

Giddi's death fit in with Starrus' plans nicely. Master Mage Balovar, head of the Great Spanglewood Forest Mage Council, was growing older. In a few years' time, Starrus was sure he'd be dead. If he wasn't, there were certain methods to help him on his way. His vacancy would make way for a new era of mages to rule the council. Starrus had been told he was in the running.

Starrus didn't want anyone—especially not a boy like Giddi— to get in his way. With a powerful young mage flashing his magic about, his plans could have easily been upset. But not anymore. He snorted. Dragon mage, indeed. Ridiculous.

Starrus took a deep breath of fresh air and strode to the water barrel. He pulled out a dipper of rainwater, swished out his mouth and spat overboard. Then he drank deeply, trying to purge the acrid bile from his throat.

Suddenly, a shadow fell over him.

He jerked his head up. An enormous beast was rising from the ocean, emerald wings dripping with water. Starrus gaped. A sea dragon.

The creature opened her maw, fangs dripping brine, and lunged toward the deck. Her talons clattered on the planks as she landed. *Wave Runner* bucked under her weight.

The captain and crew rushed over to the dragon, pointing at her back. "Look, the boy! He's back!"

Only then, did Starrus see the limp figure draped over one of the dragon's spinal ridges. He hadn't done away with the boy at all. Unless he was dead.

The captain and crew pulled the lad off the dragon's back and laid him on the deck. Giddi muttered incoherently but remained unconscious. The boy had fainted. How he'd survived so long underwater was a mystery to Starrus.

The captain spun and waved. "Come, do something. Save your boy. He's barely alive."

What rotten luck. Heart pounding, Starrus snatched up the water barrel and rushed over. When he reached the sea dragon, he bowed deeply. "Thank you, my most highly esteemed—"

The dragon roared, cutting him off and flicked her head toward Giddi. Her golden eyes slitted, she bared her teeth.

Starrus hastily barged through the crew before the dragon bit off a chunk of him. "Stand aside. Let me help my trainee." He sloshed water over Giddi's face.

Giddi spluttered and pushed himself up on his elbows, gazing around, bleary eyed.

"Welcome back." Starrus clenched his teeth but forced a smile onto his face to please the dragon. There'd be more opportunities to do away with Giddi on this journey. And if there weren't, he'd create them.

THE WASTELANDS

Giddi plodded alongside Starrus through the hot desert sands, his feet sore and his throat parched. After nearly drowning, it wasn't easy to traipse through these endless tangerine sands with the blistering sun beating down. Shimmering waves of heat danced above the dunes, making his gritty eyes squint.

He guessed it was fair that Starrus rode the only camel the captain had been able to organize in the oasis near the coast, but he couldn't help thinking that a more compassionate trainer would've let him ride occasionally—especially after his underwater ordeal.

Starrus had been the only one that seemed put out about him rescuing Queen Aquaria. Everyone else had rejoiced, but his trainer had gritted his teeth and smiled. Maybe he was afraid of sea dragons. Or maybe...

"Watch it," Starrus barked from on camel back as Giddi stumbled near the beast's enormous foot.

"Sorry, ah, do you mind if I have a swig of water?" Giddi asked.

Starrus halted the camel and passed down the waterskin. "Here," he said gruffly. The headgear his trainer was wearing made him nearly unrecognizable.

Giddi took a swig. The warm water eased his dry throat, but did little for the sand in his eyes. "How long to the Robandi assassins?"

"I think they're over the next few dunes. We'll stop and make a fire and cook the fish I caught."

Fish *Starrus* had caught? Huh! "Are you sure the assassins won't kill us?" Giddi asked. "The captain said they're ruthless."

"They have no need to. We're not about to attack them, only ask if they've seen the Scarlet Hand or know of his whereabouts."

Giddi shaded his eyes and peered up the enormous dune. It stretched higher than a towering strongwood and was stippled with patterns where the wind had rippled the sand. It was all right for Starrus, the camel was doing the hard work, not his boots. He sighed and passed the waterskin back to his trainer, who urged the camel forward.

"At least we have the fish to look forward to," Giddi said, dragging his boots through the sand.

§

The boy had sounded so forlorn when he'd mentioned the fish that Starrus had nearly given in and offered him a ride on camel back. But Starrus knew deep in his bones that this boy would one day stand between him and his chance at leadership—just the way Giddi's father, Gideon, had prevented Starrus' father from becoming a master mage. He could never let that happen, so he hardened his heart and let Giddi drag his feet alongside the camel over the dunes. The boy got slower and slower until the camel was stopping every few paces, waiting for Giddi to catch up.

The sweat on the lad's face had dried, leaving his forehead streaked with salt and orange sand grains. His eyes stared straight ahead as if he could no longer think.

One more dune ought to do it.

Starrus urged the camel and the boy on. As they crested the next dune, he caught a glimpse of what he'd been seeking to the east: the oasis where the Robandi assassins lived. A brilliant blue lake was nestled in a hollow, fringed by green palms and colorful tents. He'd had no idea the oasis was so large. Starrus gulped. He hadn't asked the captain how many assassins lived there, but from the number of tents, and the size of the camel and goat herds, there were quite a few.

"Nearly there." Nervousness skittered through Starrus' belly.

"Huh?" The boy didn't even look up at him or out at the horizon. His unseeing eyes on his feet, Giddi plodded down the sandy slope.

Excellent. Just what he'd wanted—Giddi so worn out he didn't have a drop of magic in him. Or the strength to fight.

"Only a few more dunes between us and the Robandi," Starrus said cheerfully. "Let's have a bite to eat now." He led the camel down the dune and pulled the kindling the captain had given him from the camel's saddlebag.

"Water?" Giddi asked, trying to sink to his haunches, but collapsing on the sand.

"Soon," Starrus said. No point wasting his precious resources. He tossed most of the wood on a heap on the sand in front of Giddi. "Sometimes, we'll have to use our magic when we're exhausted, which is the reason I made you walk. As part of your training, you must make this wood burn."

"Water, first?" Giddi rasped, his eyelids drooping.

"After you set the wood on fire." Starrus stood beside Giddi, a piece of wood still in his hand. "Go on," he said softly, imitating how his mother had sounded when she'd cared for him. "I know you're tired, but once the wood is burning, I can bake the fish and you can have a drink."

"Water?" Giddi's eyes opened hopefully. He pushed himself to sit, and raised a hand. A lone spark pinged from his fingertip. Then another.

More than most mages could manage when they were dehydrated and exhausted.

Starrus let the boy manifest a few more sparks, just to be sure he couldn't create more.

"Never mind," he said kindly, tossing the waterskin from the camel's back onto the sand between Giddi and the wood.

Giddi lunged to grasp the sack. Starrus raised the piece of wood and smacked the back of Giddi's head. The boy slumped to the sand, unconscious.

Laughing, Starrus retrieved ropes from the saddlebags and bound Giddi's ankles and wrists. He tipped a few drops of black bane onto the wood pile, and leaped on the camel's back, leaving Giddi face down in the sand.

Starrus shot a bolt of mage fire from his hands and hit the wood. Flames licked at the heap and dark smoke rose into the sky. He smiled. The black bane had blackened the smoke nicely, creating a sure signal for the nearby assassins. Starrus gauged the sun and angled his camel west. He snatched a goad out of the saddlebag and whipped the camel's haunches with the barbed metal tips. The beast brayed and took off across the dunes, sand flying at its feet.

Starrus struck it again and again, heedless of raising welts on it flank, nervously glancing back at the desert to ensure no assassins were on his tail.

§

It took Starrus a few hours and a lot of whipping to get his camel to the coast in time to rendezvous with the captain and *Wave Runner*. Luckily, before Starrus had departed into the desert with Giddi, the captain had fallen for Starrus' lies, and insisted that he'd wait at the next accessible bay along the coast in case Starrus had issues with the Robandi Silent Assassins.

When the sails came into sight as the camel plodded down a dune to the bay, Starrus' heart lifted. This trip had been an exhausting gamble, but one that had paid off. He was rid of Giddi. Now he could focus on securing Master Mage Findal and bringing him back to the Naobian Mage Council. Then he could return to Great Spanglewood Forest and earn the accolade of being the mage who'd retrieved Findal from the Scarlet Hand. Soon, he'd be a master mage.

He wouldn't be shunted aside—the way his father had been when Gideon rose to become a master mage. As his father had died, he'd vowed to get revenge upon Gideon for him. And now, he'd succeeded.

The captain and a few of his crew were lounging on the orange sand in the bay, a longboat moored at a crude post. As the camel's feet thudded on the sand, they jumped up, hands flying to their swords. The captain gave a sheepish grin. "We thought we'd better be prepared in case the assassins were after you." He frowned. "Where's the lad?"

Starrus shook his head and sniffed. He rubbed a finger across one eye as if he were wiping away a tear. "The assassins…" he said, and hung his head. "You were right," he mumbled. "I shouldn't have asked them for help."

"Oh gods, that poor boy." Shock strangled the captain's voice.

One of the sailors clutched at his chest. "They kill their victims slowly, peeling their skin, then leave them half alive for the vultures to finish the job."

Another sailor shuddered. "Sometimes they throw them off the cliffs and feed them to sea monsters."

"I know," croaked the captain.

"Stop. I can't bear it," Starrus cried in a husky voice. As they climbed in the longboat and rowed back to Wave Runner, he strongly resisted the urge to grin.

FIELDHAVEN

The breeze ruffled Anakisha's hair as Zaarusha spread her wings and glided through a wisp of cloud. King Syan dipped a wing and sidled alongside Zaarusha, the cloud partially obscuring his sleek black tail.

Yanir grinned at Anakisha and mind-melded, *"How do you feel about going home again?"*

They drifted lower and the cloud cleared, revealing the edge of the forest, and a village in the middle of a sprawling patchwork of fields. Anakisha's heart bounded at the gleam of yellow corn, meadows strewn with wildflowers, kohlrabi, cabbages, and wheat that swayed in the breeze.

"Fieldhaven looks like a cluster of scatter stones dumped by a littling in the middle of all those fields," she replied. *"Until I'd flown on dragonback, I never realized how small and insignificant it was."*

"It's not that insignificant. After all, the Queen's Rider was born and raised in Fieldhaven." Yanir's slow grin made her toes curl in her boots.

She smiled. *"I spent my whole life there and never realized how much more there was to the realm."*

Yanir pointed beyond Great Spanglewood Forest and Montanara, toward a distant mountain range in the north. *"If you feel like that now, wait until you get to Dragons' Hold. The fierce peaks of Dragon's Teeth are enough to make anyone feel insignificant."*

Anakisha swallowed. As soon as she got to Dragons' Hold, she'd be too busy to visit home. Even though she'd only been gone a few weeks, she'd missed Pa and Stella, and had often wanted to talk to her sister. She longed to catch up with the gossip in Fieldhaven. Were the Night Wings still fighting the Howlers? Or had the street rats disbanded now that Fox's uncle was the new arbitrator?

And what about Justan?

Her belly clenched, as if an icy fist had grasped it. The ex-arbitrator's son's handsome face, with golden hair and cinnamon eyes swam before her. He'd fooled her, sucked her in with his romantic notions, and even kissed her to convince her that she should lose the tournament so he could win and be allowed to be hand-fasted to her.

She saw his lips again, spitting, *"Lowly tavern wench."* And remembered his hands around her throat, the hard bite of the cobbles at her back as he'd straddled her and tried to kill her.

Yanir's warmth washed over her, his gentle voice in her mind, *"Anakisha, don't be hard on yourself. Justan fooled many people. He and his father put up such a good front. How could you have known what they were really like?"*

The wind sifted its fingers through Yanir's sandy hair as his smoky gray eyes met hers.

She'd misjudged him too—thought he was the arrogant King's Rider and not seen his compassion, nor how deeply he could love.

His cheeks reddened as he sensed her thoughts. *"Come on, the sooner we land and see your family, the better. It will do you good to be with them again. It will be more difficult to visit once you start your training at Dragons' Hold."*

"You'll love Dragons' Hold," Zaarusha chimed in. *"It's a wonderful place. After all, I live there."*

"Zaarusha, I'm heartbroken. I thought you liked Dragons' Hold because of my *company,"* Syan quipped.

Their chortles rumbling through Anakisha and Yanir's minds, the dragons angled their wings and shot down toward the village, the houses becoming ever larger and more distinct as they grew closer. A rabbit warren of alleys wound between the buildings, the tiles on the rooftops glistening in the early morning sun. Their dragons swooped low, aiming for the village square. A handful of stalls were set up in a corner, and people were wheeling and dealing.

"Look!" The shrill cry of a boy rose from the village square.

A cluster of people raised their faces to the sky and waved.

Anakisha grinned and waved back as Syan and Zaarusha spiraled down together to land on the cobbles of the square. A babble of voices greeted them.

"It's Anakisha!"

"She's home!"

"The Queen's Rider is back."

"And the King's Rider is here, too."

"You're the village hero now. We can't disappoint them," Zaarusha said, flexing her wings.

"Do you always play to a crowd like that?" Anakisha leaned forward to scratch Zaarusha's eye ridge and then slid off her back to greet the villagers she'd grown up with.

"Anything to make you look good."

"And here I was thinking you were making yourself look good, showing off your pretty-colored wings," Syan interrupted, nudging his queen's shoulder with his snout.

Yanir slid off Syan and was instantly mobbed by a group of littlings who wanted to sit on King Syan.

The door to the tavern burst open. Stella pelted across the cobbles and bowled into Anakisha.

Anakisha's arms closed around her sister. She inhaled deeply, enjoying the familiar floral and lemon verbena scent of Stella's hair soap. Soap she too, until recently, had used.

"I remember that scent too." Yanir quirked an eyebrow as he lifted a littling into Syan's saddle and showed him how to scratch Syan's spinal ridge.

Stella's blue eyes gazed up at her like pools of liquid fire, excitement dancing in them. "I can't believe that you're just in time, Anakisha!"

"In time for what?"

Stella frowned. "You don't know Pa and Mayfree are being hand-fasted?"

The air was sucked from Anakisha's lungs as if she'd been knocked in the chest. She opened and closed her mouth, speechless.

Behind Stella, Pa strode out of the *Dancing Dragon* into the square, holding Widow Mayfree's hand. Well, obviously not *widow* Mayfree anymore—now that she had Pa.

By the First Egg, that was quick! Anakisha had only been gone a few weeks.

Pa enveloped Anakisha in a bear hug, his bristly chin scratching her forehead. The familiar scents of the tavern—home-made bread, ale and beef stew—wafted from his jerkin. He pulled back, still clasping her shoulders and grinned down at her. "From the shocked expression on your face, I'd say Stella's blurted out the news."

With a lump in her throat, Anakisha nodded, still not sure what to say. "Hello, Pa, Mayfree." She threw caution to the dragon gods. "Pa, are you two being hand-fasted today?"

A belly laugh erupted from Pa. He threw back his head, his laughter booming around the square.

Mayfree kissed Anakisha's cheek. "You won't get any sense out of him while he's laughing so hard. No, our hand-fasting ceremony is not today. We didn't know when you could get here, so we sent a messenger bird to Dragons' Hold. We were waiting for your arrival. I'm so glad you heard and came so quickly."

A littling cried out, pointing to the southern sky. "No, she didn't come from Dragons' Hold. They came from there."

Anakisha nodded. "It's true. We've just come from Naobia. We're on our way to Dragons' Hold now."

Pa stopped grinning. "So, you didn't get our message? That explains why Stella's news shocked you." He gazed back and forth from Anakisha to Yanir hopefully. "I hope you can both stay until the end of the week? We'll have our hand-fasting while you're here."

"The immediate threat in the south has been vanquished," Yanir said. "I see no need to hurry." He slipped a comforting arm around Anakisha. "We wouldn't miss it for the world."

Anakisha squeezed Stella's hand and couldn't stop grinning as happiness blossomed in her chest like a thousand mage fires.

Robandi Silent Assassins

Giddi woke with a thumping headache, to a soft sibilant hiss like silk slipping over sand. His mouth was as dry as a desert. No, it was a desert—half filled with sand that made his teeth gritty and throat raw. His eyes were full of the stuff and his face felt like it'd been scraped raw. But his head was the worst. The back of it throbbed in time to his pulse like a blacksmith's hammer striking an anvil, pain searing from the back of his skull through to his temples with every strike.

Giddi groaned and rolled over onto his back. Oh gods. Tall figures loomed over him, the bright sun behind them casting their faces in deep shadows. The hiss hadn't been silk on sand, but their voices, whispering in Robandi as they gesticulated at him. Some of their hand movements looked violent, others were placating.

The assassins had found him and his trainer.

He moved his head, looking for Starrus—a mistake. Pain ricocheted through his skull. He lay still and breathed until the pain subsided. Then he sat up. "What—" he croaked, unable to say more. He tried to swallow, but grit coated his throat, making him cough.

What in the First Egg's name had happened? He slowly turned his head. And where was Starrus? They must've killed him already. His eyes landed on a trail of deep gouges in the sand, camel prints leading west. From the depth and the sand in disarray around them, the animal had been in a hurry. His trainer must've fled when the assassins had attacked.

Strange, he didn't remember anything after Starrus had thrown him the waterskin.

Giddi raised a hand to shade his eyes, but the instant he moved, a short assassin leaped forward and thrust a curved scimitar under his chin.

"Don't move," she hissed, her dark eyes flashing within her headdress. Now that she was out of the sun's glare, he saw her robes were as orange as the desert sands.

"What—" Giddi croaked again. Then he understood. These were the *silent* assassins who moved as softly as silk on sand and spoke only in whispers. Rumors said they trained as soon as they were old enough to hold a blade and were the deadliest creed in all of the realms. The Wastelands were their home—and theirs alone. Others who inhabited the sands of the Robandi Desert knew the assassins ruled.

Giddi wanted to swallow but didn't dare. The pulse at his throat bounded against the sharp blade as if it wanted to challenge his captor to press a little harder. These rogues must have run Starrus off.

"Why are you here?" the young woman hissed. "Why are you so close to our home?" She jerked her head at the heap of smoldering wood nearby.

Wait, Starrus had been about to bake fish and had handed him a waterskin… The assassins must've sneaked up behind them. There was no other explanation.

"Speak. Or pay with your life." She held the blade away from Giddi's throat, giving him space to form words, but when Giddi tried to speak he could still only croak. She jerked her head, her other hand flashing near her mouth and an imitation of someone drinking.

A thin man in a similar robe and headdress strode forward and unhooked a waterskin from a belt at his hip. He passed it to Giddi.

"Drink," she whispered.

Eagerly, Giddi grabbed it and took a swig, then another and another.

"Careful." Her dark eyes flashed, but it was too late.

Giddi's stomach groaned. He hunched over, vomiting in the sand at her feet. The woman flicked sand over his spew with the toe of her beaded slipper and wrinkled her nose. "Drink again, but only sips. Anything more and you'll be vomiting over my feet again, you mangy cur."

Giddi nodded and took a few short sips in rapid succession. Glad his mouth wasn't filled with grit anymore, he wiped his chin with the back of his hand and cleared his throat.

"Drink again," she commanded.

For such a young woman, she was pretty bossy, but Giddi didn't dare say a thing. Instead, he drank slowly, while all the assassins surrounded him, their hands on their wicked, curved blades.

"My trainer and I wanted to talk to your chief about the Scarlet Hand." The girl cocked her head and frowned, so Giddi continued, "He's a pirate with blood-red sails on his ship, the *Fiery Dragon*. We're searching for him because he's kidnapped Mast..., um, a friend." Better not to let on he was a mage in case he needed to use his talents. Giddi coughed and took a few more sips from the waterskin. "Have you seen him?"

The girl's frown turned into a scowl. "What trainer?" she hissed.

"The man who brought me here."

The tall man who'd passed him the waterskin pointed back at the trail leading down the dune. Giddi's tracks were barely footprints, more like long gouges in the sand where he'd half-slid and half-stumbled down the dune to collapse. Beside his prints, the camel's feet had sunk deep into the sand, leading to where Starrus had dismounted to make the fire to bake their fish.

She looked down at his scuffed tatty boots. "You mean he rode while you walked beside him like a slave." It was a statement, not a question.

Giddi snapped his head around to stare at the fire and sniffed. The wood was blackened with a heavy tang of black bane—often used for sending signals.

The man's eyes slid to the tracks created by the camel fleeing West. The men and women surrounding them gestured at the camel tracks in the sand as if they hadn't seen Starrus flee.

Giddi's head reeled and throbbed even harder.

Starrus had abandoned him and left a signal fire. His hand flew to the back of his head. His hair was matted with congealed blood over a lump the size of a dragon egg. He groaned, and when he pulled his fingers away, the tips were crusted with flakes of dried blood.

The young assassin's eyes were wide. "We found you alone. The fire was belching black smoke. Your wrists and ankles were bound. You were meant to be a sacrifice for us, but we don't prey on the weak." She sniffed, her nose high in the air and stared down it at him as if he were a sand beetle.

Who did she think she was? She was barely older than him and certainly a lot shorter. Giddi was about to protest when there was a subtle shift in the stance of the ten assassins ringing him. *We don't prey on the weak.*

So, they didn't want to fight him? That was fine. Giddi nodded, even though it sent a spasm of pain across his skull. "Thank you," he choked out.

The tall man plucked the waterskin from Giddi's hands.

The girl nodded to some men. Two of them lunged, grabbing Giddi and hauling him to his feet. His head pounded. What in the realm did they want now? The men held him up while two others searched him, patting him from head to foot, looking for weapons. Little did they know that his best weapons were his fingertips.

Giddi stood resolute, hoping it would soon be over, his head pounding.

Once they'd frisked him, they stepped back and spoke rapidly in their tongue, gesticulating and miming with gruesome gestures.

From what he could see, they weren't sure what to make of him.

A moment later they were all still, and the young woman spoke, "It has been decided that we should not kill you…" she said.

Giddi breathed a sigh of relief.

Amusement flashed in her dark eyes. "Well, not immediately," the girl continued. "We could leave you in the sands to fry in the hot desert sun, or trade you as a slave to the emperor of Metropoli for gold."

His heart sank into his tatty sand-ridden boots.

The slim girl pointed to a man with regal bearing. "However, our leader insists that we should throw you off the cliffs to appease the monsters in the deep. Often we give them dead tributes, but he has assured me that the gods want to see you alive."

Giddi pounced on her words. "Yes, they do," he said. "They want me very much alive, indeed." Now was his chance to impress them. He focused, letting the *sathir* build inside him. As he thrust out his hands, the assassins snatched their blades and rushed at him. Fire flew from his fingers, circling him in a wall of green flame that hungrily licked skyward.

From within his fiery sanctuary, Giddi bellowed in his most commanding voice. "I'm a dragon mage. I know the wishes and desires of these great monsters of the deep. They do not want me underwater. They do not want me to die. But they do want me to travel to the coast and avenge myself upon the trainer who abandoned me here in the desert."

The men and women fell back, gaping.

Giddi let the flames die down to waist height and pulled back his clothing to show the faint white scars the kraken had left on his neck and upper chest. "I have fought the monsters of the deep and survived. Earlier this morning, I rescued Queen Aquaria of the sea dragons. I have powerful friends who roam the seas and the skies. None of them want me dead."

To his surprise, the assassins fell to their knees and pounded their fists on their hearts.

He got such a shock that his flames guttered and died.

The Robandi assassins murmured, their whispers hissing across the sand.

The regal man gestured at the girl, and she spoke, "My father, the head of the Robandi assassins, wishes to apologize for our mistake. He is pleased the realm has a new dragon mage and offers his deepest respect to you. We would like to help you get revenge upon your trainer."

Sending a band of assassins after Starrus would be very sweet indeed, but he'd never find out the whereabouts of his father, and these assassins could turn upon him at a whim. He'd sleep sounder without them. "I'm honored, but I can't accept your offer. My blood is on my trainer's hands, and therefore his shall be on mine." Keeping his back straight and his head high, he stalked away from the assassins to follow Starrus' camel's prints west. He only made it half way up the dune before his legs gave out and he was face-first in the sand.

The girl ran to him and pressed a sack into his hands. "A waterskin and some food. Please, accept one of our camels." She indicated behind Giddi. "They're hobbled beyond this dune."

His aching feet and groaning belly rejoiced. "I'd appreciate a camel very much." He took the sack.

The girl thumped her hand on her heart and bowed her head. "It's my honor to serve you, tamer of monsters, honored flame bringer and dragon mage."

As soon as Giddi and his camel were over the lip of the dune, Giddi dug into the sack, pulled out a juicy date, and chewed it. It was a shame Starrus hadn't cooked their fish, but then again, maybe Starrus had never intended to.

§

Two hours later, Giddi was sure the camel he'd been given was the most stubborn creature in all the realms. It refused to follow Starrus' camel's tracks and kept shying to the left, back toward the Robandi assassins' oasis. Twice, it halted and refused to go any further.

He clung onto the saddle, snatching some dates and oranges out of the sack, making sure he drank often.

The camel stopped again, this time near the top of a dune. It brayed and bared its teeth, swinging its head back to bite him. He ducked, but it snagged the sleeve of his jerkin and ripped it. Giddi grabbed the sack and was about to slide off its back, when the camel sank on its forelegs, pitching him over its head onto the sand in an undignified heap.

Braying, it lumbered to its feet, and trotted back down the dune, leaving him stranded.

"Beastly beast," he yelled after it. Of course, the camel ignored him. He snatched up the sack, and stalked back to the tracks that Starrus' camel had left. At least he now had food and water and they'd come a distance.

The sun was slipping toward the horizon. In a few hours, it'd be dark. He pressed on, his boots trudging through the endless tangerine sand, hoping he'd reach the shore before the night gripped the desert and turned it into a chilly deathtrap.

Hopefully he could get wherever Starrus was headed and remind his trainer of his commitment to take him to Pa. Giddi trudged along the ridge, down a dune and then up another. At the top, Starrus' camel had made a wide berth to the north around a narrow basin filled with odd undulations of sand. On the far side of the basin, the camel's prints continued over a higher dune. Tired, and his head fuzzy, Giddi squinted into the basin, but there appeared to be no sign of danger. There was no point in going all the way around, so he headed down to go straight across.

At the base of the dune, his boot collided with something solid hidden under the sand. The ground shifted, throwing Giddi onto his backside. A huge orange lizard emerged from the sand, thicker than a log, with enormous squat legs and a long tapered jaw. Its tongue flicked out from its jaw and then its maw opened, exposing jagged fangs.

By the flaming dragon gods! Giddi scrambled to his feet and ran. His foot landed upon another sand-covered lizard. This one roused too. Shaking off the sand and rearing on its hind legs, it knocked Giddi onto his back. It bellowed, head raised to the sky. The sands shifted as the entire basin came to life, lizards emerging from the orange desert.

Shards! There were more!

The lizard opened its maw, exposing long yellowed fangs. Saliva dripping onto Giddi's face, it lunged at his throat.

Giddi threw up his hands. A bolt of green mage flame burst from his fingers and hit the beast's neck. The blast sheared its throat in half and its head flew through the air, in a spray of blood. Its body flipped onto its back, legs spasming in the air.

Another lizard straddled the dead lizard's belly, biting into its soft gut. Others rushed in until the beasts were a writhing mass of snapping jaws, thrashing tails and strings of green and yellow guts.

More lizards lunged at the body, blood spraying as they wrenched the limbs from its carcass.

Heart thumping like a racing camel's feet, Giddi scrambled to his feet and ran straight back up the dune. Gods, he was fool—with less sense than that dumb camel. He'd never had any idea such creatures existed. Below him, the beasts were battling, rearing on their hind legs and gnashing their jaws. Even more were rising from the ground, shaking the orange sand off their scaly hides.

A low flying gull swooped over the basin. Thank the Egg, this area must be near the coast.

A lizard lunged into air and snapped the bird in a flurry of feathers, its feet hanging from the reptile's mouth. A stocky shorter lizard snatched at the bird's dangling feet, and the reptiles scuffled in a flurry of feathers, jaws and claws.

Giddi ran down the far side of the dune and took an even longer detour than what Starrus' camel had taken. His breath rasped in his chest and his feet floundered in the sand, but he kept running. There was nothing except a slight hill to stop those ferocious lizards from chasing him—and nothing to take him to the shore except the tenuous trail of camel footprints that'd be impossible to follow when night fell.

FOX

As evening drew near, Uncle Pieter put that morning's pastries into a huge basket and handed it to Fox. There were cinnamon twists, raspberry tarts, apricot pastries, bread smothered in cheese, and bacon rolls all jammed in together. Not that Fox had much stomach for pastries anymore. After a few weeks of working in the bakery and cramming pastries down his gullet at every possible moment, the allure had worn off.

"Please take these out to Widow Samantha's farm, Curly," Uncle Pieter said. "She has a lot of hungry mouths to feed and we'll soon be baking more for tomorrow."

Fox took the basket. Uncle always called him Curly. Although his red hair had been as straight as an arrow for years, he'd been born with a thatch of ginger curls. "Uncle Pieter, you look tired. Are you sure you don't want me to knead another batch of dough for you first? Or work an extra shift when I get back?"

His uncle brushed him off. "I think we can manage. Adora's going to work late tonight and Purley will help me with the bread dough."

Purley, the ex-leader of the Howlers, bustled out to the front of the shop, sweeping the tiles vigorously with her broom. She grinned at Fox, knowing she was getting under his skin.

The Howlers—a notorious gang of street rats that had terrorized Fieldhaven until recently—used to prowl the streets, stealing and fighting. A few months ago, the ex-arbitrator's son, Justan, had asked Fox, Fox's sister Brianna, Billy, and Anakisha to form the Night Wings, a vigilante gang that had fought the Howlers.

Things had gone well until Anakisha had been attacked by Spike, a Howler, and been injured. Then Justan's cover had been blown when Anakisha had discovered that his father, the arbitrator, had been paying the Howlers to steal for him, and that he and Justan had created the Night Wings to throw people off their trail.

What a mess that'd been.

Uncle Pieter had been appointed as the new arbitrator and Fox had volunteered to run his bakery.

Fox hadn't liked it when his uncle had released the Howlers from the stocks and given them jobs in the bakery. But Uncle Pieter hadn't had much choice: his uncle's new role as the town's arbitrator kept him busy dealing with townspeople's grievances and running Fieldhaven. Justan's Pa was still locked in jail—thank goodness: he was a nasty piece of work.

Justan had been taken into prison after being accused of murdering Anakisha's brother, but he'd been set free yesterday, because no one had been able to prove it.

Fox stepped to one side as the door opened and Purley's right-hand man, Lefty, carried in a sack of flour. "Evening, Pieter, I have three more sacks in the wagon."

"Very good, Lefty, just take them out the back," Fox's uncle replied, busying himself with counting the day's takings.

Lefty carried the bulging sack to the store as Fox headed for the door and opened it for a man who came into the bakery and went to the counter.

"Good evening," Adora—also a Howler—said in her sultry voice, batting her eyelashes. "How can I serve you?"

Fox rolled his eyes. She was so flirtatious, she sounded like she was offering far more than pastries.

"A loaf of bread, please," the man replied. "I'll take the rye with walnuts."

Fox left and strolled down the street. A woman was approaching with a gaggle of children clutching her skirts and each other's hands. He nodded at her. "Good evening."

"Evening, Fox. Off to Widow Samantha's again?" She smiled.

Fox pulled a littling's hand away from the fruit seller's display next door as the lad reached for an orange. "Not now, lad, your Ma has to pay for the fruit first. Here, have a pastry instead, but make sure you share it." He passed it to the boy, who broke it and gave some to his siblings.

"You're a kind lad, Fox," the woman said. "You'll make a good father someday."

Fox's face grew hot and he blushed to the roots of his hair. "Uncle Pieter's got the soft heart," he replied. "Not me."

"Say what you like." She smiled. "You take after him more than you take after your father, thank goodness." She bustled off down the street, leaving Fox flabbergasted.

How in the name of the First Egg should he answer that? Sure, his Pa had made an error in judgment by becoming a trusted adviser to Justan's father, the ex-arbitrator, and Pa was still bitter now, but what did that have to do with him?

He shrugged and walked past a group of littlings under a plum tree. A big lad up in the branches shook them, making the ripe fruit drop. The littlings giggled and snatched up the spoils for their baskets. A plum hit a littling in the face, splattering purple globs over his cheek. The boy's lower lip trembled.

Fox stopped and bent down. "Let me help," he said, cleaning the purple muck off the boy's face with his 'kerchief. "Luckily this one was mighty ripe so it didn't hurt."

"Fank you, Fox." The boy sniffed.

Fox waved and kept walking. He stepped out of the way as a wagon rumbled past laden with goods.

Brianna strolled out of a side street, her flaming red hair bouncing on her shoulders. "Hey, Fox. Off to Samantha's?"

"I am, and you?"

She giggled. "I'm meeting Justan for some fun."

"He's no good, Brianna. Billy said he murdered Anakisha's brother."

"If he murdered Jacob, then why hasn't he been tried?"

Fox shrugged. "You know Billy—he's so shy he hardly speaks. The thought of bearing witness terrifies him."

"Well, until Justan's tried, he's not actually guilty, is he?" Brianna smirked. "Besides, he's been out of prison a whole day, so it's high time I saw him."

"Leave Justan alone." Fox shook his head. "He's betrothed to Bertha now."

Brianne shrugged her hair over her shoulder. "I don't care. He and I can do what we want. It's none of your business."

"By the dragon's claws, it's not!" said Fox. "I'm your big brother."

"You may be bigger, but you are younger. Age trumps size. Besides, I'm my own person. You don't see me running uncle's errands like a lapdog."

"At least I'm doing some good," Fox growled.

"Sure, Fox, you keep telling yourself that," Brianna taunted, rolling her eyes. "All you're doing is fattening up the townspeople with fine pastries."

"Bread is a staple, not a treat, and I'm delivering these free goods to Samantha who has no food."

"Delivery? Is that what you call it now, Fox?" Brianna simpered, batting her eyelashes. "She'd be a fine catch!"

"It's not like that! She's just a poor young widow."

"A very pretty one. I'm sure you're making her happy, *visiting* every day."

"Brianna, you're being a brat. Stop playing with Justan. I don't want to see you get burnt."

"I'll play with whom I want." She poked out her tongue and flounced off.

Fox shook his head. If only she had her head screwed on right. But what could he do? He was her brother, not her father, and Pa didn't see anything wrong with her kissing the ex-arbitrator's son. In fact, he was encouraging it, still saying Justan would be a fine catch.

Fox didn't know what had gotten into her lately, but when Brianna was in one of these moods, there was no stopping her. Most of the time they got along fine, but when it came to Justan, she never saw reason. Fox's hand formed a fist. He'd like to smack Justan's nose, but Pa had forbidden him to fight Justan, saying a couple of weeks in jail were good enough for a young man like that, and that he was sure Justan was now on the right path. Pa was blinded by status and riches, and Justan's father had possessed both of those, before he'd been found out.

But Fox had seen the way Justan had reeled in women, one after the other: first his sister; then Anakisha; and now Bertha. At least Anakisha had seen the light.

He stomped down the lane. When a pretty young girl shied away from him, he realized he must be scowling like a thunderstorm. He quickly smiled. "Good evening." He hurried on his way, adjusting his expression so he didn't scare half the township away.

A blue guard wheeled overhead, and there were a few more dragons over the farms in the distance. Fox gazed at them wistfully. He'd rather be on dragonback soaring above the countryside than delivering pastries, working with his archenemies and being taunted by his silly sister. Perhaps if Anakisha ever came back to visit he could ask her for a ride on Zaarusha. His heart bounded in his chest. That would be amazing.

He missed Anakisha. Although he still hung out with Billy and Brianna, life hadn't been quite the same since the Night Wings had disbanded and Anakisha had become Queen's Rider. He missed the nights of scampering over the rooftops with Anakisha, Brianna, Justan and Billy, fighting the Howlers. Not that he'd give Justan the time of day now.

Fox passed the stable yards on the edge of town, sidestepping a fresh pat of horse manure buzzing with flies. The scent of more horse manure was rife, wafting through the stable yard gates. Fox waved a hand over the basket to keep the flies off and hurried down a lane into the countryside.

Soon, he was at Widow Samantha's. The hinges squeaked as Fox opened the wooden gate to her farm. It slammed shut, and he made his way through the yard toward the house. Before he could get there, the door flew open.

Three littlings tumbled onto the doorstep, tripped over each other, and fell down the stairs. The smallest landed face-down in the dirt. She lifted up her curly golden head, and howled.

Fox dashed over and put down the basket. He scooped her up, dusting off her face and knees, and reached into the basket. "How would you like one of these?" He passed her a cinnamon twist.

The golden-haired girl stopped mid howl, eyes gleaming, and snatched the pastry, stuffing it into her mouth.

The other two littlings crowded around him, beaming. He passed the older girl a raspberry tart and gave the boy an apricot pastry. The three littlings grinned, stuffing their faces and thanking him in a spray of crumbs.

"Fank ooo, Fox," said the smallest. "Like it."

"Oh, this is scrumptious, Fox," the eldest said. "Please thank Uncle Pieter."

"Have you got any more?" asked the boy hopefully. "That was good."

Samantha came to the door with a crying babe in her arms, his clenched fingers stuck in her mass of curly brown hair. Her eyes fell to the basket, then shot up to Fox's face. "Hello, Fox. Nice to see you again." She jiggled the babe, trying to quiet him, but the babe cried louder, his face turning red. "Thank you for bringing your uncle's pastries. He's been so kind since Wren passed away."

"He says you're welcome." Fox carried the basket inside. His gaze flitted to her open pantry. The shelves were bare except for a pumpkin and half a sack of flour. Outside a cow lowed. "You seem to have your hands full. Would you like me to milk Bessie for you?"

She disentangled the babe's fingers and pushed her hair over her shoulder so it was out of reach. "Thank you, Fox. That would be most helpful." She crooned softly to the babe. "I need to feed him."

"I'll keep the other littlings busy," Fox called, heading out the door. Gods, he was blushing, remembering Brianna's words. He'd never thought about whether Samantha was pretty or not, but now that Brianna had put the notion in his head, he had to admit she was a very young widow, probably only a handful of summers older than him, and still a mighty fine looker.

He shook his head. His stupid sister was messing with him. He was only here to help someone in need, not find a girl and an instant family. That shrotty-tongued Brianna was doing his head in. He'd never thought about Samantha that way and he wasn't about to start just because of his sister's sharp tongue.

The three littlings were playing with a pile of pebbles in the yard.

"Come with me." Fox snatched up the smallest and headed to the barn, the other two trailing him. Bessie was already in her stall, waiting for them. He grabbed a pail from a peg on the barn wall, and then asked the eldest littlings. "Have you learned to milk a cow yet?"

They both shook their heads, their curls flying.

Fox seated them on stools beside his and perched the smallest on her sister's knee. "Hold her tightly and mind she doesn't get near Bessie."

Soon the hypnotic rhythm of squirting milk plinking against the side of the wooden pail soothed his nerves. He showed the littlings what to do, laughing as one of them *accidentally* squirted the other's face.

When they were finished, they all washed their hands at a tub near the well. Fox headed back inside with the pail in one hand and the littling on his opposite hip.

Samantha was asleep in an armchair, the snoozing babe nestled in her arms.

Fox silently bid the littlings to sit at the table. He poured the steaming milk into three chipped cups and gave them each a pastry. Fox lifted the babe from Samantha's arms without her waking, and placed the lad in his cradle in the corner of the room, tucking him in. He took the rest of his uncle's bread and treats out of the basket and placed them on the shelves in Samantha's pantry, then closed the door to prevent rats or mice from eating their supplies.

He placed his finger on his lips. The littlings nodded solemnly, chewing on their supper, as he slipped out the door with his uncle's empty basket.

Before he left, he'd take a quick glance at Samantha's vegetable patch and see what she had growing. Fox headed out the back of the house across the field to her garden, which backed onto a copse of trees.

While the west end of the garden was neat and tidy, at the other end, the veges were struggling to grow through a tangle of stray plants. Fox bent to his knees, tugging out weeds. Soon his uncle's basket was full of carrots, turnips, tomatoes and beets. He filled his arms with weeds and strode to the edge of the copse to dump them under the trees.

"Fox, you've done some good work today," a voice rumbled.

Fox spun but there was nobody there. Who in the dragon gods' name was talking to him?

"I'm here."

He spun again. There was no one in the woods, the field, the garden or near the house. Not even a creature—except for a squirrel on a nearby bough and a bird high in the sky.

No, it wasn't a bird. It was descending, rapidly getting larger by the moment. A dragon was hurtling down toward him.

"Yes, Fox, I'm coming for you."

Fox's heart pounded like a littling banging its cup on the table. "M—Me?" he stammered aloud. Gods, what had he done? Thinking about how pretty Samantha was shouldn't have gotten him in trouble with a blue guard—and it'd been weeks since he'd been out fighting on the rooftops.

"Yes, you," the dragon replied, its voice rushing through Fox's head like a river thundering down a waterfall.

The mighty blue dragon landed in the meadow, its talons gouging the earth and sending clumps of grass flying. Its scales were a wondrous shade, reminding Fox of a deep-blue lake shimmering in the sun.

"Fox, I sense that you're unhappy."

Fox shrugged. *"My life is quieter now, and has routine."*

"Some of us were born to do good and fight evil. Others are happy to stay at home and have families."

"As if I'll ever have a family." Fox snorted. He'd never thought of himself as a crusader either.

The dragon nuzzled his hand.

Energy zapped through Fox, like a lightning bolt, jolting him to his core. Every hair on his arms stood on end. Fox could've sworn he heard the beating of battle drums. His whole body was pounding, compelling him to move.

"That's no battle drum, Fox." A deep rich laugh bounced around his head. "It's your own heart racing with excitement. Follow it—do what it tells you."

Fox flung his arms around the dragon's throat and swung his body up onto her neck. She arched her neck, her head in the air. He slid down her back until he bumped a large spinal ridge. Wriggling his way backward over the first ridge, he nestled down to sit between it and the spinal ridge behind.

The dragon chuckled again. "Fox, you need a saddle."

"A saddle? Whatever for?"

"Because you're my new rider. We're imprinting. I shall take on your name and be known as Foxita after you."

"Foxita?"

"Dragons or riders take on a syllable of each other's names upon imprinting as a symbol of the deep bond between us." She turned back to gaze at him with her golden eyes, a gust of warm breath huffing over his face. "Surely you knew that?"

"Yes, but—" Fox stared at her. "This is imprinting?" This surge of something far bigger than him, filling him and making him want to burst—making him feel anything was possible, like he could conquer realms, or fight pirates, or even fly. Anything.

"I see you're a man of many questions, Fox. Thankfully they're answered easily."

They were imprinting and all he could do was repeat her words like an idiot. Fox threw back his head and laughed.

Her haunches tensed and Foxita sprang into the air. Fox's heart beat so loud he thought his eardrums would burst. As they circled the meadow, Foxita roared and her rush of pleasure coursed through Fox's veins, searing him like fire. He shrieked with joy.

Samantha and her littlings ran outside, waving and calling out as Foxita and Fox spiraled up into the sky. Soon the widow and her family were tiny figures in the meadow. The forest and farmlands receded. Tendrils of cloud wisped across Fox's face.

"Fox, are you ready to leave your home and train at Dragons' Hold?"

"Am I ever!" He hesitated. *"I'll need to tell Uncle Pieter."*

"He's a good man. I'm sure he'll understand."

"You know him?"

"More questions? Yes, we blue dragons share our knowledge of people with each other, often long before we meet them." Foxita flew over the meadows toward town. As she descended, she turned her head and huffed at him. Warm air stole over his hair, drying the misty drops left by the clouds.

Gods, this was fun. He laughed. *"This beats baking pastries any day. I'd love to ride with you and fight evil from dragonback."*

"You have a good heart, young Fox. Let's put it to use. I've seen you feeding Samantha and her family over the past few weeks as I've been learning my duties with the blue guards."

As they plunged down toward the houses, Fox hung on, his stomach dropping and his heart soaring. *"So you're new to all of this too?"*

"I certainly am," she replied. *"We'll be learning together."*

§

Anakisha took Yanir's hand as they headed down the cobbled lane to the bakery. "I hope you're enjoying my tour of Fieldhaven. I'm sorry, there isn't that much to see." Anakisha had shown him the dragon statue on the edge of town, the plum tree along a lane where she and Jacob had picked plums as littlings, and her favorite swimming hole at a river just out of town.

Yanir squeezed her hand. "This is fun. Remember, I've mainly seen this town from dragonback until now, apart from the few days here for the tournament." He grinned. "And most of that was spent in your sick room."

She laughed. "Thanks for carrying me home that night. I don't know what Spike would've done to me if he'd come back and found me unconscious. A quick dagger between my ribs was probably the most likely outcome."

He turned to her, his gray eyes grave. "Don't even joke about you dying. Gods, I would never have gotten to know you. Never had the opportunity to do this…" He gazed at her with ferocious intensity and leaned in. His lips brushed hers once, twice, and then he pulled back and grinned. "Not that once or twice would ever be enough…"

Anakisha's heart thrummed. "I know what you mean," she murmured.

"Later." He winked and inhaled. "What's that delicious aroma?"

"Probably Pieter's custard tarts or apricot pastries."

When they got to the bakery door, Yanir held it open and ushered Anakisha inside. She walked over the stoop and stopped dead in her tracks, gaping. Purley was sweeping the floor, and Adora was behind the counter.

Yanir smacked into her back, and she stumbled. He caught her around the waist. "Sorry, you stopped so—"

"What!" Anakisha blurted, staring at Purley. "You!"

Fox's Uncle Pieter came out from the back of the store. "Evening, Anakisha. Welcome home. It's nice to see you not covered in chimney soot for once."

Purley gaped back at her. "So, this is where you disappeared to that night! We hunted all over town. Never thought you'd gone down a flaming chimney!"

"It wasn't flaming," Anakisha replied dryly.

Yanir shifted beside her, resting a reassuring hand on her waist. "I gather there's a story behind this." His gray eyes turned to slate as they lit on Purley.

"We work in this shop," said Purley. "No need to look down your nose at us like that. We're re-hab— um, rehab—"

"Rehabilitating," supplied Fox's uncle.

"Yes, that thing," Purley said. "Working in the bakery to pay for our misdeeds."

"Crimes, more like it," snapped Anakisha. "Or have stealing and assault changed their status in Fieldhaven over the past few weeks? I suppose you're pilfering from the coin box while you're here?"

"No need to. We get board and lodgings out the back," Purley smirked.

Fox's uncle beamed. "Purley and her friends work for me now."

Anakisha's eyebrows flew up. She couldn't believe it. "Um, where's Fox?"

"He's running an errand for me," Fox's uncle said. "If you'd like a pastry and a drink, you can sit in the garden out the back and wait for him there. He'll be back soon. It's a pleasure to have the Queen and King's Riders here." He put a handful of dried soppleberries into a teapot.

Purley's eyebrows nearly fell off. "I heard you was Queen's Rider, but I didn't believe it," she said.

"I'll serve you." Adora batted her eyelashes at Yanir. "I didn't realize the King's Rider was quite so handsome, close-up. But I'm sure we can get much closer."

"Enough of that, Adora," said Fox's uncle. "I've told you not to flirt while you're working. Not in my shop, thank you."

"Of course, sir." Adora said demurely. "But perhaps I can after work?" she purred at Yanir.

Yanir looked anywhere but at Adora, the tips of his ears redder than the raspberry tarts on the counter.

"Two hazelnut twists, a custard tart and an apple-and-almond dragon, thank you, Adora," Anakisha said sweetly, depositing her coppers on the counter. "Come on." She tugged Yanir outside.

Fox's uncle soon followed them with a porcelain plate laden with pastries in one hand and a pot of soppleberry tea in the other.

They sat at a wrought iron table outside in a cobbled area at the back of the bakery edged by a pretty flower garden. At the end of the yard, a gardener was planting seedlings in a vegetable patch, his back to them.

Fox's uncle set the tea and delicacies on the table. "I apologize, Yanir. It's going to take Adora a while to learn the ropes."

Yanir nodded and took a quick sip of tea, his cheeks still pink.

Anakisha picked up a hazelnut twist, biting into the fine flaky pastry and gooey hazelnut paste. She stopped herself from groaning out loud. *"Yanir, these are good. You should try one."*

Yanir picked up a hazelnut twist and bit into it. *"Delicious."*

Fox's uncle gestured at a squat building near the back of the yard beyond the flower garden and the lawn. "That's where Purley, Adora and Spike sleep. It's a few notches up from the burnt-out ruins they used to sleep in."

Anakisha nearly choked on her hazelnut twist. "Spike? He's here?" she yelped.

"I'm hoping the work, lodgings, good food and respect from my customers help keep them honest." Fox's uncle shot her a reproachful glance.

"I'm sure you're giving them the best chance possible." Yanir nodded. "This twist is very tasty."

The gardener turned and smiled, exposing a row of pointy teeth. "Nice to see you Queen's Rider." He waved. "How's your head?"

Why, the nerve! Cheeky, shrotty bully. Spike had not only clobbered her on the back of the head and left her unconscious, he'd also bruised her littling sister Stella's face.

Yanir mind-melded, breaking into her thoughts, *"Maybe we should be grateful to Spike. After all, if he hadn't clobbered you, I never would've met you."*

Anakisha snapped her jaw shut and smiled sweetly at Spike. "Nice to see you." She took another bite of her pastry, but somehow, it didn't taste quite as sweet.

Yanir chuckled in her mind. *"As Queen's Rider you're going to have many more difficult political situations than this. Think of Spike as good practice."*

Anakisha's cheeks burned.

Spike puffed out his chest. "I'm the gardener. My first paying job in my life."

"And a fine job you're doing too, Spike." Fox's uncle walked back into the store.

Anakisha's cheeks burned hotter. Perhaps she'd misjudged the Howlers. Without a home or parents to care for her, maybe she would have resorted to being a thug too.

"Such maudlin thoughts when we have such fine treats before us," Yanir said. "Spike, would you like to join us?"

"That's taking it a bit too far," Anakisha snapped via mind-meld.

"Dining with your enemies is a perfectly valid strategy," Yanir replied, infuriatingly gesturing Spike to join them.

Spike tipped his head toward the vegetables he was planting. "No thanks. I'm working. It's not my break time yet." He turned and set a seedling in a hole he'd dug, and then reached for another.

"Here, Yanir, try this." Anakisha passed Yanir the dragon. Crafted of delicate layers of pastry, the dragon was glazed with honey to a deep golden hue and stippled with scales of candied apples and almonds.

Anakisha had just taken her first sip of soppleberry tea, when a shadow fell over the garden.

A dragon with scales the deep blue of shimmering water speared down toward the grass between the flower garden and the vegetable patch. Straddling the flower bed, it landed with one set of talons on the grass and the other clattering on the cobbles. The dragon tilted her head and gazed at Anakisha and Yanir. The fine creature dipped her head in respect.

Anakisha stood and walked over to place a hand on the dragon's snout. *"My Queen's Rider,"* the dragon said. *"I'd like to present my new rider. His name is Fox. And I'm Foxita."*

Behind her, Yanir's teacup clattered on his saucer.

"By the shrotty tail of a dragonet!" Anakisha exclaimed. "It's Fox!"

A Plea for Help

Giddi floundered through the sand in the dark, scanning the sand for a sign of the camel's trail. It was hopeless. Clouds obscured the moon. His hand was a pale glimmer in front of him but it was too dark to see the sand underfoot.

When he'd seen the poor gull snapped up in that lizard's jaws, he'd assumed he was close to the coast, but for all he knew he could have been wandering in the wrong direction since nightfall. Dusk had come quicker than he'd expected. His empty food sack hung from his belt, along with the waterskin that still held a little reserve water. The back of his head throbbed in time to his footsteps. A shiver wracked him as a cool breeze rose and nipped at his sunburnt face. It clawed its way through his jerkin, especially the loose flap on his sleeve where that stupid camel had bitten him. Thank the Egg its teeth had missed his flesh.

He kept trudging—he had to keep moving even if it was in the wrong direction. He'd freeze if he stopped. The Robandi Desert was a world of harsh contrasts. Her cold nights and her blazing hot sun made her a tough taskmaster for anyone who wanted to survive.

For a moment, Giddi wondered what would've happened if he'd stayed with the assassins. Would they have continued to worship him? Or would he soon have become one of their victims? He shivered again, glad he hadn't waited around to find out.

§

Giddi slumped to the ground. He was exhausted and had no idea where he was, but he had to sleep. The cold breeze ruffled the sand, spraying it into his face. Within moments of stopping, his body was wracked with shivers. He turned his back to the wind, sand peppering his jerkin with a patter that helped him drift to sleep.

Violent shudders woke Giddi, his body spasming and legs twitching. Gods, he was cold. He'd probably die here in the desert. He'd never catch up with Starrus, nor find out his father's whereabouts. Every moment training under that shrotty mage had been a waste. Every insult, every injury and even the kraken attack... What good had it done him to withstand Starrus' bullying if he died now and never saw Pa again?

"Oh gods, Ma, I miss you." Giddi's harsh whisper cut through the desert night. "And you too, Pa. If you were still here, I would've trained under you instead of being trained by that lousy Starrus."

Starrus had been his father's protégé and the last mage who'd seen Pa.

He had to find Pa. And find Mage Findal to make up for leading Frugar into battle and having him killed. Not that he could ever repay Frugar's death.

With a sob Giddi cast out his mind. *"Help me please. Help me find the way home."* Tears rolling down his cheeks, he lay his head against the cool sand. He was lost. He needed help and there was no one—absolutely no one—who cared whether he lived or died.

A dark chasm yawned inside Giddi. He was falling, drowning in a deep dark sea with no end. His back shook with sobs. "I have no one, no one except Pa who cares." And Pa had been gone for years.

"What is it you need?" a faint but familiar voice asked.

Aquaria? He was dreaming, delirious after so long in the sun. Giddi closed his eyes.

Her voice came again, still faint, but more insistent. *"Dragon Mage? What help do you need?"*

He sat bolt upright. It *was* Aquaria. He wasn't dreaming. *"I'm cold,"* he sobbed, *"And lost in the desert and I can't find the coast."*

A chuckle ran through his head. *"If you're cold, why don't you warm yourself with your mage flame?"*

By the dragons gods, what a fool he'd been. He'd been so overwhelmed with emotion, he hadn't even thought to use his magic. He rubbed his hands together, and let *sathir* flow to his fingertips. A small yellow flame burst from his fingers, lighting up the sand around him. He got to his feet and held up his hand, casting his light further, and hoping no nocturnal beasts were prowling nearby.

"Where are you?" the sea dragon queen asked.

"I don't know."

"Keep walking to the coast. I'm swimming to the shore, then I'll fly inland to meet you. It will take me a while to get there."

He didn't know where the coast was, but he had to try. Giddi stalked into the breeze.

Surely, the wind was blowing inland from the coast—or was it blowing from the desert? He sat down again, the flame still dancing at his fingertips.

A shadow moved on the crest of the dune before him. Giddi let his light flare, illuminating the small assassin, slithering over the dune on her belly. As his light hit her, she jumped to her feet and whistled. Two camels plodded up the dune behind her, one carrying the taller, thin assassin.

She planted her hands on her hips, feet apart. "Flame Bringer, your camel returned," she whispered. The thin assassin laughed, and Giddi got the distinct feeling it was at his expense. The girl glared at her fellow assassin, then continued, "My father sent me to ensure you were not lost." The corner of her mouth twitched, and the thin assassin laughed again. This time she made no attempt to stop him.

Gods, they thought he was a fool. And they were right. Giddi bristled. "Ah, of course I'm not lost."

She arched an eyebrow. "I see."

"Yes, I'm heading straight for the coast." He stalked off, his mage light held high.

"Wrong way," she called, mirth in her voice. "Unless you'd like to traverse the entire desert to find the eastern coast."

The other assassin was no longer silent, clutching his midriff, his laughter ringing out beneath the cold desert stars.

The girl nodded in the opposite direction. "The west coast is over the third dune, that way."

Giddi swallowed his pride. "You're right. I was lost. Thank you for helping me."

Her teeth flashed. "My pleasure, Flame Bringer."

Holding his flame up, Giddi backtracked then headed up the opposite dune. At the top, he let a volley of flame shoot into the sky, lighting up the sands. "Thanks again," he called.

She waved from camel back, and the two assassins and their camels disappeared into a hollow.

§

Giddi plodded up the third sand dune, inhaling deeply. A salty tang filled his nostrils, lifting his heart and making him weep with joy and exhaustion. *"I'm nearly there,"* he mind-melded with Aquaria.

"I've just arrived at the coast. I can hear you better, so you must be near."

He crested the dune and gasped. A glimmer of moonlight illuminated bright-blue light swaying like a living carpet at the foot of the dune. Breakers rolled in, limned in sapphire light, seething upon the shore of a sandy bay.

Aquaria arose from the ocean, her scales gleaming molten blue against the dark sky. She landed on the shore, luminous-blue spraying from her wings. Giddi raced down the dune, his feet sliding through the sand, then ran along the shore. He flung his arms around her wet neck, not caring that his clothes were getting soaked.

"I was far offshore. You're lucky I heard you," she mind-melded.

"Thank you." He laughed so hard, tears rolled down his cheeks. His limbs and chest were covered in shining blue. *"Thank you for coming. I have no family, no one to care for me,"* he mumbled.

"My boy, you're exhausted." The queen of the sea dragons nuzzled his shoulder. *"I care. You will always have me."*

Giddi nodded and sank to the sand, relieved he'd made it.

Aquaria flapped off and dived into the sea. Moments later, she returned with a fish speared on her talon. She roasted it on a small flame and passed it to Giddi. *"You will always have me and every other dragon in the realm at your service, young dragon mage."* She bowed her head low, then raised it again, her golden eyes regarding him. *"It's an honor to serve you. What is your name?"*

"Giddi, short for Gideon. It's my name and my father's, too." He took a bite and moaned, juice running down his chin.

"Is he also a dragon mage?"

"No. He's a powerful master mage, loyal to the realm, but no one has seen him for years."

"I and my sea dragons will help you find him."

"Only one person knows his whereabouts. My trainer." Giddi shared a memory of Starrus on the deck of *Wave Runner*.

"I don't trust that man."

"Neither do I, but I have no choice. He's the only man who knows where my father is. But he's run off and left me behind."

"Then we shall find him." Aquaria cocked her head, as if she were listening to the hiss of the waves on the shore. *"One of my sea dragons tells me that the ship you were traveling on is heading for Metropoli, the city of the shining white palace. When you've finished eating, I will take you there."*

The sea dragon huffed warm breath over him while he ate his fish, easing the chill of the night. When he was done, Giddi hooked his waterskin on his belt, clambered upon her back and wrapped his arms around her spinal ridge, and Aquaria dived into the sea.

METROPOLI

Blue light streaked from Aquaria's limbs as she swam south along the coast. Giddi was enveloped in a silver bubble of *sathir*, once again, able to breathe freely underwater.

A manta ray sped past, its coat undulating and its tail trailing a wake of luminous blue. Schools of fish darted between seaweed and dived on coral, also leaving ripples of blue. A giant turtle floated past on a current with babies swimming behind it. Everything that moved was bathed in sapphire.

"What's all that blue light?" Giddi asked.

"Algae that light up the water when there's movement. Everyone comes out to play when the algae abound." Aquaria swam past a pod of frolicking dolphins, their plaintive squeals carrying through the ocean.

"What can you tell me about Metropoli?" Giddi asked.

"Humans regard it as the richest city in the realm." Aquaria snorted. *"Poor things. A life above water has limited their under-standing of true riches."* She waved a foreleg. *"Look at this."*

Seeing the vibrancy of underwater life lit up with streaks of sapphire, Giddi knew exactly what she meant. Coral sprawled across the ocean floor and crowded the bank along the coast in giant fans, knobbly trees, mushroom-like growths and large dishes—all purple and blue in the reflected light of the moving sea life, but Giddi knew that during the day, these formations would be all the colors of the rainbow.

"I have nothing of value, only the clothes on my back. How will I find Starrus or pay for anything in Metropoli?"

"We can fix that," the queen chuckled.

"How?"

"Just wait and see."

§

A breeze ruffled Starrus' hair as *Wave Runner* pulled into the Metropolian harbor. The city was still as impressive as the last time he'd been here with Gideon. The market quarter and slums of Metropoli rambled along the foreshore with brightly-colored tents, ramshackle buildings and squat sandstone dwellings haphazardly crammed together. The hum of the market floated across the water—a familiar blend of vibrant music, the shrill tones of hagglers, and laughter.

The backdrop to the marketplace was the city proper, which rose in neat terraced switchbacks up the side of the orange cliffs. Fountains cascaded between the terraces, tumbling into pools with sweeping tiled areas around them. Orderly rows of sandstone buildings made of red and orange bricks stood sentry along the broad boulevards leading to the gleaming white building inlaid with golden stars that crowned the city—the emperor's palace.

A shiver rippled down Starrus' spine as he remembered the last time he'd dined with the emperor. His last visit to Metropoli hadn't gone well—a secret that was better left unshared. Even the two mage councils who'd sent him and Gideon on their quest didn't know what had happened on that journey. Or why his trainer had never returned. And now that young Giddi was dead in the desert, probably murdered at the hands of the Robandi assassins, there was no need to divulge it.

Starrus' grin turned feral as the sailors moored *Wave Runner* on the broad planked pier that jutted out into the harbor.

The pier and dockside were bustling, sailors loading silk, cinnamon, dried fish, fine necklaces of gold, exotic herbs and curved Robandi scimitars onto ships. A caravan of camels

EILEEN MUELLER

burdened with saddlebags was trudging away from the docks up the sandy road that wound up the hillside to the desert, their handlers walking beside them.

Situated by the largest oasis in the Robandi Desert, Metropoli was the richest city in all the realm. The emperor's fierce army and navy had seen to that. Once again, Starrus recalled the gleaming dark eyes of the emperor, eyes that had mocked him and glittered with avarice.

Starrus scanned the myriad of ships—galleys, naval longboats, hulks and fishing sloops—docked in the harbor. None of them had red sails. But the Scarlet Hand had to be here somewhere. If Starrus were the one fleeing from Dragons' Realm and the green guards, Metropoli would be the place to come. With its busy docks, sprawling markets and warrens of crowded terraces sprawling across the hillside as far as the eye could see, this was the perfect hideout for criminals.

Not that the emperor encouraged crime. His guards were vigilant, however, bribery was rife—if it suited the emperor's purposes. Although the original inhabitants of Metropoli were predominantly Robandi, many ethnicities and cultures from all over the realms now gathered here.

The captain clapped a hand on Starrus' shoulder. "Farewell. I'll be unloading my cargo, reloading with goods, and leaving in three days. Once again, I'm sorry about you losing the boy."

Starrus grimaced and shook his head. "I tried to do what I could, but there were too many assassins for me to fight them off. I should have taken your advice, Captain."

"The state of your camel's hide was sorry enough. I saw the whip welts. It must've been a furious flight to escape them."

Starrus nodded somberly, bored that they were going over his alibi again, but if it helped solidify his story, it was worth it. "If I don't get back to *Wave Runner* in the next few days, please sail without me. When you get back to Naobia, can you tell the Naobian Mage Council my trainee's life was lost?" He shook his head sadly. "Such a waste."

The captain clapped him on the shoulder again, making Starrus want to cringe. "I will, Starrus. It's the least I can do," he said gruffly. Clearing his throat, the grisly old sea dog strode along the deck to oversee the cargo being unloaded from the hold.

Starrus shouldered his travel bag, wishing his trainee was still around to carry it for him—about the only thing the lad had been good for—and strode down the gangplank onto the busy dock. He waded through the sailors and merchants unloading the cargo and reloading their ships.

Yes, part of the emperor's fortune was based on the gold he'd mined. His jewelers were among the finest in the realms, and their work contributed much to his coffers. Further along the docks, past the markets, merchants were packing goods into the bulging saddlebags on another team of camels strung together in a caravan. Within hours, they'd make their way from the docks to the desert towns and villages inland to sell their goods.

Pushing his way past the busy sailors and clamoring merchants, Starrus passed the clerks sitting at wrought-iron desks, scratching their quills on parchment to log the details of each ship and its cargo. Coins clinked as first mates and captains paid duties on the goods they were importing. No ship came to Metropoli without the emperor being aware of when she'd docked, who'd disembarked and what cargo she was carrying.

Passengers were queuing to have their names and village of origin noted, forming a line that snaked along the dock. Starrus eyed the clerk, who had her head down, scribbling frantically. He strolled along the queue in a business-like manner and, by shadowing a sailor carrying a huge sack over his shoulder, managed to slip past the clerk without being noticed.

He approached the marketplace, the scent of spicy meat and vegetables in sweet aromatic sauces making his belly grumble. Starrus pushed through the throng, noting the shifty gazes of the emperor's adviser's spies stationed among civilians on the dock side. Although his name wasn't recorded in any of the official documents, his arrival would be noted. By midday, Vizza, the emperor's adviser would be alerted that Starrus was in the city. He refused to bow his head and act like prey about to be hunted. Instead, he strode confidently through the market, fiercely meeting the gazes of the adviser's spies.

§

Nightfall found Starrus in a drinking establishment. Not a lowly tavern, but a prestigious lounge on the terrace below the palace. Starrus sat in a corner, nursing his ale, knowing it wouldn't be long until Vizza, the emperor's adviser, appeared. His eyes flicked over the patrons gathered at the crowded tables. These clientèle were not the dockside rabble or lowly inhabitants of Metropoli, but the well-shod and silk-clad upper echelons of Metropoli society.

The low hum of discrete conversation was deliberately masked by a cascading fountain that ran down a narrow channel out the wide front door and billowed over a ledge into the pool of crystalline water on the terrace below. A flautist and percussionist ensured further discretion for patrons discussing all manner of business.

At the table next to Starrus, a deal was being brokered in hushed tones between a man in a black silk robe and a woman with a tattooed cheek wearing a crimson dress. To the right, gold flashed in the candlelight as it disappeared into an official's purse—a bribe of some sort. A corpulent man at a table behind a towering potted fern shook hands with a thin wiry man, the rings on his pudgy fingers flashing in the candlelight from a blazing chandelier.

Powerful people met here every night to cement the futures of others: assassins, officials, merchants and business people—some genuine, others fronting illicit dealings.

Sure enough, Starrus' ale was only half finished when the emperor's adviser stalked through the doorway, nodding and smiling at patrons as he wound his way through the tables with crisp footsteps and well-controlled grace. Starrus wasn't fooled by his wiry build—although lean, the man was solid muscle and packed a mean punch. A head taller than most, the adviser was the canniest general in the emperor's army, a keen strategist and, unfortunately for Starrus, an excellent judge of character. Candlelight made the gold buttons in his silk tunic gleam. He was the only general not to wear the standard uniform—and his network of spies was the most formidable in the realm. Vizza's dark glittering eyes never once lit upon Starrus, until he'd greeted every other patron in the establishment.

Finally, Vizza slipped into the chair opposite Starrus, crossed his long legs and signaled the waiter. "I'll have two more ales, the same as my friend here is drinking."

His friend. Starrus knew Vizza's codes. If Vizza didn't touch his drink, the waiter would dispatch an assassin at a nearby table to deal with Starrus tonight. If Vizza deigned to take a sip, Starrus was considered no threat.

"Good evening, Starrus. I'd heard you'd arrived, but I've been delayed on business. Where is the gold you stole?" Although Vizza smiled, his voice was laced with steel.

So, they'd found out. He'd known they would. "Gone," Starrus replied, meeting Vizza's gaze.

"What are you seeking in our land?"

Without preamble, Starrus leaned in, "The whereabouts of the Scarlet Hand."

"The Scarlet Hand?" The adviser raised an eyebrow and stroked his dark goatee.

The waiter set the foaming ales on the table. Vizza pushed his aside—not a good sign.

"I've been busy in the markets today, gathering gossip."

"So I heard." Vizza's eyebrow twitched again.

Starrus ignored him, plowing on. "And I heard the Scarlet Hand obtained an audience with the emperor."

A faint glint in his dark eyes was the only sign that the adviser knew what Starrus was speaking of. Vizza tilted his head back, looking down his nose at Starrus, dark eyes flat. "The emperor's business is the emperor's business." His powerful legs thrust into the floor and he stood, boots snapping on the tiles. With exaggerated care, Vizza lifted his chair back into the table and spun away.

Gods, he was about to leave. Starrus grabbed Vizza's sleeve. "I request an audience with Emperor Haakin."

Vizza's eyes traveled slowly down his sleeve and rested upon Starrus' hand pawing at his dark silk. He disdainfully flicked Starrus' hand away and peered at the ale stains Starrus' grubby fingers had left. His eyes flashed with venom, betraying no hint of their former friendship. "You stole from Emperor Haakin. In order for you to have an audience with him, you'll have to fight in the arena."

"Accepted." The words burst out of Starrus before he could think.

Vizza gave a wolfish smile—as if Starrus had just given him what he'd come here for—and stalked out of the establishment without a backward glance, leaving his ale untouched.

Suddenly, Starrus' thirst was quenched. The arena—by the dragon gods, what had he just agreed to? He slugged back his two ales and Vizza's, hoping they wouldn't be his last.

COIN

G iddi and Aquaria soon left the luminous-blue algae behind. They flew inland to an oasis so Giddi could fill his waterskin and pick oranges and dates. Then they traveled along the coast for days, stopping to sleep on the sand early in the morning before the sun was scorching, then swimming or flying again by mid-morning each day. Aquaria fished for him, roasting his meals to perfection.

They often journeyed through the night. At times, they dived deep underwater, where the sea was dark and the fish had lights drooping off stalks on their heads. At other times, they swam on the surface among flying fish and cavorting dolphins. Occasionally, other sea dragons joined their queen, their sapphire, jade and emerald scales gleaming as sunlight rippled across them in shallower waters. And sometimes, Aquarius flew high along the rugged orange sandstone coastline—which made Giddi shudder, remembering his close call with Starrus, the lizards, and the Robandi assassins.

When Giddi and Aquaria were a day's journey from Metropoli, Aquaria dived, skimming down a cliff smothered in coral. Brightly-colored mushroom-shaped formations as large as serving platters clung to the rock face in a dazzle of purple, pink, orange, yellow and green. Yellow and blue fish with white spots on their bellies shot under them, peeking out at the mighty sea dragon. Finger-like coral projections poked out of crevices. Lobsters withdrew into holes in the rocks as they approached, their feelers the only sign of their presence. Coral rose like tiny trees, stretching out their colorful branches. Fish darted in and out, their striped scales flickering among the branches. Stars of purple and blue nestled among blobs of lime and lapis. A school of pink-and-blue spotted fish shot off, scattering like a spray of mage sparks.

Wonder blossomed in Giddi's chest until he thought he'd explode. *"Where are we going?"*

"You'll see," Aquaria hummed. *"I promised you this."*

He didn't remember her promising him anything.

Aquaria settled upon the sandy sea bed near a rocky formation that undulated through the water like a low mountain ridge stretching as far as Giddi could see. The rocks were odd, with strange silvery-tan projections all over them. *"I've never seen rock like that before,"* Giddi mind-melded.

"That's because they're not just rocks."

"Of course they are."

"Well, they are, but they're covered in oysters. This is an oyster reef."

"They don't look like the oysters shells I've seen in the market in Montanara."

Aquaria edged closer. Each projection was actually a hinged shell clamped shut. They perched on top of one another, creating an indistinguishable wall of shell, covering every surface of the rocky ridge.

An oyster reef—he'd never even known they existed.

Long fringes of wispy seaweed hung from each lower shell. *"They look like they've got beards."* Giddi pointed to the wisps waving in the water.

"That's because these are bearded oysters," Aquaria said. *"I know that humans exchange coin for things to eat, instead of plucking sustenance from nature's bountiful seas, however I don't have coin, and I promised I would help you survive in the richest city in all the realms. If you tickle under their beards, these oysters will open their shells and you may pluck out their pearls."*

"*Really?*" It seemed too easy. Giddi took a deep breath and slid into the water out of the bubble of silver *sathir* that enveloped him whenever they dived. He swam over to the oysters and ran his fingers under the seaweed hanging from the lower shell of an oyster as large as his head. The wavy, ridged shell slowly opened. Several gleaming pearls lay within the oyster's flesh.

"*Just squeeze, and the pearls will be expelled,*" Aquaria instructed.

"*Isn't that painful for the oyster?*" Giddi asked.

"*Pearls are a nuisance. They're happy to get rid of them and provide you with your means of survival.*"

Giddi squeezed the pearl through the slippery flesh of the oyster. It popped out of the flesh into his hand. He squeezed another and collected that too. And then he tried with four smaller oysters, taking a pearl from each.

"*Thanks, Aquaria.*"

"*Are you sure you have enough?*" she said.

"*Probably enough to survive a year in Metropoli,*" Giddi mind-melded. He laughed underwater, bubbles escaping his lips and his laughter reverberating through the sea.

§

Giddi and Aquaria reached the harbor of Metropoli at dusk. Wings dripping, Aquaria rose from the sea and flew high above the sandstone cliffs into the dark sky. Lit by lanterns, topped by a palatial building with an onion-shaped white dome gleaming in the moonlight, the city clung to the sloping hillside in a trail of terraces with cascading waterfalls leading into deep pools. On the hill above the city, the landscape was lush with vegetation that fringed a huge lake. Canals led from the lake to irrigate fields planted with crops. Tall plants with broad flat leaves swayed in the breeze of Aquaria's wingbeats.

"*What strange plants. What are they?*"

"Haakin, named after the emperor. The Robandi grind the black seeds to make a hot drink that they swear makes them more alert."

Odd custom. But then again, perhaps it was similar to soppleberry tea. A pang of homesickness hit Giddi. Not that there was anyone left to go home to. The only family he had left was his missing father.

They had to find Starrus so Giddi could see Pa.

Dared he nurse the hope inside him that he'd finally find his pa after two years? The mages on the Great Spanglewood Council had sent Starrus and Pa off on a secret journey. Only Starrus had returned—and none of them had spoken of Pa much since, despite Giddi and Ma's questions.

Grief knotted Giddi's stomach as Aquaria landed on a dusty strip of barren sandstone far beyond the edge of the city. *"From here, you should be able to enter the city discretely."*

Giddi dismounted and flung his arms around her warm, scaly neck. *"Farewell, Aquaria. I thank you for rescuing me and for bringing me here."*

"Without you, I'd be dead in that ship's traps."

There was no point telling her it was just rigging, not a trap—she'd still been snared in it.

Aquaria huffed warm breath over him, drying the back of his jerkin and breeches. He turned, his arms outstretched and the ragged flap of sleeve from the camel's bite hanging loose. She wafted her breath over his arms, torso and legs, drying the rest of his clothing.

"I knew a mage once that could dry his own clothes with his magic," she said. *"I suggest you learn how to do that too."*

"Good idea." Giddi chuckled. *"But until I've finished my training, I'd probably just set my breeches on fire."*

She snorted, flipped her wings, then dived back into the sea. *"Farewell, my dragon mage. Thank you, once again. I'll miss you."*

A lump rose in his throat. *"Farewell Aquaria."* Giddi blinked hard. His hand tightened around the pearls in his pocket, watching until her ripples disappeared. Once he found Starrus, they had to hunt down Mage Findal so he could clear his debt for Frugar's death with the council.

He slipped along the dusty trail toward the twinkling lanterns of Metropoli. The closer he got, the harder the nerves jangled in his belly. He clenched his hands over his stomach, willing the dragonets dancing in his stomach to stop.

He passed a few crumbling sandstone ruins. In the dim light he made out a couple of tall figures leaning against a marble statue of a sea dragon ahead on the trail. Giddi quickened his pace. A man a few years older than him pushed off the statue and stepped out onto the track, his hard gaze sweeping over Giddi, sizing him up from his tatty boots to his bushy eyebrows. "Need somewhere to stay the night?" he asked.

Of course he did, but not with that thug. "I'm fine, thank you," said Giddi. "My father's expecting me."

The man raised a disbelieving eyebrow, and let Giddi pass by, but Giddi didn't miss the thuds of footsteps behind him. He rushed toward the city outskirts. As he turned a corner to go down a winding alley between orange sandstone buildings, he glimpsed three men following him.

Not again. It was like Naobia all over again. He put on a burst of speed, dashing down a myriad of alleys. He had no idea where he was going, so it didn't matter which turn he took. Even though it was dusk, it was still warm, the sultry night air clinging to him. People fringed the streets, sitting outside on stoops, chatting with their neighbors, drinking aromatic hot drinks so dark they looked like cups of pitch.

When he was sure the men were no longer following him, Giddi slowed his pace and meandered among the alleys. He pulled his cloak over his head and around his face, using it like a headdress. The dull red of his face after days in Robandi Desert had gradually tanned on the journey here, and, although his eyes were green, they were so dark they almost looked black, especially in dim light like this. He wouldn't pass for a Robandi, but he might just pass for someone who'd lived here a while—if he was lucky.

Now, to change his pearls into local coin and find a bed for the night.

At last, Giddi found a sign emblazoned with script he couldn't read, but the emblem of the sack of gold was clear enough. The sign was hanging over a narrow entrance in a sandstone wall. The door was hooked open, lantern light spilling into the alley. The shops on either side were closed for the night. Just what he needed, a late-night moneylender.

Glancing around furtively, Giddi pushed his way past a curtain of beads and went inside. The shop was barely more than a narrow passage. A wizened old man was asleep in a chair behind a counter painted garish red and decorated with golden symbols of coin emblazoned with camels, eagles, vultures, snakes and scorpions.

Giddi drew the pearls out of his pocket and thrust four of them deep into his undergarments hoping they wouldn't roll down his leg. With the other two clenched tightly in his palm, he strode to the counter. "Excuse me."

The man emitted a snore, inhaling noisily through his hawk-like nose. His gray hair curled in wisps from under his headdress—a headdress in cloth that matched his counter: deep red with the same garish symbols, but this time in silver.

Giddi cleared his throat. The man twitched, but kept snoring rowdily.

In desperation, Giddi reached his hand across the counter in order to shake him. Halfway across the counter, his hand brushed a tripwire. A lever fell down and hit a gong with a boom that resounded through the enclave. The moneylender jolted awake and sprang to his feet, flashing his yellowed teeth in a greasy smile. He rattled off a phrase in Robandi.

Although he was taller than most lads his age, Giddi knew his voice was a sure giveaway. If the money lender thought he was a young foreigner, he'd be ripped off. He grunted and shoved one of his pearls across the counter.

The man threw his hands up in horror and shook his head, rattling off another phrase in clipped Robandi, but Giddi didn't miss the gleam of avarice in his eyes, nor the twitch of his fingers.

Giddi shrugged a shoulder and closed his hand around the pearl. The man wheedled with Giddi in a placating tone, and snatched at his sleeve. Giddi turned away. An explosive string of Robandi flew past the man's lips.

Perhaps he was now ready to trade fairly. Gods, it was hard to be sure what the moneylender was saying but Giddi had to have coin. He grunted and placed the pearl on the counter again.

The moneylender retrieved a heavy iron lock box and pulled a key out from inside his shirt. He unlocked the box, and spread a handful of coins across the counter. There were two camels, two vultures, two snakes and two scorpions. The camels were the largest and the scorpion the smallest. Giddi deliberated for a moment, wondering whether largest coins were the most valuable, or the smallest, or whether the sizes represented of the size of the animals emblazoned on them.

He held up two fingers and swept a hand across the coins, indicating he wanted the man to double his offer.

The man shook his head.

Giddi laid the other pearl on the counter.

The man's eyes boggled, flicking from the pearls to Giddi. The moneylender licked his lips and asked what sounded like a question.

Giddi grunted and drew the pearls back again, but the man quickly relented and laid out quadruple the number of coins he had previously.

He could be being ripped off. What was a pearl worth here? It didn't matter. He'd quit while he was ahead. Giddi nodded.

The man flashed an even bigger greasy smile and clasped Giddi's hand to seal the deal. He scooped coin into the leather pouch with his emblem on it and passed it to Giddi, grinning as he locked the pearls in his iron box.

At the gleam in the man's eyes, Giddi couldn't help feeling he'd been ripped off, but it didn't matter. Aquaria had provided him with the means to infiltrate the city and find out more about the Scarlet Hand and, most importantly, to track down Starrus.

Giddi extracted one of each coin and jammed the coin pouch down his undergarments, hoping it stayed firmly nestled above his thighs. Gods, imagine dropping his newfound wealth on the cobbles as he strode about the city.

As Giddi left the tiny enclave, the man restrung his tripwire, sat back in his chair, and nodded off.

Giddi bustled along the busy roads. Here the buildings were more ramshackle, and jammed together like fish in a net. The stench of human excrement hung in the air. He rounded a corner and passed an open sewage canal. He was in the poor quarter of town. He backtracked and took a side alley away from the stench, and after a while of meandering along winding streets, came to a house of ill repute. Three women fluttered their long dark eyelashes at him and called out with sultry voices, their fragrant perfume cloying in his nostrils. As he hurried past, a young woman giggled, reaching through the hole in his sleeve and ran her finger along his forearm. Even though he was barely thirteen summers, she thought he was older and mistaken him for a man—a prospective customer. Heat rose in his cheeks and his skin pricked with awareness.

He wanted to cast aside the cloak he'd used as a headdress and sprint off, but instead, he pushed his way through the streets and headed toward the sound of running water. Eventually, he came out into a cobbled area surrounding an enormous fountain lined with blue tiles that turned the water deep sapphire. Giddi pushed past the throng gathered around the fountain with large laundry pails, washing their clothes. He shoved back his headdress, plunged his hands into the water, and doused his flaming cheeks.

The terraces he'd seen from Aquaria's back rose above them up the towering cliff. Water cascaded down between each terrace in majestic waterfalls until the flow reached this enormous pool.

People were filling tubs, then washing their clothes and spreading them on the sandstone cobbles to dry. A bit pointless really—the clean clothes had orange marks on them from the sandstone. As Giddi watched a woman peel her family's dry clothes off the cobbles and shake the dirt off them, he understood. Here, it was faster to dry garments with the heat of the scorching stones than on a line in a breeze. The orange dust was a part of life. It probably got in everything, so they may as well live with it, not fight it.

Giddi dipped his hands back in the pool and gulped down the clear water. Oh, it was good after days of drinking from the waterskin—much better than the river water in Spanglewood's rivers, reminding him of a crystal-clear mountain lake. Next to the waterfall tumbling into the pool's sapphire depths, he spied some narrow steps. He had coin. If he was going to stay the night, hopefully he could afford somewhere less dangerous and provocative than the slums. Giddi mounted the steps and began to climb.

§

Vizza hadn't sent an assassin after Starrus. Instead, Vizza's soldiers had waited two days before escorting Starrus to the palace's arena.

Starrus wasn't surprised that they'd found his lodgings so easily. He also wasn't surprised at the opulent furnishings in the pristine white-tiled room he was taken to. He knew it was nothing more than a gilded cage. The lavish brocaded couches, luxurious drapes, and the enormous Robandi-style bed heaped with pillows did little to ease him.

Common criminals were tried and given a chance of a hearing if they survived the arena. But what could they possibly throw at him—an accomplished mage—that would defeat him? Vizza was up to something. Even as he had the thought, Vizza's servants closed and barred the door behind him. Unease skittered down Starrus' spine. A chill gripped him despite the scorching climate outside.

He strode to the window and looked down over the terraces and pools rippling down the hillside. There were iron bars on the other side of the glass—nothing he couldn't blast his way through or melt, but Vizza knew that. So, what did the emperor's adviser have in mind?

The setting sun cast a blaze of color over the ocean and turned the white-sailed ships in the harbor to gold. No rutting sign of the Scarlet Hand.

He had no choice but to go through with this.

Starrus steeled his nerve. He had to find out the whereabouts of the Scarlet Hand, so he'd be recognized among the mages and promoted to the council. The emperor knew something, or Vizza would not have agreed to grant Starrus an audience with him. But he had to earn that audience by providing entertainment for the unwashed masses and upper echelons of Metropoli society—while paying penance for what he'd done.

At least he no longer had to worry about Giddi finding out his secrets. By now, the vultures would have picked his bones clean and they'd be nothing but a pile of bleached sticks in the desert.

HAND-FASTING

Yanir shoved his hands in his pockets and shuffled his feet, unsure what to expect. It was strange being alone in the hollow taproom of the *Dancing Dragon*. All the tables and chairs had been taken outside, awaiting the evening's festivities, making the room feel like a tomb. Gods, he was as twitchy as a dragonet. And tonight wasn't even his hand-fasting.

He gulped—not that he ever dared hope he and Anakisha would one day be hand-fasted. Sure, he loved her, but she'd only ever known him as King's Rider. And even though he'd known her while she was working in the tavern, she didn't know the other side of him—the side everybody jeered at. Sure, he'd told her he'd been a pig breeder, but she hadn't seen him being treated like pig dung. Only as the esteemed King's Rider.

Soft footsteps sounded on the stairs.

Anakisha descended. Her chestnut hair was braided and coiled upon her head. Her face glowed, making her look like an enchantress.

He gasped. By the dragon gods, she took his breath away.

She stepped off the bottom stair into the taproom and twirled, her full skirts billowing around her, showing off an elegant emerald silk dress with dark panels of velvet and ribbons threaded around the low-cut neckline.

From the moment he'd found her unconscious in the alley, she been beautiful to him, but he'd never seen her dressed like this. She smiled radiantly—and took his breath away all over again. By the First Egg, she was a stunning, rare beauty. Her eyes caressed his face. Yanir's heart faltered. Would she feel the same way about him if he was smeared in pig muck and grime?

Her dress rustled as she walked toward him. Anakisha wrapped her arms around him, leaning her head against his chest. "Your heart is pounding as fast as if you were facing the Scarlet Hand in battle. Am I that terrifying?" Her laugh tinkled in the hollow room.

Gods, his past was haunting him here, in the happiest of moments. There was only one solution. He'd have to take her back.

"After the hand-fasting celebrations are over, I have somewhere to take you."

"Somewhere special?" she asked. "Is it a surprise?"

"Special to me," he said. "But maybe not so special to you. And yes, don't ask because it's a surprise." He took her hand and led her out the door into the crowded village square.

Villagers were seated at the tables, chatting, and more were standing, lining the square. Some errant lads were perched upon the rooftops. Musicians were clustered on a small stage. Fox was making the most of being a dragon rider, gesturing to a group of littlings who stared at him wide-eyed as he flapped his arms like dragon wings.

Near the head table, Anakisha's father was mopping his brow. By the dragon gods, the man had even shaved his beard.

"Hail the King's Rider! Hail the Queen's Rider!" Fox called.

On the far side of the square near an immense pile of wood, Syan uncurled himself and stood. Zaarusha joined him, and the two dragons lifted their heads skyward and roared. Spurts of flame ghosted from their maws and then died.

The royal dragons observed them as Yanir and Anakisha walked through the rows of tables, waving and smiling at the cheering guests.

"*This is better than a dream come true.*" Anakisha squeezed Yanir's hand. "*My old dream was nothing compared to this reality.*" She stretched up and kissed his cheek.

Yanir's face warmed to the roots of his hair as they stood beside Anakisha's father.

§

Stella clapped her hands and jumped with joy as Anakisha and Yanir stepped from the tavern and the dragons roared. Since Ma and Jacob had died, she'd hoped something special would make her family happy again.

For moons, Anakisha had sneaked out at night, fighting the Howlers, thinking Stella didn't realize what was going on. But Stella had known her sister was angry about her brother's murder and distraught that Ma had died. Stella blamed herself because Ma had caught *pilzkrank* from her mushrooms. But tonight, Anakisha was dressed like a queen, and the handsome Yanir in his fine breeches and fancy tunic had his eyes full of love.

Stella's chest was so full, she felt like she'd burst out of her skin and soar like a dragon above the square. She stepped up beside Pa, who was in front of the head table, and squeezed his hand.

Pa leaned down. "Yes, blossom, what is it?"

Stella went up on tiptoes and kissed his smooth cheek—he'd shaved for the ceremony today. It was the first time he'd been rid of his beard since Ma died, and it was good to see him without it again. "Do you think Mayfree will recognize you without your whiskers?"

"I certainly hope so." His eyes were bright with anticipation.

Stella let go of Pa's hand as Anakisha and Yanir joined them and greeted Pa.

A gasp rippled through the crowd and the chatter stopped. The gentle tones of a flute drifted through the square, floating over the waiting guests.

Stella spun.

In the mouth of a narrow street leading to the square, Mayfree appeared on the arm of the new village arbitrator—Fox's uncle Pieter. Mayfree's dress was a stunning dark-blue velvet, trimmed with pretty silver ribbons which fluttered in the breeze as she walked. Her dark glossy hair was undone from its usual bun and fell down to her waist. A garland of flowers sat upon her head and she held a matching bouquet in her hands. Stella suspected that Mayfree's two best friends, who were walking behind her with similar bouquets in their hands, had picked the fresh flowers and made the garland and bouquets that morning.

Mayfree and her party walked past the enormous pile of firewood that would be set alight when it was dark. Her shining eyes fastened upon Pa, full of love, as she approached.

Stella's heart nearly cracked in two as Mayfree took her father's hand and they turned to face the arbitrator together.

Yanir and Anakisha flanked Stella and grinned over her head at each other.

Of the four of them, Stella couldn't say whose eyes were shining more. Both Anakisha and Pa were in love. Their broken hearts had been mended. She swallowed the lump in her throat and smiled. The sight was enough to mend her grieving heart a little too, and maybe, in time, it would heal completely.

§

The arbitrator blew a ceremonial horn and the crowd quieted. "Reb, tavern master of the *Dancing Dragon,* has requested the hand of Widow Mayfree. Are there any objections to this hand-fasting?"

No one objected.

"Then we shall proceed with the ceremony," Fox's Uncle Pieter announced.

Anakisha grinned as the crowd roared their assent. Yanir's fingers brushed hers gently, although his eyes were upon the couple.

When the villagers' boisterous cheers had died into expectant silence, Pa stepped forward, gazing at Mayfree, his eyes bright with tears of joy. "I pledge to love and cherish you to the end of my days and beyond. I will lay down my life for you if necessary."

"Thank you," Mayfree whispered. Her voice rose. "And I pledge to love and cherish you to the end of my days and beyond. I will lay down my life for you if necessary. I also pledge to be fair and loving to your children."

A lump rose in Anakisha's throat as Mayfree smiled at her and Stella, then Mayfree rose on tiptoes and brushed her lips against Pa's.

Yanir's hand tightened on Anakisha's. She gazed up at him, but instead of him looking joyous, he was pale and gnawing his lower lip.

"Are you feeling well?"

"Of course," he mind-melded, flashing her a smile.

DANCING

Anakisha gave a contented sigh, her stomach pleasantly full. "That was delicious."

"It was indeed." Yanir had kept his gaze averted from the suckling pig over the embers in the corner of the square and refrained from eating any. He'd shot Anakisha a grateful glance as she, too, had chosen food other than pork. "The dessert was so tasty," he said. "I've never had such delectable pastries. Fox's uncle certainly knows his craft."

"And he's a great arbitrator. Much nicer than the last."

"That wouldn't be hard." Yanir grinned, sharing his memory of Justan's father in the stocks yelling insults.

She grinned. Mind-melding would never get old.

The arbitrator stood and rang a bell for silence. "And now the dancing shall begin." He waved a hand at the musicians waiting on a makeshift stage near the bonfire pile.

Zaarusha and Syan rose from their haunches and shot gusts of flame at the wood. It ignited, flames licking along the branches. The drummer tapped his drums, the beats soft and tentative, symbolic of a couple getting to know one another. Pa and Mayfree stepped toward each other on tiptoes in a complex series of steps. A flute joined in, the trilling notes an exciting counterpart to the ever-more-confident drumbeats. Pa took Mayfree by the waist, his other hand resting on her shoulder, and they began to dance, her face alight.

A gittern joined in, plucking an intricate melody that wove around the flute and drumbeats. The beat sped up, the music swelled. Pa swept Mayfree into his arms and whirled his new lover around the square, her dress swirling around her ankles and her hair flying out behind her.

Yanir tapped his fingers on the table in rhythm to the drumbeats. Anakisha's heart bounded. She wanted to skip in time to the music. Finally, at the height of the crescendo, Pa dipped Mayfree backward, supporting her with his strong hands. Then he kissed her.

Gasps rippled through the crowd. Applause broke out.

Amid whistles and clapping, the arbitrator yelled over the music, "Now, the King and Queen's Riders shall dance."

"Oh gods, I wasn't expecting that," Anakisha blurted via mind-meld to Yanir as he—and all the hand-fasting guests seated at the tables around them—turned to her.

"There's no getting out of it now." Yanir stood, bowed elegantly, and took her hand. He led her out from behind the table to the dance area. His gray eyes already dancing, he placed a warm hand at her waist and another on her shoulder. "You're beautiful," he whispered and swept her off her feet before she could even think.

The music got faster and faster. Pa and Mayfree twirled past them. Yanir expertly kept pace with the frenetic music. Soon, Anakisha was whirling in a blur of firelight, colors and snatches of sound. Her dress swirled as Yanir whisked her across the cobbles, making her feel as light as gossamer on a summer's breeze.

He grinned, his hair awry as he spun her in his arms.

"Gods, Yanir, this is almost as good as flying."

"Better," he replied. *"Because I'm holding you."*

The hand-fasting guests joined in, clapping to the beat. People stomped and whistled. The arbitrator hollered, "Everybody, please dance and celebrate the union of this sweet couple." Mayfree blushed bright pink as Pa kissed her again.

Although the arbitrator had flourished a hand at her father and his new lover, Yanir's face was redder than Pa's new wife's.

"Yanir, what is it?"

"I must admit, I was thinking of doing exactly the same to you, but not now, not in front of all these people." The blush faded from his cheeks as he took her hand and led Anakisha to a table laden with drinks. He passed her a cup and they drank, the cheery music wrapping around them.

And as Yanir took Anakisha into his arms and swept her onto the cobbles again, she felt her heart would burst.

"I hope it doesn't," commented Zaarusha wryly. *"I'd hate to lose a rider so soon after getting one."*

Anakisha chuckled.

"Yanir would be terribly sad if your heart burst right here on the cobbles," Syan said. *"We were hoping to welcome you to Dragons' Hold soon."*

"Indeed," said Yanir brushing a strand of Anakisha's hair back from her face.

They danced the whole night long, but no matter how often his gaze caressed her lips, he never kissed her.

§

Fox carried a pot of stew outside into the square, making his way between the feasting hand-fasting guests to the table groaning under its heavy burden of fine food. Uncle Pieter rose from his seat and came over to help him ease the pot onto the trestle table.

"Put any more on this table, and I'm sure the boards would break," his uncle said. "You've been working yourself to the bone tonight, helping in the kitchen. Take a break. Find a pretty girl to dance with."

Fox shrugged. "I don't really feel like dancing tonight," he said. "There's still lots of work to do in the kitchen." His eyes slid to his sister Brianna who was dancing with Justan.

Her red hair flew as Justan twirled her around. Brianna tipped back her head and laughed, batting her eyelashes.

Uncle Pieter nodded. "We haven't been able to pin that rat, Justan, down yet. But don't worry, Brianna's pretty feisty. She can take care of herself. I'll keep an eye on her while you're gone at Dragons' Hold."

Fox nodded, failing to shrug off the tension in his shoulders, and made his way back through the crowd past the dancing, feasting people. He entered the *Dancing Dragon*. With all the tables outside, the taproom was bare. As he made his way back into the kitchen, Billy sauntered out with a tureen of sweet potato and lemongrass soup.

"You all right?" Billy asked. "Is it your sister?"

Fox nodded. Dragon's claws, it was as if Billy had read his mind.

Billy shook his head. "Justan can't be trusted. Brianna knows that, but she likes playing with fire." He looked downright unhappy. "One of these days, I might bop Justan on the nose."

"I'd love to shake some sense into Brianna," Fox admitted.

Billy shook his head. "As if that would change anything. That's one of the best things about her—when she makes up her mind, she won't be budged." Billy's cheeks flamed.

Fox stared at the red spots on Billy's cheeks.

Billy ducked his head shyly, and rushed out the door into the square, his cheeks flaming.

Gods, Fox'd known Billy had a crush on his sister years ago. They'd even kissed, according to Brianna, but he hadn't realized Billy still liked her—or how much. He bit his lip, watching Billy go, then strode into the kitchen to face the Howlers.

Purley was slaving over the hearth, stirring a cauldron of stew. Adora had her hands in a tub of water, washing plates and stacking them on the bench. Snitch was ladling pudding into tiny bowls and Spike was sawing at the bread as if it were a tree trunk, not a loaf. Fox smothered a chuckle. Spike made a better gardener than cook.

Eileen Mueller

Billy stomped into the kitchen, scowling.

"Something wrong?" Fox asked quietly.

Billy snorted. "Your sister's gone off with that slimy toad. Gimme that." He snatched the knife off Spike and hacked into the bread, crumbs flying.

"Impressive." Spike grinned, showing his vicious teeth. "Want me to take a chunk out of Justan?" He gnashed his teeth together. "Or perhaps Brianna."

Billy ignored him, throwing thick slabs of bread into a basket.

Snitch chuckled. "Come on, Spike. No gossiping. While I'm in charge of this kitchen, you have to work." He passed Spike a ladle. Spike groaned, took the ladle and doled pudding out into bowls alongside Snitch. Occasionally, he gnashed his teeth—and Billy twitched every time.

Purley turned on Spike. "No one needs you to bite them."

"Least of all my sister," Fox added. "Although I must admit your offer to gnaw on Justan is pretty tempting."

"Don't you ever touch his sister," Billy snapped, his massive upper arms flexing as he hacked the bread. He glowered at Spike, who whistled as he ladled out more pudding.

The kitchen door slammed and Brianna stormed in, her green eyes fiery and her red hair flouncing on her shoulders. "That Justan is a heap of shrotty, flaming dragon dung."

Adora plunged a pot into the soapy water. "Why are you so mad? Is he a bad kisser?"

A hand on her hip, Brianna snorted. "Of course, he kisses well. But that's the problem: he kisses too many women well."

Spike sniggered. "So, who else was he kissing tonight? Was there a long line of them?"

At least it wasn't Anakisha anymore. Justan had kissed Anakisha at the tournament. Fox had seen them going into the trees, but luckily Anakisha had quickly seen sense. Hopefully his sister would do the same.

"I knew he was betrothed to Bertha," Brianna continued, "but he told me he didn't like her. I didn't think he was kissing her already. I figured I could mess around with him until he was officially hand-fasted."

Spike chortled. "He's probably kissing more than just the two of you."

Brianna held up her fist triumphantly. Her knuckles were bruised and bloody. "Not tonight. And he won't be kissing anyone else for a week." She grinned. "Not with a split lip and the bloody teeth I gave him."

"'Atta girl." Billy slung an arm over Brianna's shoulders. "I knew you'd come through." He ducked his head shyly and kissed her cheek.

Brianna beamed and slipped her arm around Billy's waist, her eyes dancing mischievously. "I didn't know you still cared."

"'Course I do," said Billy. "I was just waiting for the scales to fall from your little dragon eyes." He grinned, looking as happy as a bear with a honey pot.

Brianna leaned into Billy and wrapped her other arm around his waist. "I'm glad you didn't give up on me," she said.

The Howlers cheered. Purley banged a spoon on a pot lid. Spike stuck his fingers in his mouth and gave a shrill whistle. Snitch clapped, and Adora cackled her head off.

Suddenly Fox knew that although he was going to Dragons' Hold to train as a dragon rider, his sister would be all right. His uncle, the Howlers, and his old friends from the Night Wings would look after her.

Brianna let go of Billy and poked her tongue out at Fox. "No need for you to play the protective bigger brother anymore. And remember, I'm older than you."

Fox grinned and hugged her. "I'm going to miss you, Bree."

"We won't miss you," she said, swiping a tear from her cheek. "You're far too bossy." She slugged him on the arm, and they all laughed again.

"Goat stew's ready," Purley announced.

Fox scratched the back of his neck. "Could you two give me a hand, Billy?" He gestured at the enormous cauldron.

"Sure." Billy took one cloth-wrapped handle and Fox took the other. Brianna picked up the basket of bread and followed them through the deserted taproom out to the square. As they made their way through the tables, there was a shriek.

Bertha, clad in a peacock-blue dress, stood. "You're nothing but a lowly cad," she screamed at Justan.

All the chatter and hubbub died down. Everyone swiveled to stare.

Bertha up-ended a wooden tankard of foamy beer over Justan's head and stalked off, leaving the caramel-eyed son of the imprisoned ex-arbitrator with beer drenching his golden hair, shoulders and chest. Justan glowered and raced after Bertha amid taunts and jeers, leaving a sopping trail in his wake.

Brianna hooted, Billy sniggered, and Fox laughed. It was nice to see the tables turned on that shrotty louse who'd once been the leader of the Night Wings.

§

Anakisha picked up the last chair in the square and carried it back into the taproom. Pa and Mayfree were long gone. They'd slipped off in the midst of the revelry to Mayfree's cottage for a few days. The Night Wings—apart from Justan, who nobody wanted to see again—and the Howlers had helped her and Yanir move all the furniture back into the tavern. They'd finished the last of the dishes, and the kitchen was in pristine order, ready for the tavern to start functioning when Pa returned in a few days.

"There you go. It's all looking good," Yanir said.

When everyone had said their goodbyes and headed out the back door, Yanir led her outside and held her hand, facing her by the glowing embers of the dying bonfire. "Thank you for a lovely evening," he said. She stepped closer, placing a hand on his chest. He bent his head.

Anakisha closed her eyes.

His breath whispered across her face, and his lips brushed her cheek. "I'll see you tomorrow," he whispered, and walked off into the night to meet Syan.

Disappointment lanced through Anakisha.

Once again, he'd had the opportunity to kiss her properly, but hadn't. What had changed? What was wrong? She wracked her mind, but couldn't think of anything she'd done.

Anakisha slipped inside, went upstairs and took off her dress.

"Anakisha." Stella sat bolt upright in bed.

"Are you still awake?"

"Oh, Anakisha, I'm so happy," Stella said.

"I am too." She sighed. "Well, I'm sad I'm leaving you. I didn't mean things to turn out that way."

Stella shrugged. "It's not every day my sister gets to become Queen's Rider, so I'll forgive you." She grinned. "Although, officially, you still owe me a ride on Zaarusha."

"I do." Anakisha hung up her fine dress and pulled her riders' garb out of the closet. She had to do something to shake off the feeling that things weren't right between her and Yanir. Besides, she wanted Stella to be happy. "How about now?"

Stella squealed and jumped out of bed. She raced over to the closet and pulled out some breeches and a shirt.

"You need something warm as well," Anakisha reminded her.

"I know." Stella grabbed a knitted hat and tucked her blonde braids up into it, then pulled a thick leather jerkin from the closet. "Mayfree made me this in case you ever took me for a ride."

Tears welled in Anakisha's eyes. "That was kind of her," she said, swallowing the lump in her throat. It was just the sort of thing Ma would have done.

Stella's eyes shone with tears too. "I'll never forget Ma, either, Anakisha, but I'm so glad we have Mayfree, especially now that you're leaving." She bowled into Anakisha, nearly knocking her over.

Anakisha flung her arms around her sister and kissed her little hat. "I'll always love you, Stella. No matter what happens, I'll never forget you. I'll come back and see you often."

"And take me for more rides on Zaarusha?"

Anakisha nodded fiercely. "And take you for more rides on Zaarusha."

When they headed outside, Zaarusha was waiting. *"I've been looking forward to taking Stella into the skies,"* the dragon queen said in Anakisha's mind. Zaarusha snuffled Stella's palm, huffing warm air over her.

Stella squealed again, a grin breaking over her wee face.

"Anakisha, help your sister into the saddle."

Anakisha hoisted her littling sister into the saddle on Zaarusha's back. "Let's fasten the straps tight," she said. "I don't want to lose you on your first flight."

"Neither do I," rumbled Zaarusha as Anakisha slipped onto the saddle behind Stella and wrapped her arms around her sister's waist.

Stella leaned back against Anakisha's chest.

"You might feel your stomach drop as we're airborne, but that's normal."

Zaarusha tensed her haunches, springing above the dying embers of the bonfire, up over the village square and into the starry night.

Stella squeaked and grasped Anakisha's forearms. "Look down at the lanterns, Anakisha. They're like tiny twinkling stars from up here. This is wonderful. I feel so… so…"

Anakisha grinned. "I know. It's great, isn't it?"

They winged on into the night, over dark fields and rushing rivers, wind gusting into their faces. They reached a forest, the rustling leaves like a sea undulating in the moonlight. Anakisha cradled her sister in her arms, wishing this flight would never end.

When Zaarusha landed in the village square, Billy was standing by the bonfire staring into the embers, Brianna at his side.

"You two are still up?" Anakisha slid to the ground and helped Stella out of the saddle.

"We were waiting to talk to you," Billy said. "Anakisha, we'll look after Stella while you're gone. She has a new brother." Billy thumped his fist on his breast.

Brianna held her fist to her chest too. "And a new sister."

"Thank you." Stella hugged them both, then turned and patted Zaarusha's flank. "And thank you, Zaarusha." She yawned and went into the tavern. Moments later, the candle in the window above the tavern's main door extinguished.

Billy shuffled on his feet and ducked his head. "You wanted to talk to Anakisha, didn't you, Brianna?"

Brianna nodded and bit her lip, staring pensively into the embers, the glow glinting off her red hair.

This was awkward. They'd both cared about Justan, both been used by him, and Brianna had fought her tooth and nail when Justan was trying to kill her.

Anakisha met Brianna's gaze, waiting.

A moon ago, she would've been ready to fight Brianna, even moons after what happened. Now, with a new future at Dragons' Hold, that part of her life no longer seemed relevant.

Brianna cleared her throat.

Billy nudged her and grinned. "Go on," he said. "If I can forgive you for kissing that slimy toad, so can Anakisha." He strode off to stand on the other side of the fire, giving them space.

Brianna tossed her hair over her shoulder, suddenly looking vulnerable and years younger. "I'm sorry. I shouldn't have fought you that night in the warehouse. Justan lied to me and I fell for his lies. I shouldn't have attacked you, taunted you or been mean to you. I knew you were Fox's good friend. Justan was the one that deserved a knife between the ribs, not you."

"He was very convincing. I fell for him too." Anakisha nodded. "But I've forgiven myself and so has Yanir, so I can forgive you too."

A moment later Anakisha was enveloped in Brianna's arms.

"Thank you," Brianna mumbled. "Take care of Fox for me. He's stubborn. Worse than me." She sauntered around the embers and took Billy's hand. "Go on, Billy, your turn."

Billy took a deep breath. "I'm going to bear witness against Justan for killing your brother, Jacob. Fox's uncle will put him on trial." He stared into the embers. "I'm sorry I've waited so long. I was afraid he'd burn my Ma and sister in their sleep like he threatened."

"But he can't if he's behind bars," said Brianna. "And I'll bear witness that he tried to kill you too. Me and Billy will support each other."

"We mean what we said," said Billy. "We'll help take care of Stella."

"Thank you."

Nodding goodnight to Anakisha, they wandered out of the square and were swallowed by the night.

Anakisha sighed. Although she wouldn't be here for Stella, it seemed like half the village would be.

Dark wings blotted out the stars above, and a breeze ruffled her hair. Syan and Yanir landed, the King's talons clattering on the cobbles. *"Anakisha, it's going to be all right."* Yanir's voice was gentle.

"I know," she said, *"but I'm still going to miss my sister and Pa."* She clambered up in front of Yanir. He wrapped his arms around her and they flew into the night. Although things would be fine in Fieldhaven, she had no idea what awaited her at Dragons' Hold.

Marketplace Mayhem

Giddi tossed and turned all night, dreaming about Starrus, the Scarlet Hand, Master Mage Findal, and his underwater adventures with Queen Aquaria. In his dream, the oysters opened their bearded mouths, but as he touched the pearls, the oysters devoured his fingers, leaving his hands in a bloody pulp. He destroyed them in a blaze of mage flame, only to see his father dying in the flickering fire.

Hair slicked with sweat and heart still pounding, Giddi woke, made his way downstairs and left the boarding house. Gods, he missed Pa. He felt like he'd lost him all over again. Was it a sign? What if his father really was dead?

When Pa had first gone missing, he'd asked Ma, but she'd refused to acknowledge the possibility of his father's death. Her words came back to him.

"What if Pa is dead, Ma?" he asked. "What then?"

"He's a powerful mage, son." Ma hugged him, stroking Giddi's hair. "Your pa is busy with the realm's secret business, protecting people and fighting evil. He'll be home when he's done."

Giddi sobbed. "I don't want to him to protect everyone else. Starrus came back. Why can't Pa? I want him here with us."

Just remembering Ma and Pa was enough to turn his limbs into a trembling mess.

He ran a hand through his hair and fastened his cloak around his head as a makeshift headdress. It was still early. Hardly anyone was about. Perhaps a drink of that haakin stuff Aquaria had mentioned would help steady his nerves. Giddi made his way along the sandstone house-lined terrace, back down the long flights of stairs by the waterfall to the markets. Perhaps he should also buy a headdress and some local clothing so he didn't stand out so much. Being a young foreigner alone in a huge city was sure to make him an easy target for hustlers and thieves.

The marketplace was humming. Giddi strode past the fountain into the market and was swept up in the crowd. People were haggling and toting their wares in shrill voices, the Robandi accents like waves cresting and breaking over him. He didn't understand a thing, but being among a crowd of people helped shatter the shock of his dream. There were armed soldiers dressed in military robes and headdresses with swords at their hips stationed throughout the marketplace as shoppers went about their morning business. Giddi discretely observed people haggling for food, watching what coin they used. Despite being the largest, the camel was worth the least, and the scorpion worth the most.

Giddi pulled out a camel and passed it to a young boy selling fresh buns sprinkled with hazelnut pieces and topped with sweet glaze, and cups of haakin poured from a long-spouted tall silver pot. The boy pocketed the coin and passed him two sticky buns and a cup of the steaming black beverage. Balancing the buns on one palm and holding the cup in the other, Giddi made his way toward some benches at the edge of the square, beyond the throng near a barren garden of cacti. A bitter aroma wafted from the hot cup, but it was the scent of the buns that made his mouth water.

Giddi sat on the end of the bench, near two elderly gentlemen with wrinkles that reminded him of the patterns left by the winds on the Robandi sands. A crowd of littlings played with stones in the sand at the men's feet near baskets of yellow tubers. A soldier was stationed at the edge of the garden, his eyes constantly roving over the littlings, the men and the crowd. As Giddi bit into his bun, a woman collected a basket, balancing it on her head, and took two of the littlings by the hand. Smiling her thanks at the elderly gentlemen, she made her way up the broad road that led to the terraces higher up the hillside.

Giddi sipped the haakin. Gods, the stuff was bitter. He was tempted to spit it out, but didn't dare, in case he breached some local taboo. He swallowed the vile scalding stuff and set his cup on a stone. Perhaps he could accidentally tip it over before he returned the cup. He wouldn't bother wasting his coin on another. The bun was good, the crunchy nuts and sweet topping hitting Giddi's tongue in exactly the right spot. He sighed, feeling the warmth of the early morning sun on his face.

He had yet to find Starrus, but somehow, he'd manage. If not, as long as he wasn't mugged, his pearls should get him a passage back to Naobia.

A waif-thin young girl with huge brown eyes carried her littling brother on her hip over to the elderly men. The wee boy, only about three summers old, cried and clung to his sister, but she patted his back and handed him to one of the men, who took a firm grip on him, crooning in Robandi. The girl, who must've been only about six summers, stole off to the market with more than one backward glance at her littling brother.

He wouldn't stop crying, his arms outstretched toward his sister and the outline of his bony ribs poking through his ragged shirt. The man sat the boy on the seat between him and Giddi, still crooning gently. The boy's eyes lit upon Giddi's bun. He stopped crying, his large eyes fixated on the bun as Giddi took a bite. The lad's cheeks were sunken, his bones sharp through his skin. The lad wet his lips with his tongue.

Giddi broke off the bitten end and gave the rest of his bun to the boy. The lad grabbed it and ripped off a bit, then ravenously stuffed the rest into his mouth, chattering in Robandi.

With a final glance back at her brother and Giddi, and the flash of a smile, the thin girl sidled over to a bread stall. Giddi waved his second bun at her, but she wasn't watching. The poor thing looked hungrier than her brother. They were obviously poor—her dress was ragged and the trail of bruises on her arms didn't bode well.

Giddi stood, about to follow her and offer her the bun, when she snatched a loaf of bread off the stall, shoved it down the front of her dress and dashed into the crowd. The stall owner yelled and gesticulated at the fleeing girl. A soldier whipped about and rushed into the throng, giving chase. People parted like wheat in a storm, opening a path for the soldier. Although the girl was fast, he caught her in moments.

The elderly man next to Giddi gasped and clutched the boy in his lap, burying the lad's face against his chest, uttering what Giddi guessed was the longest oath he'd ever heard.

Moments later, the soldier dragged the girl back through the crowd. Her face was pale and her legs were shaking. She kept her eyes downcast, not meeting the elderly men's gazes. One of the old men held her brother close, obscuring his view of his sister while the other walked over to the solider.

After a heated discussion with lots of wild gesticulation, the elderly gentleman's shoulders slumped and he dragged his feet back over to the bench. He sat down, shaking his head. When he spoke to his companion, his voice cracked and tears sprang from his eyes, running in rivulets down the wrinkled channels in his face.

The solider bound the girl's hands and marched her at sword-point up the broad road leading to the terraces. The boy in the man's arms swiveled, caught a glimpse of his sister and howled, his wails drowning out the hubbub of the marketplace as she disappeared around the corner.

Giddi suddenly lost all desire to eat. He passed his second bun to the littling, who promptly stuffed it in his mouth—silencing his own wails. "What will happen to her?" Giddi couldn't help himself—he had to know.

"You're a Northerner?" The man cradling the boy asked, his shrewd eyes peering at Giddi. "Then you wouldn't know. She'll be tried before the emperor."

The other man nodded. "She has no chance, so now it will fall to us to care for this littling. His father died in the mines last week."

"Are you part of his family?" Giddi gestured at the boy, who was chewing the bread, his long-lashed eyes regarding Giddi solemnly.

"We look after littlings while their families are at the market. This boy's mother is ailing and his sister was trying to find bread for the family." He shook his head sadly. "If only I'd known she had no coin…"

The weight of his coin pouch suddenly dragged against Giddi's thigh, where he'd suspended it on string on the inside of his belt that morning. He still had four pearls and a pile of coin. He could've easily given the girl and her family a scorpion.

He raced after her to plead with the guard, feet pounding the cobbles. As Giddi rounded the corner, the street was blocked by a troop of soldiers marching downhill.

"Where are they taking the girl?" Giddi asked a huge soldier with a bristly beard and a chest as broad as a shield.

"None of your business, Northerner," the soldier said, jabbing his spear at Giddi. "Back to the market."

More soldiers flanked the one who'd spoken, forming an impenetrable barrier across the road. Behind them, the girl disappeared, she and her guard swallowed by another bend in the road. Giddi sighed. There was no point in fighting these guards. That wouldn't help him find Starrus or Master Mage Findal.

"March," the soldier bellowed.

The soldiers flanking him marched, forcing Giddi back around the corner down the road. He retreated to the garden as soldiers nailed pieces of parchment to wooden posts, stalls and the fronts of buildings. More soldiers strode through the marketplace hollering and waving their arms toward the road uphill. Murmurs built in the crowd, and ignited like wildfire. People flocked past the garden and raced to the road, chattering excitedly and waving at friends and family to join them.

Parents dashed over and snatched up their littlings from the elderly men, then joined the crowd.

"What is it?" Giddi yelled to be heard above clattering boots and boisterous voices.

"The emperor's entertainment. A northerner is fighting in the arena," the elderly gentleman holding the boy said, shaking his head.

"Who is it?"

The men shrugged. "The guards only said he's a traitor and deserves to die."

Not Starrus then, but with so many people heading to one place, maybe someone had seen him.

The men grimaced and shot looks at each other. "We won't be going. We're too old to hike up the hill."

With a nod, Giddi pushed his way back against the tide of humanity to the parchment fluttering on the post. There was a picture of a circular arena and some indecipherable Robandi script. That much he'd known already. The artist had painted a camel coin in the bottom corner. So, there was an entry charge for this entertainment.

Giddi was swept up in the throng, pressed between a sweaty corpulent man that stank of garlic and a bony youth his own age. He pushed ahead through the crowd, jabbed in the gut by elbows, the sharp edge of a chicken cage and basket handles. On the first terrace, near Giddi's lodgings, a soldier in a crisp military uniform stood on a wall, calling instructions out above the crowd and waving them upward.

The second terrace was thronging with foot traffic, everyone making their way up toward the gleaming white dome of the emperor's palace. Giddi pressed on, his long legs climbing up the switchbacks until he was amid the crowd on the terrace below the palace.

An enormous plateau had been carved into the sandstone hillside. The arena was ringed by a wall. The entrances were choked with people. Soldiers waved citizens around to entrances on the other side of the arena, and Giddi followed, asking people if they'd seen a man with straw-blond hair. Some muttered and gesticulated at him in Robandi, others shook their heads and rushed into the crush of people, eager to get a good seat.

Maybe he'd have better luck finding someone who spoke his tongue when he was inside.

Giddi dropped his camel into a pail held by a beefy soldier, and was swept through the dim low-ceilinged entrance corridor by the pressing crowd behind him. Tiers of seats rose above him, towering above an oval arena, and running around three-quarters of it. Soldiers were stationed at the end of every row, overseeing people as they slid into seats, their hawk-eyed gazes roving over every person.

A thin soldier curled his lip as he waved Giddi into a seat in the second row, next to a family.

To his surprise, the littling girl next to him asked the man next to her, "Who will be playing today, Uncle?"

The rotund man, who was in the middle of conversing with his wife in Robandi, turned and replied in Giddi's tongue, but heavily accented. "Isobella, my fair one, today they're not playing. They're punishing a terrible criminal who committed a crime against Metropoli."

"What sort of crime, uncle?" Blonde curls peeked from the edge of the girl's headdress and although her skin was dark, her eyes were a startling blue. She was a northerner, too.

"A terrible crime, my love." He waved an airy hand. "Many do not survive the arena, but do not be alarmed. It's an honor to fight and die in the arena."

The arena was paved, but covered in a fine layer of tangerine sand, except where the sandstone cobbles peeked through around the edges. Huge double wooden doors were barred shut at the west end, closest to the harbor. At the east end of the open space, there were barred cages, but it was too dark inside to see what beasts the cages held.

The area above the cages was free of seats. The naked cliff rose above the arena and a gleaming white marble balcony jutted out over the top. Soldiers flanked a man seated upon a raised throne—the emperor. Dressed in a white silk robe, his gold buttons glinted in the sun, and diamonds set in gold rings flashed on his fingers. Behind him, a row of army officers—probably the emperor's generals—stood stiff-backed, gazing impassively over the arena.

A powerfully-built man in a black silk tunic with gold buttons was at the edge of the dais. The emperor lifted a hand from the arm of his carved throne and inclined a finger. The man clad in black silk moved with the grace of a panther to stand behind the emperor's right shoulder. He nodded as the emperor spoke, his glittering gaze sweeping the arena.

If gazes could kill, there'd be a sea of dead before this man in moments. Giddi made a mental note to never cross that man—or the leader he served. Giddi shuddered and turned away. From this high, he had a fine view of the harbor. He scanned the docks. There were no red sails in sight—so the Scarlet Hand wasn't in port, his ship was running white sails, or he'd already been caught.

Giddi leaned over the littling and spoke to her uncle. "Excuse me, I'm a visitor to Metropoli. Do you mind explaining how the arena works?"

The man spun. "So, you're a northerner, too, like my niece?" He flashed a dimpled smile. "I can certainly explain. Sometimes Emperor Haakin has games here. Sometimes they bring criminals here to be tried and pitted against foes."

"Do you mean criminals such as the notorious pirate, the Scarlet Hand?" Giddi asked.

The man's brows shot so high they disappeared into his headdress. "Has the Scarlet Hand been captured?" He tilted his head and ran his fingers through his goatee. "I heard that the one chosen to fight today is of great repute, but the emperor's soldiers have not divulged who it is—only that it's a Northerner."

"What's great repute?" the littling asked, turning her startling blue eyes upon Giddi.

Before Giddi could think up a suitable answer, her uncle tucked an arm around her shoulders and said, "That means everybody has heard of them doing evil deeds." He looked at Giddi. "The Scarlet Hand? It could be him," he said doubtfully.

"He's been terrorizing the Naobian Sea further north," Giddi offered.

The man gazed around furtively and then leaned over the littling's head to whisper, "His ship was sighted in the harbor. Rumors say he recently had an audience with the emperor. The next morning the *Fiery Dragon* was gone, and her blood red sails graced our harbor no more." The man's eyes narrowed. "Why are you so interested in the Scarlet Hand?"

"Oh!" said Giddi. "Um, he has something that belongs to me." Master Mage Findal actually belonged to Naobia, not him, but the man didn't need to know that.

"Then I guess you'd best kiss that something goodbye. You'll never recover anything that he's stolen," the man whispered. He shot Giddi a shrewd look. "Something or someone? Did he steal your girl? Or was it a relative? They say he's now trading in slaves."

Giddi rocked back in his seat. Slaves! By the First Egg.

A trumpet blasted. Soldiers bristled, their backs straightening and the crowd was instantly silent.

§

EILEEN MUELLER

A trumpet blasted, and the crowd roared. Vibrations ran through the ceiling of Starrus' opulent dwelling. As opulent as it may be, and although he'd been treated like royalty and served the best food, the moment the doors had shut, he'd become Vizza's prisoner.

Four soldiers arrived to guide Starrus through a corridor to a small holding chamber. They arrayed themselves around him, spears bristling. He didn't know why they bothered. He could blast their spears to ash within moments. Fingers twitching, he restrained himself.

Above them, a trumpet rang again, and the same vibration pounded through the ceiling.

Starrus grimaced. Whatever it was, if it kept up, he'd soon have a headache. "What's that pounding?" he asked, refusing to be intimidated by the guards' haughty stares and blank faces.

His question fell upon seemingly-deaf ears.

Beyond the guards, enormous wooden doors were sealed shut, barred on the inside by two logs thicker than Starrus' body—as if there were a threat outside, waiting to burst through those thick doors and into this finely-tiled holding room.

Starrus turned to the youngest soldier. "Soldier, I asked what that noise was."

The young soldier gave a grim smile. "That would be the crowd, sir. It's their feet pounding the ground."

The crowd—the audience to today's debacle. Starrus flicked lint off his sleeves. The sooner he could get this over with, the sooner he'd be taken to the emperor. He could handle whatever they threw at him.

His eyes flitted to the barred door. "And that? Why are the doors barred?"

A sly smile slid across the impassive face of the eldest guard, malice glinting in his eyes. "These doors are barred to prevent you from coming back in when you flee in terror."

A horn rang out. Muscles bulging, two guards lifted the top log down while the others stepped closer to Starrus, their spear points almost touching his garb.

Starrus gazed down his nose at the vermin. "Don't damage my cloak, gentlemen, or you'll be paying for a new one."

The guards removed the second log, staggering as they placed it in iron brackets on the wall above the first one.

Whatever they were keeping must weigh as much as a dragon. Perhaps it was a dragon. He knew how to deal with those. Starrus smiled. Forewarned was forearmed. "What's—"

"No more questions, sir," an old guard smirked. "It's your turn in the arena."

The younger guards pushed against the doors. They thudded open with a hollow boom that echoed through the chamber. Starrus squinted against the bright light that flooded over him.

A wooden cage was wheeled inside. The guards jabbed Starrus with their flimsy spears—made of shafts he could burn and tips he could melt in an instant. Very well, if the emperor wanted to play with him, he'd let him. Starrus stalked into the cage and held his head high as the guards slammed the cage door and fastened it with chains and locks. A team of slaves in nothing but loincloths tugged the cage out into the center of the arena, their bronzed bodies gleaming with sweat.

As the slaves ran from the arena, escaping down a narrow tunnel, Starrus faced an audience who were watching with bated breath.

Very well, let the show begin.

§

The double wooden doors at the western end of the arena boomed open. A team of nearly-naked slaves heaved a wheeled wooden cage outside. Gasps and muted whispers of "Northerner," rippled through the audience.

EILEEN MUELLER

Giddi lurched in his seat. By the dragon gods and the holy First Egg! Starrus was standing proudly in the wooden cage at the center of the arena, his straw-blond hair gleaming in the sun and his rich midnight-blue cloak wrapped around him.

Giddi's hands clenched the wooden slats on his seat as the slaves disappeared into a narrow tunnel, the door clicking shut behind them. Another trumpet blew and the crowd expectantly turned to the balcony, murmuring.

A wooden ramp slid out from the marble wall and the emperor's right-hand man strode out on it, the snap of his boots on the plank resounding over the arena. Giddi caught himself holding his breath as the plank bounced under the man's weight. At the man's raised eyebrows, the soldiers in the arena thumped their spears in unison. The last few murmurs in the crowd died down.

The man bowed, spoke in Robandi, then repeated himself in Giddi's tongue. "I, General Vizza, the emperor's adviser, welcome a traitorous Northerner to our arena—Mage Starrus of Great Spanglewood Forest, an inconsequential territory in the north."

The crowd booed and jeered. Starrus remained haughty, ignoring them.

"This man is an enemy to the emperor. He has betrayed him once before and has dared return to our fine city," said General Vizza. "He had the audacity to request an audience with our highly-esteemed leader. To determine his worthiness, he shall have to pass three tests. In the first test, he must escape this wooden cage unscathed."

There must be a trap. It was too easy.

No sooner had General Vizza finished speaking, Starrus waved his hands. In a flash of blinding light, the cage was on fire, luminous green flame licking up the wooden struts, burning the framework around him.

People gasped. Cheers and shouts broke out. The littling girl next to Giddi clutched her uncle's arm, whimpering.

Giddi's grip on his seat tightened. As much as he resented Starrus, he didn't want him to die. If Starrus perished, he'd never know the whereabouts of his father. With Ma dead and their cottage in Great Spanglewood Forest abandoned, his father would never find him. The only chance he had of being reunited was to find his father himself—via Starrus.

The flames died and Starrus was left standing on a charred wooden platform among a pile of ash, charred wood and buckled metal wheel rims. He kicked at one of the charred wooden bars and jumped through the gap as it crumpled into a pile of ash and the burnt ceiling caved in.

Starrus landed nimbly and stalked into the center of the arena. The crowd went wild, pounding the floor with their feet and screaming as he bowed to the emperor and his adviser, his gleaming straw-blond hair stained with flecks of ash. The ruins behind him were still smoking, and his face soot-smeared, as he waited under the hot desert sun for his next test.

MONTANARA

S yan, Zaarusha and Foxita wheeled over the bustling city of Montanara.

Yanir mind-melded with his onyx dragon. *"Syan, could you please drop us out on the edge of town?"*

"No," Syan rumbled. *"I'm dropping you right in the city square. There's no need for you to skulk and hide on the outskirts. You're the King's Rider and I'm the King of Dragons' Realm. We won't come to Montanara through the back door just to make you more comfortable."*

Yanir was glad that Anakisha wasn't mind-melding with them at that moment.

But Zaarusha chipped in anyway, *"Anakisha wouldn't care. She loves you as you are, so stop worrying."*

Easy enough for Zaarusha to say. Nothing could stop the worry gnawing at Yanir's gut.

Zaarusha, Foxita and Syan tilted their wings and swooped down between the stone buildings to land in the city square. Yanir thanked the dragon gods it wasn't market day, or the square would be crowded and there'd be a right fuss.

A couple of people going about their business stopped and waved to him. Yanir waved back.

"The King's Rider's home," a woman called.

People turned to stare. Some pounded their hands on their hearts, others bowed their heads.

"The Queen's Rider, too."

"Who's the red-headed rider? Is he a new blue guard?" Murmurs built and people crowded around them to meet Anakisha and Fox and welcome Yanir home. Storekeepers and customers rushed out of shops.

Yanir groaned. *"You're a treacherous dragon."*

Syan preened his scales. *"This respect befits a King's Rider."*

Not that Yanir cared. He'd rather stay low in his own town. He slapped Syan's onyx shoulder as he dismounted. *"You're a vain dragon, Syan."*

"Vanity is my prerogative. After all, we dragons are magnificent creatures."

Yanir chuckled and helped Anakisha out of her saddle. *"Not that you need help,"* he melded. *"But there's no harm in being gallant, is there?"* He turned to the crowd to introduce her. "Please welcome Anakisha, the new Queen's Rider of Dragons' Realm, who is on her way to Dragons' Hold. Please also welcome Fox, a new blue guard."

Anakisha grinned cheekily. "Thank you, kind sir." She turned to face the people thronging forward to shake her hand.

"Are you the new Queen's Rider?"

"Nice to meet you. Zaarusha's so beautiful."

"Did Yanir say your name's Anakisha? Such a pretty name."

Fox slid from his saddle with a jaunty smile, bathing in the Montanarians' admiration and shaking their hands, too.

Reluctantly, Yanir joined in. *"Next time, we'll land by my parents' farm,"* he growled at Syan, smiling at a merchant as he shook his hand.

"I'm glad you're intact," the man said gruffly. "We heard rumors of battles in the south against pirates."

Yanir nodded. He wasn't about to admit to any Montanarians that he'd been injured, in case word got to the wrong ears. "Yes, we fought the nefarious Scarlet Hand, a vicious new pirate captain who has a sea dragon. Unfortunately, he's escaped to the southern Naobian Sea, but he'll be back again."

"How bad is it?" The merchant's eyebrows drew down and he wrung his hands. "Has his crime affected the silk trade?"

"He's taken a few ships, but it's hard to tell at this stage. The blue guards' reports will keep the town arbitrator up to date."

The crowd waned and eventually people went back to their business.

Fox grinned at Yanir and Anakisha. "Nice to be royalty,"

Anakisha slugged him on the arm. "Yanir and I aren't royalty. That title goes to our dragons. We're only their riders."

"Only?" Zaarusha mind-melded.

"Yes, only. Without you I'd still be serving ales in the Dancing Dragon."

And he'd be minding pigs. Yanir hid the thought from Anakisha, Syan and Zaarusha, suddenly embarrassed, now he was so close to home.

A dragonly chuckle was Zaarusha's only answer.

Fox scratched the back of his neck. "I've never been to Montanara. Do you two mind if I take a look around?"

Yanir shrugged a shoulder. "Sure. We'll only be here for a few hours to see my family, then we'll head on to Dragons' Hold, so feel free. Syan or Zaarusha will let Foxita know where to meet us when it's time to go."

"I'll see you then." Fox nodded and headed through the throng.

"Come with me," Yanir said, tugging Anakisha's hand.

"Where are we going?" Clad in her riders' garb, her hair tangled and cheeks flushed from the wind, she was breathtaking.

He noticed the eyes of passers-by glancing at her more than casually, and kept hold of her hand. A fierce protectiveness stole over him, and he squeezed her hand a little, reassured when she squeezed his back.

Gods, in his hometown he felt less than a man. Less than the King's Rider. And less than worthy of her, the woman he loved.

§

They meandered through the township, Yanir occasionally greeting people he knew, but as they grew closer to the outskirts, his shoulders grew tight and his eyes wary.

Anakisha glanced around, but couldn't figure out what was wrong. *"Are you all right?"*

"Fine." He smiled, but as they kept walking, his eyes darted down the lane that headed out of town.

They approached a rowdy tavern. Three men slightly older than them staggered down the steps. The largest, a thickset lout with a pug nose, sneered at Yanir, "Oh, look at what the dog dragged home—dragon dung."

Anakisha opened her mouth, about to yell, but Yanir yanked her onward, ignoring the men, his frame rigid. *"Don't respond, Anakisha."*

She snapped her jaw shut and they kept walking. How dare they treat the King's Rider like that! It made her seethe. *"Yanir, what's going on?"* There was no answer.

A man with broad shoulders stepped into the middle of the lane, blocking their way. "Forgotten your old friends, have you, Yanir?"

"Where are you headed to?" a good-looking blond asked, stepping out beside him. "Back to lick your pig's butts clean?"

"Have you missed your little porkers?" Pug Nose taunted, joining the other two, blocking their way.

"We all know you're a pig lover!"

Anakisha broke away from Yanir's grip, her fists swinging, but before she could get far, Yanir mind-melded, stopping her. *"Anakisha, no! Don't make things worse. They're not worth answering."*

"*No, they're not. But you're worth fighting for.*" She stalked up to the man who'd first spoken and thrust her chin out, stepping into his space so he took a step backward. "I suppose the only way you feel good and strong is to put others down?" she snapped.

He folded his arms in front of his chest. "So, what if it is?" he sneered. "What's the tough dragon lady going to do to stop me?"

Anakisha's hand flew to her dagger. She'd teach these bullies a lesson.

"*Anakisha, no!*" Yanir mind-melded. "*Just leave them.*"

"*I'll handle this,*" Syan said. "*No one insults the King's Rider and gets away with it.*"

"*Very well.*" Anakisha replied, slowly withdrawing her hand from her weapon. She smiled sweetly at the bully and tapped his chest with her forefinger. "I'd watch it if I were you. Dragons have long memories." She barged past him, making the man jump aside.

Yanir followed her without speaking to the men.

"*I don't understand,*" Anakisha said. Yanir was strong. Together, they'd easily beat these louts.

"*I'm not always here,*" Yanir mind-melded, "*and they live too close to my family for me to risk fighting them.*"

Anakisha turned to him.

His eyes glinted dangerously and his jaw was tight.

"*All right,*" she said, squeezing his hand.

Dragon wings swished above them. King Syan's maw opened. A plume of fire blazed down between the buildings singeing the cobbles near the men. They yelped and scurried back into the tavern.

"*Syan,*" Yanir complained, "*I told you I don't need you to fight my battles for me.*"

"*Why? Someone's got to teach those louts a lesson,*" the onyx dragon replied.

"I'm sorry, Yanir, but I agree," said Anakisha. *"They shouldn't get away with bullying."*

Yanir shrugged. "It harms no one but my pride." A slow smile stole over his face. "The only thing that matters is who I am, not what they think of me. By fighting them, I'd sink to their level."

§

It was true. With a jolt, Yanir realized he'd risen above the petty insults of the bullies he'd grown up with.

"So what was all that about?" Anakisha took his hand as they strolled away from the tavern.

"Since I was tiny, those three teased me about being a pig farmer." Shards, it'd embarrassed him his whole life. And now Anakisha and Syan had stood up for him. But he hadn't wanted to fight. Fighting had never gotten him anywhere with those boneheads. And she'd been angry at those men, not thought less of him. He smiled.

"There's nothing wrong with being a pig farmer." Anakisha's eyes were earnest as she gazed up at him, their steps in rhythm.

So, she didn't mind pigs. He'd find out soon enough whether that was right. "Nor being a tavern wench," Yanir replied ruefully. "Not that I ever thought of you as a wench," he added hastily, "but I heard what some of those men said."

Anakisha snorted. "No one can determine who we are or what we become," she said. "Only we can determine that ourselves."

"I know." Yanir slung an arm around her waist. "Come on. Let me take you home to meet my friends and family."

When they reached the farm, instead of taking Anakisha inside to meet his parents, Yanir skirted around the farm and approached from the meadow, nearest to the pigs.

Oinks, snorts and grunts filled the air as they rounded the old pig shed. A huge bay hog with black spots ran to the fence of the pen, nosing through the palings. Yanir held out his hand and she snuffled it, tickling his palm. He scratched her behind the ears.

"This is Bertha, funnily enough," he said chuckling as he remembered the indignant woman who'd dumped the pitcher of beer over Justan's head.

"You haven't been back here since the tournament, so I assume you named her before you met Justan's betrothed?" Anakisha giggled. "Poor piggy, sharing a name with her. She's much more handsome than Justan's Bertha."

"I raised her by hand after her mother died. Although she's a mother herself, now."

Beige and black spotted piglets rushed out of the shed, squealing and butting each other in their eagerness to greet him.

Yanir scratched one's back and fondled another's ears.

Anakisha reached through the fence and let a piglet snuffle her hand. "Hey, that tickles."

"These are her yearlings. Would you like to hold one?" He clambered over the rail and Anakisha followed him, her boots squelching through the mud.

Yanir picked up a piglet and handed it to Anakisha. She held it, its hooves scrabbling against her jerkin. Anakisha grinned and patted its ears. The piglet grunted. "She's adorable."

"Sorry," he said. "She's made your jerkin dirty."

"It's just a little mud. It'll wash off."

"It certainly will, "Yanir said, beaming. Gods, she was too good to be true.

"Watch out!" Anakisha cried.

Something bowled into the back of Yanir's legs and knocked him to his knees in the mud. Great way to impress a girl. "Yes, Boris, I've missed you too, you mad monster." Yanir flung his arms around the black boar's neck and scratched his back, just the way Boris liked it. Boris oinked and stomped off through the mud to the pig trough to snaffle a few scraps. Yanir got to his feet, his lower legs plastered with mud.

Anakisha was laughing so hard, she lost her grip on the piglet and it scrambled out of her arms, splattering them both with more mud as it landed in the sty.

"Boris is Bertha's mate." Yanir pointed at the sow's heavy teats. "Bertha was pregnant last time I flew through, so I'd say she has a litter of sucklers inside."

Anakisha's eyes lit up. "Can I see them?"

He offered her a mud-stained hand, but it didn't matter—her's was just as muddy. "Come inside the sty. This is where I spent most of my younger years. I was in charge of the pigs while Pa, Ma and my sisters looked after the rest of the farm."

He took Anakisha inside. Bertha ran to the corner, nosing in the hay. Yanir and Anakisha tiptoed after her. "Look," he whispered. Bertha lay down and eight tiny piglets, nestled in the hay, grunted and butted at her teats, then latched on to feed.

"Yanir, they're so gorgeous. Look how tiny they are, and how fine their hair is." Anakisha turned to him, her eyes bright.

"We don't kill the pigs," he said. "I refused to when I was young, and my family understood, so we sell them live to other people who want to breed them."

Anakisha nudged him. "You big softy."

He ran a hand through his hair. "Hmm, I know. But they're just so sweet, I couldn't bear it."

"Now I understand why you don't eat pork," she said.

"Or bacon or ham," he added.

She grinned and turned to him. In the shaft of sunlight streaming through the door of the pigsty, with mud smeared on her face and her hair in a tangled mane, she was the most beautiful woman he'd ever seen. "Anakisha," he stepped closer, gently placing his hands on her upper arms.

She raised her eyes to his, still smiling. "Yes, Yanir." She took a step closer. Placing a hand on his chest, she reached up her other hand and entwined her fingers in his hair.

He smiled at her, his heart soaring, and brushed his lips against hers. Oh gods, they were the softest thing he'd ever felt. He cupped her cheek. "You're so beautiful."

"Even smeared with mud?" she asked, laughing, her breath ghosting across his lips.

"Covered with mud, you're more beautiful than ever. Although I'd told you, I was never sure if you'd accept me as a lowly pig farmer from Montanara."

"I don't," she said laughing again. "I accept you as the King's Rider and a *distinguished* pig breeder from Montanara."

He laughed and hugged her. "I knew my true love would be someone who loves pigs as much as I do."

"Well, maybe not quite as much as you do, but they are sweet."

There was a squeal, but it wasn't a pig, because it was accompanied by a giggle, snorts and whispers.

Yanir lunged out the pigsty door, leaped the fence, and snatched at his littling sister. She ducked, evading his grasp. She sprinted off, her blonde pigtails flying as she and the neighbor's girl raced back toward the house, shrieking, "Yanir's home! He's kissing a pretty girl."

Anakisha came out into the sunlight, blinking. "Is that your sister?"

Yanir groaned. "I'm afraid so. Well, one of them. Sorry, Anakisha."

She giggled. "I remember teasing my brother when he got his first kiss. I never let him live it down."

Yanir brushed the mud off his hand and took her hand in his, and they strode across the meadow toward the farmhouse. "Ready to meet my family?" he asked.

Anakisha laughed again. "You have a family, other than the pigs?"

"You have a point." He grinned. "The way my sister squealed, I think she's part porker."

ARENA

High on the gleaming marble balcony, the emperor nodded, and General Vizza walked out onto the plank again.

"Now that our mage has warmed up, we have a slightly more difficult challenge for him." General Vizza smiled. "He must escape this trial unscathed. If he is injured, he won't progress to the next round."

At Vizza's words, a team of bolt-flingers stepped up to the edge of the balcony and trained their crossbows on the mage.

Vizza's teeth flashed in a broad smile, as if nothing pleased him more than the prospect of seeing Starrus die. "Please commence the next trial."

Giddi had been clenching the seat in a death grip for so long, his fingers were numb. He shook out his hands as one of the cages at the opposite end of the arena slid open. Unconsciously, he leaned forward as the crowd craned their necks to see what beast emerged.

A collective sigh of relief rippled around the arena as slaves wheeled out another cage. Made of metal, it consisted of four layers of complex filigree, each from a metal of a different shade— bronze, iron, silver and gold. Interlaced, the layers formed a web of intricate patterns that were so fine it was almost impossible to see through them. The precious metals gleamed in the sun, an ostentatious show of wealth for wealth's sake.

Starrus shook loose ash from his hair as he waited for the slaves to wheel the low platform holding the cage closer. When they were half a dragon length from him, he flung out his hands as if he were going to smite the slaves. A poor slave turned and ran.

The crowd watched in stunned silence, waiting for a bolt of mage flame to end the hapless slave's life, but Starrus dropped his hands, his laughter ringing through the arena.

The crowd laughed too, jeering at the fleeing man.

Before the slave could reach the slave's narrow passage and safety, a crossbolt flew into the man's bronzed back. He dropped dead, a bloody stain spreading on the arena's orange sand.

The man next to Giddi shaded his niece's eyes. Giddi spun in his seat. Vizza nodded at the crossbowman. His dark gaze swept the arena, and the crowd fell into shocked silence. Giddi swallowed. This was no laughing matter: a man had just died due to Starrus' joke.

Ignoring the slave's body, Starrus bowed to general Vizza and stalked to the filigree cage.

The remaining three slaves stood fast, avoiding the sight of their dead friend. They each opened a door in the cage: the first slave opened a door in the outer layer of bronze; the next slave opened an iron door within it; and the third slave opened the silver door. The innermost gold door was still shut. A quick glance between the slaves, who were studiously avoiding glancing at their colleague, showed whose door this had been. One more glance, and the man who'd opened the silver door took charge of the final door and opened it.

Without a nod or the slightest acknowledgment of these men's recent loss, Starrus stalked inside and waited while the doors were each locked. He was still visible through the inner gold door, which was formed of flames of gold metal. The next door was fashioned with tiny crests of silver, like the rolling waves of the sea. The iron door was made of branches and leaves. And the final outer door of bronze comprised of people joining hands in a huge orb that encompassed the other cages within it.

As the last lock snapped shut, Starrus was lost within the myriad of metal shapes that surrounded him. Giddi stretched out his legs and folded his arms. This was easy, Starrus could be out within moments. All he had to do was melt the metal and step free. Giddi smothered a yawn, then quickly sat upright when he noticed a solider taking a keen interest in him. He leaned forward again, his elbows on his knees, making sure he stayed focused on Starrus.

The soldier gazed up at Vizza's platform as the general spoke again, "To escape, our traitor must melt each layer of metal so that it does not contaminate another layer. If the metals blend, my crossbow team are under strict instructions to shoot him." The general paused dramatically. "Furthermore, I have personally tasked every one of these crossbowmen to shoot one of their individually-fletched bolts into his traitorous body. We will check the fletching. If one of them fails, they will be executed as well."

Giddi's head spun—melt those metals without them running into one another. How in flame's name was that possible?

The general signaled. "Slaves, we require the thousand-beat drum. To live, Mage Starrus must complete his task by the thousandth beat."

Two of the slaves retrieved a set of double drums and they sat, beating a slow rhythm. From within the latticework, a pale-green mage flame glowed. By the time Giddi had counted to a hundred beats, not even a trickle of metal had leaked from the latticework.

By the dragon gods, Starrus was going to end up a pincushion for the emperor's bolt-flingers.

§

Only a thousand beats? It was nearly impossible—but Starrus had done the impossible before. Aware of the ten cross bows trained on his torso, he focused, sensing the *sathir* of only the outermost cage—the bronze people holding hands. If he could melt that first, maybe, just maybe, he'd survive.

He stretched out his senses, reaching past the gaudy playful *sathir* of the gold, the quiet hum of the silver and the dark presence of the iron, to feel the dancing *sathir* of the bronze. He closed his eyes, sweat beading on his brow, and saw the interlinked hands that joined to form this beautifully-crafted prison. His fingers tingled and he felt flames spring from them, but these were not his purpose or his means, merely a by-product of his concentration.

The beats of the drum droned on and a remote part of Starrus' mind kept count as he felt the essence of the bronze filigree.

§

No one stirred in the arena. Six hundred beats, and not a single shred of metal had melted. Giddi's clenched jaw ached. His entire body was coiled tight, ready to jump into the arena—although he wouldn't be much help to Starrus with a cross-bolt through his heart.

High on the balcony, the bolt-flingers' nocked bolts were trained on the filigree cage. A young bolt-flinger at the end of the row quivered with tension, her bow trembling. With a twang, her bolt flew free, straight for the cage.

The crowd drew in a collective breath.

The bolt punched a hole the first two layers of the cage. Giddi's heart lurched as fragments of bronze and iron scattered over the sand.

Then the bolt flew backward, expelled by some invisible force, clattered into the wall of the arena, and thunked to the sand.

A tiny jet of mage fire shot through the bolt hole in the filigree and morphed into a roiling fireball of luminous green flame that sped up to the balcony. The fireball hit the bolt-flinger and blew a hole through her stomach. The young woman toppled over the edge of the balcony, hit the wall of the arena and thumped onto on the sandy cobbles, her neck and limbs sprawled at impossible angles.

Blood seeped from the gaping hole in her belly and pooled around her head.

"Hold steady," General Vizza commanded his bolt-flingers, a thunderous scowl darkening his features.

Splattered in the young woman's gore, they kept their bows trained on the cage housing Starrus.

The littling next to Giddi whimpered, and flung herself into her uncle's arms, burying her face against his chest. Around the arena, cheers rang out as some of the crowd clamored in blood lust. Other people stirred in shock, cradling their littlings against them, their cries of horror punctuating the drumbeats. Gods, seven hundred beats, a dead bolt-flinger, and still not a tiny scrap of melted metal.

Perhaps Giddi needed to help his trainer. But with his untamed raw power, he didn't dare. He'd obliterate the cage and Starrus in one untrained blast. This was a task that required finesse and years of training. He clenched and unclenched his hands, helpless.

What was that? A breeze stirred at the front of the cage, disturbing the sand and scattering it so the cobbles were bared. Coppery drips ran from a corner of the outer cage door—the bronze filigree was melting. Giddi watched, fascinated, as the emblems of people's joined hands became a molten mass of running liquid and the bronze door disintegrated into a pool of molten fluid.

The sand gusted away from the base of the cage and the rest of the bronze structure melted into a deep pool around the base of the cage. The wind gusted a channel through the sand to the south side of the arena, then blew the sand into a heap against the wall. Slowly, the liquid flowed along the channel and pooled at the base of the sand pile.

Goosebumps pebbled Giddi's skin. He'd never realized how strong and focused Starrus' power could be. He was lucky to have survived the kraken attack that Starrus had engineered, and his stint in the desert.

Green flame glowed from deep within the cage, but Giddi couldn't make out much else of Starrus except his shock of straw-blond hair.

Oh gods, he'd stopped counting. He listened for the beat, waiting for the drummers to mark eight hundred with a heavier boom of the drums.

§

Only a few drops of melted iron had dribbled to the ground when the drums boomed the eight hundredth beat. Starrus swallowed. Two hundred beats left. He was out of time. It had taken him over a hundred beats from the first drip of bronze to melt the entire outer layer of this dragon gods' forsaken cage, and he'd only just started with the iron.

His body was aching, cramps building from his lower back and rippling up his spine and across his shoulders and neck. His arms spasmed and the drips slowed. He had to focus, not worry about the crossbows that could kill in an instant. If necessary, he'd blast the lot of them and every member of the emperor's guard. He'd show that stupid Vizza he wasn't to be tangled with.

The thought gave him a surge of power, but he had to rein it in or he'd melt the silver too, and make the metals impure. Whoever had thought of this nasty test had known what they were doing. Through the latticework, a smile danced across General Vizza's face.

If he had the chance, Starrus would kill the emperor's shrotty adviser. But first, he had to find out about the Scarlet Hand so he could regain his status and rise through the mage ranks to become the head of the Great Spanglewood Mage Council.

§

As the boom for nine hundred beats rang out, Giddi kept count, feverishly hoping Starrus could make it. His trainer had siphoned the iron off to a molten pool near the cages in the eastern arena wall. But Starrus still had the silver waves and the golden flames to get through.

How in the realm's name Starrus was managing to isolate and melt each layer of metal was beyond Giddi, but it didn't matter—Starrus had to survive. Giddi had to find out the whereabouts of his pa.

The silver waves dripped to the naked cobbles around the cage. Starrus' hands moved within the gold and silver latticework and the silver dripped faster.

People were perched on the edges of their seats. Whispers ran through the arena like the rustle of dried leaves as the drummers reached nine hundred and fifty beats.

Giddi's fingers twitched. If only there was some way to help... But he didn't dare disrupt Starrus' finely-balanced magic.

Above the crowd, the bolt-flingers were ready, bolts aimed, and vengeance on their faces. Starrus had made enemies of them all today. He was good at making enemies. What in the name of the First Egg had his trainer done years ago to anger the emperor and his general?

General Vizza's smirk grew as drips of silver plunked into the molten pool around Starrus' prison. Giddi would do anything to wipe that smirk off the shrotty general's face, but there was nothing he could do.

Wait, perhaps there was.

Giddi reached out and sucked in *sathir*, letting the power in his core build until he was trembling.

The littling looked up at him. "You're shaking. Are you all right?"

Giddi gave her a tight smile. "I'm fine."

Nine hundred and eighty beats. The silver cage was only half disintegrated. Starrus was exhausted, his magic wavering. Giddi willed him to rally.

At nine hundred and ninety beats, the silver was in a molten pool around the cage and Starrus was slumped, hands trembling as he tried to channel it away so he could melt the gold. His face was lined with fatigue and his hair was drenched with sweat as rivulets of silver trickled away from the cage at a snail's pace.

Giddi drove a fierce blast of wind at the silver, shunting the liquid to the northern side of the arena, then he threw every scrap of his *sathir* reserves at the golden filigree cage.

§

It was over. Five beats to go and he'd be dead. Starrus had no *sathir* reserves left, not even the strength to push the silver away from the cage so he could melt the golden-flamed filigree. And the emperor's bolt-flingers would kill him anyway if the two metals mixed. Anger rose in his belly, its embers stirring to life and igniting a fire of hatred.

Curse the golden cage. He wouldn't even bother trying. With one blast, he'd kill those shrotty southerners instead. Starrus comforted himself with the knowledge that he'd take the emperor, Vizza and the bolt-flingers with him. If he still could.

A freak gust of wind pushed the molten silver away from the cage.

With three beats to go, Starrus didn't question his strange luck.

The cage was now clear of silver. The gold was his to melt. He doubted his efforts would be enough, but he had to try. He let his hatred stoke his power and blasted the cage with everything he had. The gold softened and caved slightly, but held fast, still caging him. He panted and tried to drag more *sathir* inside him, but his breath came in shallow gasps and he swayed on his feet.

A voice ripped through his mind. *"Starrus, you owe me your life."*

Giddi?

The cage exploded in a shower of molten gold. It whirled in a hurricane around him and dribbled into a molten pool in the center of the arena.

Starrus' heart thudded, louder than a dragon's roar, as the thousandth drumbeat boomed across the arena.

BEAST

General Vizza signaled the bolt-flingers to stand down, and narrowed his eyes, staring at the cocky northern mage in the arena. Starrus had done the impossible. The pools of molten metal dispersed around the arena were testament to that.

Within the last few drumbeats, a mage wind had sped the silver away from around the cage, giving the mage space to melt the gold.

And melt the gold he had—with a theatrical display that had made a mockery of this trial. Mind you, the emperor's trials were a mockery in themselves. Very few made it through to a formal hearing. Vizza stroked his chin.

The emperor raised a finger on the arm of his throne. Vizza strode over and lowered his head to listen to his leader's command.

"And now?" the emperor asked.

"I suggest we unleash the beast."

"Which one?"

"The one that will kill this mage the fastest."

"While the mage is shackled." His leader nodded. "Give him someone to save. That usually motivates the vilest of criminals."

"It shall be done, my highly-esteemed emperor." Vizza strode off to issue orders. If that scoundrel Starrus survived this next trial, he'd kill the mage himself.

§

The crowd roared, screaming and stomping, the reverberations running through the ground under Starrus' feet. His body was an empty dried-up husk. He swayed, wishing there was a bench he could sink onto. He'd felt the wind that had swept away the silver, heard Giddi in his head, and seen the hurricane of swirling gold, yet he still couldn't believe it. His trainee had survived.

And by the dragon gods, Giddi had helped him. The fool. The last thing Starrus wanted was to be indebted to that boy. Sweat ran down his forehead into his eyes, stinging as he scanned the crowd looking for Giddi. He blinked the sweat from his eyes and tried again to pinpoint his trainee in the crowd. But the faces of the spectators blurred and merged into one everlasting round of color.

Starrus staggered and sank to his haunches. He was past caring if Vizza saw he was exhausted. Perhaps the crowd would take pity on him and plea for his life with the emperor. Gods, that was a fanciful thought—about as likely as a dragonet giving up its first taste of meat.

Or as likely as Giddi surviving the Robandi assassins.

Soldiers marched from the double wooden doors and grasped Starrus by the arms. They hauled him over to six metal stakes in the ground near the west end of the arena. Slaves rushed from the passageway, iron chains looped around their shoulders.

The soldiers shoved Starrus to the ground and spread his legs and arms. The slaves wrapped their chains around his thighs and all the way down his legs, and the soldiers chained him to the stakes at the ankles. For good measure, they looped chains round his body and arms and fastened him via the neck, torso, and both wrists to the remaining four stakes.

The only thing free was his head. Starrus glared at the soldiers. The chains were damnably uncomfortable, digging into his spine and the base of his skull and constricting his movement—of course. Starrus tested the chains, wriggling his leg. They clanked but held fast.

As the soldiers and slaves retreated, he decided this trial wasn't so bad after all. He could lie here as long as he needed to recoup his *sathir* and then melt his way out of the chains. No problem. All he needed was time.

Vizza's voice rang over the arena, "Bring out the sacrifice."

A sacrifice? That didn't make sense. He wasn't about to kill anyone. Starrus lifted his head, but it was yanked back by the chain at his neck. Slowly he raised it again to see a tiny girl led out and staked nearby. Not fair, her chain was much flimsier than his.

"To gain an audience with the emperor, you must save the girl from the beast." There was an audible smirk in Vizza's voice.

What beast? Starrus cast about, but the chains at his neck prevented him from seeing everything.

"Open the cage," Vizza bellowed.

The sound of scraping metal shuddered through the arena. Something clattered on the cobbles. Cheers and terrified screams rang out.

Starrus strained, raising his head. The towering beast on the far side of the arena made the blood in his veins turn icy.

EILEEN MUELLER

Dragons' Hold

Anakisha eyed the steep mountain peaks looming before her, Syan, and Foxita. "Zaarusha, what if I get dizzy again and fall off?"

"I asked a blue guard when we were in Montanara. One of them told me that his rider always got height sickness from thin air until he learned to breathe correctly."

"I'm glad I'm not the only one."

"Try what he suggested. Draw as much air into your lungs as you can, then hold it."

Anakisha gulped.

"No, not in a great gulp. Inhale slowly through your nose, gradually drawing the air in for ten heartbeats."

Anakisha drew a thin stream of air in through her nostrils. Her lungs slowly filled, but when she was about to exhale, Zaarusha interrupted, *"Now hold it for ten heartbeats."*

She did, hoping her lungs wouldn't burst.

"When you exhale," the dragon queen advised, *"do it slowly, counting for as many heartbeats as you can. Then take the next breath slowly again."*

Her lungs straining, Anakisha's air trickled out of her.

Zaarusha chuckled. *"It'll take us a while to get up the mountain, so you have time to practice. Keep doing that the whole way up. Holding air in your lungs regularly as we fly higher will help your body cope with the thinner air over the mountaintops."*

Zaarusha slowed her pace and Syan and Foxita matched it. They zigzagged lazily up the mountainside.

"*Welcome to Dragons' Hold, Anakisha.*" Zaarusha said. "*These are the fierce peaks of Dragon's Teeth, the sentinels around our stronghold.*"

"*They're too steep to climb, so the only access to Dragons' Hold is on dragonback,*" Yanir explained, Syan's dark wings flashing against the snow. They winged past an ibex perched on a rock jutting out from the slope at a ridiculous angle. "*You think they'd fall off,*" Yanir melded. "*But in all my time here, I've yet to see an ibex lose its footing.*"

"This is amazing," Fox called, his red head bobbing above Foxita's cobalt wings. Startled by his yell, marmots whistled and ducked behind rocks.

The air grew cooler as they traversed past the snowy upper reaches. Anakisha concentrated on her breathing. "*It's working, Zaarusha. I haven't gotten dizzy yet.*"

"*Good, don't stop now.*"

They shot up over the mountain top, slipping over a crest alongside an even taller peak that towered above them.

"*That's Heaven's Peak,*" Yanir melded. "*It's the tallest mountain along the southern end of Dragon's Teeth.*" He pointed to the north where the sun glanced off a towering pinnacle. "*And that's Fire Crag, the tallest in the entire ring.*"

Anakisha's breath caught. Dragon's Teeth were indeed like a gaping ring of dragon fangs. But instead of opening to a dark cavernous maw, inside was a picturesque basin. Dragons wheeled in the sky, most carrying two people—one clad in riders' garb and the other in a mage cloak. The riders shot arrows at targets on the slopes, then the mages aimed bolts of mage fire. The air was filled with catcalls and whistles when someone hit a target and friendly taunts when they missed.

"*So many dragons,*" Anakisha mind-melded.

"*Well, it is called Dragons' Hold,*" Zaarusha commented.

"*For a reason,*" added Syan. "*Who did you think trained here? Chickens?*"

"*No, but—*" She gasped as a dragon zipped across the basin, the rider hanging off the saddle at a dangerous angle. He loosed an arrow that thudded into a wooden target. Cheers rang out.

Anakisha had thought she was good at archery. She'd have no chance at a tournament against an archer like that. None at all. She swallowed.

A group of dragons swept past them in single file. They swooped down over the stony clearing beneath them, then fanned out to fly over meadows, fields and orchards. The dragons shot over a bristling pine forest, a silver lake nestled in its close embrace, and flew out toward a tangled wilderness, staying in tight formation.

"*Flight training,*" Yanir said as Syan swooped down the mountain ahead of them.

Zaarusha tipped her snout down and followed. Anakisha's stomach dropped.

"*Let's take her to the main cavern to meet the council.*" Syan shot over the stony clearing and through a tunnel in the hillside.

Zaarusha flew through another tunnel, Foxita following them. The rustle and flap of the dragons' wings bounced off the walls like cascading stones. They shot out into an enormous cavern, many times larger than the village square in Fieldhaven, and wheeled down toward Syan, who'd landed on a huge natural shelf of rock. Although steps led from this natural stage to the lower floor of the cavern, Yanir dismounted and waited for them to land, a torch in a nearby sconce sending light flickering across his face. He helped Anakisha off Zaarusha.

Foxita sank to her haunches, and Fox slid off. "She's tired," said Fox. "It's been a long journey."

"I don't blame her. I am too," Anakisha replied.

Fox scanned the cavern. "This place is huge."

A ruby dragon swooped down. A tall, broad-shouldered man with a tough, pitted face and a shock of dark hair nimbly leaped from the saddle and strode over. His cloak swirled around his legs and daggers jutted from his boots.

Yanir shook his hand. "Master Taren this is Anakisha, the Queen's Rider, from Fieldhaven. Anakisha, meet Spymaster Taren."

"It's about time," Master Taren smiled, shaking her hand. "Zaarusha's been pining for a rider for years."

"Pining?" Anakisha asked the queen.

"Of course not." Zaarusha snorted. *"A queen would never pine."*

Master Taren narrowed his eyes, staring at the queen of the dragons. "If I know Zaarusha, she'll be denying it, but we all know dragons are never quite complete without their riders. Just as we are completed when we meet our dragons. Welcome to Dragons' Hold."

Despite his tough exterior, his smile was warm. *"He seems nice."*

"He's as tough as old boots, but has a heart of gold. Not that I'd ever want to cross him—he has a mean aim with a dagger." Yanir suppressed a smile, waving a hand between Fox and Spymaster Taren. "And this is Fox, a newly imprinted rider, also from Fieldhaven."

The men shook hands and exchanged greetings.

A familiar blue dragon and two riders swooped into the cavern and landed on the stone stage. The blue guard dismounted, flicking his sandy hair out of his face and turned to help a man wearing a mage cloak dismount.

"Hello, Seppi," Anakisha called out. She hadn't seen the leader of the blue guards since after the battle in Naobia against the Scarlet Hand.

Seppi hugged Anakisha. "Good to see you finally made it here." He grinned and gestured to the mage, who was striding over.

The handsome mage in his early thirties thrust his hand out at Anakisha. "My name is Balovar."

She was so tired, if anyone else shook her hand, it would probably fall off.

"By the way," said Seppi. "Balovar heads up the Great Spanglewood Forest Mage Council."

Balovar snorted. "Not that titles are important." He gave a grin, making his face light up. Smile lines crinkled his brown eyes.

"No, but you're important," Seppi insisted. "And it's important that Anakisha knows who she's dealing with."

So, he was head of the Great Spanglewood Mage Council. Anakisha raised an eyebrow at the mage. "Oh, so you'll know our good friend, Giddi?" she asked. "We left him in Naobia. He and Starrus were heading south to search for Master Mage Findal. I expect they've found him by now."

Balovar nodded. "How is Giddi doing?"

"Our dragon mage is doing well, but he still has a lot to learn. There was an unfortunate incident…" Anakisha shrugged, not sure how much she should say.

"I don't know how much he knows," admitted Yanir via mind-meld.

Balovar nodded. "Spymaster Taren informed me about Lush Valley." He shook his head sadly. "Hopefully finding Findal and getting some training will help restore Giddi's esteem. But what's this you said about a dragon mage?"

Anakisha smiled. "Giddi can mind-meld with any dragon."

Yanir nodded. "It's true. The first dragon mage in years."

Balovar's eyebrows shot up. "An interesting development."

Seppi smacked his forehead. "Dragon's claws, with the excitement of battle and Frugar's death, I forgot to tell you."

Spymaster Taren scowled. "As the leader of the blue guards we expect you not to forget momentous details, young Seppi."

Seppi nodded.

"Right," said Yanir. "Now that you've met the Dragons' Hold Council, we should summon the riders to meet you both."

"We'll do the honors," Zaarusha mind-melded. She roared and Syan joined in, shaking the stone floor underfoot.

The deafening flap of wings ricocheted down the tunnels leading into the main cavern. Dragons shot out from the tunnels overhead, spiraling down to land on the floor below the natural rock stage. Riders whooped, hanging off their dragons at crazy angles. One rode in standing on her saddle. More dragons poured through the tunnels—of every size and color imaginable: rust, ruby, sapphire, jade, gold, tangerine, beige, lemon, scarlet, canary-yellow, violet, bronze and even silver. And so many shades of blue: cerulean, cobalt, lapis, peacock, lake-blue and sky.

Dragons flew around the cavern, their wings stirring Anakisha's hair around her face. They landed, hundreds of dragons crowding the cavern floor until Anakisha thought every space was filled. Yet more landed, others moving over in a rippling sea of colors. Some perched on ledges halfway up the walls, others circled and alighted at the edge of the stage.

A mage rode in on the back of a mossy-green dragon, shooting mage fire at an unlit torch, which burst into luminous green flame. She and her rider laughed and they shot up to land on the highest ledge, near the cavern's rocky ceiling.

"Excuse me, Anakisha." Master Mage Balovar flung out an arm. An arc of flame swept around the cavern, torches springing to life in its wake, spluttering green mage flame and bathing the entire cavern an eerie glow. Balovar twitched his fingers. Tiny balls of glowing flame flitted from his fingertips, darting into the air and careening around the cavern.

"You have to love mage lights," Yanir said. "There's nothing quite like them, is there?"

"This is your home?" Fox gaped. "It's incredible."

"It's yours now, too, Fox," Yanir replied, his warm gray eyes on Anakisha. *"Do you think you can be happy here?"* he mind-melded, biting his lower lip, looking like a nervous littling.

Anakisha's breath exploded. She hadn't even realized she'd been holding it. *"Of course, Yanir. It's wonderful."* Gods, she yearned to hug him, nestle in his arms away from the prying eyes of the waiting riders and mages gathered on the floor below—and others flying in on more dragons. But there'd be time enough for that later.

Yanir strode to the front of the stage and the dragons stilled. "We would like to present Anakisha, Zaarusha's new rider," he called out, his voice carrying through the cavern. "As Queen's Rider, Anakisha will rule beside me, Syan and Zaarusha, with the help of our council, protecting Dragons' Realm." Yanir scratched his neck, then held an arm high. "Do you swear your allegiance to Anakisha?"

Hundreds of heads bowed and fists thumped chests, echoing through the cavern like a stampede.

"I pledge to serve you, Zaarusha and Dragons' Realm," Anakisha called out.

Zaarusha roared, making Anakisha's neck hairs stand on end.

Fox nudged her, chuckling, "No pressure."

Anakisha mind-melded with Yanir, *"I'm nobody special, just me. How can I rule these people?"*

Yanir grinned. *"That's exactly how I felt. You'll learn. Syan and Zaarusha are good coaches."*

Zaarusha's rumble echoed through her mind, *"You're special. You're courageous. You've always fought for the downtrodden and those who couldn't fight for themselves. I chose you, so trust me."*

Anakisha nodded, but as riders and mages cried out her name and dragons roared, her trickle of doubt grew into a torrent. Dragon's claws, how could she prove herself to these people?

Fox nudged her. "I never knew you'd be this popular. I guess I'm lucky to know you."

Anakisha grinned. "Soon, you may have to pay a golden dragon head to have an audience with me."

"Of course, I'd pay to see you, my honored Queen's Rider," he bowed low.

Anakisha laughed. Thank the First Egg Fox was here to help her laugh at herself.

Yanir raised his arm again, and the crowd quieted. "Please help Anakisha and our new rider Fox to get to know their way around Dragons' Hold. We thank you for your support."

The rustle of wings as dragons departed was like a hurricane that left Anakisha reeling. By the shrotty tail of a dragonet. So many riders. So many dragons. All more experienced than her. All better.

The cavern emptied and just the three of them and their dragons were left. Yanir turned to Anakisha and Fox. "Enough politics and business for today. We'll show you your quarters, give you a tour, and then you'll need a bite to eat."

"I'm famished," Fox piped up.

"Luckily, our cooks here are excellent." Yanir grinned at Fox and patted his stomach.

With the weight of the realm pressing on her, the last thing Anakisha felt like was eating.

DEATHSTALKER

Taller than a man, the monster scuttled along the wall at the far end of the arena, waving its enormous pincers in the air. It's thick, curved tail held a barbed stinger that made Starrus' mouth turn dry.

The dragon gods help him! Not only was it a giant scorpion, it was a black death stalker. With its spitting tail, it was the most venomous scorpion in the Robandi desert. The beast's slick black carapace gleamed as it skittered along the wall, the crowd only half a dragon length above its curved tail—which was thicker than Starrus' thigh and had a wicked barb at the tip.

Thank the First Egg it hadn't seen him yet. Or the girl. Starrus grinned. Thank the dragon gods, the girl was between him and the scorpion.

Starrus strained to melt the chains wrapped around his body. A flicker of *sathir* glowed in his belly, then died. He tried again, but nothing happened. He'd burnt himself out melting that stupid fancy cage.

The scorpion reared on its legs and leaped, scrabbling at the arena wall. Good. If it climbed into the spectator area, he'd be safe for a while yet. Maybe he'd have a chance to replenish his *sathir*.

The beast's pincers scraped the arena's walls, making Starrus' blood curdle. The black death stalker fell back to the cobbles among the scattered sand, and raised its tail, aiming its barbed tip at the seats. Dark liquid sprayed from its barb and hit a man's neck. His skin bubbled in angry red blisters. The man screamed and writhed in his seat, his eyes rolling back in his head. A woman next to him shrieked and clutched at him. Panic broke out around her and people fled.

Spectators in the stands screamed. Those in the front rows at the east end of the arena pushed their way through the crowd, scrabbling over people and seats to flee to the narrow exits. Starrus didn't blame them. If he were free, he'd be running too.

The scorpion raised its tail again. The woman let go of her husband, and scrambled over the seats. A jet of dark fluid flew from the scorpion's barb, staining the woman's white robe. The fabric disintegrated before Starrus' eyes and her flesh bubbled in a mass of red blisters.

High on the balcony, Vizza grinned.

Oh yes, the emperor's adviser was getting revenge on him. Even if he got out of this, the people would hate Starrus and blame him for Vizza's debacle. They'd probably rejoice in Starrus' execution.

Starrus cursed himself. He'd been so eager to get recognition from both mage councils he hadn't stopped to think before coming to Metropoli. He'd thought he could waltz back in here and pick up where he'd left off. With his eyes on rescuing Master Mage Findal and becoming a master mage himself, he hadn't stopped to consider that Vizza might have found out the depth of his treachery.

Starrus tried to swallow, but his mouth was too dry. He slowly drew in *sathir* from the people around him, from the sand and from the very chains that bound him. He was still weak, but if the scorpion was distracted long enough, maybe he'd have a chance to build up his reserves.

§

Giddi sat frozen as a woman at the west end of the arena fell onto the seats with her back in a mass of blisters. Her body twitched and convulsed. Everyone around her fled. No one stopped to help her. And that smarmy general stood on the balcony impassively, watching the chaos and carnage.

Giddi pushed his way through the crowd, trying to get to the injured woman and her dead husband, but the flood of people shoving past him, fleeing to the nearest exit, caused a bottleneck. It was impossible to get through. He was trapped in the crowd near the flimsy rail around the arena.

Behind him, a trumpet blew. Giddi spun.

The giant scorpion froze, its tail in midair, and trembled—its enormous carapace shaking and legs quivering. There was a short blast on the trumpet and the beast slowly turned.

By the puking dragon gods! That horrible thing was trained. General Vizza had let it attack the spectators. And now, he would turn it on Starrus.

Two more blasts and the creature stepped slowly toward the center of the arena, carefully stalking its prey.

Giddi's heart stopped as he recognized the girl who'd stolen the bread at the marketplace. Her eyes were as large as dragon eggs. Oh gods, if only he'd helped her earlier. She faced the advancing scorpion, her leg shackled, her head high and back straight, with the bleak stare of a warrior facing death.

Starrus lay bound with chains from neck to ankle, only his head, feet and hands visible. Whatever he'd done to annoy the emperor must've been bad. Very bad. But surely, Giddi's trainer would melt those chains and save the girl.

The scorpion's feet skittered across the cobbles as it advanced on the girl and Starrus.

What was Starrus waiting for?

The scorpion stalked the girl, getting ever closer. The crowd had stopped fleeing—and was now rooted to the spot, staring at the pitiful waif in the arena.

PLANS

Anakisha and Fox made their way through the tables in the mess cavern with their trays laden with bread and soup.

"Evening, Queen's Rider, Fox." A dragon rider stepped to one side so they could squeeze between the crowded tables.

Mages and riders nodded as they passed. In a corner, a mage was flourishing bouquets of fiery flowers at a red-headed rider, who was blushing furiously as the riders and mages at her table whistled.

"I'm starving." Anakisha wished Yanir's council meeting was over so he could join them.

"Me too." Fox smiled at a group of riders as they edged between the full tables. "Mind you, I always have an excellent appetite after a hard day's training."

"You make it sound as if we've been here for years when it's only been a week."

"Good evening, Queen's Rider." A blue guard laid his fist upon his heart and nodded. "I trust you've enjoyed your first few days here?"

"Yes, thank you." Anakisha nodded back. She and Fox continued to wend their way between the tables, the hubbub of the evening conversations rising around them.

Anakisha deliberately chose an empty table in a quiet corner where everyone was out of earshot. They sat down, putting their trays on the table. "I wish they'd really respect me," she said to Fox.

"Everyone here respects you." Fox ate a spoonful of soup. "This is good."

Anakisha leaned in. "I know they appear to respect me. They have to because I'm the Queen's Rider. That makes it even worse, because I feel as if I haven't earned it. I want them to respect me for a real reason, not just for my title."

Fox cracked a smile. "And to think you once wanted to gain respect by being hand-fasted to Justan because of his father's position. That was all about title and not about you at all."

"Ugh. Gods, I was a fool." She rolled her eyes. "But I don't want that with Yanir. He matters too much for me not to be his equal." She tried to swallow down the fear that kept niggling at her. If she mattered to him, wouldn't he have done something about it by now? She'd half expected him to ask her to be hand-fasted at Pa and Mayfree's ceremony. Then again in his pigsty—of all places—when he'd last kissed her.

Maybe he wasn't as keen on her as she'd thought. Maybe...

No, she squashed that thought before it could grow. Yanir wasn't like Justan. He didn't have other girls hiding at Dragons' Hold, waiting for him. But perhaps he thought she wasn't the one for him. Otherwise, why wouldn't he have asked her by now? Or at least, kissed her again. He was always hesitant, holding back.

Anakisha sighed and toyed with her soup, trailing her spoon back and forth. She lifted a spoonful of soup and eyed it before taking a sip.

"I thought you said you were starving," Fox said, eying her bread.

"I am. I'm just thinking."

"Well, don't think too long or I'll bolt the lot for you," he said, tucking into his own dinner with gusto. "So, what makes you think you're not respected?" he asked after a few mouthfuls.

"Everybody here is so good at everything. The mages are brilliant at shooting their mage flame, even the young ones who're still learning. The archers are fantastic—every bit as good as I am.

And on dragonback, they're even better. At least in Fieldhaven, I stood out. Here, I'm supposed to be Queen's Rider, but the only outstanding talent I possess is that I imprinted with Zaarusha."

Fox used his bread to mop up his soup, and chewed it, gazing at her thoughtfully while she ate hers. Finally, he pushed his empty plate aside and spoke. "Anakisha, you're right. I'd like to tell you not to worry because Zaarusha chose you and she knows best, but you're used to being good at things. In Fieldhaven, everybody knew you were a great archer. In the Night Wings, you were respected for your courage. And even in the tavern, you were a quick hand to pour a beer or wipe a table down before anyone ever noticed the beer had spilled. Now, you're here and you're supposed to rule with Yanir, Syan and Zaarusha, but you're a novice."

She beamed. Thank the dragon gods, someone understood.

"You need to gain a talent that makes you stand out from other riders. Something that helps you feel that the accolades they give you are deserved."

"That's exactly it." She couldn't stop her grin growing wider. "Any ideas?"

"Nope, not a thing," said Fox. He winked at her. "But don't worry. Sooner or later, we'll come up with something."

CHAINED

The scorpion was advancing on the girl. Starrus had been feeding off the *sathir* of the fleeing crowd, tugging in their energy and spooling it deep into his core. It wouldn't be enough to save himself and the girl, but he had to try something. Sweat trickled down his forehead and ran into his ear, making him twitch. The chains at his neck rattled.

The scorpion jumped, angling its body toward him.

Oh gods, the clinking chains had attracted it. Starrus' bowels shuddered. Gritting his teeth, he clamped his buttocks until the feeling passed.

A breeze drifted across the arena, ruffling his hair. The scorpion jumped closer. His shrotty blond hair—his pride and joy—had grabbed the creature's attention. Starrus gulped.

The girl was frozen, as still as an opaline statue, as the scorpion passed her and stalked toward Starrus.

He trembled, his chains clattering. Oh gods, oh gods, oh gods. He hadn't trained for all these years just to lose control now. Starrus yanked on every bit of *sathir* he could and coiled it tight inside his belly. The scorpion's shadow fell over him. The enormous creature raised its pincers and lunged. The beast plunged its pincer at his leg, grasping the chains. The shock jolted Starrus and he nearly lost control of his *sathir*. The beast recoiled and clacked its pincers, the echoes skittering down Starrus' spine.

The black death stalker lunged again, this time, to grasp his arm. The thud of the pincer hitting the iron chains reverberated through Starrus' bones. It tried again, lunging, its pincers clattering off the chains that bound his chest. The blow sent pain ricocheting through Starrus' ribs. Gods, he couldn't lose control. He had to have more *sathir,* or he'd never get out alive. The scorpion pounded the chains on his chest again, making his rib cage ache.

This close, Starrus could see the scorpion's four beady eyes, two on top of its head and the other two on either side of the bulge, above the suckers it would use to drain his body fluids when it had him in its grasp. It peered at him, pincers waving above his head, the fine hairs bristling on its jaws.

Shaking like a leaf tossed on a storm, Starrus sucked in *sathir.* His clanking chains angered the beast, as if it thought it was being challenged, but Starrus couldn't help trembling as he faced certain death.

The death stalker reeled back, raised its tail, and squirted dark venom over Starrus' face. Starrus screamed, his mouth filling with the bitter stuff. His tongue curled and spasmed, growing thick in his throat. Venom ran under his eyelids, burning his eyeballs. The fluid seared across his skin, scraping it raw. His face felt as if it was about to erupt.

In a blaze of pain, Starrus let go.

§

Giddi jumped the barrier without thinking. He thudded to the arena's cobbles, a jolt of pain running from his ankle to his knee. Ignoring it, he raced across the arena toward Starrus. His trainer was screaming in agony, his face covered in venom and bubbling into blisters. The scorpion towered over Starrus, tail raised to strike again.

Starrus' scream was cut off in a blast of lightning that flashed across the arena. Molten iron burst from the chains around Starrus' body, spraying the walls and hailing down on the cobbles. It peppered the scorpion.

His trainer had burst his chains.

Starrus leaped to his feet and ran toward the barred double doors behind him. Mage flame shot from his hands, blasting through the wood and making a hole in the door. Starrus vanished into the hole.

The scorpion reared, flecks of hot metal shining on its black carapace. It landed on its feet and twisted and writhed, trying to buck the steaming metal off its shell.

And then it spied the girl, still chained to the stake in the center of the arena. The scorpion made a beeline for the girl, pincers out and tail raised.

By the dragon gods! Giddi shot a blast of mage flame at the girl's chain, shearing it in two.

"Run," he bellowed. "Run!"

Dust gusting at her feet, the girl scampered after Starrus.

Leaving Giddi to face the enraged beast.

A sheet of dark venom flew at Giddi. He ducked and shielded himself with a gust of wind that drove the venom back at the black death stalker. The venom hit the scorpion, sliding off its shell. Carapace dripping, the scorpion writhed and bucked, slashing at its eyes with its pincers.

Giddi flung out his hands and released the *sathir* that had been building as he'd anxiously sat through the trials. A wall of green flame shot from his hands. Oh gods, no! He could set the whole arena alight. Remembering the Fieldhaven tournament, he forced the flame into a spear that hit the scorpion, obliterating it and spraying the walls of the arena with chunks of carapace and splattered scorpion guts.

A smoking leg flew through the air and landed at his foot. He kicked it and strode from the arena, a trumpet blast ringing in his ears.

ZAARUSHA

Anakisha stretched out in the four-poster bed in her cavern. They'd spared no effort in making her feel at home, providing her with a huge cavern, a closet full of riders' garb and beautiful robes, and an enormous metal tub to bathe in. During the day, sunlight streamed through a hole in a stone ceiling, but now the stars twinkled in the clear night sky.

"Do you want me to close the skylight?" Zaarusha asked, snaking her head through an enormous archway that led out to her den and the ledge they regularly took off from. *"There's a stone I can roll over it if it rains."*

"No, I'm enjoying the view." Anakisha's breath huffed out in the cool air.

"Aren't you cold?"

"My quilt is warm enough." She wriggled further under the mound of snowy-white fabric. *"Although it would look better if I embroidered dragons on it. I saw some gold thread in a cupboard yesterday. Maybe I'll embroider gold ones that look like you in a sunrise."*

"I'm flattered." Zaarusha went back into her den. Soon, dragon snores rumbled through the cavern.

Anakisha punched her pillow and rolled over, but she couldn't sleep. She'd tried to talk to Yanir about how she'd felt, but he'd been distracted with preparing for yet another council meeting. And while Fox understood, he hadn't come up with any brilliant ideas yet. Neither had she.

She rolled over again, counted a few stars and gave up trying to sleep. She mind-melded with Zaarusha, *"Zaarusha?"*

"*Yes?*" the queen answered sleepily.

"*I have to prove myself as Queen's Rider.*"

Zaarusha's sigh was like the rustle of autumn leaves. "*I've told you that you don't have to prove anything. Everyone accepts you.*"

"*How does that help me if I can't accept myself? I need a talent, something I'm really good at. I have to do something different. Anything.*"

"*You did do something different. You imprinted with me. Besides, you're an excellent archer,*" Zaarusha replied.

Anakisha pulled the covers up under her chin. "*I know, but I'm only as good as many of the riders here. It's not enough. I need to be more.*"

"*You're enough for me.*"

"*But I'm not enough for myself.*"

"*That's troublesome.*" The queen snaked her head into Anakisha's chamber, huffing warm air into her cavern. "*What would you like to do?*"

"*What are the qualities you chose me for?*"

"*Your courage, bravery and determination.*"

"*Therefore, I need to be determined to have courage and be brave.*"

The Queen chuckled. "*You already are—it's in your nature.*"

"*But nobody knows that—and I'll never have a chance to prove myself unless it's in battle.*" Anakisha nestled into the soft white pillows.

"*They'll see it in time.*"

A moment later, Anakisha was bolt upright in bed. "*In return for visiting Lush Valley, Yanir promised me that I could determine my own training.*"

Zaarusha's golden eyes regarded her steadily. "*But we didn't visit Lush Valley. He was shot instead.*"

"*No we didn't, but it was no fault of mine. He still gave me permission to determine my own training regime.*"

"I remember it well. I'm assuming you'd like to fall off dragonback so I can practice rescuing you?"

Anakisha grinned. "No," she said. "I'd like to go further than that. I'd like to be known as the most daring dragon rider in the realm. And I'd like to start now."

"Now? But you're in bed."

"Not for long." Anakisha leaped up and grabbed her riders' garb. "Fox will be thrilled to hear we have a plan. Please mind-meld with Foxita and ask Fox to meet us at the plateau above the training grounds."

Emperor Haakin

Starrus' facial wounds were doused with water and treated with a salve against the venom. The guard who treated him said he'd been lucky he'd been bathed in sweat because the layer of moisture had prevented the venom from doing more damage.

Giddi hid a grimace. No doubt Starrus' buildup of sathir had helped too. But the damage was bad enough: Starrus' face was raw and covered in blisters; one of his eyes was swollen shut; and his hair had turned white from shock. The dragon gods knew what he'd look like when he was healed. One thing was sure: Starrus would no longer have the pretty face he'd been proud of.

As slaves cleaned the arena and ushered spectators away from the scorpion's carnage, six guards marched Giddi, the girl from the market, and Starrus—whose face was now swathed in bandages— up a terrace behind the arena to the emperor's palace.

The final stretch of road to the palace was laid in white marble tiles. A broad sweeping staircase rose to a terrace in front of the palace which was shaded by an elegant porch supported by pillars, all in the same gleaming white marble. The palace's pristine marble walls were inlaid with stars of glistening gold. A broad expanse of tiled ground ran around the palace, bordered by lush vegetation and towering palms. A river flowed through a marbled channel into a pool, then ran off into a waterfall that cascaded down to the lower terraces. The palace was at the heart of the oasis.

The guards kept their spears at the ready, their eyes sliding to Starrus' and Giddi's hands as if bolts of mage flame could fly from their fingers at any moment. Giddi snorted. If he and Starrus were threatened, the guards' fears could be realized, but he'd had enough theatrics for one day. He wanted to know where the Scarlet Hand was and get on with hunting down Master Mage Findal.

The girl slid her hand into his and looked up at him with her large brown eyes. Giddi squeezed her fingers, glad the young girl was still alive.

She murmured something in Robandi.

Starrus gave a snide smile. "She says she'll protect you because you protected her."

He smiled at the girl and nodded. If only his trainer would also protect him, but Giddi had no illusions about Starrus. He'd not only resented his intervention in the arena, but resented him since his powers had manifested. The shrotty idiot should be thankful he was alive. After this, Giddi would insist Starrus take him to his father.

The guards halted on the terrace. From here, beyond the hillside cascading with pools and terraces of sandstone houses, the harbor was a sweeping crescent fringed with piers and docked ships, and edged by two tangerine hills that jutted out at either end. Giddi checked again—all the sails in the harbor were either white or the beige-gray of dirty canvas.

Starrus leaned in. "The emperor met with the Scarlet Hand. Rumors say he knows where the pirate is—that the Scarlet Hand may be about the emperor's business."

"I know."

"What do you mean, 'you know'?" Starrus hissed.

With his bandages over his face and his eye swollen shut, his trainer would've looked comical if he wasn't so pitiful. Giddi waved an airy hand. "It's common knowledge around here." Thankfully, the girl next to him in the arena and her uncle had spoken his tongue.

The guards marched them past wrought-iron tables and cushioned benches on the terrace and took them through an arched entranceway. "We'll wait here," one said, pausing on a rug that stretched from wall to wall and ran the length of the broad hallway. Decorated with cavorting sea dragons in lapis and jade on a creamy background, the rug was so thick that Giddi's boots sank into it. He wished he could remove them and feel the soft pile against his bare feet.

Oh gods, he longed to go home, wished he could be with Ma and Pa, sitting on their rug in front of the hearth as a littling again, listening to Pa's tales of the quests he'd been on and how he'd wielded his magic to protect the realm.

"I saved your life," Giddi muttered to Starrus. "I expect you to take me to my father as soon as possible."

Starrus turned to Giddi stiffly, wincing at the movement. "I'll take you to him today."

Today? Pa was in Metropoli! By the First Egg! Giddi's body coiled with joy. He automatically tightened his grip on the girl's hand. She cried out. "Sorry," he mumbled, dropping her hand.

A servant in a long red robe with dark hair that hung to her waist and a headdress edged with golden discs approached them and led the party down the long hallway.

The little girl hung back, until Giddi placed a reassuring hand on her shoulder. The guards surrounded them and marshaled them after the servant, who led them to a white door, also embellished with painted sea dragons.

"You have an audience with the emperor," she said to Giddi. "You have the right to ask one question only, so make sure you ask it well."

"We will," Starrus answered.

The servant appraised Starrus, staring down her nose at him. "You don't have the right to ask anything. General Vizza informed me that you abandoned the girl to the scorpion and left her undefended—therefore you did not pass your final trial."

"But, I—" Starrus blustered.

"I heard you did admirably on the other trials," she added with a charming smile, leaving Starrus gaping. She turned to Giddi. "You saved the girl. Do you wish these two to accompany you or do you wish to see the highly-esteemed Emperor Haakin, ruler of Metropoli, alone?"

Haakin—so Aquaria was right. The drink was named after the ruler. "I-I, ah, all of us," Giddi stammered. Gods, he hadn't expected that.

Starrus glared out of his bandages, his only open eye wild. His fists were bunched at his side as if he were straining not to kill Giddi in a blaze of mage flame.

The servant ushered them inside a wide white-tiled room, with tapestries on the walls. On the far side of the room, the emperor was seated on a carved throne edged in gilt. General Vizza was standing at his right shoulder. He and Emperor Haakin were flanked by two bolt-flingers with cross bows trained on their visitors. Three guards stood to either side of the bolt-flingers, spears at the ready.

Power was in every line of the emperor's body: the hard set of his jaw; the coiled muscles of his thighs draped in pristine white silk; his blunt fingers with carefully-manicured nails. The same golden buttons adorned his tunic as General Vizza's. Giddi arched an eyebrow at the sea dragon emblems on those buttons. Perhaps the emperor knew Aquaria. Perhaps she could influence him if he needed it.

The emperor's glittering gaze landed on Starrus, then slid to Giddi.

Giddi's palms broke out in beads of sweat. His scalp prickled under that hard, unwavering gaze. This was a man who never made compromises. Who'd never had to beg for bread in the market. He was in absolute power over his dominion with an army at his manicured fingertips.

The young girl at Giddi's side trembled.

"Ah, Starrus, we meet again." Emperor Haakin nodded, his gaze as sharp as daggers.

So, Starrus had not only crossed the emperor, but knew him. News indeed.

"And who is this?" the emperor asked General Vizza, waving a hand at Giddi.

General Vizza leaned in. "I'd guess he's the son of Gideon. You see the resemblance?"

"He is," said Starrus. "His name is Giddi. He's my trainee."

"For his sake, I hope you treat him better than you treated your master," General Vizza snapped.

"You know my father?" Giddi blurted. "Do you know where he is?"

A short nod was the Emperor Haakin's only reply.

"Focus," Starrus hissed. "You only have one question."

A smile broke across General Vizza's face, reminding Giddi of a viper about to strike. "You have used your single question and the highly-esteemed Emperor Haakin has given his answer with his nod."

"But—"

"There are no buts, Giddi, son of Gideon. When I knew Gideon, he was a man of honor and understood the rules of this court." General Vizza's black gaze landed on Starrus as if he could sear him to the core and obliterate him, the way Giddi had destroyed the scorpion.

"I agree." The emperor nodded again, as if to rub salt in Giddi's wound. "Escort them out of Metropoli. They killed my black death stalker. I never want to see them again. Consider it a favor that I don't have them executed on the spot."

"And the girl?" Giddi interjected.

Emperor Haakin raised an eyebrow. "She has served her purpose. If she is caught stealing again, I will kill her."

General Vizza repeated the phase in Robandi. The girl touched her shaking hand to her heart and bowed deeply. Then the general addressed the emperor. "Would you care to execute Starrus for his past crimes, highly-esteemed Emperor Haakin?"

The emperor waved a hand. "The entertainment we had today in the arena has paid his debt, and Starrus will continue to pay it every time he sees his face in a looking glass. I'd rather he lives and suffers."

"Very well," Vizza replied. He gestured to the guards.

The guards marched Giddi, the girl and Starrus out of the room at spear point, the bolt-flingers following with their bows trained on their backs. When they were out on the terrace, a servant brought four black stallions to the foot of the stairs. The horses stamped their hooves and tossed their heads, their glossy midnight flanks rippling.

"We can't leave Metropoli," Giddi said to Starrus. "I have to see my father."

"Don't worry. He's not in the city center. In fact, he's near where they'll probably drop us," replied Starrus. "You'll finally get to see your pa. I bet you're looking forward to it."

With all those bandages over his face, Giddi couldn't tell what Starrus was thinking, but there was an odd edge to his voice that made Giddi's neck hairs prickle. But right now, despite his excitement at soon seeing Pa, he had to take care of the girl.

Crouching in front of her, Giddi extracted a pearl and a scorpion from his coin pouch. The girl's eyes widened. "You mustn't steal again," Giddi whispered.

She took the gift silently, then flung her arms around Giddi's neck, clinging to him, as the guards helped Starrus onto a horse. Giddi hoisted the girl onto another and clambered up into the saddle behind her. The two bolt-flingers mounted their horses, taking turns at training their arrows on Giddi.

Starrus rolled his good eye, no doubt annoyed that the bolt-flingers considered Giddi the greater threat.

The guards bound Starrus' and Giddi's hands—as if that would stop them using mage flame—and the horses trotted down the terraces, crowds of people coming out to stare at them as they made their way down toward the marketplace. Some waved, some booed, and some called out to the girl on Giddi's horse.

When they reached the barren cactus garden and the old men on the benches, the crowd at the market had thinned to a few early evening hagglers and some stall holders still plying their wares. The old men were still on the benches, but only one child was with them now—the girl's little brother, asleep in the fleshier man's arms. The girl turned in the saddle and flung her arms around Giddi again, her little heart beating like a trapped bird against his chest. With his hands bound, he was unable to hug her back, so Giddi kissed her hair. Gods, without hands, he had no way of stopping his horse to let her down.

One of the guards clucked his tongue and all of the horses halted.

"Well-trained. Fine horseflesh, these Robandi desert horses," Starrus muttered to no one in particular.

The girl slid off the horse, giving Giddi a quick wave, then raced over to the two elderly gentlemen and her brother. Sobbing, the thin man bounded to his feet and swept her into his arms, spinning her around. The girl pointed at Giddi and babbled in rapid Robandi, gesturing at the treasure enclosed in her fist. The man's sobs turned to laughs and tears ran freely down his face.

Soon. Giddi swallowed. Soon, he would be reunited with his father. With someone who loved him.

The horses picked their way through Metropoli's winding alleys until they reached the dusty strip of road where Giddi had arrived with Aquaria. Gods, had it only been yesterday? It felt like a lifetime had passed since he'd been abandoned by Starrus in the desert.

A guard cut their bindings, freeing their hands. Starrus and Giddi dismounted. Giddi shook the blood back into his fuzzy fingers, flexing them.

One of the bolt-flingers swiveled, training an arrow on Giddi. "Keep your hands still."

"I'm not stupid enough to try anything," Giddi muttered.

"Just stupid enough to ruin our only chance to ask Emperor Haakin about the Scarlet Hand," Starrus snapped.

Giddi's shoulders slumped. "At least I killed the scorpion," he hissed.

"Which is why Emperor Haakin is mad with us." Starrus' one-eyed glare could peel skin.

Giddi stifled a smirk. No one was in danger of having peeled skin around here except Starrus.

The guards broke into their argument, gesturing to the docks where ships were moored along the coast. "Book your passages to Naobia," one of them said.

A bolt-flinger nodded. "You'd better book tonight, then stay on board. Tomorrow, we'll scour the city for you. There will be no warning, only an arrow through your hearts if we find you."

Giddi swallowed. He would finally find his father, only to have to leave him again. His chest ached. He'd been so close. He'd messed up. Perhaps he could disguise himself, hide out somewhere and stay...

But where? The Robandi dessert was inhospitable, and he was banned from Metropoli.

Starrus nodded at the guards gruffly. "Thank you for your escort, gentlemen. We'll be on board a ship tonight and gone by tomorrow."

The guards and bolt-flingers left, their horses' hooves stirring the dust and leaving Giddi and Starrus coated in fine grit.

"By the flaming butt end of a dragon, you've promised me forever that you'd take me to Pa, and now that we finally have the chance, I'll have to leave again." Giddi glared at his trainer, wishing he could blast a nearby date palm into smithereens.

"Follow me," Starrus said. "You'll see your Pa soon enough, but you may not like what he's become."

"Don't be stupid," Giddi snapped, suddenly weary.

Starrus led him along the narrow strip of dusty land. They came to the base of a cliff that jutted out into the harbor, forming half of the crescent that shaped the bay, and followed the trail out onto the spit. Halfway along the thin strip of sand, the trail headed up the hill through some desert scrub.

Not yet recovered from the venom, Starrus huffed and puffed up the sandy trail, while Giddi meandered after him. What a strange place for Pa to live, out here on a spit on the edge of the bay. There wasn't even a house in sight, just a few boulders at the top of the cliff.

Giddi grinned, remembering the time Pa had helped him build a tree hut in the woods. He'd been about six summers old and come home long-faced and glum after his efforts had failed.

With Pa's arm around Giddi shoulders, they strode back into the woods. When they reached the site of Giddi's fort, Pa nodded wisely and pointed to a lone stick Giddi had managed to place across two sturdy strongwood boughs. "So, I guess that's the floor?" Pa asked. A couple of sticks were propped on the boughs, leaning against the branches above. Pa waved a hand at them. "And this is a wall, isn't it?"

Giddi nodded, embarrassed that his hut was so spindly, but gratified Pa had at least recognized his efforts.

"You've chosen an excellent site, son. These boughs are strong enough to support a small hut. And look at the great pile of wood you've collected." Pa gestured at the heap of sticks and branches at the base of the strongwood trunk. "That must've taken you all day."

"It did." Giddi sighed, his shoulders slumping.

"I guess your biggest problem is that at six summers old you can't reach things very well."

A fat tear rolled down Giddi's cheek. "I worked all day on this, Pa." And he'd failed.

Pa nodded grimly. "And the sun is about to set. Your ma wants us home soon for supper." Pa scratched his chin and crouched down to Giddi's height. He wiped Giddi's cheek with the edge of his sleeve. "Would you object if I helped you?"

Giddi clapped his hands. "Oh, Pa, I was too afraid to ask." He sniffed. "I thought you'd think I wasn't a real man if I asked for help."

"One of the keys to being a real man is knowing when to get help and how to learn from those who help you," Pa said sagely. "You've just passed that test, son. I'd be honored to help you if you'll let me."

"Please, Pa."

Pa beamed as if Giddi had just given him a delicious treat on market day. "Thanks, son. However, it's your fort, so I'll need some guidance. Would you like me to finish the entire fort for you, or would you rather do some work on it yourself?"

Giddi gauged his father. "Um, I'd be happy to do the inside," he said hopefully.

Pa laughed. "If we're going to get home in time for supper, we'll need to be quick or Ma will send us outside to eat with the chickens." He winked. "Shall we use a little magic?"

Giddi grinned.

Pa waved his hand, and two stout sticks from Giddi's pile rose into the air and wended their way through the branches to land across the boughs. More sticks from the pile followed, neatly landing on the boughs side by side, until a floor had formed. "Do you think it'll hold like that?"

"I doubt it," Giddi said. "Not in a storm."

"Good thinking. What could we use to bind them to the boughs?"

Giddi gazed around the forest. "We'll harm the strongwood if we use nails, so I thought I could use those vines." He strode to some bushes and yanked at the end of the thick vines wrapped around them. The harder he tugged, the tighter the vine's grip grew. He panted and turned to Pa. "I guess I need more help or Ma will make us eat with the chickens."

"And sleep with the wolves outside," Pa said in mock seriousness. He waved a hand, and the vines whipped through the air, untangling themselves, then wrapped themselves around the sticks, fastening them to the strongwood boughs.

The forest had grown darker. Somewhere in the distance a wolf howled.

Giddi stepped closer to Pa, relieved when his father's warm arm rested on his shoulder again. Tiny pinpoints of light darted among the strongwood branches around his tree hut. "Pa, what are those?"

"Spangles, my son. You're very lucky you have the gift of seeing them. Most can't."

"What are they doing?"

"I guess they approve of your dwelling. Well done, son."

Giddi yawned.

"I'm pretty exhausted after all that," Pa said. "Shall we head home for supper now, and come back to do the walls tomorrow?"

At Giddi's eager nod, Pa draped his mage cloak over his son's shoulders and they strode home together, planning how Giddi could decorate the inside of his hut.

Perhaps Pa worked here out on the spit, or lived on the other side of the hill in the next bay. That must be it. "How long does it take to get to the next bay?" Giddi asked. Dusk was closing in.

"Don't know," Starrus panted, stopping to gaze back at Metropoli.

"Come on," said Giddi. "I know you're tired, but this is the only chance I'll get to see Pa in years, and we barely have any time." He pushed past Starrus up the path, racing until he reached a cliff-top plateau covered in boulders and low scrub.

The bay swept to his left in a huge curve, the docks and ships visible in the lights of the lanterns from Metropoli. On the other side of the cliff, rugged coastline stretched to the north, towering sandstone cliffs hiding the inlets and bays he'd visited on his way here with Aquaria. There were no houses, not a single cottage in sight.

Starrus staggered onto the sandy plateau, and leaned on a boulder.

Giddi rounded on his trainer, his hands on his hips. "Is this your idea of a joke?"

Starrus' uninjured eye was grave and his voice somber. "No, it's not funny at all. I told you for years I'd take you to your father."

"And now you can't?"

"Yes, I can." Starrus took a few deep breaths and then led Giddi past the boulders, through a trail in the scrub. They came to some paving stones set in the sand. Mage light flared at his trainer's fingers, casting the paving stones in an eerie green glow.

There were names on each of them. Names. Ashad, Metzfar, Rotan and…

… Gideon.

Graves.

Starrus had brought him to his father's grave. Starrus had known for years that his father was dead, and never told him. Never told Ma.

"How did he die?" A hoarse whisper ripped from Giddi's throat.

Starrus shrugged. "Does it matter?"

"Yes. It matters. He matters to me." Giddi pounded his chest, a violent shudder ripping through him. He wanted to curse these stones, blast them with mage flame, and shatter them into tiny pieces.

And then ram them down Starrus' throat.

He'd stayed with this vile man, been strangled by a sea monster, hurt, humiliated and maltreated—all so he could see his father again. And this was it. A shrotty stone on the sand in a land he could never visit again.

Giddi pounded his chest. "I wanted to see my father," he cried. "You promised me."

He'd lost the last member of his family. He was orphaned.

"I promised you nothing except to show you the whereabouts of your father, which I have done."

It was exactly what Starrus had promised him each time he'd asked.

Another shudder ran through Giddi. He dropped to his knees in front of the stone, and held up his hands, crackling with light. He ran a finger over the letters of his father's name.

G. Pa had loved him.

I. He'd loved Ma too.

D. Pa was a powerful mage, one of the best.

E. He never would've abandoned them.

O. Something must've happened.

N. Starrus knew.

"I asked you how my father died."

Starrus' gaze slid out to sea, then flitted back to Giddi. His mouth tightened, but he remained silent.

With a jolt, Giddi knew. He struggled to restrain his power as his magic crackled through his veins. "How did he die?" he demanded. His scalp prickled, the static from his magic making his hair stand on end.

Starrus compressed his lips and shrugged.

Giddi stood over him, lightning crackling from his fingertips and flying into the ground around Starrus' feet, carving channels in the earth. Dust flew and particles of sandstone pelted their breeches. Gods, he was losing it. Giddi reined in his power, pulling the bucking mage flame back into his core.

The dust settled, leaving dark furrows in the ground around Starrus. Pale-faced, Starrus babbled, "It wasn't my fault. It was an accident."

"What happened?"

"The story is not mine to tell."

"You're talking about my father, you good-for-nothing, shrotty, trumped up piece of dragon dung. How dare you refuse to tell me." Two forks of lightning bounded from Giddi's hands, surging over Starrus' body, wrapping themselves around his neck and lifting him into the air. The stench of fresh lightning left a bitter tang in Giddi's nostrils.

Giddi gasped as his trainer hung suspended by the light flying from his own fingertips. And then General Vizza's words came back to him: *"Starrus, I hope you treat Giddi better than you treated your master."*

"You killed him, didn't you?"

Starrus replied smoothly, "Of course not."

"I know you did. How did it happen?" Giddi shook his hands, rattling Starrus' jaw and making his feet sway in the air.

"He forced me. It was a magical accident. He pushed me too far and my powers exploded. It wasn't my fault."

"Just like the sea monster wasn't your fault. Just like leaving me tied up in the desert wasn't your fault. What in fang's name did you do to Pa?"

Starrus gurgled, grasping at his throat. His eyes bulged.

Giddi's heart faltered. By the dragon gods, he was killing his trainer.

He was as bad as Starrus.

ANTICS

Zaarusha rose off the ledge outside her den into the dark sky. She glided along the peaks on the south side of the basin and flapped up to land on a plateau high above the main cavern. Apart from Foxita, who was lifting off a ledge outside Fox's cavern, there wasn't a dragon in the sky. Most of the dragon riders were in bed, except Yanir, Master Taren, Seppi and Master Mage Balovar, who were deep in a council meeting.

She sighed, relieved she was still in training and didn't yet have to make some of the weightier political decisions that faced Yanir. Although all those endless council meetings and her rigorous training schedule did mean she was spending less time with him than she'd like.

Far beyond the dark fields, nestled in the blackness of the forest, the lake shone silver in the moonlight. The same rays glimmered on snowy peaks of Dragon's Teeth that ringed the quiet basin.

"Dragons' Hold is beautiful, Zaarusha. Thank you for giving me a new life beyond Fieldhaven, a life far bigger than anything I could've found myself."

"You're welcome. My life is complete with you as my rider and Syan as my mate. Together, with Yanir, we'll protect Dragons' Realm."

With Yanir. There was that. He'd been carefree and loving in Naobia, distant when they'd reached Montanara—until he'd kissed her in the pigsty—but since then, he'd been aloof again. He was always respectful, fun, and full of admiration, like a best friend. But Anakisha didn't want a best friend. She wanted more. *"Men are so complicated, Zaarusha."*

"They are," she agreed. "*Dragons are much simpler. I knew Syan liked me when he bit my tail.*"

"*He bit your tail?*"

"*He did indeed. That was before he bit my throat. Then I knew he loved me.*" She snorted, her breath steaming in the cool night air. "*Human mating rituals are so complex. I don't even try to understand them.*" She hesitated. "*There's no point in me suggesting you bite Yanir's tail to tell him you're interested, because he doesn't have one. Biting his neck may not help either.*"

Anakisha leaned over the saddle and flung her arms around Zaarusha's neck. "*Thank you.*"

"*Whatever for?*"

"*Making me smile.*"

Foxita arrowed down to land on the plateau near the dragon queen, her talons scrabbling among the shale.

Fox clambered off her back and strode over to Zaarusha and Anakisha. "Foxita tells me you have a daring plan?"

"I do indeed," Anakisha replied. "You remember how you taught me to jump the roofs in Fieldhaven?"

"Yes." He nodded, his freckles standing out in the moonlight. "It was all about the right approach. Your run up and the way you positioned your feet determined your success in leaping the gap to the next gutter." He grinned. "And even though you doubted yourself, you made it every time—as long as you followed my instructions."

"Now we're going to follow Zaarusha's instructions. Foxita is young and still in training, but Zaarusha reassures me that her reflexes are just as fast as any dragon's. You're agile and fit, and so am I. There's nothing to stop us attempting what I'd like to do. Please, place your hand upon Zaarusha's forehead. She'll show you what we have in mind."

Zaarusha turned her head, angling it down toward Fox. He placed his hand upon the queen's head. A wild grin broke out across his face. "I'm in," he said. "This looks like fun."

"We'll take turns," said Anakisha. "I'll try first, then you and Foxita can mimic what Zaarusha and I do. But be careful," she said. "It's risky."

Anakisha undid the straps of her harness as Zaarusha took off into the night sky. The swish of her wings was the only sound above the deserted basin. They scaled the mountain peak, climbing higher, the snow glimmering in the faint moonlight.

"Are you ready, Anakisha?" Zaarusha asked. *"Let your body loosen. If you're scared or tense, you could break a bone when I catch you, so relax. You do trust me, don't you?"*

"I do." Anakisha let go of the saddle and tilted her body sideways, slipping off Zaarusha's back. Air tugged at her hair, whipping it across her face. She tumbled through the sky, deliberately letting her body stay limp.

Exhilaration rushed through her, setting her veins on fire. But, as Zaarusha rapidly grew smaller, terror gripped her, stiffening her bones and making her muscles rigid. Oh gods, oh gods, she was going to die. Her foolish vanity—her need to be someone special—would be the death of her. A scream built in her throat, but before it released, Zaarusha was in her mind. A wave of comfort rushed over her.

"Anakisha, you said you trusted me. Relax. Let your muscles go loose." Zaarusha dived, her wings tucked tightly against her body, racing after Anakisha.

"I can't." Her whole body was coiled, braced for impact.

"Close your eyes and imagine you're in a warm bath."

Anakisha forced herself to take a deep breath as she hurtled through the air. She didn't dare close her eyes, but she did breathe slowly, concentrating on her muscles loosening, until she was a limp as an empty sack.

"*That's it.*" Zaarusha was nearer now. Anakisha could make out her golden eyes. "*Stay relaxed.*"

Anakisha twisted. The treetops were racing toward her, but she was no longer afraid.

Zaarusha's wings swished. A jolt ran through Anakisha as her dragon plucked her up in her talons. She reached up and clung to Zaarusha's forelegs, her heart pounding and her blood singing.

"*That was incredible. I've never felt anything like it.*"

"*I'm glad you enjoyed it,*" the queen thrummed. "*Next time, I'll dive a little sooner.*" Her wings beat strongly and the wind caressed Anakisha's face as she hung, her body loose and as light as a feather in the queen's grip as they winged their way back up the mountainside into the dark sky.

Zaarusha shot up to the top of the mountains and Anakisha breathed deeply, filling her lungs with air and holding it before exhaling.

"*The air at Dragons' Hold is thinner than in the flatlands where you grew up, but your body will soon adjust,*" Zaarusha said. "*In a few weeks you won't have to deep breathe anymore.*"

"*It feels so different traveling beneath you instead of riding you.*" There was nothing below Anakisha's boots except empty sky and the snowy peak. No saddle, no scales, just air. It was the strangest sensation—she felt as free as a bird. Or a dragon.

Zaarusha chuckled. "*We'll try again, but Foxita is getting impatient, so we'd better make sure she and Fox don't do anything silly.*"

"*As silly as us, you mean.*" Anakisha chuckled. "*I'm ready to try again when you are.*"

Zaarusha gently spiraled down to the plateau.

When she was an arm's length above the rocky plateau, Anakisha mind-melded, "*You can let go now.*"

Zaarusha's talons uncurled. Anakisha dropped and rolled, then sprang to her feet.

Fox raced over, his face alight. He grabbed her arms, grinning. "You're mad, absolutely mad! By the First Egg, I'm glad you're alive." He hugged her.

"Me too." She grinned so hard her face hurt.

"I can't believe it, Anakisha! That was amazing. Can I try too?" Zaarusha nodded.

"Whatever you do, you must relax or the impact of Foxita grabbing you might break a bone," Anakisha warned him.

Fox bounded like a deer over to Foxita, then climbed into her saddle. Foxita was airborne moments later, flying up the mountainside.

"I'll make sure we don't lose anyone tonight." Zaarusha sprang into the air and flew down to circle above the forest. *"If Foxita misses him, I'll be waiting."*

"Good plan." By the First Egg, if they lost Fox tonight, it'd be her fault for suggesting such daft training.

Foxita was high above the mountain peak when Fox jumped. He was a tiny dark blob plunging through the air down the snowy mountainside.

Anakisha's pulse hammered. By the dragon gods, what had she been thinking?

Foxita dived after Fox, her tail streaming out above her. Anakisha held her breath, unable to rip her eyes from that tiny figure dropping toward the rock face and trees below.

Fox's blue dragon swooped and plucked Fox out of the air with her talons. Anakisha's breath whooshed out of her. She drew in great gulps of air. Thank the dragon gods he was all right.

Foxita swooped onto the plateau and let Fox down. "I did it! I did it! I did it!" he cried, jumping around like an excited rabbit in springtime.

She couldn't help laughing. "Not too loud or we'll have all the dragons in the realm finding out what we're up to."

He grinned. "After your next turn, I want another one, too."

They took turns, practicing for over an hour until Zaarusha decided they'd had enough. *"It's late and you both have training tomorrow, but I've told Foxita we'll meet here again tomorrow night,"* Zaarusha mind-melded. *"I'm afraid regular flight is going to seem rather boring from now on, but I'm sure we can achieve some fancy stunts that will truly make you a respected and revered Queen's Rider."*

"Zaarusha's asking if you want to meet again tomorrow night?" Anakisha raised her eyebrows at Fox.

"We'll be here." Fox grinned. "And I promise we won't breathe a word to Yanir or King Syan."

Anakisha cringed. Despite their agreement near Lush Valley, Yanir would be livid if he knew what they were up to.

REVELATION

Starrus dangled in midair suspended by Giddi's crackling power, his feet swaying and body juddering. Giddi slipped into his mind. He was about to demand again how his father had died, when a sequence of rapid memories rushed through Starrus' head.

Starrus strode down an alley in the poorest quarter in Metropoli. It was halfway between midnight and dawn, the best time for clandestine business. Glancing around, he sidled up to a warehouse door, opened it, and slipped inside. Making his way through the dimness, past bulky barrels of aromatic oil and crates laden with goods, he headed toward the faint glow of a lantern behind the stacks at the back of the storage facility.

Light was glimmering at the end of a long passage between crates piled higher than two men—the perfect setup for an ambush. For a moment, Starrus hesitated, his pulse pounding in his temples, then he remembered why he was here and plunged into the narrow corridor between the goods. Edging sideways through the gap, he made his way toward the dim glow. He rounded a corner, and a burly figure leaped toward him, blade flashing as it angled toward his throat.

Mage fire sprang to life at Starrus' fingertips. "It's just me." He held his hand up, illuminating his face.

White teeth flashed in a smile. The thug sheathed his blade and clapped Starrus on the shoulder. "Along here."

They rounded the pile of crates. A small chest of honeyed wood was bathed in the lantern's glow. The lid was carved with sea serpents, the golden flakes on their scales gleaming. With their claws out and their fangs bared, the creatures were a majestic sight.

"I wasn't expecting such an ostentatious case," said Starrus. Lifting a hand, he let a mage light spring from his fingertips. The blob of flame bobbed over the chest, illuminating the detail of the fine carvings.

"And I wasn't expecting such ostentatious lighting." The thug grinned, pushing back the sleeves of his sweater, revealing anchors tattooed upon forearms that were as thick as the trunk of a young strongwood. "Show me the gold and I'll show you what you're here for."

Starrus extinguished his mage light. "I could blast you with a plume of mage flame that would leave you as nothing but ashes." He gave an arrogant laugh. "What makes you think I bothered to bring the gold?"

"Because you want the goods." The thug let his gaze travel from Starrus' boots, up his body and over his head.

Slowly, Starrus tilted his face up to the roof.

His pulse thundered. By the shrotty dragon gods. It was a set up. Perched on the rafters were four archers with arrows nocked to their bows, aiming right at him. He could toss a sweeping arc of mage flame and exterminate them like pesky vermin, but one was bound to kill him first.

He smiled. "Well played. Of course, I was only joking."

"I wasn't." The man's gaze glittered like black pearls. "Now, shall we get this over with? The gold, please."

Starrus reached inside his cloak into a hidden pocket. His hand grasped the solid weight and lifted it out. He opened his hand to display a gold nugget half the size of his palm. It was stamped with a star—Emperor Haakin's insignia.

The man sucked in his breath. His eyes shot to Starrus' face, his gaze suddenly penetrating. "You expect me to take gold stolen from the emperor's mines?"

Starrus closed his fingers over the nugget and pretended to slip it back into his pocket.

"No, wait." The thug licked his lips.

"Hey, boss, should we kill him and take the gold anyway?" one of the archers hissed.

The burly sailor shook his head. "No, let him have the dragon egg. With that older mage poking his nose around, these things are getting too hot to handle. I'd rather have gold any day, even if we have to melt it down or sail offshore to use it." He flipped back the lid of the chest.

Nestled in sheep's wool in the hay-lined chest was a stunning creamy egg mottled with orange veins. In the lamplight, the egg took on a golden hue. Starrus snapped his fingers. His tiny mage light floated through the air and hovered over the egg, bathing the shell in its mossy-green glow.

"Very nice." A warm glow of satisfaction trickling through him, Starrus snapped his fingers again, extinguishing the mage light. "That chest is rather ostentatious, but I do like it. How do you propose I transport the egg without being noticed on the streets?"

The man stepped behind a crate and pulled out a leather rucksack. He opened the top flap. The entire thing was lined with thick sheepskin. "That'll keep this little beauty warm. If you want this treasure to hatch, make sure you leave it near a hearth or it'll be missing its mother's body warmth." His eyes slid to Starrus' fingers. "Although I doubt you'll have an issue finding fire to warm it."

Starrus gave a wry smile. "Indeed."

"You can leave the chest here and collect it tomorrow, if it's easier."

And walk back into this den of thieves? He'd only survive that once. "I'll take it tonight." The chest was much too fine to leave behind. "This chest will be a distraction. If anyone steals it, they'll probably ignore my rucksack."

The crook held the flap of the rucksack open.

Starrus lifted the dragon egg out of the chest. A peculiar thrum emanated from the egg, making his heartbeat race and his fingers tingle. Soon, he would be a dragon rider—even better, a dragon-riding mage. That would give him power to rule the Great Spangle-wood Forest Mage Council. Instead of his stupid master, Gideon the traditionalist, or his chum Balovar, the stuffy head of the council, he would be in charge.

Hands buzzing with the strange energy from the egg, Starrus gently lowered it into the rucksack and pulled the straps tight. He slipped the bag upon his back.

The thug bent and passed him the chest. Starrus tucked it under an arm—he always left a hand free to create mage flame, especially in the lair of an enemy.

"Thank you." Aware of the archers with their bows still trained on his back, Starrus strode through the narrow corridor hedged by towering crates and out into the main area of the warehouse. He was making his way alongside a stack of crates toward the door when he heard the twang of a bowstring.

He dropped the chest and ducked, blasting a swathe of fire up into the rafters. The arrow thudded into a crate next to his face. The archers screamed, engulfed in flame. A dagger flashed through the air. Starrus dropped to the ground and the blade thunked into a barrel, splitting it. Oil spurted from the rent in the barrel, running over the flooring. Starrus scrambled to his feet and raced for the door, flinging more mage flame behind him.

The oil caught, flames blazing. A barrel exploded, spraying flaming oil and shards of burning wood across the warehouse. Crates went up in flames, crackling tongues of fire licking up the towers, devouring everything. Thick smoke roiled through the air, carrying the stench of pungent oil and cooked meat.

No one in the rafters was screaming now.

That stupid shrotty archer. So much for keeping things clandestine. The blaze was currently contained within the warehouse, but at any moment, the roof and walls would catch and everyone in Metropoli would be rushing in.

Starrus paused by the door and held out his shaking hands. He focused, sucking in the *sathir* from the flame. The fire closest to him extinguished. Sweat beading his brow and his legs trembling, he slowly sucked in more *sathir*, killing the flames and leaving the contents in the warehouse in smoking, blackened ruins.

He deliberately didn't scan the charred mess for bodies, but they were there. The sickly-sweet stench of burnt flesh, charred wood and acrid burnt oil coated the back of his throat. His stomach roiled.

Leaving the smoldering barrels and charred corpses behind him, Starrus swallowed his rising gorge, opened the door and slipped into the night.

By the shrotty dragon gods, this had all gone wrong. If Master Gideon caught him now, his whole life would go up in flames—literally. Any chance of becoming a master mage and getting onto the council would be ruined.

Smoke leaked through the cracks in the warehouse and filled the air in the narrow alley.

Although his legs and body were filled with coiled energy from the *sathir* he'd sucked in, Starrus didn't bolt. Gods, he wanted to, but he couldn't arouse suspicion, so he kept his pace crisp and businesslike. Nearby, a door flew open. A cry ripped through the air. "Fire!" in Robandi. More doors opened and windows flew up. People repeated the cry. Feet pounded the cobbles.

Heart pounding like a pestle on a mortar, Starrus nipped down the next alley and hid in the shadow of an archway as figures raced through the night toward the warehouse carrying pails of water.

When they'd passed, he strode—again, without running—down tiny alleys and narrow lanes until he was on the far side of town. He sucked in huge gulps of air. Gods, he'd killed men. He hadn't meant to, but they'd shot at him. His hands still shaking, he realized he'd left *the pretty chest in the blaze—a shame, because he'd quite liked it. Starrus rolled his shoulders, the comforting weight of the dragon egg in the rucksack reminding him that although things had gone wrong, his trade had been successful.*

Starrus was halfway down an alley when stealthy footsteps scraped on the street behind him. The hairs on his neck and arms stood on end. He spun, gazing into the shadows and peering up at the rooftops, but no one was there. He slipped down a side alley and then another, then broke out into a piazza. Starrus raced across, the rucksack thumping against his back, his hands free to weld mage fire.

A myriad of alleys faced him, but instead of choosing one of those, Starrus chose the long dusty road that led out beyond the harbor to a deserted peninsula. There, he would hide from Gideon's gaze for a few days and try to hatch his dragonet.

He strode along the deserted dusty road, edged on one side by the sea. When the last of the houses and seaside cottages petered out, he increased his pace until he was jogging.

There were muted thuds behind him. Were those footfalls or echoes of his own feet? He spun again. No one was there.

Starrus kept on running, puffing as he drew in breath in short gasps. Ahead was a copse of low scrub. He raced up to the bushes and ducked behind them, waiting, his head cocked. Over the hiss of the tide, the faint scrape of leather on dirt reached his ears, but no matter how he peered into the dark, no one came along the dusty trail.

The shock of the fire had addled his wits. He was going out of his mind, hearing things. Imagining people chasing him. Perhaps this is what a life of crime did to you—made you mad and suspicious when there was nothing to be worried about. He hefted the rucksack on his shoulders and stood. Still shrouded by scrub, he waited, listening again.

There was nothing but the sea hissing on the sand below the trail.

Starrus set out, walking briskly along the road until he reached the peninsula that stuck out like a crescent moon into the ocean north of the harbor. He smiled to himself—he'd timed things perfectly. The fishermen were still snoozing and wouldn't be up for another hour, and the merchant ships would be berthed in the harbor until dawn.

Starrus traipsed along the dusty trail until it petered out. He trudged across the sand to a goat track that made its way up to the head at the top of the peninsula. It took him a while to battle up through the scrub to the top of the hill. By the time he reached the top, his legs were shaking.

The headland was covered in huge boulders and scrub. In the day, the sandstone would be tangerine, like the desert stretching out behind him. But in the dim before dawn, everything was dark. He gazed back at the harbor to the south across the black expanse of ocean. Lanterns flickering on posts along the docks were the only sign of life.

A chill wind blew off the ocean, cutting through Starrus' robes and making his skin ripple with goose flesh. He had to keep the egg warm. Starrus ducked behind some towering boulders so any mage flame wouldn't be seen from the harbor. He gathered up some branches and sticks that were strewn on the ground and snapped more off bushes, throwing them into a pile.

Thrusting out his hands, he set the wood alight, shuddering as green tongues of mage flame licked into the dark sky. Starrus tempered the fire, sucking some of the *sathir* inside himself so the flames weren't visible beyond the rocks.

He sat on the ground, set the rucksack on the sandstone near the fire, and opened the flaps. "Ah, my sweetie, you'll be warm here." He reached into the bag, his fingers brushing the shell, surprised the egg was still warm. Once again, that familiar hum buzzed through the shell, making his fingers tingle. The fire warmed his face, chest and arms as he nestled the egg in his lap.

A puff of dust rose from the sand on the far side of the fire. Then another.

Starrus squinted, gazing past the flickering flames. Yes, the ground was being disturbed as if something was stalking him. His gut wrenched. He had been followed—by something invisible.

Or someone.

Starrus cradled the egg closer, pretending not to notice as he gathered sathir deep into his core until his veins were bucking with power. He ran his fingers over the egg's smooth shell. Soon, this dragonet would hatch and be his. Soon, he'd have the respect of all the mages in Naobia, Great Spanglewood Forest and the entire realm.

But first, he'd get rid of this enemy.

The sand alongside the fire rippled as the being made its way toward Starrus. He leaped to his feet, clutching the egg to his chest and thrusting out a hand. His veins crackled. A fireball blasted from his fingertips toward his unseen foe.

The fireball bounced off an invisible shield and dissipated in a blast that lit up the boulders.

The air rippled. A hand appeared at chest height. With a swish of fabric, Master Mage Gideon was suddenly in front of him, a thunderous scowl upon his face and his arms outstretched ready to attack. "You despicable sneak. We're here to prevent egg smugglers, yet you join them?" His bushy eyebrows drew down further, and he lunged, grabbing the egg.

"G—Gideon?" Starrus was so shocked, he lost grip of his precious bounty and reeled back, stumbling into the sand.

Gideon strode to the fire, holding the egg aloft to inspect it. "You're lucky you didn't kill this dragonet." He ran his hands over the egg with the same practiced ease Starrus had seen on many occasions when he and his master had retrieved eggs from smugglers.

Starrus had never been allowed to inspect the eggs. Master Gideon had always reserved that privilege for himself.

Gideon's signet ring glinted, the firelight catching on the flame motif that he used to seal his letters.

As Starrus scrambled to his feet, Gideon's face broke out in a beatific smile.

The egg cracked. A dragonet as orange as the desert sands flew out. Her wings flapped once and she landed on Gideon's jerkin, clutching the fabric on his chest with her talons. Master Gideon's smile grew even wider. He stroked her back, crooning to her.

By the dragon gods and the flaming First Egg! His master was imprinting with the dragonet!

"No!" Starrus bellowed, charging at Gideon. A burst of flame shot from his outstretched hands, hitting the dragonet. The flimsy tissue between her wing struts burst into flame and she writhed in pain. A high-pitched scream exploded from her tiny fanged maw, piercing Starrus' heart.

The dragonet's body twisted and slumped, and she was silent, hanging from Gideon's jerkin by her talons.

Gideon clutched at his chest, cradling the dragonet, his face ashen. "By the dragon gods, Starrus, what have you done?" His hand still on his chest, he keeled over in the sand, smacking his head on a boulder.

The dragonet's body slid from Gideon's chest, her wings in burnt tatters, her maw still open, her still golden eyes wide with terror.

Oh gods, oh gods, oh gods! Starrus knelt by Gideon's body, listening for a heartbeat. Although his master's heart was silent, his corpse was still warm—as if he'd waken at any moment and chide him for being careless with his mage power. But it was an illusion: he'd killed his master and the very dragonet he'd coveted.

If he was discovered, Emperor Haakin would throw Starrus to a wild beast in the arena for stealing his gold and committing murder.

Or he'd be hung at dawn. Or even worse, thrown to the sea monsters that roamed the deeps.

Maybe that wasn't such a bad idea. Tossing Gideon's corpse into the sea would ensure the beasts or fish devoured him before anyone would find him.

Starrus piled the dragonet onto Gideon's chest and hefted his master in his arms. *Dragons' talons, he hadn't wanted to kill Gideon, only get the dragonet off him so he could imprint with it. But when he'd seen Gideon imprinting with the little beauty, the power he'd coiled inside his core had exploded.*

His limbs trembled as he carried Gideon beyond the boulders and scrub, out toward the sandy tip of the peninsula. His foot scraped on a flat stone, and then another. Placing Gideon on the sandstone, he let sathir trickle into his hand. A soft green glow pooled in his palm. There were several stones set into the ground. Each had a name on it: Ashad, Metzfar, and Rotan.

He'd unwittingly stumbled upon a graveyard.

Burying his shrotty master in plain sight would prevent anyone from finding him or prevent his half-eaten carcass from washing up on shore.

Starrus plowed his hands into the earth, releasing sathir from his hands. The ground shook, dirt flying, creating a deep channel. Panting, Starrus made the channel deeper. And deeper.

Soon he was kneeling amid heaps of dirt.

Starrus rolled Gideon's body into the trench and pocketed his signet ring. He picked up the dead dragonet and stroked its burnt wings. *Gods, he'd done that. But it was Gideon's fault—if only he hadn't followed him and snatched the egg. The sneaky tyrant had gotten what he deserved.*

Starrus threw the dead dragonet into the hole on top of Gideon's corpse. *If Gideon wanted the dragon, he could have it.*

He sent a breeze skittering back to the fire site and collected the egg shards in a swirling tendril of wind. The wind whipped most of the fragments into the hole and sent the rest off the edge of the peninsula, scattering them over the ocean.

Starrus plowed his hands into the dirt pile. Using sathir, *he shook the dirt until it cascaded into the open grave, burying Gideon and the evidence of Starrus' treachery. He dug his hands into the next mound of freshly-turned earth and the next, until Gideon was well and truly buried. Then he stood and swept his hands in an arc, blowing orange sand over the fresh grave until it was indistinguishable from the ground around it.*

He was about to turn away when he had a thought. At some stage, the Great Spanglewood Mage Council would want to know where Master Gideon was. If there was no grave, it would look suspicious. Starrus spun and shot a bolt of mage fire at a boulder, shearing off a thin slab of rock. He dragged it over and placed it at the head of Gideon's grave.

Starrus used his mage flame to burn Gideon's name into the stone. Then he sank back on his haunches and wept.

Giddi's gut hollowed and his hands trembled. Starrus jerked in midair, his boots clapping together.

"How could the mage council let you get away with this?" Giddi yelled.

Another memory flashed through Starrus' mind.

"I'm sorry, Master Mage Balovar, but Master Gideon has been delayed in Metropoli hunting down a ring of dragon egg smugglers." Starrus passed Balovar a message bearing Gideon's flame seal.

Master Mage Balovar nodded, reading the message.

Starrus spread his hands. "I'm afraid he'll be gone some time. Of course, Gideon suggested a new master mage be appointed in his stead until he returns. He thought I may be up for the job."

"*You?*" Master Balovar snorted, tossing the message in the flaming hearth. "*The Robandi sun must've addled his brain. You're not even fully trained.*"

Starrus smiled, suppressing the rage seething through him. He'd bide his time. Sooner or later, he'd have control of the council.

Giddi's mind reeled. Pa was dead. Killed by this monster. Power coursed through Giddi's body, rushing along his arms. It flickered across Starrus' neck, crackling like lightning.

"So, boy, what are you going to do now?" Starrus asked, his voice strangled. "Kill me, too?"

Giddi rocked back on his feet, his power sputtering. Starrus dropped a hand span, his feet swinging in the air and his boots thudding against each other.

Kill Starrus? He ought to. The shrotty maggot had killed his father. And forged messages, giving him and Ma hope.

Frugar's body flashed to mind, then Joris' angry scowl as the Lush Valley archers nocked their bows.

Giddi had enough blood on his hands already. Screaming, he threw his hands wide, releasing Starrus.

His trainer dropped through the air and landed in a heap on the ground. He scrambled to his feet, and scurried off into the brush.

Arms still outspread, bolts of lightning speared from Giddi's fingers. Luminous emerald light blasted through the sky, lighting up the peninsula, the sea, the entire harbor and the city of Metropoli. The air sizzled. Wind whipped Giddi's cloak around him, wrenching off his tattered, camel-bitten sleeve.

Still screaming, Giddi plunged to his knees and thrust his hands onto the gravestone, as if he could reach through it, retrieve his father, and yank him from the earth into his embrace. The stone shattered, flying into hundreds of tiny shards that peppered Giddi's hands, breeches, jerkin and face.

Roaring, he staggered to his feet and ran to end of the cliff.

Far below, white foam thrashed at the foot of the sandstone drop. As the last of Giddi's violent wave of power died and the green flash faded from the sky, he threw himself off the edge into the dark churning sea.

STEALTH

Every night for an entire moon, Anakisha, Zaarusha, Fox and Foxita waited until Dragons' Hold was quiet and Yanir was deep in council meetings, then they slipped up onto the plateau to practice diving.

One night, after they'd just finished some tricky stunts and landed back on the plateau, Spymaster Taren flew over Heaven's Peak.

Anakisha quickly grabbed Fox in an arm lock. He twisted out of it and wrestled her to the ground.

"Good to see you're getting in extra practice," Master Taren called as Renath winged past. "Sorry, I can't stop to help you. I'm late for our council meeting. Fox, next time you twist out of that lock, keep your head down."

"Yes, sir." Fox called, grinning as the ruby dragon dived down to the council chamber ledge. He turned to Anakisha. "That was close."

They kept up their pretense of combat practice until Renath had hunted and returned to her den.

"I don't know how you did those somersaults and rolls tonight before Zaarusha caught you," Fox said. "I'm happy to leap from dragonback, but I'm not up to those fancy stunts you're doing. When I tried to roll, the stars tilted and it made me dizzy."

"Maybe you'll get the hang of it." Anakisha was glad she no longer felt dizzy in thin air.

"I doubt it, but I'm happy with what Foxita and I have achieved. I don't know anyone else who can leap from their dragon for fun— except our honored Queen's Rider, of course."

EILEEN MUELLER

A rumble, like a giant cat purr built in Foxita's throat. She nestled her head on Fox's shoulder. "She's tired." Fox yawned. "And I think I need to get to bed too."

Anakisha hesitated. "Go ahead. I'll go to bed soon. Zaarusha and I want to try one more trick, but I'll see you in the morning."

"We can stay," Fox said, stifling another yawn.

She laughed. "I'll be fine. We've been out here for a whole moon. Everything's gone well. What could possibly go wrong?"

Foxita and Fox winged off down the mountainside toward Fox's cavern.

Anakisha clambered onto Zaarusha's back and slipped into the saddle.

"What would you like to try this time?" Zaarusha asked.

"Just falling," she said. *"To tell the truth, I've enjoyed Fox and Foxita's company, but tonight I just wanted some time with you."* Time with Yanir would be good too, but there was no likelihood of that with him so busy, so she'd take what she could get.

Return to Naobia

When Giddi clambered off Aquaria's back onto a cove on the Naobian coast, a green dragon was wheeling in the air above him.

"We've been expecting you," Rengar mind-melded. *"Starrus arrived last week, so the Mage Council instructed Goren and I to keep an eye out for you."*

Giddi sighed. *"And I was hoping to slip in unobtrusively with everyone unawares."* He turned back toward the ocean depths of the crystalline sea.

"Farewell, Dragon Mage," the queen of the sea dragons said.

"Thank you, Aquaria. Your friendship means the realm to me."

"As yours does to me. You saved my life, Giddi. I will always be grateful." Her ripples faded and the queen of the sea dragons was no more than a dark shape arrowing out to sea.

Rengar landed on the beach, spraying sand around her talons. Goren swung out of the saddle and ran across the sand. He grasped Giddi by the shoulders. "By the dragon gods, I've been worried about you. When Starrus returned without you, I was worried he'd done you in. Gods knew, he'd already tried hard enough before." He clasped Giddi in a bear hug that nearly crushed him. "No matter how the mage council questioned him, he refused to say where you were."

Giddi raised his shaggy eyebrows. "That's because he didn't know, and Starrus never likes to admit his ignorance."

"By the First Egg, anything but that." Goren rolled his eyes, eliciting a chuckle from Giddi, then clapped Giddi on the back. "Come on, let's get you a change of garb and a decent meal before I take you to the mage council."

Giddi's rumbling stomach asserted its agreement. He clambered onto Rengar's back behind Goren, and they winged over the beach toward Naobia, the waves crashing on the shore behind them.

§

As Goren rapped on the ornately-carved door at the mage chambers, Giddi wasn't nearly as intimidated as he'd been the first time he'd been here, over a moon ago. By the dragon gods, so much had changed. It was good to be back on dry land.

Takoda opened the door, and Giddi swept past him down the hallway, letting the new boots Goren had given him snap on the tiles in a crisp staccato as he strode toward the mage chamber. Goren and Takoda trailed him.

Giddi threw the doors opened and stalked in.

A man with brown, puckered skin and snowy-white hair was in a plush chair next to the master mages' table. For a moment, Giddi didn't recognize Starrus. He glanced again. Yes, it was that heap of steaming dragon dung, all right. The bandages had been removed from his face. His skin was permanently discolored from the scorpion venom and as wrinkly as a walnut shell—and his hair was snowy white. Starrus' mouth was turned down in a grimace— no doubt due to his ruined good looks.

Giddi almost felt a pang of pity for him—almost—until he reminded himself that this man had killed a dragonet and his father. This mage had almost killed him, too, multiple times. His trainer had also been a charmer, often using his good looks to lure in women so he could force himself upon them, so perhaps it was just as well his pretty face was buried under scorpion venom scars, so he could no longer hide his abusive nature under a charming facade.

"Welcome back, Dragon Mage." Master Mage Lucinda nodded at him. "Starrus has explained how you were unable to locate Master Mage Findal or track down the whereabouts of the Scarlet Hand."

Giddi held his head high, refusing to be cowed by their authority. Sure, he'd made some terrible mistakes. But, at thirteen summers, he'd befriended the queen of the sea dragons, been to the Wastelands, and survived the arena—then lit up the sky in Metropoli like a glowing green sunrise. He'd never cower before a council again. "We did discover that Emperor Haakin has dealings with the Scarlet Hand, but we were unable to determine where the pirate had gone."

The gray-haired crone nodded tersely. "We will oversee this matter ourselves. We've designated the green guards to patrol the coast and the isles and report the whereabouts of the *Fiery Dragon* or the Scarlet Hand immediately. We will hunt him down and retrieve Master Mage Findal."

"Good idea, Flisa," Takoda said.

The mages nodded, as if it were an easy task.

Giddi declined to comment.

Master Takoda gave an obsequious smile. "Thank you for attempting to track down Master Mage Findal. We appreciate your efforts." The mage's snide tone sounded more like a thinly-veiled insult than appreciation.

Master Quam cleared his throat. "However, we'll now dispatch you back to Great Spanglewood Forest where you may continue your training with Starrus."

"No!" The word shot out of Giddi's mouth like a lightning bolt and echoed around the room, startling the mages behind the majestic table. Oh gods, he hadn't meant to react that violently.

Goren gave a wry smile.

Master Mage Lucinda arched an eyebrow and asked, "No? Please explain. Master Starrus has reported that you saved his life in the Metropolian arena when he faced a black death stalker. Receiving further training at his hands seems appropriate."

Starrus blustered. "We mustn't pressure the boy."

Giddi smiled. "My desire to return to Spanglewood Forest has been altered by news I received. I request to remain here and train with the Naobian Mage Council, as Master Mage Balovar and other Spanglewood mages have previously done."

"What news changed your mind?" Lucinda arched her other eyebrow.

"My father's dead," Giddi said.

Shock rippled across the faces of the master mages. "Your father's dead?" Master Jaedak spun to Starrus. "You told us that Gideon had stayed in Metropoli," he barked. "What's going on?"

"He did stay in Metropoli," Starrus replied.

"Under a slab of stone," Giddi said dryly.

"He died in a dueling accident."

So that's what Starrus was now calling it. He'd had a whole moon to conjure up a good story.

Lucinda snapped, "This is most irregular, Starrus. Why was this not reported when you returned? We demand an explanation."

"He was training me. We were dueling and he stumbled, so my mage flame hit him in the chest. Gideon grasped his heart and fell dead." Starrus shook his head, his eyes mournful. "His heart stopped immediately. I only hit him with a light flame, one that shouldn't have injured him, so I don't understand it."

That was as likely as a dragonet with a pig's tail. Giddi refrained from snorting. A mental image of a curly-tailed dragonet flicked into his head and he smothered a bitter laugh. "As you see, there are irreconcilable differences between me and my trainer." Power crackled along his arms and his fingers dripped sparks onto the tiled floor.

Quam's eyes flitted down. "Dragon mage or not, you definitely need more training."

"I agree," Flisa said.

Even though it was true, Giddi bristled.

Jaedak beamed. "I can see how it would be difficult to continue training under Starrus under these circumstances. I have long been seeking a mage to learn how to create magical talismans." He gestured at the other mages behind the table. "However, young dragon mage, you'll also be required to train with each of the mages on the council to ensure you have a more, shall we say, well-rounded instruction." The man smothered a smile and, although he refrained from glancing in Starrus' direction, Giddi understood that Master Mage Jaedak knew about Starrus' deficiencies.

"Very well," Giddi said. "I look forward to it. Goren will bring me to your quarters tomorrow." He turned on his heel and pushed through the doors, leaving the master mages gaping behind him.

Goren scampered after him, catching up with him halfway down the hallway. "I met your father when he and Starrus traveled through here a few years ago. He was a fine man and I'm sorry for your loss."

Giddi swallowed. Although he'd had a whole moon traversing the Naobian Sea on Aquaria's back, relaxing on isles, fishing, harvesting luscious fruit and enjoying the sunshine, he was aware of the raging grief inside him. It could grow like a dark canker, taking over his soul if he let it. And having Starrus around would only make it worse.

"Welcome to mage training in Naobia, Giddi." Goren clapped him on the shoulder. "You got what you want, I assume?" He chuckled. "You sure showed them that you're not to be messed with. That giant scorpion seems to have done you good."

Giddi arched an eyebrow. "You don't face down a venom-spitting death stalker and expect to remain unchanged."

"I noticed that when Starrus returned." Goren grinned. "I've been dying to ask you what happened to his pretty face? He looks much improved."

Giddi grinned back. "Scorpion venom."

"That explains it. I'll have to show you some of our secret fishing spots and the best stalls at the market," Goren chuckled. "We can start tonight with a fabulous fish hotpot, so spicy it'll blow even your shaggy eyebrows off."

They laughed as they exited the mage hall and strode into the streets of Naobia.

YANIR'S PLEDGE

The hard council seat was wearing on Yanir's sit bones. To tell the truth, he was sick of the sight of the council chamber. For the past moon since returning to Dragons' Hold, he'd been tied up in council meetings every night. It was fair enough, because he'd been gone for over a moon on his trip to Fieldhaven and Naobia, but it was frustrating that he never spent more than moments with Anakisha.

Every day, she'd been training with the sword, the bow, or in personal combat. Not to mention knife throwing, fitness, agility and dragon flight. Sometimes he'd see her in training, or even have a chance to instruct her, but by the time he got out of council meetings at night, she was usually in her cavern, asleep.

Yanir ran a hand through his hair, then nodded to Balovar, Seppi, and Master Taren. "I'm happy with the review we've conducted on our new trainees. Is there any further business?"

"I'm satisfied too," said Balovar. "It's good to have a few promising young mages moving up the ranks. However, there is one other matter, if we have time."

Something else? Between the spymaster's findings and news from the Head Master Mage, they were always busy. "Yes?" Yanir asked, resisting the urge to tap his fingers on the granite horseshoe-shaped table.

Seppi leaned in, resting his wiry arms on the table. "What is it, Balovar?"

"A messenger bird arrived this evening," Balovar said. "Master Takoda of the Naobian Mage Council is setting out to seek Master Mage Findal, who was kidnapped by the Scarlet Hand."

Master Taren's eyes narrowed. "Aren't Starrus and young Giddi chasing Master Findal?"

Yanir nodded. "They were when I left Naobia."

"Apparently, they've returned to Naobia. Starrus and his trainee Giddi didn't have any luck. In fact, Giddi is staying on in Naobia to further his mage training, and Starrus is being sent back here to Great Spanglewood Forest. They say he was rather tough on the boy."

Yanir refrained from wrinkling his nose. Rather tough was an understatement.

Taren chuckled. "So, your ploy to ship Starrus south wasn't successful?"

"I never had a ploy to send him south," Balovar blustered.

"But you did take the first possible opportunity. I recall a rumor among the mages that you told Starrus not to return unless he'd found Master Mage Findal."

"I did."

"Well then, has he found the mage?" Taren demanded.

"No. And before you ask, the Naobian Council have forbidden him to stay in the South. Apparently, he's been accused of killing Giddi's father, Gideon, in an accident."

Gideon, Giddi's father, was dead? This was disturbing news indeed.

"I thought Gideon was in Metropoli on a secret quest to infiltrate the ring smuggling dragon eggs. He's been there for years, hasn't he?" Taren asked.

So that's where Gideon had been. It had all happened before Yanir had imprinted as King's Rider, but gossip and speculation had been rife when he'd arrived at Dragons' Hold. No one had mentioned Gideon's exact whereabouts, but apparently he and Starrus had gone off on some sort of quest and Gideon had remained when Starrus had returned home. Yanir should've realized that the head master mage and the spymaster would've known what was going on.

Elbows resting on the granite, Balovar steeped his fingers. "Furthermore, Giddi is claiming that Starrus tried to kill him and actually murdered his father Gideon."

"It's true," Yanir said. "Starrus did try to kill Giddi."

"Then he must be tried and punished," Taren snapped. "That arrogant young fool has gone far enough. He's ambitious and would stop at nothing to become head of the Mage Council."

Balovar snorted. "He's got a long way to go before he can best me in a mage duel. Besides, Giddi has refused to give any evidence against him. Lucinda, who's standing in for Findal as head of the Naobian Mage Council, wrote that Starrus has suffered injuries in Metropoli and now has a facial disfigurement, so Giddi's decided to leave it at that."

"Facial disfigurement?" Yanir said. "Scars are only skin deep. People learn to live with them and grow beyond them. Surely murder deserves greater punishment?"

"Starrus claims Gideon's death was an accident," Balovar replied.

"There's nothing anyone can do if Giddi refuses to bear witness," Seppi said.

Taren nodded. "Seppi's right."

"I want to know what Takoda is up to," Seppi said. "If Starrus and young Giddi didn't have any luck, why does that jumped-up fool think he'll do any better at tracking the Scarlet Hand?"

"Apparently, the pirate rogue is sailing the seas south of Metropoli on clandestine business for Emperor Haakin." Balovar sighed.

Yanir shook his head. "Good luck to Takoda if he thinks he can succeed where Starrus has failed."

"How long was that message?" Seppi laughed. "The poor bird must've been weighed down to carry all that news."

Taren stroked his chin. "Those dragon egg smugglers have been a difficult ring to crack. My Dragon Corps spies in Naobia are still working on infiltrating their ring. It's a shame Gideon was lost. He was a valuable mage and a trusted friend. I wondered why we hadn't heard anything from him directly."

"Yes," Balovar said. "It was convenient that all of Gideon's messages were sent to Starrus, but I didn't really think anything of it at the time." He shook his head, his mouth grim. "From now on, I'll be keeping a very close eye on that shrotty upstart."

"I'm warning you, don't keep Starrus too close. He's bad news. It was in his father's blood and it runs in his."

"Excuse me, but shouldn't we have some sort of ceremony to mourn Gideon?" Yanir asked.

"Yes," said Balovar, "but not until Giddi returns. I wouldn't want the boy to miss it." His voice grew husky. "Gideon was one of my best friends. When he returns, I'll ensure the boy is looked after." He rose. "I bid you goodnight. I'm sorry I saved this dire news until last." He stalked from the council chambers, the heavy double wooden doors thudding shut behind him.

"This sad news is weighing heavily upon Balovar," Seppi said as he stood. Master Taren remained seated. "Was there anything else?" Seppi asked.

"I'd like a quiet word with our King's Rider, if you don't mind," Taren said.

"Very well." Seppi nodded and left the chambers.

Taren cleared his throat. "This is a little awkward, Yanir. I have a personal matter I'd like to discuss."

From Taren's tone, Yanir gathered it wasn't Taren's personal matter, but his own. "Yes?"

"You know my allegiance is to the King and King's Rider, but also to the Queen and Queen's Rider?"

"Yes, Taren. What is it?" It wasn't like Taren to beat about the bush.

"You like Anakisha, don't you?"

Yanir bristled. "Of course, but I don't see how this is anyone's business."

"On the contrary, your happiness is everyone's business. You, King Syan, Queen Zaarusha and Anakisha lead our realm. If you'd like to be hand-fasted to Anakisha, I'd suggest you move quickly before someone else does."

A cold fist clenched in Yanir's gut. No!

Taren continued, "It will be a much smoother reign if you and her are hand-fasted, than if she's hand-fasted to someone else while you're trying to rule together."

"What in flames' name are you talking about?" Yanir thundered. Anakisha liked him. He knew she did. And he loved her. "Speak up, man. Be straight with me."

"Spymasters often see things others don't. Anakisha has been out at night training with another rider while you've been busy in council meetings. It wouldn't surprise me if she turns to him instead of you when she needs comfort. After all, we know association breeds familiarity, which can breed feelings of comfort—and even love."

There'd be no breeding of anything if Yanir had his way. Well, except their future children— if she'd have him. "Who has she been seeing?"

Taren rose and stalked to the door. "I'd suggest you ask her. After all, if you need to ask me, then you really haven't been spending enough time with the woman you love."

Yanir slumped in his seat. He'd been wondering if there was another rider worthier of her. Whether his role as King's Rider would stand in the way of who she wanted to be. These flaming council meetings, the duties, the never-ending tasks before him… Yanir sprang to his feet. Things had to change. There was no time like now. *Syan, are you nearby?*

"*Waiting on the ledge outside the council chambers. Renath said you might be needing a ride somewhere.*"

That wily old spy was manipulating him, but Yanir didn't care, because he did care about Anakisha and couldn't risk losing her. By the First Egg, what had he been thinking? His own insecurities weren't worth risking the only woman he'd ever loved.

And neither were these shrotty council meetings.

Yanir rushed to the ledge and patted Syan's flank. "*When we imprinted, you didn't mention all these boring meetings.*" He clambered into the saddle.

Syan gave a dragonly grin. "*I didn't want boring administration to put you off riding me, did I?*" The onyx king tensed his haunches and leaped off the ledge into the darkness.

Yanir's stomach dropped as they swooped through the air. That feeling would never get old. Exhilaration charged through his veins every time they were airborne. He relaxed, letting the sensation sweep through him, enjoying every moment.

Syan banked and rose up the mountainside. Someone else was out flying too, a dark spot high up against the snowy range. "*Who is it, Syan?*" Yanir asked.

"*Zaarusha,*" Syan answered, beating his wings to catch up with them. In the moonlight, Anakisha was a tiny speck upon the queen's back.

"*Let's sneak up behind them and surprise them. Don't say a word.*"

"*I wouldn't dream of it,*" replied Syan.

As they winged up the snowy peak, Yanir smiled. Anakisha sat nicely in the saddle. She'd always flown well from day one, but over the last moon, he'd noticed she now had more confidence. It was in the way she rode, how she talked with the other riders, and in how she handled herself. She was developing into a fine Queen's Rider worthy of leading the realm.

"*I agree,*" said Syan. "*And she rides a fine Queen.*"

The mighty onyx dragon's love for Zaarusha swept through Yanir, warming him. He grinned, rejoicing in the wind tugging at his hair as they sped through the night to join Anakisha and Zaarusha.

As they danced along the snowy slope, sneaking up on Zaarusha, Anakisha slipped from the saddle. Her arms and legs limp, she plummeted through the air.

"*Quick, Syan! She's falling.*" They raced, plunging down the mountainside, arrowing toward Anakisha.

Zaarusha dived too, her wings beating strongly.

It was too late. They'd never get there in time. Memories flashed through Yanir's mind: him holding Anakisha unconscious; healing her with piaua juice; her triumphant smile upon winning the tournament; he and Anakisha borne on the backs of the villagers in Fieldhaven to the *Dancing Dragon;* her joyous laughter; her kissing him only a moon ago in the pigsty.

Oh, gods, if she died right now, he'd never have another moment with her. Yanir tried to mind-meld with Anakisha but her mind was closed to him.

His heart in his throat, he laid himself flush on his dragon's neck, urging him on. "*Syan, hurry! Quick! Save her!*"

Anakisha was plummeting toward the sharp tips of the pine forest. Gods, they were like a hundred angry warriors, waiting to spear her. He shook his head. No. No, this couldn't be happening. He'd wasted his chance. Not even told her how much he loved her.

In a blur of color, Zaarusha streaked ahead of them. The queen stretched out her talons and plucked up Anakisha's body with a jolt that could've broken her bones—within dragon lengths of the bristling pines.

Syan leveled out and followed Zaarusha up the slope.

Yanir's breath gusted out of him. *"Thank the First Egg, Syan."*

Syan rumbled an agreement, *"That was a close call."*

Zaarusha and Anakisha landed on the plateau and Syan landed moments later.

Yanir leaped out of the saddle and dashed over to catch Anakisha in his arms as she slid off Zaarusha's back. "Anakisha, oh gods! I thought I'd lost you."

Anakisha's laughter was her only reply.

Syan reared on his hind legs and beat his wings, his fury burning through Yanir's mind. *"They were playing,"* the onyx dragon said scathingly. *"Only playing games."*

§

Anakisha laughed, exhilaration burning through her. "That was the lowest Zaarusha has ever let me fall," she said, grinning. "It was great." Yanir was here, his warm arms around her.

"Great?" Yanir scowled, his face thunderous. "That nearly stopped my heart. Don't ever do that again, Anakisha. I can't lose you, not like that."

She gaped. "You thought I was falling?"

Yanir nodded, his gray eyes like slate. "I thought you were about to die. By the dragon gods, girl." He pulled her against him, then bent and kissed her with a ferocity that took her breath away.

Anakisha buried her fingers in his hair and tugged his head down closer. His warm lips moved against her cold ones.

He pulled back, staring at her fiercely. "Anakisha, I love you. I never want to lose you. I've been holding back, waiting until I thought you were ready, waiting until I thought I was worthy of you." He shook his head. "But, gods, now I don't care." His breath whooshed out of him and he kissed her again. He pulled back, gazing at her with fierce intensity. "Would you be hand-fasted to me, Anakisha, and help me lead Dragons' Realm with Queen Zaarusha and King Syan?"

Anakisha's heart soared on dragon wings. She kissed Yanir again and grinned against his lips. "I will," she said and kissed him back just as fiercely as he'd kissed her.

Zaarusha mind-melded with Syan, letting Anakisha and Yanir hear her thoughts, *"About time. She's been wondering when he'd ask."*

Syan rolled his slitted pupils. *"I know. I've been egging him on. He's always been too shy. After all, what would you expect from a pig breeder from Montanara?"*

"Hush, you two," Yanir snapped via mind-meld. *"Can't you see I'm busy kissing my future wife?"*

Anakisha couldn't resist having the last word. *"Would you two mind turning away and giving us some privacy?"*

Zaarusha paced over to Syan, her talons crunching on the shale. The onyx king wrapped a wing over his queen's back and she nestled in against his side. With their tails entwined, the two dragons sat staring out over the dark basin of Dragons' Hold.

Yanir chuckled. *"They look so sweet, don't they?"*

"Sweet?" Syan huffed, shooting a plume of fire over the edge of the plateau.

"Very sweet." Anakisha kissed Yanir thoroughly and properly, the way she'd wanted to for weeks. Together, their hearts soared.

MAGE TRAINING

Master Mage Jaedak opened a drawer in a cabinet of honeyed oak and passed Giddi a fine silver chain holding a flat crystal disc about as thick as his finger and the size of a small plum. "The first task in crafting a talisman is having an object that will hold power. The purer the element the talisman is made from, the more *sathir* it can hold. Crystal, silver, opaline or gold are often materials we mages use. Surprisingly, cotton and wool work as well."

Giddi rubbed the amulet. Its surface was as smooth as silk and it was cool to the touch. If he'd had one of these, he could've shielded himself against that kraken when he'd been at sea. Or shielded himself against Starrus. "How do I make one?"

"Today I'm not going to teach you how to craft a talisman, but how to use it—if you can." Although his eyes were full of challenge, Master Mage Jaedak's ruddy face split in a grin.

"How?"

"That's up to you."

"I don't have the faintest idea." Giddi scratched the back of his neck.

"But I do. It's my job to teach you, so you'll have to trust me." Jaedak passed Giddi another amulet. "This is how your amulet should feel when you're finished."

Giddi cradled the warm pear-sized talisman in his hand. The crystal crackled with magic, and the scent of fresh lightning clung to it as if he were standing in the middle of a storm. This was a powerful tool. A tremor of excitement ran through him. "What can we use talismans for?"

"You'll see. Now that you know how it feels, see if you can store power in yours." Jaedak twitched an eyebrow and gestured to the cottage door. "However you do it, I suggest you try outside," he said wryly. "I don't really want my home to catch on fire."

"I wouldn't—"

"You must learn control. From what I've heard, in the past you've had a tendency to be impulsive and brash."

Giddi nodded. "I have been—on occasion." He hadn't killed Starrus. As much as he'd wanted to, he'd restrained himself.

Master Jaedak continued, "Coupled with the immense power you hold, that could be fatal. You'll try this exercise and fail, but hopefully you won't harm yourself or anyone else, and you'll learn a lot on the way."

"How long did it take you to master the art of talisman magic?"

"Ten years."

"Ten years?" That was most of his lifetime.

Master Mage Jaedak laughed. "Yes, but you'll be different. You have much more power." Giddi beamed until Jaedak added, "But only a fraction of the control that I had at your age."

Giddi sighed and traipsed outside. He strode down to the rocky cove below Jaedak's cottage. His boots sank into the narrow strip of damp sand as he strode toward the rocky outcrop at the end of the bay. The sea hissed as the breakers rolled in and receded. The tide was going out, and, except for a ship on the horizon and a few gulls wheeling above, the cove was deserted. But Giddi wasn't taking any chances. Without any instructions, Giddi had no idea how he was supposed to store his power in a talisman—and he didn't want to hurt any onlookers.

When he was between two large outcrops of rock, he took the crystal amulet from his pocket and cradled it in his hands, letting a tendril of power flow from his fingers. Nothing happened.

He tried again. Still nothing. He sighed and tried again. And again.

He'd have to use more power. He glanced up the hill behind him and peeked out from behind the rocks to check the beach. No one was there. Good.

Giddi set the crystal on a broad flat rock in the middle of the sand. He stood, legs braced and hands a body-width apart. The breeze ruffled his hair and the salty tang of the sea filled his nostrils. No matter how long he stayed here, he'd probably never get used to the salty air, instead of the dank scent of leaves and moss he'd grown up with.

Giddi tugged on the *sathir* coiled in his belly and drew energy in from the sea, the air and the grasses on the hill above him. His body buzzed as the *sathir* inside him built. Still, he absorbed more until his stomach was a roiling ball of heat and his forehead broke out in a sweat. He released the *sathir* into his limbs. Fire coursed through his veins and charged into his hands. Giddi held it there until his fingers were throbbing.

His hands shook. He counted to ten, letting the energy build.

He let it loose.

A blast of green lightning erupted from his fingers and hit the crystal. The amulet shattered, peppering him and the surrounding rocks. A fragment flew into his face, and he cried out, clutching his searing cheek. Warmth trickled over his fingers, accompanied by a coppery tang—blood.

Green flames danced over the surface of the flat rock, and a clear substance dribbled down the sides.

He flung out a hand and clenched his fist, extinguishing the fire.

He strode to the rock and dropped to his knees to examine it. A pool of clear liquid dribbled over the rock's surface—melted crystal shards.

"So much raw power and no idea how to use it." The voice came from the hill behind him.

Giddi spun.

Master Mage Jaedak shook his head. "We've got our work cut out, young man. You can start by learning control." His new trainer scrambled down the grassy verge and jumped onto the sand.

Giddi bit his lip and nodded meekly.

His eyebrows shot up as Master Mage Jaedak burst out laughing. "Don't look so taken aback. As I mentioned, you've got lots of raw power. If you learn how to tame it, you'll go far."

"Master Starrus said I was clumsy and had no talent for magic. That I was too impulsive to learn control."

"Master Starrus is an ambitious, jealous man. I take it you didn't learn much from him, except how to pander to his wishes. Forget about him."

Giddi nodded again, this time with his head held high. That was the most intelligent thing he'd heard since his thirteenth name day. "I agree," he replied.

"Good," Master Mage Jaedak said. "I see you're now ready for your first lesson."

§§§

FREE NOVELETTE—SILVER DRAGON—RIDERS OF FIRE

Marlies is good at healing. But she wasn't good enough to save her friend. Now the Nightshader gang are after her.
They're fighters - strong, fast and mean. And they know where to find her. But when Giddi, the Dragon Mage, calls Marlies deep into Great Spanglewood Forest, she finds something she never expected...
What's waiting for Marlies in Spanglewood? And how will it change her life forever?

Find out what happens to Marlies, and how it shapes Ezaara's life, in *Silver Dragon,* exclusively on Eileen's site and only available for a limited time. EileenMuellerAuthor.com/Readers-Free-Books

DRAGON PIRATE
RIDERS OF FIRE DRAGON MASTERS, BOOK 3

A vengeful dragon.
A lucrative trade in a damnable cargo.
And a pirate captain with nothing left to lose.

Master Mage
Riders of Fire Dragon Masters, Book 4

Three mages:
A powerful dragon mage.
Another plotting to kill him.
And a temptress, hungry for power.

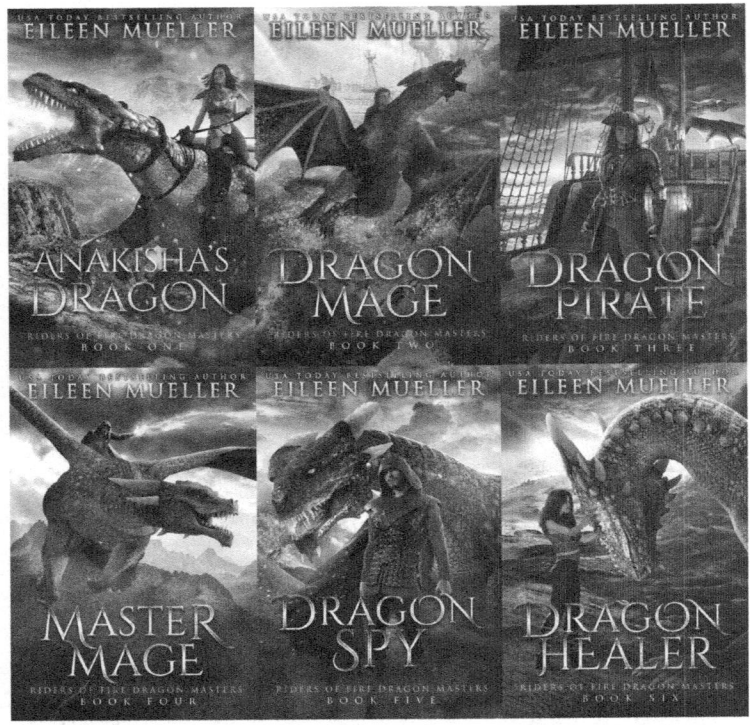

Riders of Fire
Dragon Masters

Anakisha's Dragon—Book 1

Dragon Mage—Book 2

Dragon Pirate —Book 3

Master Mage—Book 4

Dragon Spy—Book 5

Dragon Healer—Book 6

Dragon Rider—Book 7

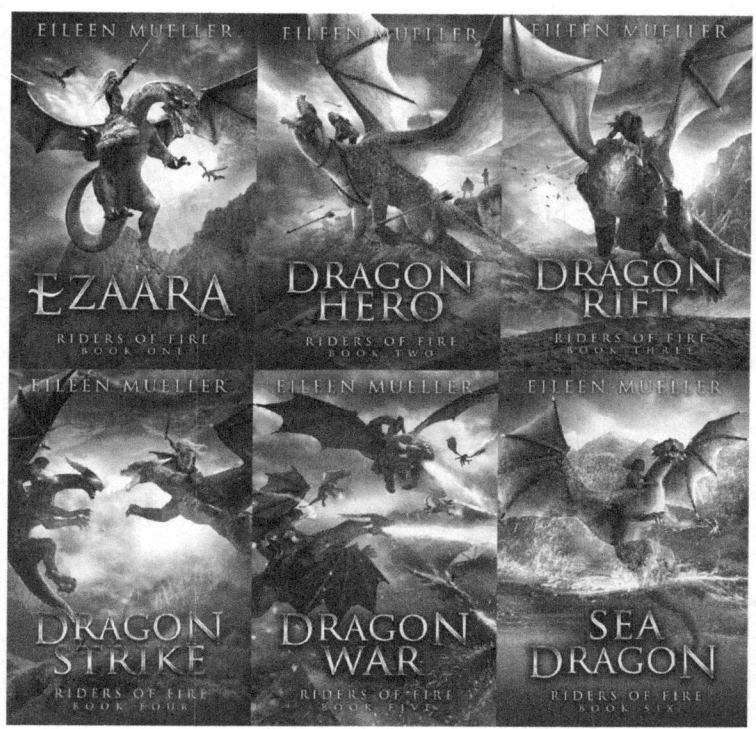

RIDERS OF FIRE

COMPLETE SERIES AVAILABLE NOW

EZAARA—BOOK 1

DRAGON HERO—BOOK 2

DRAGON RIFT—BOOK 3

DRAGON STRIKE—BOOK 4

DRAGON WAR—BOOK 5

SEA DRAGON—BOOK 6

Praise for the Riders of Fire series

Winners Storylines Notable Book Awards 2019:

Ezaara & Dragon Hero

**Quarterfinalists 2019 Epic Fantasy
Fanatics Reader's Choice Awards:**

Ezaara & Dragon Hero

Dean O'Gorman, actor, Fili the dwarf in The Hobbit

"A great fantasy read."

"Played like a movie in my mind."

"An explosive novel."

"A lot of heart and a lot of action."

"The details are so vivid."

"New stories in same genre as Anne MacCaffey's Pern books. About time someone took up the torch."

"A spellbinding story from a powerful and equally promising new voice in epic fantasy."

"A page turner that is literally impossible to put down."

EILEEN'S DRAGON ADVENTURES FOR YOUNGER READERS

Acknowledgments – Is your name here?

Dragon Mage has been a bundle of fun to write. Giddi is such a cool character. Those of you who have traveled with him through Riders of Fire and the terrible wars against Commander Zens and his tharuks, know of Giddi's dry sense of humor, despite the heartbreak and trials he'll meet in this Riders of Fire Dragon Masters series.

I'd like to thank you, my readers, for your patience. When I started Dragon Mage, I envisioned a few short scenes detailing Giddi's backstory at the start of the book, and then his journey to becoming a master mage and meeting Mazyka, his lover. However, Giddi's story as a teenager developed into its own volume, so it will be a while until the rest of his story unfolds. And before we can explore his story in Master Mage, I must chase the Scarlet Hand and try to retrieve Master Mage Findal—or the wrath of the Naobian Mage Council will be upon me. I hope you join me in that journey soon in Dragon Pirate. I'm bound to be brainstorming pirate, mage and dragon rider antics in my Facebook group, so feel free to join in.

Another huge thank you to my readers and reviewers. Your energy and enthusiasm for my stories keeps me penning dragonback adventures. It's awesome knowing you're waiting for my stories! I love your emails, messages, posts and letters, and enjoy having fun with you in my Facebook group. You provide me with joy when I've spent long hours toiling over my keyboard.

Thank you to my editor, Charlotte Jardine, who believes in me and buoys me up with her humor. I'd like to thank my writing buddies A.J. Ponder, Peter Friend, Charlotte Kieft, Kevin Berry, Angel Haze, Jeff Kohanek, Andy Peloquin, Deb Potter and my awesome teen beta reader, Ash Rachel. Ash, you deserve a medal! A shout out to Indie Fantasy Addicts, the Epic Fantasy Fanatics crew, IFA Bookwyrms, and to Christian Bentulan who designs my exquisite covers!

I also thank my kids for cheering me on and kicking me into my office to write. "Go and write Mum," they say, their eyes glazing over as they plan their next construction in Minecraft! "Seriously, Mum, we'll be fine without you." And they are! (And if they're not, they come and get me immediately!) My kids care deeply about each other and support each other through life. We all encourage each other. What more could a parent want?

Lastly, I'd like to thank Mum and Dad for believing in me and cheering me on in this past year, despite some huge challenges in all of our lives. Bob Waters has a hoard of engineering gear that would make any dragon green with envy. Karen Brookes is an adventurer, always out and about hiking in the New Zealand bush. Although very different, you're both wonderful parents. I love you and treasure you.

Now, for the drumroll… Did you name a character in Dragon Mage?

My readers suggested hundreds of names for riders, dragons and mages. Thanks to everyone for joining in the fun!

Kevin, the young cheeky dragon, is named after my accountant, Kevin Newson, who enjoys counting treasure and good books! Thank you for your help over the years, Kevin. It's always great to work with you.

Sandy Fosdick named Wave Runner, the merchant ship that took Giddi and Starrus to the Wastelands. Master Mage Jaedak was named by Beth Harris. Master Mage Takoda was named by

Heather Price. Master Mage Flisa was named by Stacy Floyd, and Master Mage Quam was named by Mandie Sagen.

The healer's littling son, Borlan, was named by Joseph D, and the healer's littling daughter, Eliona, was named by Georgianna L George. Gayreth Walden named Ook, the dead sailor, the character with the tiniest part in the book!

Glenda Jaquez Dykstra, thank you for winning the simile contest in my Facebook group with 'tossed like an egg shard' in this sentence:

He desperately clung with frozen hands to the rail, praying to the dragon gods that he wouldn't be tossed like an egg shard into the swirling mass of sea.

I love it when my readers participate in my writing process and show such enthusiasm for my work.

There will be plenty of pirates to name in Dragon Pirate, because half of the Fiery Dragon's crew were killed off in battle in Anakisha's Dragon. I'm sure the Scarlet Hand will rustle up more crew as he scours the Naobian Sea!

Riders of Fire Dragon Masters is a series that features the events that led up to my award-winning and bestselling Riders of Fire series, which has been hailed as "an explosive series."

Some of these books were originally planned as books 7-9 of the Riders of Fire series, however, I realized that new readers may want to read the adventures in chronological order. Splitting out the prequels into a separate series as Riders of Fire Dragon Masters allows people to do this.

Thank you again to everyone for your support. I love my readers and the indie community which is full of wonderful authors and fantastic adventures. Enjoy them.

Please check out my reader's group on Facebook, if you'd like to say hi! Riders of Fire: Eileen Mueller's Fan Zone and **join my newsletter at www.EileenMuellerAuthor.com**

ABOUT EILEEN

Eileen Mueller is a USA Today bestselling and multiple-award-winning author of heart-pounding fantasy novels that will keep you turning the page. Dive into her worlds, full of magic, love, adventure and dragons! Eileen lives in New Zealand, in a cave, with four dragonets and a shape shifter. She writes action-packed tales for young adults, children and everyone who loves adventure. Visit her website at www.EileenMuellerAuthor.com for Eileen's FREE books and new releases or to become a Rider of Fire!
Please check out Eileen's readers' group
Facebook.com/groups/RidersOfFire

PLEASE PLACE A REVIEW

I absolutely love reviews! Hear the dragons roar and me squeal with enthusiasm when you post one. Readers are my lifeblood, so I'd love you to pop a line or two on Amazon, Bookbub or Goodreads. Thank you.

HERBAL LORE IN DRAGONS' REALM

Arnica—Small yellow flower with hairy leaves. Reduces pain, swelling and inflammation. The flower and root are used in Marlies' healing salve.

Bear's bane—Pungent oniony numbing salve with bear leek as the primary ingredient.

Bergamot—Citrus fruit with a refreshing scent.

Clean herb—Tangy, pale green leaves with antibacterial properties.

Clear-mind—Orange berries, used to combat numlock. Stronger when dried, but effective when fresh.

Dragon's bane—Clear poison that, when it enters the blood, makes wounds bleed excessively, and then slowly shuts down circulation and breathing.

Dragon's breath—A rare mountain flower that, when shaken, produces a soft glow.

Dragon scale—A gray powder that when swallowed gives the appearance of being numlocked, i.e. gray eyes and fingernails.

Freshweed—A weed that is chewed to mask the user's scent.

Healing salve—A healing paste that contains arnica, piaua juice, peppermint, and clean herb, and promotes healing.

Jasmine—Highly-scented white tubular flowers. Promotes relaxation.

Koromiko—Thin green leaves that, when brewed as a tea, prevent belly gripe.

EILEEN MUELLER

Lavender—Highly-scented lilac whorled
flowers. Relaxant, refreshing.

Limplock—Green sticky paste with an acrid scent
used to coat tharuk weapons. Acts on the victim's
nervous system, causing slow paralysis, starting with
peripheries and making its way to the vital organs.

Limplock remedy—Fine yellow granules that reverse the effect
of limplock. Dose: one vial for an adult; three vials for a dragon.

Numlock—Thin gray leaves, ground into a tangy powder.
Saps victim's will, determination and coherent thought.
Used by Zens and tharuks to keep slaves in submission.
Creates a gray sheen over the eyes and fingernails.

Owl-wort—Small leaves that enable sight in the dark.

Peppermint—Dark green leaves with aromatic scent.
Good for circulation, headaches and as a relaxant.

Piaua juice—Pale green juice from succulent piaua leaves.
Heals wounds and knits flesh back together in moments.

Piaua Berries —When eaten, these berries cause a coma
that simulates death. The only remedy is piaua juice.

Rubaka—Crushed leaves produce a pale green
powder used as a remedy against dragon's bane.

Skarkrak—Bitter gray leaves. A Robandi poison. In mild doses
causes sleepiness and vomiting; in strong doses, death.

Swayweed—Fine green tea. Reverses loyalties and allegiances.

Woozy weed—Leaves that causes sleepiness and forgetfulness.

Made in United States
Orlando, FL
06 May 2024

46551045R00176